LINDSAY McKENNA

RUNNING FIRE

HQN™

HQN™

ISBN-13: 978-0-373-78893-4

Running Fire

Copyright © 2015 by Nauman Living Trust

Recycling programs for this product may not exist in your area.

www.HQNBooks.com

Printed in U.S.A.

Gary Amato, US Air Force firefighter,1973–1977. Joined West Point Volunteer Fire Department before he went into the Air Force. Then, returned and got his fire science degree from Stark Technical College, Canton, Ohio. He then became a Lieutenant. I met him then, when I joined the WPVFD. Gary took me under his wing and made me a good firefighter, the only woman on the WPVFD. He was a great officer, great strategist and tactician at any type of fire. I ran on 400 of 600 fire calls that we had in our township over three years. Gary is a true hero, a military vet who has given from his heart to the surrounding area where he lives. He later became Assistant Fire Chief until 1989, when he retired. Thank you for your service to all of us, Gary. You rock in my Book of Life.

Dear Reader,

Army Chief Warrant Officer Leah Mackenzie leads a double life. Women who have gone through spousal abuse usually do. At work, they seem normal and can handle their job without a problem. But going home? They revert into an abuse victim. Leah didn't start out to become one, but several tragic events concerning her family when she was just a child stamped and molded her differently. And because her famous Army helicopter-pilot father ran a black ops squadron, he was married to it and not his family. When tragedy strikes, Leah is left alone with her grief and pain, and her father isn't there for her. She grows up in his powerful and authoritarian shadow.

The only way Leah can get her father to love her is to join the black ops squadron and excel at what she does so well: skillful flying in combat. That way she gets some of his attention. She has poor social skills as a teenage girl growing up with no mother and an absentee father. In the Mackenzie family, she was a quiet shadow to her older brother, whom her father doted upon. He had great dreams for his son and none for his shy, unsure daughter who only wanted his love. And she never received it. When Leah tries to save her brother in a wintertime accident but fails, she blames herself. And from this loss, her entire family is torn apart forever.

Such family dynamics, of coming out of an abusive/dysfunctional family, can set up a woman to be attractive to a man who becomes her spousal abuser. So many women caught with a brutal physical, mental and/or emotional abuser get beaten down and they give up. But Leah somehow found the courage to not give up. As she grew, matured and became an adult, she divorced her abuser. But the real problems began then, because her ex-husband was the commander of the squadron she flew for in Afghanistan.

On a stormy and dangerous night, Leah and her copilot fly her MH-47 helicopter into the maw of Taliban territory to pick up two SEALs who have completed a mission. Only, things go terribly wrong. And the resulting crash, which could have ended her life, was saved by a third SEAL, a sniper named Kell Ballard, who was on an entirely different mission in the same area. That rescue changes Leah's life. Kell wasn't expecting to meet a woman in this war-torn country. And he sure as hell didn't expect to fall in love with the raw courage she has to not only survive her past but change the course of her life with his support. That one decision sets another series of events tumbling down upon Leah, and she's not sure she can survive them.

I hope you enjoy the many layers, twists and turns of this story! Please run over to my website and sign up for my quarterly newsletter (free). It contains exclusive information and surprises that only my subscribers will receive! I love to hear from my readers, so make yourself known to me at lindsaymckenna.com.

Lindsay McKenna

CHAPTER ONE

"READY, LEAH?" CAPTAIN Brian Larsen asked.

Chief Warrant Officer Leah Mackenzie picked up the mission information from the US Army 80th Shadow Squadron office. She looked outside, getting a bad feeling. It was raining at Camp Bravo, an FOB, or forward operating base, thirty miles from the Pakistani border. "This is a lousy night," she told the MH-47 pilot. She saw Brian nod.

"It sucks," he agreed. "But we gotta make this exfil."

Leah followed him across Operations, helmet bag in one hand, kneeboard in the other. It was 2400, midnight, and they were to pick up a SEAL team one mile from the Af-Pak border. They had thirty minutes to meet the black ops team who had been out for a week hunting high-value-target Taliban leaders.

Her heart picked up its pace as they walked quickly from Operations onto the wet tarmac. Their MH-47, a specially equipped Chinook helicopter that could fly in any kind of weather conditions, had been prepped by the ground crew and ready for them to board.

The cold rain was slashing down and quickly soaked Leah's one-piece desert-tan flight suit. It was June 1, and Brian had told her rain was unusual at this time of year in eastern Afghanistan.

Bravo sat at eight thousand feet in the Hindu Kush mountains. Leah had arrived three weeks ago, acclimating and learning the Shadow Squadron area that they operated within. She had replaced a pilot who had gotten appendicitis. Being the only woman in the 80th, she stood out whether she wanted to or not. It was time to take to the sky. Soon, they were in the air, heading toward their objective.

"This is a shitty area to pick anyone up in," Brian muttered. "You remember? It's that very narrow valley? With the mountains on the east side at fourteen thousand? And on the west side, at ten thousand?"

"Yes," Leah answered. She'd worked hard to commit the terrain to memory. Black ops never picked up a team at the same spot twice—ever. It could be a trap or ambush the second time around. "What I don't like is that we're landing too close to a series of caves. The Taliban routinely hide in them."

"Roger that one," Brian agreed grimly, studying the all-terrain radar on his HUD, or heads-up display. "The SEALs said they couldn't locate any tangos nearby, but that means squat. The Taliban hide in the caves and pop up with RPGs after we land. It's a game of Whack-A-Mole."

Leah nodded. Her adrenaline was already flooding into her bloodstream. Should she tell Brian she had a bad feeling? That when she did, things usually went to hell in a handbag? "Is there any way this team can meet us out in that narrow valley?"

"No. Then they become targets for any Taliban sitting up high in those caves."

Mouth quirking, Leah felt her stomach tighten. She flew the Chinook in the long, flat stratus clouds, the rain slashing downward at four thousand feet. In ten minutes, they'd hit the last waypoint and start descending into the exfil area to pick up the awaiting SEAL team.

She heard Brian talking with Ted and Liam over the intercom. The two crew chiefs on board would have to lower the ramp once they began to descend into the pickup zone. Brian had made his authorization request with Bagram Airfield where the major part of the 80th Shadow Squadron was stationed. No mission went down unless authorization had been given by everyone in TOC, Tactical Operation Center. And it had just been approved. It was a go.

Leah listened to all transmissions while her gaze roved across the cockpit instrument panel. Everything felt good and solid to her. Since age sixteen, she'd flown by the seat of her pants, which was when her father, full-bird Colonel David Mackenzie, had taught her how to fly. The reason she'd gotten into the Shadow Squadron was because he was the commander of this particular battalion. She was the only woman in it and Leah hoped other deserving women pilots would be allowed to follow in her footsteps sooner rather than later.

"I'll take the controls," Brian said.

"You have the controls," Leah said, releasing them. Brian was worried about this pickup area and she was happy to allow the more experienced pilot to fly them in and out. She busied herself with talking to the SEAL team on the ground and preparing the helo for the pickup with her crew chiefs.

At one thousand feet, she gave Ted the order to open the ramp. Instantly, a grinding sound began throughout the hollow fuselage. The closer they descended to the ground, the harder it rained.

The hairs on the back of Leah's neck stood up. A sense of real danger washed through her. Compressing her full lips, she watched as the Chinook came out of the low-hanging cloud cover at three hundred feet. Looking to the east, she saw the caves, all black maws. Their exfil was down below them, on a gentle slope that would be easy to land upon. Her heart rate picked up and she felt a strong thrust of adrenaline burning through her.

NAVY SEAL CHIEF Kell Ballard lay in his hide, fourteen hundred yards west of where he saw the Shadow helicopter dropping below the low cloud cover. He was hidden and dry, his .300 Win-Mag sniper rifle covered with fabric to camouflage it from enemy eyes. He'd been watching through his Night Force scope for any thermal activity other than his two SEAL brothers on the opposite side of the narrow valley who were about to be picked up. The problem was that the rain was so heavy that Kell knew Taliban could be in those caves and even he wouldn't bc able to spot them.

The whumping sounds of the twin-engine MH-47 Chinook vibrated the air throughout the narrow-necked valley. He panned his rifle slowly, looking through his infrared scope at the helicopter descending.

Then, he moved his scope farther down and to his left. He saw two thermal images of the SEALs, hiding behind brush, waiting for exfil. They'd been in contact with one another all week, although Kell's single-sniper mission was different from theirs. He'd already been out here three weeks, waiting for an HVT to slip into Afghanistan. He was sitting on the mountain to intercept the bastard when it happened. So far, he'd just waited and watched.

He'd been in touch with one of the pilots on board the Chinook, a Captain Larsen. Having the daily code word and radio contact channel for any Shadow helo, Kell had warned him earlier that Taliban could be hidden in those caves. He had no way to find them unless one of them rose up and fired an RPG at the helo. He turned his scope toward those caves once more, trying to protect the helo, just in case.

Kell watched the Chinook swing over the valley, staying as far away from those caves as possible. But the valley was exceedingly tapered in shape and the huge rotor circumference on this transport helo forced it to make a long, wide turn.

The Chinook was at one hundred feet, descending rapidly. Shadow pilots got in and out as swiftly as possible, knowing they were always vulnerable when landing and taking off.

Kell inhaled deeply, the night air moist and the rain punctured by the heavy echo of thumping blades. His heart rate slowed and he focused on the caves, watching the helo cautiously approach the exfil point.

His intense focus was primarily on the caves. He panned his rifle scope slowly, right to left and then back again. No heat signatures so far. His finger was on the two-pound trigger. He had a bullet in the chamber and two more in the magazine. The wind gusted and whipped around his hide. The rain thickened, making his visual blurry. Kell's heart suddenly plunged. He saw three heat signatures suddenly pop up from a cave.

Son of a bitch!

All three Taliban had RPGs on their shoulders, ready to fire! There was no time for a radio warning as the first enemy fired his RPG at the helo. Kell pulled the trigger, taking out the second Taliban. Moving swiftly, he scoped the third one, firing.

Too late!

LEAH SAW A FLASH off to the right, out of the corner of her eye, as Brian brought the Chinook down onto the slope.

"RPG!" she yelled. And then, the entire center of the helicopter exploded, shrapnel, fire and pressure-wave concussions slamming Leah forward. She felt the deep bite of the harness into her shoulders. Brian screamed as the fire roared forward. Leah ducked to the left, toward the fuselage at her elbow, feeling the burning heat and the precious oxygen stolen from their lungs.

A second RPG struck the rear of the helicopter. The thunderous explosion ripped off the rear rotor assembly, the blades flying razors shrieking out into the night.

Leah's head got yanked to the right by the second RPG hit. The entire cockpit plexiglass blew outward. Thousands of shards shattered and rained around her, glittering sparkles catching the fire within the bird. She heard Brian screaming, fire enveloping the entire cockpit. She smelled her hair burning.

The fire was so intense, Leah couldn't reach out and get to Brian's harness. With shaking hands, she found the release on her own. The whole helo was tearing in two. Metal screeched. She heard the rotor, just behind and above her head, rip off. A loose blade sailed through the cockpit. Because she was out of her harness, she avoided most of the slicing blade's action. It cut the other pilot's seat in half. Sobbing, Leah knew it had killed Brian instantly.

Escape! Egress!

Choking on the smoke, Leah felt her fire-retardant uniform was going to burst into flames any second now. Fire roared through the inside of the broken bird. Gasping, she crawled to the blown-out window to her left. Shoving her boots up onto the seat, she launched herself out the window. Leah felt immediate pain in her right arm, slashed by a jagged piece of plexiglass left in the aluminum window frame.

She fell ten feet, hitting the rocks and mud below, tumbling end over end. Dazed, blood running down the right side of her head, she tried to get up. Her hands and legs wouldn't work. The black clouds of smoke enveloped her. The rain slashed at Leah's eyes—part of her helmet visor was broken, exposing her face to the violent weather. Coughing, gagging, she felt smoke smother her. She got on all fours and moved away as fast as she could. Air! She had to get air or she'd die of smoke inhalation!

The rocks bit into her hands and bruised her knees. Disoriented, Leah heard gunfire from her right and left. Collapsing to the ground, she crawled on her belly, so damned dizzy she wasn't sure where she was at or where she was headed. There was another explosion behind her. The Chinook ripped in half, the aviation fuel exploded. The pressure wave struck her, smashing her helmet into the rocks. It was the last thing Leah remembered.

KELL CURSED RICHLY, leaping out of his hide and leaving his sniper rifle behind. He pulled the SIG pistol from his drop holster, crouching, then sprinted down the slope. He had fourteen hundred yards to run before he would reach that pilot he'd seen fall out of the Chinook's starboard-side window near the cockpit.

Slipping and sliding, the rain so heavy he could barely see even with his NVGs on, Ballard watched for more trouble. The two SEALs waiting for extract had immediately broken contact and were already on the run toward the cave where the RPGs had been shot from. They'd have to contact the platoon at Bravo for another pickup at a later date.

Kell breathed hard. The slippery soil slowed him down. He had dispatched all three Taliban. But were there more of them around that he hadn't seen through his scope? He flipped up his NVGs because the roaring flames around the destroyed helo blinded his night-vision capability.

The last he'd seen through his scope, the pilot was about a hundred feet west of the wreckage. He'd disappeared beneath the roiling, thick smoke. Where the hell could he be?

Circling the helo, staying well away from it, Kell entered the heavy smoke. Immediately, he started choking and gagging. Crouching low, moving swiftly, Kell began a hunt for the pilot. He had no idea if the man was dead or not. He was amazed even one of them had managed to get out of that flaming helo alive.

Kell almost stumbled over the body. He fell to his

knees. The pilot was on his belly, arms stretched out in front of him, thrown forward by the second, bigger blast. Gasping, unable to see except by feel as more smoke poured into the area, Kell grabbed the man and threw him into a fireman's carry across his shoulders. Only, to his shock, he felt breasts resting against his shoulders.

What the hell? A woman? Not in the Shadow Squadron! That was a men-only combat slot.

It didn't matter. Kell heaved to his feet, holding on to the woman pilot, crouched, angling to get the hell out from beneath the toxic fumes and smoke. She weighed a lot less than a man, he realized, as he trotted out from beneath the cloud.

Halting, he pulled his NVGs down so he could see into the night. Keeping his hearing keyed, Ballard slowed his pace once he was across the narrow, flat area. Ahead of him was the slope.

As he began the climb, the rain lessened. The wind gusted fiercely, gut punching him, throwing him off balance. Cursing softly, panting from the exertion up the steep, rocky slope, he moved toward his hide. And then, Kell heard a snap and pop nearby. *Damn!* The Taliban had spotted him! Now his hide was useless!

Kell leaned into the hide, grabbing his rifle and his ruck. More bullets snapped by his head. Others struck the rocks around him, sending off sparks and ricocheting. Grunting, he was now weighed down with not only the unconscious pilot, but an eighty-pound ruck and a twenty-five-pound sniper rifle.

And the Taliban had him in their sights.

Angling up through the wadi, or ravine, Kell knew the Taliban were shooting wildly because they didn't

have thermal-imaging capability. They couldn't see
what was out there in the night and rain. But even
they got lucky sometimes. As he hoofed up the slope,
weaving between straggling trees and thick bushes,
he headed higher.

His lungs were burning. His legs felt tortured and
were starting to cramp. The bullets were going wide
of them now. Moving deeper down into the wadi, Kell
knew no Taliban were there because this had been
his home for three weeks. He knew every bush, tree
and rock.

The rain eased, the wind gusting less as he popped
out of the top of the wadi, a thousand feet higher. He
was rasping for breath, his calves knotting painfully
with fist-size cramps in each. Clenching his teeth, he
pushed through the pain, knowing he had to get to
a certain chain of caves and tunnels or they'd both
eventually be found and killed. Slipping, sometimes
falling to his knees, Ballard scrambled like a damned
mountain goat and kept fighting the slope with his
three heavy loads.

Finally, he reached a small cave about ten feet
high and six feet wide. Carefully slipping inside, Kell
dropped his ruck on the dirt floor, set the sniper rifle
against the wall and then knelt down, easing the unconscious pilot off his shoulders. The wall of the cave
hid them. Breathing hard, sucking oxygen that wasn't
easily available at nine thousand feet, Kell steadied
himself. He pushed two fingers against the pilot's
neck. She was a woman. That still stunned the hell
out of him. He saw dark blood down the entire left
side of her face. Her lips were slack.

There! He felt a pulse. That was good news. Unable to do much here, he pushed his wet fingers beneath the fabric of her soaked flight collar. He fumbled and finally located her dog tags. Angling his head, he read, "Mackenzie, L., CWO, US Army." Dropping them against her chest, he keyed his radio mic close to his mouth.

"Redbud Main, this is Redbud Actual. Over." Ballard gulped for breath, waiting. Sometimes, being in a cave stopped transmission.

"Redbud Main. Over."

That would be Ax, Master Chief Tom Axton, who ran their Delta platoon. Quickly, Kell explained what had happened. The Taliban were on their trail, following them. It would be impossible for a helo pickup. He was going into the cave system and would try to lose them. Kell told the master chief about the woman pilot, L. Mackenzie.

"Roger Redbud Actual. Egress. We've already been in touch with Raven Actual. There are two Apaches underway to the crash site as I speak. Take evasive action. Out."

Kell signed off and raised his head, listening intently. He'd murmured in a quiet tone. A whisper would have carried even farther. Looking out, he spotted five Taliban climbing toward the cave. *Damn!* Turning, he saw the woman pilot had remained unconscious. She was still wearing her helmet. He almost pulled it off, but thought better of it because if the Taliban searched the cave and found it, they'd know she was nearby.

Not good.

Kell strapped the sniper rifle onto the outside of the ruck. Pulling the pilot over his shoulders again, he picked up the strap of the heavy ruck in his left hand. He kept his right hand on the woman's slack wrist over his chest so she wouldn't slip off. After getting a few minutes of rest, he swiftly moved to the rear of the cave. In a minute more, his NVGs would be useless. He knew this tunnel and jogged down it, blind in the pitch darkness, but knowing exactly where he was going.

Kell continued the swift pace, his calves knotting up in excruciating protest. He needed water, dehydrated from the long burst of speed to get this pilot to safety. But water could wait. He sped past two more caves, locating a fork and then moving up a steep tunnel.

His breath came out in explosions, sweat running off him as he pushed hard, forcing his tired, burning legs to perform. As a black ops SEAL, he knew he could ignore pain and keep on going. There wasn't a choice, anyway. Luckily the Taliban wouldn't know which way he'd chosen to go in this system. The dolomite-rock tunnels didn't reveal boot tracks, thank God.

His heart was pounding like it was going to tear out of his chest as he climbed toward the ten-thousand-foot level. He was going into a cave that had probably never been used by anyone. *Yet.*

The reason Ballard knew about it was that he'd accidentally discovered it three weeks ago. There were no animal or human prints in the soft, fine dirt of the cave floor where he was headed. It was hidden well enough that he felt it was the right place to hide for now. Even better, there was another exit tunnel out of it, so if his hiding spot was compromised he could egress to freedom with the injured pilot.

Kell was soon operating in pitch darkness. At a juncture, he halted, leaned forward so the pilot wouldn't fall and grabbed a small penlight out of his cammie pocket. Shifting it to his left hand that was now numb, the light would enable him to traverse the caves. He pulled his NVG goggles down around his neck. They were of no use now. Breathing out of his mouth to quiet his jagged rasps, he turned, his hand on the pilot's shoulder to steady her position on him, listening. There were no Taliban voices in either Arabic or Pashto floating up toward him in the complex tunnel system. Kell knew his enemy well enough to assume that they'd probably given up, more interested in hiding because they figured Apache combat helicopters were coming to find them. They couldn't be discovered in a nearby cave where they might be seen, so they'd hunker down in a wadi and wait it out. That was fine by him.

He reached the small cave chamber. Luckily, it contained a small pool. As Kell entered it, he heard the rush of water. Figuring the rain from far above was leaking down through the fissured limestone, he pushed toward the rear of the cave. There was an alcove, a thin wing of dolomite rock that acted like a wall, hiding the mouth of the cave from where he was standing. It would also hide the pilot and his gear from Taliban eyes. That was a small advantage.

Breathing hard, Kell dropped the ruck, making sure the sniper rifle sat on top of it. He couldn't afford to have the Win-Mag damaged. Grunting, he slowly crouched, his sore knees settling onto the fine but

gritty surface. Easing the pilot off his shoulders, he
kept his hand beneath her neck and head as he got her
straightened out, laying her down.

Placing the light at an angle against the rock wall,
he shifted into combat-medic mode. Opening the ruck,
he grabbed his sleeping bag, rolling it out. He picked
her up and placed her on it. Next, he located a pair
of gloves in his ruck and he pulled them on. Kell un-
strapped her helmet and gently lifted it off her head.
Putting it aside, he got a look at her for the first time.
Her ginger-colored hair was in a ponytail and he saw
thick, welling blood on the left side of her skull. Studying the helmet, Kell realized it had been cut open by
something. Maybe a flying blade? Whatever it had
been, it had created a one-inch gash in her scalp, the
blood still leaking out of it and down the left side of
her temple, cheek and neck.

He placed his fingers on the inside of her wrist after
pulling off her Nomex flight gloves. She was medium
boned, her skin ivory colored. Her pulse was strong
and steady, a hopeful sign. Kell began to breathe a
little easier.

He put a small blanket he kept rolled up in his ruck
beneath her head and tilted her neck back slightly to
open her airway. Quickly and expertly, he examined
her for other injuries, burns, bullet wounds or broken
bones. She was unconscious and he was fairly sure it
was due to her head wound.

Still, Kell missed nothing. Rolling her toward him,
the front of her body resting against his knees, he
checked her back and legs for exit wounds and injuries. There were none. Turning her back over, he concentrated on her left lower arm. Her flight-suit sleeve

had been ripped open from her wrist to her elbow. There was a three-inch gash that she'd probably gotten egressing out of the cockpit window, Kell guessed. It was deep and oozing blood, but it was not life threatening. It would need a lot of stitches, though.

He placed another blanket beneath her knees, bringing the blood back to the center of her body to halt the devastating shock. He then went to work on her head wound. In a cave, Kell wouldn't be able to use his radio or his satellite phone to reach help. They were cut off from everyone due to the thick rock. For now, Kell was all right with that, so long as the pilot hadn't sustained a life-threatening concussion. If she had, then it became a very dicey situation because the Taliban were actively hunting them.

Pulling a bottle of water out of his ruck, he drank deeply, replenishing badly needed fluids lost in the run for safety. Taking a washcloth he always carried in a plastic storage bag, he poured sterilized water from another bottle onto it and began to carefully wash the blood away from her head wound. He had to see how deep it was and if her skull had been fractured.

To his relief, it was merely a flesh wound, but these types often bled like a stuck hog. It took him several minutes to clean it up. Getting out a surgical needle and thread, he carefully stitched the wound closed. Most important was sterilizing the area before and after. Brushing antibiotic cream over the sewn area, Kell placed a battle dressing across it. In minutes he had the wound protected, the white gauze around her head. He noticed it damned near matched the color of her flesh right now.

Hauling the ruck closer, he pulled out a syringe and

a bottle of antibiotics, giving her a maximum dose in her upper arm, wanting to stave off any bacterial infection. That was the last thing she needed.

All the while he worked over her, his hearing was keyed to outside the cave. The tunnel systems within the mountain were both a labyrinth and an echo chamber. Glancing at his watch, he saw it was 0200. He was exhausted, but pushed through it.

Trying to ignore how attractive Chief Mackenzie was, Kell went to work on the gash on her arm. It was then that she groaned.

He stopped, watching her shadowed face. Her softly arched brows moved down. Her mouth—and God, what a mouth she had—closed, and then she licked her lower lip. Any moment now, Kell knew she'd start to become conscious. Her right arm lifted toward her head. He caught her hand.

"Chief Mackenzie? You're safe. You need to lie still. Do you hear me?" Kell leaned down, a little closer, watching her thick lashes quiver. Another groan tore out of her and her nostrils flared. Kell knew she was in pain. Probably from the wound on her arm.

And then his breath jammed in his throat as her lashes drifted upward. She had incredibly green eyes, although Kell couldn't tell much more than that with the deep shadows in the cavern. Her gaze wandered. They were glazed over with shock. Finally, they wandered in his direction and stopped. Kell could see her trying to think, to remember what had happened.

Her pupils were dilated and he checked them closely. Both were of equal size and responded. Relief moved through him. If one pupil was fixed, larger or smaller than the other, it meant she'd sustained serious head trauma.

She had beautiful eyes, the kind a man could get lost in. They reminded him of the summer-green color of the trees in Sandy Hook, Kentucky, where he had been born. Pushing his personal reaction to her aside, he said quietly, "Can you hear me, ma'am? I'm Navy Chief Kelly Ballard. You're safe here with me."

Leah heard the man's soft, Southern drawl, but she couldn't understand what he was saying. Her head throbbed with pain and her vision was blurred. She felt white-hot heat throbbing through her left arm. The pain was overwhelming and she struggled, feeling as if trapped in a netherworld. Her vision cleared for a second. She was staring up at a man with a deeply tanned, craggy face, whose intense, narrowed gray eyes studied her. Oddly, she wasn't frightened of him. He was dressed in SEAL cammies. Her vision blurred again. Leah shut her eyes, struggling to remain conscious. Where was she? Where was Brian? What had happened?

CHAPTER TWO

LEAH FELT THE man's calloused hand on her left arm that hurt so damn much. She felt nauseous, dizzy, and couldn't think coherently.

"Ma'am," he drawled, "just be still. You took a bad bump to your head. Things will clear if you don't struggle so much."

This time, she heard what he was saying. It was low in timbre. Caring. His tone calmed her frantic, chaotic mind. Her whole body hurt. Leah felt as if she'd been in a major car wreck.

Opening her eyes, she blinked, staring up into the deeply shadowed face of the man kneeling beside her. She noticed the lines around the corners of his eyes. Laugh lines, maybe? Her mind was wandering, shorting out. He had an oval face, strong chin and large, intelligent-looking eyes. The word *rugged* had been created for him. He wasn't pretty-boy handsome at all. Rather, it looked as though his face had been hewn and sculpted out of mountain rock. His nose reminded her of a hawk's.

It was his eyes that snagged her attention the most. Wide spaced, gray with large black pupils and a black ring outside of the iris, they also gave the impression of a hawk. Maybe an eagle. And then her gaze wandered down to his delicious-looking mouth. Leah saw a lazy smile spread across it, and she felt relief tunnel through her. As hard as this man looked, his mouth was his saving grace. It was chiseled, the lower lip slightly fuller, the corners curved naturally upward. This man laughed a lot, Leah thought. His black hair was longish, almost to the nape of his neck, his face bearded. That made sense if he was a SEAL. They always wore beards and had long hair in order to fit in with the male Muslim population of Afghanistan.

"That's it, Sugar," he soothed, "just rest. You're going to be fine. I'll take good care of you."

Those last words rang in her mind. *I'll take good care of you.* Leah closed her eyes, his hand cradling her left forearm as if he were holding a much-beloved child. A large hand, the fingers so long that Leah could feel their length against her upper limb. His hand was calloused and felt rough on her sensitive skin. Her mind was cartwheeling between the past and present.

Hayden Grant, her ex-husband, came out of the blackness and threatened to engulf her. His leering features, those pale blue eyes that looked almost colorless when he was going to beat her, stared back at her.

The man with the Southern drawl broke the hold of her building terror. He would take care of her. No man had ever done that before. Not her father. Not her ex-husband. Yet, as Leah felt herself fighting not to lose consciousness, she honed in on this stranger's quiet, soft voice.

"Now take some slow, deep breaths. You need oxygen. That's it, just take it nice and easy, you're doin' well. We'll get you up and over this shock you're wallowing around in right now."

Leah had no way of explaining why his drawl had

such a powerful impact on her, but it did. She listened
to his voice, caressed by its natural warmth, and for
the first time in her life she trusted a man. He was
leading her out of the dark, pulling her into the light,
and she desperately wanted to rid herself of Hayden's
sneering face, his colorless eyes locked on to her, coming after her, his fist cocked to strike her.

Leah quivered, and a rasping cry lodged in her
throat. And then, Hayden's face disappeared, drowned
out by the man speaking to her, calling her back to
the here and now.

Frantic, Leah struggled to hone in on his voice,
trying to understand his instructions. More than anything, that physical link with him, his large hand swallowing up her forearm, was like a beacon of hope, an
anchor in her world of chaos and distortion.

"You're coming around," he told her. "A couple
more slow breaths ought to do it."

Leah felt weakness steal through her even though
she wanted to wake up. And then, she felt a cool,
delicious cloth move across her wrinkled brow. The
coolness felt refreshing against the heat of her skin.
Her skin was tight and smarting, as if she'd been in
strong sunlight far too long. The cloth caressed her
right cheek, and then her left one. She felt the coolness
encircle her neck and Leah swallowed, her mouth so
dry it felt as if it were going to crack. She was suddenly so thirsty that it drove her to wakefulness.

"Hey," Kell called softly, giving her an easy smile,
"welcome back to the land of the living. Do you understand what I'm saying?" He studied her eyes, and
he could see she was starting to register his voice. As
a combat medic, he knew a concussion, even a mild

one, rattled a person's brain. As she barely turned her head, his face so close to hers, he could see her eyes were a deep forest green, reminding him of the trees on the hills around his parents' home in Sandy Hook, the dairy farm that was surrounded by the Appalachian Mountains. That midsummer green was found in the oak, elm and beech trees, identical to the shade of her breathtakingly beautiful eyes.

Kell knew the advantage of talking slowly, soothingly, to someone who had just survived near death. He'd done it for members of his SEAL platoon over the years. Taking the cloth, he wiped away more of the dried blood along the slender column of her neck. Touch was important. It anchored a person who was disoriented and it helped them focus.

He continued to cradle her arm because he didn't want her trying to use it while it was open to infection. As soon as he could get her conscious, Kell would explain to her what he was going to do. Then he could get on with stabilizing the pilot.

Leah slowly licked her lips and frowned, staring up at him. Kell would give anything to know what she was thinking. Strands of ginger hair fell across half her brow.

He set the cloth on his ruck and with his long, spare fingers, eased the strands away from her face. Her cheeks had been wan, but now he was starting to see a bit of color flood back into them. That sinner's mouth of hers was his undoing. The woman didn't wear any makeup. There was no need for any, Kell observed. Her hair glinted in the light thrown out by his LED flashlight. He saw some auburn strands mixed with red and gold ones. There was a light covering of freckles across her cheeks, as well.

His medic's eyes noticed her nose had been badly broken. It didn't lessen the impact of her face, which grabbed simultaneously at his heart and lower body. Still, Kell wondered how she'd broken it. And why hadn't it been reset? Some doc hadn't done his job, that was for damned sure.

Picking up the washcloth, he continued to gently move it across her brow, cheeks and neck. Kell could tell she liked it because the tension flowed out of her. What had she cried out about earlier? Pain? He wanted to give her a small dose of morphine, but didn't dare until he could fully assess her head injury.

Leah closed her eyes, suddenly weary. The coolness of the cloth against her skin felt heavenly. It struck her spinning senses that it could be a lover gently and tenderly caressing her. She'd never known such a touch. Never would. But his ministrations helped her battle back the darkness that once again wanted to engulf her.

She felt the cloth lift. Missing his touch, she forced her eyes open. This time, her brain registered how tall and lean he was. There was kindness in his gaze and it shook Leah. A man who was kind? In another lifetime maybe. Her stomach rolled and she felt the acid in the back of her throat. It came on suddenly, out of nowhere. And then, it subsided. Breathing irregularly, Leah put her hand against her stomach. At least she was feeling better than before.

"Are you thirsty?"

Leah nodded only once because her head hurt so damn much when she moved it. He was wrapping something around her lower left arm. And then, she felt him leave her side. Opening her eyes, she saw his darkly shadowed shape move from her left side, stop near her feet and retrieve something out of a bag and then straighten. He was lean and graceful, reminding her of a wild animal, a predator, bonelessly moving in her direction. She closed her eyes, her cartwheeling imagination out of control.

Her mind halted as Leah felt his arm slide beneath her neck. He slowly raised her up into a semisitting position. She was too weak to open her eyes.

"Don't drink too much water. Your stomach's probably raising hell on you about now."

Leah felt the press of the bottle lip against her mouth, tasted the first of the water. She was so thirsty. He didn't allow her a lot of water and she made an unhappy noise in her throat, a protest, when he withdrew the water bottle from her lips.

Weak, her head lolled against his shoulder. Leah inhaled the odor of male sweat and the damp fabric he wore. Automatically, her nostrils flared. He carefully laid her down.

Leah felt her stomach lurch and she rolled herself onto her left side, heaving. Her stomach emptied and the dry heaves took over. Leah hated vomiting more than anything, the bitter taste of acid coating her mouth. Her eyes watered. Her nose ran like a faucet. Feeling a mess, the man brought her back into his arms. Breathing hard, Leah weakly tried to wipe her mouth to get rid of the horrible taste.

"Easy," he soothed near her ear, holding her in his arms. "I'm going to give you a little more water. Hold it in your mouth, swish it around and then spit it out."

His instructions were easy enough for Leah to follow. Opening her eyes, she spat the stuff out onto the cave floor. Her mind felt more clear, less gauzy and incoherent. He gave her more water and she did the same thing.

"A concussion will do that to you," he told her quietly. Kell knew he shouldn't enjoy holding this woman officer in his arms, but he did. She looked so helpless.

But he knew that wasn't the case if she was a Shadow pilot. She had a set of invisible titanium balls as far as he was concerned, and he smiled a little. His respect for her was solid. SEALs held all Shadow pilots in high esteem. They risked their lives every time they went out on a mission to pick them up or drop them off in enemy territory. This woman was no weakling. And damn, he liked a strong woman, someone who had backbone coupled with grit woven with a stubborn spirit. Just looking at Chief L. Mackenzie, Kell knew she encompassed all those qualities. And like it or not, he was drawn to her because of it.

Leah lay in his arms, her cheek resting against his broad chest. She could hear the slow, steady beat of his heart beneath her ear, feel the slight rise and fall of his chest.

Under ordinary circumstances, she'd have pushed away and not allowed a man to touch her, much less hold her intimately like this. Her senses were warped, and she swore she could feel his incredible concern radiating from him to her, enveloping her, holding her safe. Never had she felt anything like this from any man. It just wasn't possible. It was her imagination.

Yet, when he caressed her gritty, dirty cheek, his fingers rough against her skin, tears burned against her closed eyelids. The gesture wasn't sexual. It was caring. More tears welled into her eyes and Leah wished somewhere deep within her that, when she'd been eight years old, her father had held her like this. Held her, protected her, let her know that he loved her even though... Leah shut the ugly door on that time in her life, serrating pain squeezing her heart.

As he laid her down, Leah felt abandoned. She wanted those arms around her. She already missed the momentary sense of safety he'd afforded her as she'd lain against his chest. Battling back the tears, Leah gulped several times, her emotions running rampant. She could barely control them. Lifting her lashes she saw the man walk around and kneel at her left side once again. There was concern in his eyes, care burning deep within them. She could feel it, sense it.

"Wh-who...?" she managed, her voice cracking. She saw him tip his head, study her in the silence. For once, she didn't feel like she always did when a man looked at her. All they saw were her breasts, her ass and her long legs. They didn't see her as a person, only as a sexual object, just as Hayden had.

"Welcome back," he said, that easy smile shaping his mouth. "I'm Navy Chief Kelly Ballard. I rescued you after you egressed out of that burning helo."

Swallowing hard, Leah stared into his shadowed, hard face. It it weren't for his Southern accent, that hint of a smile tugging at the corners of his well-shaped mouth, she'd have been scared. Because most men scared her. "K-Kelly?" Her mind was trying to wrap around all the information. It was too much for her to process.

"Most folks just call me Kell," he offered.

That was better. It was simple. Her mind could handle four letters. Leah looked up. It was dark. She tried to see where she was. Only a small light cast shadows between them. She could see nothing else. Her brows drew down and she tried to think, but damn, thoughts were elusive. "Where?"

"In a cave," he told her quietly. Kell could see her fighting to put it all together. He saw her confusion. Her eyes were more alert looking. He added, "You're safe. I want you to just relax."

Safe. Leah closed her eyes. She couldn't understand why she trusted this man. This stranger with the soft, deep Southern voice.

"I need to tend to your arm," he told her, placing it across his thighs. "You cut it badly. I need to clean it out and stitch it up. Think you can lie still while I do that?"

Arm. Yes, it hurt like hell. Slowly moving her head to the left, because movement made her dizzy and then nauseous, Leah saw her lower arm wrapped in white gauze. She saw dark coloring across the dressing, slowly realizing it was blood. Her blood.

He was pulling medical items out of his ruck and laying them neatly next to where he knelt on a small blanket. He donned a pair of gloves, and then took a syringe and poked the needle into a bottle he held.

"Y-yes, I won't move," she managed, her voice raw, her throat feeling dry and hot.

"You're a real trooper," he murmured. "I'm going to take off the dressing and then I'm going to give you several shots of Lidocaine that will numb the area I have to clean out and then stitch up. You ready for that?"

"Y-yes." It took such effort to speak. Leah wondered if he was a doctor, because he seemed completely confident in what he was doing. The bloody gauze came off. He cradled her arm across his hard thighs. The pricks of the needle were uncomfortable, but nothing like the pain she felt in her arm.

"Good going," he praised, setting the syringe aside. "Now we'll give it a couple of minutes and then I can clean it out and stitch it up."

Frowning, she studied him. "Doctor?"

"No, ma'am. Combat medic." He gave her a lazy grin. "But you're in good hands, so no worries."

She did trust him. What was it about Kell? The earnestness in his expression, a face that had been so harshly weathered? That kind, understanding look in those dark gray eyes of his? The way his mouth moved when he spoke to her in that rich, country-boy dialect that just naturally set her at ease? Leah felt as if her world had not only been pulled inside out, but upside down. A man could never be trusted on a personal level.

Oh, she trusted the pilots she flew with, but that was different. There were no emotional ties with them. It was professional, detached, and they all had a job to do.

And then, the crash slammed back into her memory. Leah gasped, her eyes widening. She tried to get up, but he gently placed his hand on her shoulder and kept her down.

"Sugar, you're not ready to get up just yet. What's wrong?"

Her emotions ran wild. Grief tunneled through her. "M-my crew..."

Kell saw tears jam into her eyes, heard the rasping terror in her voice. He kept his hand on her shoulder more to comfort her than anything else. "I'm sorry. They didn't make it. Only you managed to escape." His heart wrenched as huge tears rolled down her pale, tense cheeks. Oh, hell, he hated when a woman cried. "Your helo got hit with two RPGs," he told her. "You were lucky you survived."

Leah lifted her right hand, covering her eyes, a sob rocking through her. Brian, Liam and Ted gone? Dead? She couldn't help herself. She began crying, softly because every time her body jerked she felt bruising pain in her head and left arm. She felt Kell's large hand on her shoulder, patting it gently like he would pat a child who was upset. She let her hand fall away from her eyes and she gave him a pleading look. "Are you sure they're dead?"

It hurt Kell, but he said, "They're gone. I'm sorry," and he gently pressed his fingertips here and there around the gash. She showed no reaction to his touch. "Can you lie still now for me? I need to stitch this closed and I can't do it if you're moving around. Okay?"

Leah collapsed against the makeshift bed he'd placed beneath her. She dragged her good arm across her eyes, grief-stricken over the loss of Brian and their crew. "Yes, go ahead," she choked out brokenly, her voice gutted with grief.

It didn't take Kell long to clean and stitch up the nasty gash. He could feel grief rolling off her. Kell understood loss because he'd lost some of his best SEAL friends over the past nine years. There was nothing he could say or do. Grief had its own way with a person and sometimes nothing could stop it, lift it or dissolve it.

As he finished placing a waterproof dressing over most of her lower arm, he gently laid it across her belly. Getting up, he put everything back into his ruck where it belonged. Glancing at his watch, he saw it was nearly 0300. It was time to check out things around their hide. Kell never took anything for granted. The Taliban were sniffing around for them and he knew it. They were premier trackers, never to be underestimated.

He knelt down on one knee and touched her shoulder. She pulled her arm away from her reddened eyes. "I need to do a little recon," he told her. "I'll be back in about thirty to forty minutes." He pulled his SIG pistol out and placed it near her right hand. "You know how to use a pistol? It's got nine rounds in the magazine and there's a bullet in the chamber. There's no safety on this model. If I don't come back, then know there's a tunnel—" and he pointed toward it "—over there. If you hear Taliban coming, get my ruck, put it on your back and take that tunnel out to the side of the mountain. It's got a compass and map, plus a sat phone in it. You can call for help. Okay?" His gaze dug into hers. Kell could see she understood his instructions.

"I can do that," Leah said, her voice husky with tears.

Kell reached out and gently touched the crown of her head because he saw the look of terror and abandonment in her eyes. She was still fragile from the head injury. "I'll be back, Sugar," he promised.

Leah watched as he took long, lanky strides and disappeared into the darkness with his Win-Mag

across his shoulder. She turned, realizing the penlight was the only light source for her to be able to see
the area where she lay. Slowly, Leah weakly pushed
herself into a sitting position. She was on a sleeping
bag with two rolled-up blankets, one for a pillow, the
other beneath her knees.

Emotionally, she felt demolished, the tears still falling over the loss of Brian, Liam and Ted. She scrubbed
her eyes, finding her left arm painful to raise. Staring at the dressing, Leah began to appreciate Kell's
medical skills.

Gazing around, she heard running and dripping
water to her right. She picked up the penlight and
flashed it in that direction. There was a small pool of
water. Leah realized water was leaking from above the
cave roof, finding its way down into the pool. They
had water. That was a good thing.

Her head ached like hell. Every time she turned it,
dizziness struck her. Leah knew if Kell didn't return,
she wouldn't have much of a chance of survival by
herself. Not in her present injured condition.

She was exhausted and lay down on her right side.
Less pain in her head that way. The cave was chilly, so
she reached down and took the rolled blanket, smoothing it out across her damp flight suit. Finally, she was
warm, and she shut her eyes and spiraled quickly into
a deep, healing sleep.

KELL RETURNED AN hour later. He moved without a
sound as he entered the cave. Turning on his other
penlight, he saw the woman pilot asleep. *Good.*

Wearily, he propped up his Win-Mag against the
cave wall. Picking up his pistol, which was very near

her right hand, he brought it to the other side of where she slept. There was nothing to do now but rest. He stretched out on the cave floor and pulled his ruck up as a pillow for his head.

Two feet away from him Chief Mackenzie slept. He felt compelled to curve himself around her body, but knew that he couldn't. She was an Army warrant officer. He was an enlisted Navy SEAL. The two would never meet rank-wise. And besides, he liked a woman to come to him on her own rather than imposing himself on her. Closing his eyes, Kell dropped off in minutes.

An hour later, Kell was snapped out of his sleep by a voice. Instantly, he pulled the other rifle he carried, the M-4, into his hands, trying to peer into the utter darkness. And then he realized it was the woman pilot talking in her sleep. She was restless, moving onto her back.

Worried, Kell set the rifle nearby and turned on the penlight, propping it against the cave wall, close enough so he could assess her condition. Slowly getting to his knees, Kell saw her throw her right arm across her face, as if someone were hitting her. Her cries were soft, almost like a rabbit crying after being caught by a predator. What in tarnation was going on here?

"No…"

Hesitating, Kell sat paralyzed for a moment, unsure whether to wake her up or not. A lot of people in his business had nightmares. It was just part of the PTSD they all got sooner or later.

"No! Hayden! Don't hit me!"

His heart plummeted. Someone was hitting her?

No way. Yet he saw her trying to use her right arm to defend herself from unseen head blows. What the hell? And then, Kell saw her jerk her left arm up. She cried out in pain, waking herself up.

Kell moved to Mackenzie's side, gently catching her left arm, bringing it down against her belly. "Hey, Sugar, you're having some bad dreams. I need you to wake up." She was breathing unevenly. He placed his fingers inside her wrist. Her pulse was pounding like a freight train.

When her eyes opened, he saw them glazed with terror. Her soft, full mouth was contorted, the corners pulled inward. Automatically, Kell smoothed her hair across the top of her head, crooning to her. She was still caught in whatever the nightmare was. Kell didn't want to believe that a man was hitting her. Maybe just a bad dream about the crash?

Leah moaned and covered her eyes with her right hand. "Oh, God, I'm so sorry," she muttered, her voice low and hoarse.

"It's all right," Kell murmured. He liked the soft strands of her hair. It was strong, thick hair. The strands were silky and sifted through his fingers. He saw his touch was having a positive effect on her. He kept his other hand over hers, keeping that injured arm on her belly, unmoving because it was such a long, deep gash. Sudden movement could rip the stitches he'd so carefully put in.

Kell's hand on hers felt warm and dry. Leah felt sweaty. She was trembling from the nightmare that came too often and usually left her up the rest of the night, adrenaline screaming through her body to run and escape.

She needed Kell's firm, warm touch. His hand was so much larger than hers, spreading out across her abdomen. The more he moved strands of her hair through his fingers, the more she calmed down. Leah wondered if he was like a horse whisperer, having magical qualities in his hands and voice to tame even the most violent of human beings. Whatever it was, maybe because he was a combat medic, he had a healing touch. And she trusted him.

Kell saw her start to pull out of it and removed his hands. He rested them on his thighs, absorbing her beauty. Probably married. Yep, someone as pretty as she was would definitely be married. He felt sad about that, but he was a realist. Even if she hadn't been, it would never work. It was against the UCMJ for an officer to fraternize with an enlisted person. Both could receive a bad conduct discharge, which would leave their careers effectively destroyed.

Yet, as he absorbed her, his heart reached out to her. That was silly and he snorted softly. He had a family called the SEALs. Getting involved again was not in the cards. It was a high-stakes poker game and the last time Kell had played it, he'd lost.

His lawyer wife, Addison, had hated his long periods of being gone, his having to spend six months in combat. She told him she felt as though she was marrying the SEALs and not him. Sadly, there was a lot of truth to her incisive statement. Kell had learned the hard way women weren't meant to be married to a SEAL for long. There was a 90 percent divorce rate among them. And if a marriage lasted ten years, that was considered a long time. That should have warned him off, but it hadn't. Now, he was a part of that sad statistic.

Leah opened her eyes, released from the nightmare. She felt Kell's presence to her left and slowly turned her head. He sat back on his heels watching her. There was such calm in his face. His shoulders were so broad, as if they could carry more weight than a normal person's. Even dressed in SEAL cammies, she could see his chest was broad, hips narrow. He was probably around six foot, maybe a little more. Her gaze drifted down to his hands resting on his long, hard thighs.

Healing hands. Hands that did not hurt her, but took her pain away. She closed her eyes. The agony of her abusive marriage had taken a chunk out of her fractured soul. Hayden had taught her about the dark side of a man's nature. He'd been a sexual predator, physically, emotionally and mentally abusive to her. He'd needed to control her, remind her who was boss.

How had she survived it? There were times when Leah thought for sure Hayden was going to kill her. He'd come close three different times. And all three times, she'd ended up in the hospital. Desperate to forget it, Leah opened her eyes and met Kell's curious gaze.

"I'm sorry for waking you…"

"It happens," he said with a slight shrug. "Want to sit up?"

Nodding, she whispered, "Yes, but I feel like a damned puppet."

Ballard gave her a lazy grin and came over and helped her, placing the blanket behind her back so the rough cave wall wouldn't tear at her or her flight suit.

"You will for a couple of days." He brought over her helmet. "Take a look at this." He turned it so that it showed where part of it had been split open.

Drawing in a deep breath, Leah's eyes widened. "That was the blade," she rasped. "It came flying into the cockpit." And it had struck Brian, and part of it had cut into her helmet. She whispered tearfully, "Jesus…"

"Yes, I suspect Jesus did have something to do with saving you tonight," Kell murmured, placing the helmet aside. He saw the stark reality in her eyes, the understanding that she could have been decapitated if she'd been at a different angle in that cockpit. *Just inches…*

"I'm not a religious person," Leah muttered, closing her eyes, remembering the blade slicing like a saber through the cockpit.

"All men find religion in foxholes," he drawled. "Death makes for a lot of converts."

Opening her eyes, she looked over at him. She was feeling better but only marginally. "I never told you who I was. I'm Leah Mackenzie. Thank you for saving my life."

Heat coursed down through Kell. The expression in her eyes touched his heart. His whole damn body was on fire. No woman had ever affected him so powerfully. He could see the gratefulness in her green eyes, in the way her mouth went soft. So damned kissable. *If only…* He cleared his throat. "It's nice to officially meet you, ma'am."

"Don't go there," she protested. "Just call me Leah. Please?" She gave him a pleading look. "I don't think the UCMJ is out here looking over our shoulders right now, do you?"

He managed a one-cornered grin. "No, I guess not. That's a pretty name you have, Leah."

"An old-fashioned name. I was named after my grandmother, who I loved so much."

"Nothing wrong with being a bit old-fashioned," he said. "I kind of like it." Hell, he was devouring her with his eyes. Kell didn't think she really knew how beautiful she was. There was no arrogance about her. No sense of entitlement that some gorgeous women demanded. She appeared homespun to him and that just added to his desire for her.

"How did you know my name?"

"When you were unconscious, I pulled out your dog tags." He motioned to them hanging outside her flight suit. "I called my master chief, reported what happened. Told him I had you and gave him your name and number. I didn't want your husband and the rest of your family thinking you'd died in that crash."

Touched by his thoughtfulness, the honesty and concern in his gaze, she admitted, "I don't have a husband." Thank God for small and large favors. "And my father—" she shrugged painfully, her whole body feeling massively bruised "—he'll see this as a pain in his ass, one that I've always been to him. It's just one more thing he's got to 'handle.'" Bitterness coated her tone. "I don't know whether he'll be relieved or not."

Stunned by her admission, Kell sat down, crossing his legs, his long, spare hands resting over his knees. He saw grief in Leah's eyes, even though she tried to sound tough, as if she didn't care. But she did. He could feel it.

Kell couldn't be dishonest with himself. He was glad to hear she wasn't married, but that surprised the hell out of him. "I can't think any parent wouldn't want to know their child was safe."

Mouth thinning, she sighed. "Not all families are happy families, Kell."

"If you don't have a husband, then maybe a significant other?"

"No." Her voice hardened. "I don't ever want to be in a marriage or a relationship ever again."

Chills went through Kell. The look in her eyes was that of a trapped animal who hadn't been able to escape. And then he remembered the name she'd cried out during the nightmare: Hayden. Was that her ex-husband? "What about a mother?"

"Dead," Leah said, closing her eyes for a moment, wanting the pain in her head to reduce. "She's better off that way."

"Sorry to hear that," Kell said, meaning it. When she opened her eyes, he saw moistness in them. "Listen, let me do a quick exam on you. If your pupils stay equal, I can get you some morphine to kill that pain." He looked at his watch. It was 0530. It was June 2 and the sun would be rising early. They could stay awake or sleep. No. He desperately needed some more sleep.

"Sure," Leah said. She watched Kell open the ruck. He pulled out a penlight. And then he got up on one knee, his large hand engulfing the right side of her face as he cradled her jaw. He leaned forward, maybe six inches between them.

"Just look at my nose," he instructed. "I'm going to pass the light from one eye to the other. If all goes well, your eyes should dilate equally."

Her cheek prickled with heat, his fingers rough, but somehow, incredibly gentle. Hayden had never touched her like that. Not ever. All he knew how to be toward her was rough and hurtful.

Leah kept her eyes trained on Kell's intent face. He passed the light slowly from right to left. And then back again.

"You're good to go," he murmured, pleased, as he switched off the light. Kell wanted to keep his hand on her jaw. God help him, but he wanted to kiss Leah senseless. That mouth of hers, full, exquisitely shaped, was wreaking hell on his sense of control. Forcing himself to break contact with her, Kell leaned over and rummaged around for a syringe and another bottle. He put just enough morphine in it to dull pain while still keeping Leah alert, not sleepy.

Rubbing her upper arm with an alcohol wipe, he gave her the shot. "There, you're going to feel a whole lot more perky in about ten minutes." He gave her a warm smile and sat back down, putting the medical items back where they belonged.

"Thanks," Leah whispered. "How did you know I was in pain?"

Shrugging, Kell murmured as he closed the ruck. "I sense it, I guess. Taken care of a number of my SEAL buddies in my platoon over the past nine years. I don't know if I'm seeing it or feeling it. SEALs usually hide their pain, so I'd have to say it's probably my gut instinct telling me."

"Something I'm sure all you SEALs have in spades," Leah said, watching the grace of his long fingers. Kell was boneless, she decided. Ruggedly handsome, in top athletic shape and very kind. That wasn't the picture of a SEAL she'd expected. But then, Leah didn't have that much contact with them, except to pick up and drop off teams. There was no time for chit-chat when that was happening. She saw he was tired.

"Maybe we could sleep for a while longer? I don't know what your plan is for me."

Lifting his head, Kell said, "We've got a whopping amount of Taliban all around us right now. They're starting a push through the border area. My master chief said for us to sit tight if possible. It might take us days or maybe a week to get picked up. Either that, or try walking back into Bravo, which would be very dangerous."

Staring at him like he'd grown two heads, Leah said, "What?" No rescue coming?

"We're sandwiched in," Kell explained, his voice becoming serious. "Master chief knows I know these mountains and caves better than anyone. And I was on a sniper op, waiting for an HVT when your crash occurred. He wants me to stick around to try to nail the HVT, and I want too, also."

"Okay," she said, understanding.

"You'll be safe here," Kell assured her. "And you aren't in any serious medical condition, so the plan changed a bit. I need to take care of you, which I will, but I also have to nail that HVT. I've been sitting out here three weeks waiting for him." He smiled a little. "What's one more week? Besides, with that head injury of yours, the flight surgeon will put you on medical waiver for at least two to three weeks. You won't be able to fly, anyway. Consider this a vacation of sorts."

All that was true. Even now the pain was easing in her head and for that Leah was grateful to Kell, for his care and continued thoughtfulness. She had a deep, scary feeling that her entire life had just changed, but she couldn't predict the outcome of it, or understand the challenges that would come with it as a result. Yet...

CHAPTER THREE

"ARE YOU HUNGRY?" Kell asked her. Leah looked pensive after he'd given her a seven-day sentence of remaining in this cave with him.

Rubbing her stomach, she said, "I think so. Not sure..."

"Shock," he murmured. He pulled out a bottle of water and opened it for her. "Keep drinking all the fluids you can. I know you're close to dehydration."

Her fingers touched his. Leah was starved for Kell's touch. Since when did she ever entertain the idea of any man ever touching her again? Hayden had cured her of that. Yet, she trusted Kell. And why shouldn't she? She'd be dead now if not for his intervention. His heroism under fire, hauling her sorry ass out of that deadly situation, deserved a medal in her book.

Leah drank deeply. How did Kell know she was near dehydration? Was the man a mind reader? Was it his large, thoughtful-looking gray eyes that gleamed with intelligence? The natural kindness that glowed in their depths?

She watched Kell get up and, with lanky strides, leave the cave, make a right turn and disappear down a tunnel.

Realizing there was more light in the cave, Leah looked up. Just above her was a huge hole in the cave wall. And it was filtering in dawn light. Leah felt a sense of relief after the overwhelming blackness. Kell returned with some items in his large hands.

"Breakfast," he said, opening up an MRE and setting it in her lap. "You need to eat whether you feel like it or not. This cave is about as safe as it gets, but it's never totally safe. Today, I need you to eat, drink and sleep."

He was all business now. Leah could see he had a mental checklist of things he had to do. After all, he was a sniper. And he had other fish to fry besides babysitting her. Lamenting the loss of his warmth and attention, Leah set the half-emptied water bottle beside her. "Thanks," she said.

Kell watched her mouth tighten. It was her left arm. "Tell you what," he said, rising and moving to his ruck. "I'm going to fashion you a sling so you can get that arm parallel to your body. The more the arm hangs down, the more blood collects in the lower part of it, which makes for a lot more pain and swelling." He opened the ruck and pulled out a sealed plastic bag that contained a dark green triangular cotton cloth folded up in it.

Leah watched him, mesmerized by his grace, those long fingers of his quick to fashion a triangle out of the light cotton fabric. He knelt down on one knee, gently placing the sling beneath her left forearm. His face was inches from hers as he brought the ends up and quickly tied them behind the nape of her neck. He smelled of sweat, dirt and male. It did something internally to Leah; as if some primitive part of her were responding to his nearness, her body reacting to his earthy male scent. Something she'd never noticed with another man before.

"There," Kell murmured, looking pleased with his efforts. "How does your arm feel now, Leah?"

She felt her heart open just a crack as her name rolled softly from his lips. It sounded like a prayer. A beautiful prayer. "I-it feels good, Kell." She looked up into his hooded eyes and gave him a grateful look. "I feel spoiled, to tell you the truth. You've taken such good care of me. Thank you…"

He gave her a lazy smile. "Medics are like that," he drawled, easing to his feet, shutting up the ruck and then sitting down near her. He opened the MRE for her and warmed the food in the heating pouch.

"I've never been on the receiving end of a combat medic before," Leah admitted. Now, with her arm in a sling, she only had one good hand and found herself fumbling with the other packets.

The next moment, Kell was kneeling next to her, his knee nearly touching her thigh. It happened so fast, so silently, that Leah began to realize what SEAL meant. The man moved like a shadow. She'd been focused on trying to open the packet of food, distracted, and he'd just shown up like magic at her side.

"Let me do that," he murmured, taking the bag. He tore it open, looked at the rest of the MRE and got everything open and available for her to eat after it was heated up. He took the plastic utensils out of their wrapper, as well.

"I'm not used to feeling helpless," Leah muttered uncomfortably, giving him an apologetic look.

"Everyone needs to lean on someone at some point," Kell said philosophically, easing back to where his MRE sat. Leaning up against the wall, one long leg hitched up, he quickly consumed everything in the MRE.

Leah thought about his words, slowly testing the food. If her stomach rebelled, she was not going to eat even if Kell wanted her to. Somehow, she knew he'd understand.

Kell tipped his head back and glanced over at Leah. He'd seen her brows dip over his comment. "Tell me about your family. Where were you born?"

The questions, softly asked, made Leah's stomach clench. She owed him, so she said, "I was born in Istanbul, Turkey. My father is in the Army. He was stationed there with our family."

"Turkey? You're exotic, then," he teased, smiling at her. Kell saw her look awkward. Why? "That was a compliment," he added. And she was exotic looking, her green eyes slightly tilted, giving her a mysterious quality. But in truth? He also saw a haunted look in them, as well. Kell couldn't figure out why she was so wary of him. So troubled.

"I'm hardly exotic," Leah muttered darkly. It thrilled her that he saw her like that. At the same time, she remembered Hayden making fun of the tilt of her eyes, saying she looked ugly. She looked different. No other man would want her. She was lucky to have him. *Oh, yeah, real damned lucky.*

"Listen," Kell said gently, "if you're uncomfortable with me because I'm an enlisted person and you're a warrant officer, you just tell me."

Stricken, Leah felt her lips part as she stared in shock over his statement. "What? No. Of course not. You saved my life, Kell. I've never been one to make a big deal that I'm a warrant. I work with enlisted people all the time and I see them as part of my team. I respect them."

"That's good to know," he said, holding her upset gaze. "You just need to speak up and tell me what's comfortable for you and what's not. I have a feeling you aren't too good at communicating to others on a personal level." He added a slight grin to take the sting out of his observation.

Leah was hiding a whole helluva lot and he felt as if she was a mine field he had to negotiate. He wasn't sure where to step with Leah without her becoming defensive. Like she was right now.

Leah scowled, hit hard by his comment. She was too tired to put up her normal defenses to keep the world—and him—at bay. Kell had been nothing but kind, caring and supportive toward her. Leah waffled between evading what he'd asked and telling him the truth. She put the MRE aside, no longer hungry.

"It's hard for me to open up," she admitted, her voice strained.

"Maybe a trust issue?"

She stared at him. Good God, he was a mind reader! Leah saw no judgment in Kell's expression, his expression sympathetic as he held her shaken gaze. She leaned back against the rock wall and closed her eyes. "I don't trust too many people," she admitted wearily.

Well, if she had been a real mine field, Kell told himself grimly, he'd have just lost his leg. The look on Leah's face bothered him. She was a beautiful, confident, intelligent woman. A powerhouse, because she was a ball-busting Shadow pilot. Only the cream of the Army's helo pilots ever got invited to join the 80th. And she was one of them.

He ate the rest of his MRE in silence. Looking at his watch, he knew he had to get going to find a new hide. His old one had been compromised last night.

Silently rising, Kell went about putting on his H-gear harness, placing six mags of bullets for his .300 Win-Mag rifle in the front pockets. Automatically, he checked his SIG Sauer pistol, made sure a bullet was in the chamber and slid it back into his drop holster.

His mind was moving over a mental list of what he had to do. Dawn was a good time to search for a new hide location. Usually, the Taliban didn't start moving until after first light. Prayers and tea, in that order, first. By that time, the sun was well above the horizon. He set the rifle on the wall near his ruck.

Leah watched him, the silence heavy in the cave. It was because of her. Her prickly defensiveness. She never wanted a man to get inside her walls again. Never wanted a man to know who she was, her vulnerabilities and weaknesses. Hayden had exploited every one of them against her, took her power and controlled her to a large extent. Kell had scared the hell out of her with his simple observations. He was right that trust didn't come easy to her. Compressing her lips, she asked, "How long will you be gone?"

"Until nightfall," he answered. Kell handed her four bottles of water from his ruck and set them beside her. "I want to see these empty when I get back tonight," he told her, giving her a serious look. "There's a cave to the right of this one. There's all kinds of foodstuffs, ammo and boxes of water. I don't know how steady you'll be on your feet today, but if you get bored, look around a little."

"Okay," she said. He was so damned swift and efficient, his hands flying over his gear, pulling the ruck up on one shoulder, the Win-Mag in his large left hand. He settled the boonie cap on his head. He had a pair of wraparound sunglasses hanging out of one of his cammie shirt pockets.

Kell strode out of the cave, turned right, and Leah could hear him repacking his ruck. When he came back, he set the ruck down, strapped the Win-Mag on the back of it and then hauled on the pack. Moving his hands along the thick straps, he belted it up so it rode comfortably on his shoulders and around his waist.

"I'm taking the sat phone," Kell told her. "There will be no way for you to contact me." He gestured to the cave. "No signals get in or out of here." And then his voice became teasing. "If I had an iPod, I'd give it to you to listen to some good bluegrass music, but it's back at Bravo."

She managed a slight smile, drowning in the warmth of his gray gaze. "I like bluegrass."

"Really?" Kell was pleased. "We have something in common." He patted his left breast pocket. "I always carry my harmonica with me."

"Where were you born?" Leah couldn't stop the personal question from flying out of her mouth. She had a million questions for this man who had saved her life.

"Sandy Hook, Kentucky. My folks are originally from Alabama and moved us up north when I was a year old." He crouched down near her, his eyes becoming serious looking. "Now listen, Sugar, you take it easy on yourself today. I know you're a Type-A hot-shot pilot, but right now, your wings are clipped and you need to stand down for just a bit."

Leah felt like the sun had suddenly come out and incredible warmth encircled her. It was Kell. It was his genuine care and concern for her. She felt heat moving from her neck into her face. At twenty-eight she was blushing? His eyes were large, intense upon her, as if she were his whole world in that moment. The sensation was hot, alive, and Leah suddenly felt her body respond to him as a man. Rocked by the unexpected sensations, she managed in a whisper, "I'll be good. Don't worry."

Kell grinned and reached out, moving a few strands away from her flushed cheek and eased them behind her delicate ear. He'd seen his care make an amazing difference in Leah. It struck him that she wasn't used to a man's attention. And that she was innocent. As if she didn't know how to handle him or his teasing. Kell tucked that knowledge away, not wanting Leah to feel threatened by him. In the back of his mind, he was very sure some bastard had really hurt her emotionally. She reacted like an injured animal that was constantly being threatened. And he saw her eyes suddenly go soft when he'd tucked those ginger-colored strands behind her ear.

He liked touching her, understanding she craved it. He craved her. That was a far different scenario. This was his territory, his world, and she was a stranger to it, thrown off guard and out of her element. It was up to him to make her feel welcomed and a part of it.

"Take care out there," Leah whispered as he rose fluidly to his feet.

"Always," Ballard promised. He lifted his hand and then walked silently out of the cave.

KELL SAW A SMALL penlight on as he approached the cave many hours later. He turned the corner and saw Leah sitting up, her gaze on him as he appeared around the wall of the cave. "How are you doing?" he asked quietly, coming over and shrugging out of the ruck.

"Okay," she murmured. "How'd it go out there today? Any luck?"

He knelt down on one knee, setting the ruck up against the wall. "No luck. I had to find and build a new hide today. Took most of the day, and the Taliban was quiet in the area." He gave her a glance, seeing that her eyes looked dull. "Are you in pain?"

"A little," Leah admitted, pointing to her arm in the sling.

"I should have left you some pain pills," he said with apology, opening his ruck. "Here—" he handed her the medication "—this will stop the pain but keep you clearheaded."

"Thanks," she murmured, popping the pill in her mouth and drinking the last of the water in the fourth bottle.

Leah didn't want to admit she'd looked forward to Kell coming back to the cave. His skin gleamed with sweat and she could tell he'd been running. His trousers were filthy, probably from digging a hide into a rocky mountain slope. He tossed his boonie cap over on his sleeping bag. His hair was dusty, as well.

He took off his H-gear, setting it next to the ruck. "Have you been up and about?"

"I tried." She pointed to her bandaged head. "Dizzy."

"Were you wanting to pitch forward?" he wondered, sitting down on the sleeping bag and unlacing his desert boots.

"Yes. How did you know?"

He smiled tiredly. "That's a deep cut on your scalp. And I think you have a pretty good concussion. Probably a level-two variety. Most people get nausea and dizziness for two or three days after the incident." He pulled off his boots and his dark green socks that were soaked with sweat. Rubbing his fingers across his aching feet, he said, "I'm taking a bath over there in that pool," and pointed to it. "Need to get clean."

"I've been looking at that pool, too," Leah said wistfully. She wrinkled her nose. "I'm filthy."

"Easy to get that way out here," Kell agreed, standing. "I can carry you over there. Give you a sponge bath?" He entertained the thought of helping her undress. All day, off and on, he'd wondered what her body looked like beneath that sexless flight suit of hers. Kell knew he'd been out here way too long.

"No, I think I'll be able to walk tomorrow. Maybe get cleaned up while you're gone." Her body reacted hotly to his suggestion, however. Leah found herself like a greedy little beggar, wanting any touch he'd bestow on her. What the hell was the matter with her? Why couldn't she hide behind those elaborate walls she'd built up since her divorce?

Grunting, Kell said, "I'll get you a towel, a washcloth and some soap."

She watched him disappear into the cave where he had all his supplies hidden. Tomorrow, she wanted to get over there and explore his stash. Kell came back with the articles and set them near her. He had a towel draped over his shoulder.

"Now, unless you want to see me buck naked, you might want to just lie down and face the other way?"

"Right. No problem," Leah muttered, embarrassed, turning over so that her back was toward the pool. Her heart was pulsing. Her desire to see him naked surprised the hell out of her. She was so drawn to his large hands—those fingers that were almost artist-like. And when Kell touched her…groaning softly to herself, Leah listened. And she wished, as she heard him walk into the pool, that she could turn around and appreciate him from a purely aesthetic standpoint.

Kell felt incredibly clean. The water was freezing cold, dripping off the tops of the mountains that remained snowbound all year-round. He tucked a towel around his waist and walked into the other cave to retrieve a clean pair of cammie trousers and a desert-tan T-shirt. He wiped his hair dry as he reentered the cave. Leah was sitting up once again. "All clear."

She gulped, her gaze moving to his broad set of shoulders and his deep chest. The T-shirt stretched tautly across his upper body and it made her feel shaky inside. What was going on with her? Why was her body behaving like this? Kell looked almost boyish, that easy grin across his mouth, his gray eyes alight with mischief. The transformation was amazing. Breath-stealing. His hips were narrow, and those long legs of his… Leah felt helpless in a feminine kind of way. She'd had very few experiences with men. And they hadn't been good ones. Did sexual libido build up after a while? Hell, she had *no* idea and she felt like an idiot of sorts. She could fly into the most danger-

ous of situations and not bat an eyelash. But let this
Kentucky SEAL, with that loose, boneless walk of
his, and that warm smile, walk into her life, and she
was turning into a sexual puddle of sorts.

"Hungry?"

Oh, that was a pointed question with all kinds of
innuendos, Leah thought. "Yes," she managed, swallowing nervously.

Kell pulled the towel across his shoulder and left for
a moment, returning with two MREs in hand. Leah's
breath hitched as he knelt down on one knee near her
right side. She could smell the Afghan lye soap on his
flesh, his male scent that was sending her body into
spasms of heat and hunger. Kell didn't seem to be at
all aware of his effect on her. He quickly opened the
MRE, tore open the packets and put the plastic ware
on the tray for her. Within a minute he had the main
dish cooking in the heating bag.

"There you go," Kell murmured. "Spaghetti tonight." He lifted his head. He was in such deep trouble. Leah's eyes were huge, such a rich, dark green,
and Kell saw gold within them. His gaze dropped to
her lips, which parted as his eyes took them in. That's
all he needed right now, an erection stirring. *Damn.*
He wanted to kiss Leah. Hell, Ballard had entertained
the thought of feeling those lips beneath his mouth
from the moment he'd seen her face, when he'd laid
her down, unconscious, on this floor.

Kell forced himself to get up and move. If he didn't,
he was going to be in such deep shit he'd never be able
to dig himself out. She was an Army warrant and he
was enlisted. He couldn't go there even though his

heart and body could give a damn less about military regs or the UCMJ.

Feeling shaky, Leah watched Kell rise. He was at least six feet two inches tall. The breadth of his shoulders, the power of those ropy bicep muscles attested to his superb athletic condition. Mouth dry, she dropped her gaze to the food. Again, she felt heat sweeping up her neck and into her face.

Flustered, she focused on eating. Kell was going to kiss her. She saw it so clearly in his eyes, that for a split second, she couldn't breathe. What would it have been like to kiss this man? Leah wanted to find out, despite her past. Against her screaming brain and her memory, she *wanted* to kiss this SEAL! Worst of all, he was enlisted and she was a warrant. She knew better. Officers were to uphold the UCMJ, not disobey it.

Kell sat down with his MRE, leaning against the cave wall. "When I left the cave complex this morning, I called the master chief first thing and gave him an update on your medical condition." He glanced over at her. "He said a Major Hayden Grant was demanding you be airlifted out right now." Kell saw her freeze. The flush in her cheeks drained instantly to white. Her mouth compressed, as if in pain. Leah looked like a deer caught in headlights, he supposed. Paralyzed. And then, Kell remembered she'd been screaming a name during the nightmare. The name Hayden. Scowling, Kell put it together, realizing it was probably the same man. But he wasn't sure. He cleared his throat. "You okay, Leah? You look a little shaken."

Leah closed her eyes for a moment, wrestling with myriad emotions, mostly fear and, yeah, raw damned terror that was gutting through her right now. But

Kell's deep, drawling voice broke through the bar-
riers that had suddenly imprisoned her. She put the
packet aside, having absolutely no appetite. Looking
over at him, she realized he was worried—for her.
There was another emotion she felt him directing toward her: protectiveness. And she felt it surrounding
her right now, invisible, but so very real and incredibly
comforting to her. Kell must have seen or sensed her
terror. "I, uh— That's my ex-husband. He's the commander of the 80th Shadow Squadron that's stationed
at Bagram." Her voice sounded dry. Scared. Licking
her lips, she said, "He's always like that."

"Like what?"

"A control freak," Leah muttered with distaste. And
sexually and physically abusive toward her, playing
with her mind, her emotions. A shiver coursed through
her and Leah forced herself to hold it together.

Kell saw genuine terror in Leah's eyes. She was
easy to read, plus he had his SEAL instincts that never
led him wrong and had kept him alive throughout the
years. She was frightened. Of her ex? It seemed like
it. He watched as her right hand shook as she placed
the packet on the MRE bag.

Something repulsive hit him. Ballard couldn't define it. Didn't know what it was about, but God help
him, he felt it around Leah. Like a dark, ugly shadow.
And she wouldn't look at him.

Leah forced herself to speak. "What was the decision?" The last place she wanted to go was Bagram,
where she'd have Hayden in her face, making her life
utterly miserable.

"Master Chief told him no," Kell offered. "I was
going to add that the CIA is picking up a lot of radio

and cell-phone chatter around the border. When that happens, it means a big push by our enemy is coming shortly. And right now, every forward operating base is on high alert. We've got air assets piling in to be used and every SEAL is out in teams at choke points, working with the Rangers and Delta Force operators. It's a big assault that's coming our way."

He held her shattered-looking gaze. More gently, Kell added, "You're safer here with me for now, Leah. I know this isn't great digs and I'm sure you're looking forward to a hot shower and hot food…" And he was going to miss her when she left. All day, he'd been looking forward to coming home tonight, seeing her here. Talking with her. Getting to know her. Kell couldn't ever recall a woman making him feel like this. It was Leah, he realized. There was a special connection between them. Kell had felt it from the outset. Now, it was stronger, tighter, more palpable than ever. He could feel it and he knew Leah did, too.

"I'd rather stay here, Kell, if I have any say in it."

"You have every right to have a say in your rescue. The master chief asked me what I thought you'd want to do and I took a risk and said you'd rather stay with me until we can get a safe opening to get you out of here." His mouth crooked. "Glad I made the right call."

Relief flooded through her. "You did." And then Leah shook her head. "Sometimes I think you know me better than I know myself." She said it in jest, but Kell had shown repeatedly he could read her, see right through her, ask the right question or have the correct observations about her.

"Aren't you going to eat?" Kell urged her in a quiet tone.

"No. I'm…not hungry."

"Because you're upset?"

"Yes." She shouldn't bare her soul to Kell, but dammit, she felt like doing exactly that. He was a good listener. But she was afraid Kell would judge her if she told him the sordid story of her marriage to Hayden Grant. "I'm just not feeling good," she muttered, setting the MRE aside.

"What can I do to help?"

Leah sat without reacting, but inwardly, her heart just somersaulted and her pulse began to race. Her lower body went hot and dammit, she felt the dampness between her thighs. *Again.* Pushing her fingers through her dirty hair, she growled, "Nothing."

Kell got it. Another land mine. Only this time, it had a name attached to it: Major Hayden Grant. He didn't know the Army officer, having little interface with the 80th except to hitch a ride on one of their MH-47 helicopters.

He finished his MRE and stood up. He had an idea, maybe something that could divert Leah's attention to something a little more positive. He walked over and picked up her uneaten MRE. She was pale, agitation in her eyes. Kell could feel the terror around her, even though she didn't say anything.

Going to the other cave, he picked up a large aluminum bowl, found some unscented shampoo he kept for whenever he got a chance to wash up on a sniping mission, and brought it back to the other cave. Going over to the pool, he got fresh, cold water by holding the huge bowl over the drips coming off from the rocks above.

Leah frowned as he brought the bowl of water over

and set it nearby. "What's that for?" She met his gray eyes and felt some of her terror dissolve. That power- ful sense of protection wrapped around her with just Ballard's kind gaze.

"I think you'll feel better if you can at least get your hair washed." Kell set up the other sleeping bag, roll- ing it out and putting his ruck where a pillow would have been.

"But…I can't wash my hair," Leah said, longing badly to get the dirt off her scalp, get rid of the dried blood so she'd stop smelling it. "I only have one hand."

"I'll do the washing," Kell told her. Holding out his hand, he said, "Come on, I have to move you over here. I want you to lie down on your back and let your head hang over the end of my ruck."

Leah sat there, stunned. He was serious. Her heart opened, catching her off guard. "But—"

"When my grandma Inez was alive, I used to wash her hair once a week. I was a kid, only thirteen, but I usually did a pretty good job. She was happy with my efforts and my mother was relieved I didn't dump the water all over her bed." Kell gave a bashful grin. "I'm not a hairdresser, but I am pretty good at wash- ing a woman's hair. Want to give it a whirl? Live dan- gerously?"

Leah stared at his long fingers, seeing the calluses on them, the width of his palm, the inherent strength of him as a man. Hesitantly, she placed her hand in his. Fingers warm and strong around hers, Kell easily lifted her to her feet. Dizziness struck Leah big-time and she felt herself pitching forward.

"I got you," Kell rasped, placing his arm around her waist and holding her upright. "A little walking is going to be good for you, anyway. It will force your brain to get back to normal quicker."

Leah's mouth went dry. She was plastered against Kell's body, felt the hardness of his muscles, his stability and strength. Her heart was tripping all over itself. Overwhelmed with too much going on, she simply surrendered to Kell and let him slowly guide her over to the other sleeping bag.

He handled her as if she were a feather in his arms and she knew she wasn't. The man's strength was hidden, but she felt it now as he lowered her to the floor.

Closing her eyes for a moment, Leah wanted to cry. The tears came out of nowhere. Kell was being incredibly gentle with her. As if she were a rare vase that might shatter between his hands if he wasn't careful enough with her. Compared to Hayden's heavy-handedness, his need to hurt her, make her scream for mercy, Kell was the exact opposite.

Somehow, Leah forced back the tears as Kell guided her shoulders onto the ruck, making sure she was comfortable. The difference was pulverizing. Eye-opening.

CHAPTER FOUR

"This is very cold water," Kell warned her, settling the bowl between his knees and sliding his fingers through Leah's thick, tangled hair.

"It's okay. I'm just so glad you're going to get the blood out of my hair. The smell is terrible." Leah bit back a gasp over the pleasure of his fingers sifting through her strands. It was sensual. Heat scattered from her scalp, down to her breasts, tightening them and then flowing to build in her lower body, making it clench and grow needy. She closed her eyes, dragging in a deep, unsteady breath.

"I understand," Kell soothed. Cupping his hand, he drizzled the water across her scalp. With his other hand, he supported her neck and the back of head, feeling the tension in her.

As he worked with her hair and scalp, Leah gradually began to relax and surrender to him. It was such an intimate act to Kell. She trusted him with herself. Another man might have tried something stupid, to take advantage of her in such a compromised position. He would never do that to any woman. Instead, Kell took pleasure in simply washing Leah's hair, cleansing it of the blood and matted, muddy areas. Knowing how a woman always wanted her hair clean, it was a small gift that he could give to Leah. And soon, her eyes closed and she fully relaxed, her soft lips parting.

Smiling to himself, Kell knew the luxury of having one's hair washed because his grandmother used to lie there and sigh with pleasure, too. Leah didn't, but that was all right. He could see all the tension dissolving from her face and the length of her body.

"I'm afraid my shampoo has no smell to it," Kell told her, opening the bottle. "Out here when I'm hunting, the Taliban can pick up on a foreign odor and know there's an enemy nearby. I learned a long time ago to get lye soap that has no scent to it."

"Wise choice." Leah sighed, feeling his fingers gently begin to massage her scalp. He had removed the dressing from her head earlier and he was very gentle and very careful around the stitched wound. Still, just to get the blood out of her hair, Leah was utterly grateful for his thoughtfulness. "I've never had a man wash my hair before," she admitted, her voice sounding breathless even to her.

"Well, if this doesn't go right, don't blame the next male hairdresser you get." He laughed.

"No…you're doing…wonderfully. It feels so good," Leah whispered, feeling the tingles his fingers were creating by lightly massaging her scalp. Leah had no idea how much tension she'd been holding until it disappeared beneath his seductive fingers.

"Oh, good, then you're not going to fire me." Kell grinned, rinsing the soap from her sleek, gleaming strands. He heard Leah laugh, his hand cupping and supporting the back of her head. Her skin felt like soft, warm velvet to him. Feeling a bit like a thief, Kell enjoyed touching Leah. He felt good making her laugh.

It was better than seeing stark terror lurking in her eyes. Who had scared her so much that she reacted with such a deep, automatic fear?

Once her hair was rinsed free of the soap, he put the bowl aside. Kell held her head up and awkwardly placed a towel around the dripping strands of her hair. "Okay, I'm going to get you up into a sitting position. You ready?"

Leah was sorry it was over. "Yes." She felt the towel around her head and held it in place with her right hand. Kell gently eased her into a sitting position and then came around to her right side.

"Here, let me? Tough to dry hair with one hand." Kell took the towel and carefully dried her long, thick hair. Taking a look at the gash on her skull, he said, "The cut is healing nicely. I think we'll let it air-dry tonight. I'll put some antibiotic ointment on it and that's all it should need."

"I have a medic and a hairdresser all wrapped up in one," Leah teased. "That feels dry enough, Kell, thank you." She wanted his hands on her, but at some point the surging pleasure rippling through her would stop. Kell was so damn personable. He slid inside her heavy, protective walls as though they'd never existed.

Kell stood and pulled out a comb from his pocket. "Here you go," he said, handing it to her. Wanting to sit and watch her, he forced himself to move away from Leah. Watching her was a sensual pleasure all its own in his world. He emptied the water into a channel leaving the pool and hung the wet towel and wash-cloth in the other cave on some rocks to dry. When he ambled back in, he smiled. Leah had finished combing her hair. The ends were damp and slightly curled across her shoulders.

"Now, don't you feel better?"

Handing him the comb, Leah admitted softly, "I feel a million times better. Thanks so much, Kell." And she wished she could do something to repay him for his generosity. She watched as he sat down against the wall after moving his sleeping bag over to it.

"My grandma, who had bad arthritis in her hands, would always bake me chocolate-chip cookies as a thank-you for washing her hair weekly." Kell smiled fondly, remembering those good times.

"I'm afraid I'm a nonstarter in a kitchen," Leah admitted.

"Tell you what. Next time we happen to both be at Bravo, you can buy me a beer over at the canteen. Fair enough?" He caught her gaze. She looked infinitely better. The tension was gone. So was the terror. Instead, Kell saw her green eyes radiant with warmth. Was that warmth for him? He could feel it, but didn't try to interpret what it meant. That would get him into dangerous quicksand real fast.

"That's a deal," Leah promised, her voice passionate. "I need to thank you for everything you're doing for me, Kell. I really appreciate it."

"No need to pay me back," he murmured. "My ma always taught me you treat others like you would like to be treated. It's been the rule I've lived my life by."

"Tell me about yourself. You said your parents moved from Alabama to Kentucky. How did you become a SEAL?"

"The short version," he said, pushing his long legs out in front of him. "My pa, who is a dairy farmer, was in the Army for four years. He thought it was good I do my duty to my country, so I joined the Navy. I'd heard about the SEALs and applied. I got in, managed to survive BUD/S, and here I am."

"You didn't want to be a farmer?"

"No. I'm a rolling stone." Kell chuckled. "I liked being outdoors, I liked challenges and I was a pretty active kid. I liked what the SEALs offered me. I believed I could make a difference in the world, take out the bad guys so the good men and women could live."

"You don't strike me as being black-and-white," Leah murmured. "You're a good observer of the human condition. That encompasses a lot of gray areas."

Shrugging, Kell said, "I'm aware of the gray areas. But when it comes to a bad guy who's going to kill one of my brothers, or anyone on our side who is fighting over here, I'm very clear about pulling the trigger. I don't enjoy it, but I know someone has to do it. Does that make more sense?" Ballard absorbed her thoughtful expression. Shadow pilots were aggressive in combat, too. They didn't just drop black ops men off from a helo. They were often in direct combat protecting men on the ground, too.

"Makes sense to me," Leah agreed. She moved her fingers through her clean hair. It felt like she'd lost a pound of dried blood, sweat and dirt out of the strands. "I have a tough time seeing you in the role of a hunter-sniper."

"Oh, you met the nice side of me is all," he said, chuckling. "I'm not out there offering to wash a Taliban soldier's hair, believe me."

Leah laughed with him. "Point taken."

"You have any brothers or sisters?" Kell asked. Instantly, he saw he'd just stepped on another land mine with her. *Damn.* If she'd had a miserable marriage, which is what he surmised by her reaction earlier, *and* an unhappy childhood, it was no wonder she was so closed up. Kell could feel her hiding; had sensed it all along.

"Yes," she said, her voice low. "Evan was my older brother by one year." Leah tensed and then figured to hell with it. "When I was eight, Evan was nine. My father was on assignment in Rhode Island and when winter came, we'd go for walks. One morning, after a heavy snow, Spike, our dog, went running out into a field where we were walking. He fell through the ice and into a frozen pond." The corners of her mouth drew in. "Evan went to rescue him and so did I." She looked up and held Kell's somber gaze. "We didn't realize the ice would break. Evan fell in. And then I did, too. The dog managed to climb up my back and got to thicker ice. I tried to rescue Evan, but he disappeared below the water and I was so cold I could barely move. Somehow, I pulled myself up on the ice. About that time, my father found us."

"I'm sorry," Kell offered. Was that why she looked so haunted? "Did you blame yourself for not rescuing Evan?"

Giving him a dark look, Leah nodded. "My parents were grief-stricken. A month afterward, my mother had a heart attack and died. I'm sure Evan's death triggered it. My father went into deep shock."

"So you were a little eight-year-old girl who was grieving for two losses, then."

Touched by his awareness, Leah said heavily, "I was devastated."

"Was your father able to comfort you?"

Shaking her head, Leah said, "No." And then, "I sort of became a shadow in his life until I was about sixteen. He loved my mother so very much. Looking back on it, I now realize that his love for her was so powerful, so real, that her getting ripped out of his life like that devastated him in ways I can't even understand to this day."

Kell wanted to go over and sit down and hold her. He heard the quiet pain in Leah's low voice, saw the haunted look back in her expression. "But who took care of *you*?"

"No one, I guess. My father was a major in the Army, and he was up for light colonel. His life revolved around the Shadow Squadron." *Not me. Never me.*

Rubbing his jaw, Kell asked, "Did he ever remarry?"

"No." Leah looked up, giving him a sad smile. "I got to see what head over heels in love really meant. My father was utterly devoted to my mother. They lived a love I've never seen since." She opened her hands and gave a strained laugh. "I remember as a kid looking at the love my father had for my mother, wishing someday I'd meet someone who felt like that. Someone who thought I was the most beautiful person in the world. Someone who wanted to love me, care for me and support me like my dad supported my mom."

And it didn't happen, Kell thought, knowing what little he did about her marriage. "My ma and pa are like that," he offered. "Pa thinks the world revolves around Ma. Still does to this day. They're in their early sixties and they're completely devoted to each other. And to us. They spread their love around."

"You're lucky," Leah said, feeling a bit jealous. "My father...well...he had great plans for Evan and none for me."

"Ah, the favored-son routine?"

"You could say."

"How did that change your relationship with your father after Evan died?"

"He basically ignored me until I was sixteen. And then, one day, he told me to get into a helicopter and I did. He started teaching me how to fly. I found I loved it. The freedom..."

"And then you went to college?"

"For two years. I wanted a four-year degree in electrical engineering, but I quit after two years. I was always fascinated with how things worked. Not exactly a girlie girl growing up."

"Could have fooled me," Kell said. "You are one heck of a good-looking woman even if you're forced into wearing that bulky flight suit."

His compliment was sincere and Leah absorbed it. "Thanks...kind of hard to be very feminine out here in the badlands."

"Don't kid yourself," he said, smiling a little. "You give that flight suit a whole new, better, meaning." He saw her blush and she wouldn't meet his eyes. Her shyness bothered him. Again, Kell was seeing her inability to deal with a sincere male-to-female compliment. He wasn't flirting with her. He was being honest. She didn't know the difference.

"I'm pretty much focused on my career" was all

Leah could manage. There was no question Kell was interested in her. Leah felt the same toward him, but didn't dare let him know it. There was just no room in her life, with her career as a warrant officer, to allow a potential relationship to work. She looked over. "Are you married, Kell? Have a bunch of children?" Because looking at him, he looked like the father type.

"Was," Kell admitted. "I met Addison, who was a criminal-defense lawyer, in San Diego. Married at twenty-three and divorced at twenty-seven. She couldn't take my long deployments, and I didn't want children while I was in the SEALs. I'd never be home often enough to be a father to them. My training and deployments kept me away from home so much of the time. I did want children, but I wanted to be a father who was home and there for them, like my pa was for us."

"You'll make a wonderful father someday," Leah said. Mentally she was comparing her father to Kell. There was a Grand Canyon of difference between the two men. Her father was cold, bottled up, frozen in time and bitter. Kell was warm, kind and caring. He was able to show his feelings.

Leah wondered if things would have been different between her father and herself if her mother hadn't suddenly died. She had felt abandoned and alone after her mother was gone. She cried for months, every night, sobbing into her pillow, missing Evan and her. Her father was unable to care for her. He couldn't even care for himself, as crippled as he'd been by the multiple deaths.

"I have a good role model," Kell admitted. "My pa. I have two younger brothers, Tyler and Cody, and we used to have so much fun with him. He taught us how to hunt, fish and care for the land. The three of us grew up milking dairy cows."

"You've got a good work ethic," Leah said, trying to imagine Kell when he was younger. She'd bet he was the brother who played humorous jokes on others. Not mean ones, but funny ones, because he was so laid-back and easygoing.

"We all worked hard," Kell agreed, smiling fondly, remembering those days, "but we also played hard."

"What sports?"

"I went into track and field. Ty and Cody went into football."

"You look like a quarterback to me."

"Nah, my two younger brothers were good at it. I wasn't. I'm six-two and they're both six-four and outweigh me by thirty pounds. I didn't see any sense in getting the shinola kicked out of me on the football field. Running was something I was very good at. It came naturally."

"You've got long legs," Leah agreed. She visualized him running and imagined he would have looked to her like a cheetah with swift, boneless grace.

"Did you ever go into sports?"

"No. I found my love, my passion, when I was sixteen. I loved flying. I still do."

"What does it give you?" Kell wondered. He looked forward to talking with Leah. She was intelligent, well grounded in reality and funny.

"I guess…my freedom. When I'm flying, I'm above all the crap that I carry around with me. Up there—" she pointed toward the ceiling of the cave "—I'm in the arms of the sky."

"Maybe an invisible, loving mother of sorts?"

She stared at Kell for a long moment. He was extremely intelligent, able to put seemingly disparate pieces together and make them fit like a completed puzzle. "I never thought of that way, but yes. I always feel protected up there, guarded, maybe." She'd just walked away from a helo crash that should have killed her. Kell had been her guardian angel this time around.

"Without a mother to hold you," Kell said, "you probably didn't get a lot of that maternal nurturing we all need as kids growing up."

"I've thought about that, too. Maybe that's why I love going out into the Afghan villages, bringing clothing and shoes to the kids. I work with a local charity that is run by a husband-and-wife team, Emma and Khalid Shaheen. Both were Apache pilots and then Emma got kidnapped by the Taliban. She was injured and received nerve damage to her left hand. The Army doesn't let you fly if you don't have feeling in all ten fingers. But when Emma married Khalid, she got to fly his charity's helicopter, a CH-47. A year ago, when my squadron was at Bagram, I took my off days and flew with Emma."

"You like kids?"

"Just a little." Leah smiled, tipping her head back against the wall. "Before we lost Evan, I loved taking care of him. I spoiled him rotten." She laughed softly, a warm, good feeling flowing through her. "Kids should be spoiled with love."

"Evan will always own a piece of your heart."

"One of the good parts," Leah agreed quietly. "The rest of my heart feels like it's been cut up and buried."

"Because of your marriage?" Kell knew he was getting into dangerous territory, but he wanted to understand her ex-husband. He saw her give him a grim look and her lips thinned as if she was weighing whether to say anything or not.

"Let's just say I had lousy taste when it came to choosing a husband."

Kell looked at his watch. "Time to go to bed." It was a piece of information about Hayden Grant. Maybe, in time, Leah would trust him with the rest of the story, but he wouldn't push her. As a sniper, he could look at a lawn and tell which blades of grass had been moved by an animal or a human. In the same way, Leah was giving him tiny signs and in his mind he was putting them together. Eventually, a pattern would emerge and he'd see the whole picture. He wanted to know because he had feelings for Leah. No one was more surprised than Kell. He wasn't looking for a woman. Sex with the right woman? Yes. But as he pushed off his boots and got comfortable, he wouldn't lie to himself. His heart was involved in this equation. What was he going to do?

As he made sure Leah was settled in for the night before turning off the light, Ballard sensed, or maybe intuited, she liked him just as much. They were two planets on a collision course with one another that could never have a happy ending.

THE NIGHTMARE STARTED *insidiously for Leah. She and Hayden were camping out in the hills of Georgia; something he liked to do. It was August, the humidity high, the mosquitoes pestering her nonstop. Hayden was in a bad mood. Her father had been busy reviewing the fitness reports for every officer. Hayden was a captain and he wanted early major in rank. He was worried her father wouldn't give him the marks he needed to make that early rank. He was busy building a fire, throwing heavier limbs on it, the smoke billowing up through the dense pine forest surrounding them.*

"You need to talk to your father," he growled. "I need a perfect score on this next fitness report."

Leah's hands shook as she began unpacking the food from the cardboard box sitting in the rear of their SUV. "If I say anything, Hayden, he'll suspect you put me up to it. You know that."

She hated these conversations. Assessments came every six months, and officers and enlisted persons alike were given a score. Those that had the highest grades would automatically be put up for early-promotion consideration. This was the first time Hayden could be put up for it by her father, the squadron commander.

"You have to say something," *he ground out, standing, wiping his hands off on his jeans. He glared at her. "Figure out a diplomatic way, Leah, but get it done, dammit!"*

She winced as he cursed. Hayden was building into one of his rages and it scared her to death. She dropped the bread on the ground, then quickly picked it up. Breathing unevenly, her mind awash with fear of what he might do, she said, "I'll talk to him."

He walked over and stood beside her. He was six feet tall. She was five feet seven inches tall. Staring down at her, he jerked her hair back, hard. "Monday. When we get back. Take him to lunch."

"Ow!" Leah cried, her scalp radiating pain. Her

hand had gone up to the side of her head. "Stop hurting me, Hayden! You don't have to worry, I'll talk to my father."

"LEAH! WAKE UP!" Kell dodged her fist and it landed hard against his chest, a lot of power behind her swing. She'd screamed and scared the hell out of him, jerking him out of his sleep. Worse, if there were Taliban nearby, they'd have heard it.

Gripping her arm, Ballard gave her a small shake. "Leah! Wake up. It's just a dream!" He saw her face twisted and contorted, her mouth opened to scream again. What the hell kind of nightmares was she having to make her twist and buck against him? He had knelt down, dodging her flailing fist. It was lucky for him her other arm was in a sling or he'd have been in trouble.

"Sugar. Come on. It's Kell. You're safe. No one is attacking you…"

Kell's voice broke through her nightmare and Leah snapped awake. Her eyes widened enormously as she sucked in ragged gasps of air. Kell's darkly shadowed face was so close. His eyes narrowed, filled with urgent concern. She felt his one hand on her shoulders, the other carefully holding her right wrist. With a groan, she pushed him away. He instantly released her.

Sweaty, shaking, Leah pushed herself up into a sitting position. Kell sat back on his heels, guardedly watching her.

Rubbing her face, her hands trembling, Leah muttered, "I'm sorry…I'm sorry…I didn't mean to hit you…" She couldn't tear Hayden's glare out of her mind, the one from after she'd struck him in the face.

That time, she wasn't raped. How many times had he done it to her over the years? She'd lost count.

"Do you want some water?" Kell asked her quietly, watching her hide her face behind her trembling hand. He could feel she was embarrassed and he wanted to give her some room.

"P-please."

"Be right back." He got up and walked over to his ruck near his sleeping bag.

She couldn't cry! She had stopped crying years ago. No help had ever come. Leah had felt something precious break inside her soul once she realized there was no way out of that nightmare marriage to Hayden. Scrubbing her face, Leah forced all the tears deep down inside herself.

Kell knelt at her side, opening the bottle. "Here," he offered her quietly, holding it out toward her.

Leah slid her shaking hand around it and drank deeply. Her throat hurt. She couldn't look at Kell. She was too ashamed. Finally, she stopped drinking and gripped the bottle in her lap, hands white-knuckled. "I didn't mean to wake you."

Kell moved his hand lightly across her hair. "Do you have these nightmares often?" He was thinking maybe the crash was resurrecting a lot of ugly events in her life, replaying them now, one after another. He saw the agony in her eyes as she looked over at him.

"Not like this," Leah quavered. "Maybe once a month." Rubbing her aching brow, she tried to draw in a deep breath. Her heart was skipping so hard, she felt like she might have a heart attack.

Resting his hand on her right shoulder, Kell said, "It's probably because of the crash. You could have died in it. That sort of thing can raise all kinds of monsters we hide from ourselves."

"*Monster* is the right word," Leah rasped unsteadily. She gave him an apologetic look. "You need your sleep, Kell. You're working twelve hours or more as a sniper every day." She swallowed hard. "Maybe I should move my bed into the other cave. At least you'll get some undisturbed sleep that way."

"That's not happening." He saw her eyes turn sad. Kell sensed such deep grief within her, but he couldn't plumb it with just his senses. Whatever it was, it was tragic. He wanted to hold Leah but he could tell she was tense, as if struggling to contain all those runaway terrors. She was trying to stuff them way back down into herself once again. Kell wasn't going to force her into his arms. If she didn't come of her own volition, he couldn't help. Leah didn't know that, though. "I wake up so many times a night," he told her sincerely, catching her downcast eyes. "SEALs don't sleep like regular folks. We catnap for five, maybe ten minutes, and then we snap fully awake. And then, we go back into a catnapping cycle again." He gave her a small smile meant to make her feel better. "No harm, no foul. Okay?"

"Okay," she whispered brokenly, feeling as if she were falling apart.

"Why don't you lie down? I'll get the blanket and cover you up with it."

Leah nodded and whispered her thanks, lying on her right side. She felt him cover her with it, gently tucking it in around her hunched shoulders like a mother might for a child. Shutting her eyes tightly, biting back a sob, she realized Kell's touch was stunningly different from Hayden's. She'd been such a coward. Looking back on that three-year marriage, Leah knew she should have gone to her father. But even now, she wasn't sure he'd believe her. He still thought of Hayden as the son he'd lost, Leah thought bitterly. Hayden replaced Evan in her father's world. And Hayden wanted to show him he could one day replace him as commander when he retired.

She heard Kell lie down, the cave going to blackness once more as he turned off the small penlight. The darkness hid her and maybe that was a good thing. Leah figured Kell telling her that Hayden had demanded her immediate return had probably brought up their sordid past. Pushing her face into the scratchy wool blanket, she was so glad Kell had told him no. Leah *never* wanted to see Hayden again face-to-face. She wasn't sure what she'd do, there was so much rage built up inside of her from three years of being beaten and raped by him.

She had five more days, possibly, before they had to leave this cave. Hayden couldn't hang around Bravo forever; he had a squadron to run at Bagram.

Leah prayed he wouldn't be there once they were picked up by helicopter. She wanted to leave her past behind her.

CHAPTER FIVE

KELL MOVED SILENTLY down the long tunnel enclosed in complete darkness. He'd made this trip so many times, he didn't need any light. His hearing was keyed for any slight change of sounds from what he knew to be normal.

His heart was pounding hard. He'd been jogging for two miles from his hide back to the cave complex. His heart yearned for Leah. No matter what he tried to do, Kell couldn't get her out of his mind, his heart or his body. Damn, but the woman attracted him.

He held the Win-Mag easily in his right hand, beginning the ascent that would take him home. *To her.* He was late by two hours and he hoped Leah hadn't worried. Being a sniper wasn't a nine-to-five job.

As he approached the cave, he saw a very faint light, indicating she had a penlight on. His nostrils flared and he could smell an MRE that she was eating. *Spaghetti.* Grinning to himself, he rounded the entrance and found her standing, alert, watchful. Had she heard him? And then, with a jolt, he realized she was dressed in one of his clean, tan T-shirts and a pair of his cammie trousers. The long legs of his trousers had been rolled up to her ankles. Halting, Kell took off his damp boonie cap.

"Looks like you raided my fashionable-clothes

closet," he teased, coming forward. Kell saw that Leah had bathed. His gaze missed nothing. She had taken the sling off, too. Even in the shadows, he could tell she was stronger, a confident look gleaming in her eyes.

"Guilty." She pointed to her flight suit that she'd washed and was drying on a rock near the pool. "It should be dry by tomorrow morning." Leah felt her pulse rise as Kell moved like a silent shadow toward the rear of the cave where she stood. "Is everything okay?"

Hearing the worry in her tone, he set the sniper rifle against the wall, got out of his H-gear and set everything near his sleeping bag. "Yes. Sorry I'm late. No way to contact you." Kell glanced over at her, his gaze automatically falling on her lips. What would it be like to touch that mouth of hers? If he kissed Leah, would she respond? Or push him away? His gaze went to her eyes. He could see she looked much better.

"I was worried," Leah admitted. "I got out an MRE for you. Are you hungry?"

Kell straightened, rolling his shoulders, getting rid of the tension in them. "Yeah, I'm a starving cow brute. You've been busy," he commented, giving her a grin. "Place looks clean as a whistle." He gestured around the area.

Pleased he'd noticed, Leah stepped forward, handing him the MRE. When their fingers briefly touched, she felt a powerful yearning radiate outward within her heart. A burning in her lower body went from simmer to boil.

The look in his eyes changed, grew turbulent as their fingers met. Kell felt it, too—an invisible magic that seemed to exist between them. Shaken, Leah stepped back, unsure of herself, not him.

She sat back down on her sleeping bag, drawing up her knees and placing her arms around them. "I feel pretty much back to normal," she told him as he sat down. Kell looked tired. Leah could see the strain by the way his skin stretched across his cheekbones. "Wish I could do more. You look whipped." And of course, she'd awakened him last night, causing him more loss of sleep. It wasn't a good thing and Leah knew it.

"Tough day at the office," he said, eating hungrily. "The assault's underway. I was on the sat phone with the master chief just before dark, giving him more intel on what's coming over the border. There's been nothing but clashes going on down in the valley area all day long."

"So, you were very busy." She knew snipers often were the eyes and ears for high command, so that timely decisions could be made. They were a very important force multiplier tool out in a constantly changing war like this.

"Very. I wasn't bored." Kell lifted his head and grinned over at her. "Did you get the note I left you?"

"I did. That was so sweet to leave me candy." Leah smiled into his dark eyes that burned with a look that sent fire streaking through her. "I loved the M&M's. Thank you."

Shrugging, he said between bites, "I figured you could use a lift. Chocolate does it for me and I was hoping it would do it for you, too." Well, it did only so much for him. Kell's desire for Leah was so damned urgent and constant, no amount of chocolate would douse the fire in his groin or the need for her growing in his heart.

"It was wonderful," she admitted softly. "And thoughtful of you." She saw him nod, those stormy gray eyes of his making her feel desired. Leah forced herself to quit watching his lips move as he ate. Kell's mouth was chiseled and somehow, Leah sensed he'd be an incredible kisser. Groaning to herself, she felt sensitized to his gaze. Even her breasts were tightening beneath his too-large T-shirt. She'd washed her cotton bra, too, but it was still damp.

Keeping her arms across her breasts stopped her nipples from standing out from the fabric. Now, she wished she'd put on the damp bra.

Kell put the MRE aside, wiping his mouth with the back of his hand. "What else did you do today?" He saw she was protecting her breasts, understanding her only bra was hanging off another rock near the pool. Forcing himself to keep his eyes above her neck, he had no desire to make her feel uncomfortable.

Leah gestured toward the other cave. "After I got clean in the pool, I went looking for something to wear," she admitted. "I found your clothes thrown all over the place. That cave was a mess, so I spent part of the day just folding clothes and organizing a few things."

"Bored, eh?" Kell chuckled. Getting up, he said, "Let's go take a look." Leah stood and joined him. He watched her walk. "No more dizziness?"

"None, thank goodness," she murmured, walking at his side. He was so tall she felt somewhat dwarfed by his size, the breadth of his shoulders and chest. He moved without a sound and she was always impressed by his silence.

"And your left arm?" he asked, rounding the corner.

"Okay. Sore and tender. I really missed using my arm." She held it up, moving her fingers. "It feels pretty good today, thanks to you."

Kell halted inside the cave and flashed the penlight around. "Amazing," he murmured. "You moved a lot of stuff around." He had used this cave off and on over the years and he had to admit he wasn't exactly organized. At least, not like now. The woman knew how to get things done and done right.

"You okay with it?" Leah asked, feeling trepidation. Hayden hated her moving anything around. He wanted everything in a very specific place. If she moved it, he flew into a rage. He was a total control freak. A fanatic.

"Sure 'nuff," Kell murmured. "I like what you've done. I can see the MREs are all in one place, the boxes of water in another. Makes it easier to find them than in the mess I had." He chuckled. Looking down at her, Kell said, "Makes me wonder what you'll do for an encore tomorrow while I'm gone."

"Not much," Leah said wryly, following him to the other cave.

"Uh-oh," Kell teased, placing the penlight between their beds, "I can tell you're getting restless."

She sat down, legs crossed, facing him. Kell joined her and took off his boots. "For sure. Are you going to get washed up?"

"Yes, my skin's crawling with that fine dirt. Drives me up a wall." He pulled off his sweat-soaked socks and put each one on a small rock outcropping to dry.

"I've gotten spoiled having this place to land. Sometimes, I'd be out on a sniper op for two or three weeks, never getting a chance to get one shower. That's when the baby wipes I always carry in my ruck come in handy."

Leah watched him unwind. His male grace was breathtaking. She got to her feet. "I'll head to the next cave while you get cleaned up," she told him.

Kell nodded, thinking that he'd like to slowly undress Leah and go to that pool so they could wash one another. It was a lost cause, but he couldn't stop his heated thoughts. "Sounds good. I won't be long," he promised.

Leah grabbed the other penlight he handed her and made her way to the other cave. He followed her and found a clean T-shirt and trousers sitting on top of one box, waiting for him. If nothing else, Kell knew she was thoughtful. She sat on a box, turned off the light, probably not wanting to waste the batteries.

Leah could hear the splash of water and closed her eyes, imagining what Kell looked like naked. Licking her lower lip, she swung sharply from wanting Kell in every way to abject fear of ever having any kind of relationship with a man again. But Kell made her want to jump back in and take a chance.

Shaking her head, Leah knew she was still working out the shock of the crash. And the tragic loss of Brian, Liam and Ted. Leah figured that by now, their families had been notified. She wasn't even sure if there would be any evidence of their bodies being found at the wreckage site; no doubt they'd been burned into oblivion. She couldn't imagine how Brian's wife would

take it, not even being able to have closure because
he'd probably been burned up in the fire.

Sadness cloaked her. There was nothing good about
war. All it did was take, not give. Except, she thought,
hearing the splashing of water as Kell washed himself, it had given her him. What would it feel like to
have Kell touch her? Really touch her, like a lover
would his woman?

She was a mess and she knew it. Leah had felt enclosed and safe since the divorce from Hayden. She
never saw him; they were never in the same country at the same time. Now, he'd returned. And in her
backyard.

"It's safe to come out now," Kell called in a quiet
voice.

Rising, Leah turned on the penlight and walked
slowly from the cave and into the larger one. When
she entered, she saw Kell pulling a tan T-shirt over his
broad, dark-haired chest. The man was an incredible
specimen. He was in top shape, but not heavily muscled. Most SEALs she'd met were lean, not bulked-up
muscle mass. Their work was so damned demanding
that their bodies never had an ounce of extra fat anywhere on them.

Leah sat down on her sleeping bag, watching Kell
pull on a pair of clean socks. He had such large feet,
but then, he was really tall. She enjoyed watching his
hands as he tugged on the socks. "Do you feel better?"

He lifted his head, smiling. "A hundred percent." He
saw the emotion in her eyes, his senses open to her. Kell
wanted Leah. All of her. Yet so much stood in the way.
It seemed insurmountable to him at present. Leah's
hair was combed and formed a soft frame around her

face. She was peaceful and that was good. "I'm going to need to change that dressing on your arm."

Looking at it, she nodded. "Okay."

He stood, opened his ruck, taking out a number of medical items. "Do you feel any more pain from it?"

Leah leaned against the cave wall, leaving him room to sit down on her bag. "No. Just tender if I twist and turn it too much." She managed a slight smile.

Kell knelt near her left side, his knees almost contacting her hip. "That's good to know." Pulling on a pair of latex gloves, he lifted her arm and placed it across his thighs. He tried to ignore her nearness, but that was impossible. Taking a pair of blunt-nosed scissors, he quickly cut away the old dressing. "Things are heating up out there," he told her, removing the dressing.

Sliding his fingers beneath her arm, he held it closer, carefully examining the long gash. The flesh was healing fine and he was pleased with his small, careful sutures. Leah might have a slight scar, but over time, it would disappear.

"How bad?" Leah asked, trying to concentrate on his words, not his touch. His fingers were gentle and her skin ignited with wild tingles beneath the roughness of his pads. She tried not to imagine those hands all over her body, eliciting all kinds of reactions from her. But she did. Closing her eyes, Leah felt her breasts tightening. And her nipples hardening. Groaning inwardly, she hoped it didn't show through his T-shirt. She couldn't put her arms across them right now. *Oh, no...*

"The Taliban are hanging around in our area. That's

why I was late. I was watching to see where they were going to make camp for tonight."

Kell felt her breath hitch for just a moment as he moved his fingers along the line of her forearm. And as he glanced momentarily in her direction, he saw her nipples standing out against his T-shirt. His body instantly tightened. *Damn.* She liked his touch as much as he liked touching her. And he saw she'd closed her eyes, her head tipped back against the wall, that long, slender throat of hers exposed to him.

He fantasized about kissing Leah's skin, licking it, nipping it here and there, creating pleasure within her. He felt her tremble inwardly as he worked over her arm. Kell swallowed hard, trying to control his body, his erection. Leah had given him no outward sign that she wanted anything from him except medical help.

Kell swore softly to himself, feeling trapped in a new and different way. He quickly applied more antibiotic to the healing gash and placed a new, waterproof dressing over it.

Leah opened her eyes as he laid her arm against her belly. "How close are they, Kell?"

He leaned back on his heels, pulling off the gloves. "Very close. They're about two caves down from us. Maybe one tenth of a mile as the crow flies." He saw her eyes go wide with fear.

"It's close enough. There's a group of about two hundred Taliban, all on horseback, taking up that group of caves," he explained.

"Then let me help you," she said, her voice becoming firm. "I want to leave with you tomorrow and do something to support your efforts."

Kell heard the sincerity in her voice. "It's mountain-goat work," he explained.

"I'm in very good shape."

He had to agree, but for different reasons. "You can stay here and rest. Just because you're not dizzy today doesn't mean you're completely recovered, Leah. Head trauma takes time to clear."

"You're used to having a spotter. Right?" Leah didn't want to spend one more day in this cave if she could help it. She'd go crazy with nothing to do.

"SEALs sometimes work without them, but I do work with a spotter when I can," he agreed. Kell searched her face. Her chin was stubborn for a reason.

A part of him felt uneasy about leaving her alone and unprotected with the Taliban so close. He knew Leah was trained and could shoot, but with so many enemies gathering a short distance away, he weighed the options.

There was a side to him that was damned protective of women and children in general. Yes, Leah was military, and she sure as hell could kick ass when it came to flying. But on the ground? Ballard wasn't so sure about leaving her alone, open to possible attack. She'd be outgunned.

"Okay," he said, "I'll let you go with me. We'll be getting up before dawn, though. I have to find a hide on a ridge that looks down on those caves. I have to get a count of men, weapons, and try to look for their leader, Khogani. A lot of what snipers do is recon and that's what we'll be doing. I'm not about to shoot and give away our position. Are you up for that?"

"Anything is better than staying here alone," Leah

said, relieved. "I'm a fast learner, Kell. If you tell me to do something, I will."

He rubbed his palms slowly up and down his thighs, thinking about her flight suit. "We're going to have to fix you up a set of my cammies to wear."

Leah got up. "Okay," she said, "give me those scissors. I'll alter the pant-leg length. If you can get me a cammie blouse, I'll do the same for the arm length."

He liked her attitude. The Shadow pilot was emerging, in charge, confident and assertive. He liked it a whole hell of a lot. "I have a second ruck in the other cave. While you're cutting a pair of my trouser legs off, I'll get it, stock it and bring the shirt back with me."

Her spirits rose as she sat down and began to cut the thick fabric, making the trouser length shorter for her legs. Kell's T-shirt was huge on her, but she wasn't going to cut it.

Kell came back about ten minutes later. In one hand, he had a ruck just like the one he wore. In the other, his blouse. He handed it to her.

"Put it on and I'll shorten the sleeves for you with the scissors," he told her.

Getting up, Leah saw the trousers length was fine. She'd taken dark green nylon rope this morning and fashioned a makeshift belt out of it, the trousers staying around her waist instead of sliding down to her hips. She shrugged into his blouse. It was huge on her, his shoulders were so broad.

Kell grinned, taking the sleeve that hung below her long, beautiful fingers. "You're a little thing, aren't you?" he murmured, quickly cutting away the extra fabric. She turned, holding out the other sleeve.

"Little but mighty," Leah said, smiling up at him. If Kell was upset with her going along, he didn't show it.

"That you are," he agreed gruffly, the cuff material falling away.

"This is fine," Leah said, her hands visible now. She turned and looked at the ruck. "What's in it?"

Kell put the scissors away and walked over to the ruck, opening it up. Kneeling down, he said, "It's an identical copy to the one I wear. SEALs believe one is bad and two is good. Your ruck is going to weigh around fifty pounds. I'll transfer most of the mags out of it and into mine. I don't want you humping sixty or seventy pounds. It will really throw you off your stride and quickly tire you out." His eyes narrowed. "And you need to remind yourself that you're not fully recovered yet, Leah. We don't need to go far tomorrow, which is good, but the heat out there is a killer, too."

"As long as I have water and a hat, I'll be fine."

"Ever done any covert intelligence work?"

"No."

Kell double-checked the ruck, took out a boonie hat and then closed it up. "You're going to have to stay close to me, Leah. There's a lot to stalking and you're going to have to learn it on the fly."

"I'll learn, Kell. And I won't be a pain in the ass."

Shaking his head, his lips curved. "You would never be that to me, Leah. Come on, let's get all your gear ready now before we bed down for the night. Tomorrow, when we get up, we're going roll fairly quickly, then eat a protein bar once we get set up for the recon."

For the next half hour, Leah felt as if she contributed. Used to working as a team, pilot and copilot, she felt excited about being Kell's partner. An ignorant one, for sure, but she promised herself she'd catch on fast so she wouldn't be a distraction.

Finally, she sat down on her bag after everything she needed was nearby. Surprised, Kell came over and knelt down beside her, his face unreadable

Resting his hands on his thighs, he frowned. "I'm worried because you've had a nightmare every night you've been here."

Leah nodded, feeling guilty. "And that's not good," she agreed, apologetic. Voices carried. And in a cave system like this, Leah realized she could possibly alert the enemy to their whereabouts. "What can I do? I know I'm a liability." Feeling bad, there was no way she wanted to put them at risk. Maybe stuff a sock in her mouth? She cast around for solutions and found none. "Maybe I could go sleep in the other cave?"

He shook his head. "No. If you screamed like you did last night, Leah, we'll be in trouble no matter where you're sleeping."

"Do you have a sleep med on you? Something I could take that would knock me out?"

"I do, but they don't work like that," he admitted, his voice low as he held her guilt-ridden gaze. "It doesn't guarantee that you won't have another nightmare and wake up screaming again."

Groaning, she rubbed her face, frustrated. "I'm sorry. I wish I could control it."

"It's not your fault, Sugar. You've been through hell and it's the shock working out of your system, is all." Giving her a slight smile, Kell saw how anguished she'd become over their dangerous situation.

Desperate, Leah tried to think of a way to not

scream or make sounds as she slept. Every time he called her Sugar, her heart opened just a little more to Kell. "I don't want you discovered by the Taliban because of me," she managed, suddenly emotional. "This is my fault—"

"Whoa," he said, touching her shoulder, "don't go there, Leah. None of this is your fault. You're human. You're hurting. Shock and grief wreak hell on all of us. On you." He saw her eyes grow moist, felt her sudden desperation. His fingers became more firm on her shoulder. He could feel the soft firmness of her skin beneath the material, and wanted to feel more. Kell felt he was caught in a special hell with her.

"Maybe I'll try to stay awake tonight?" She dug into his narrowing gaze. Her conscience ate at her.

"You'd never make it staying awake all night," Kell murmured. He dropped his hand back to his thigh. "Besides, if you're working with me tomorrow, you have to get some sleep in order to be alert. I've given it a lot of thought," he told her hesitantly, frowning.

"Did you come up with an idea?" Leah saw him shrug, his expression suddenly uneasy. Why? Maybe take her up that other tunnel and sit her outside to sleep tonight?

"You probably won't like the idea," he began, holding her gaze. "But I thought if I held you…if we slept together, it might make you feel safer."

Stunned, her breath jammed in her throat. She stared at Kell, fear sizzling through her. "What?" she gasped.

He opened his hands. "It's the only thing I can think of, Leah. I know you're an officer. I'm enlisted. I'll just hold you. I promise not to do anything to make you uncomfortable. It's just that we have to do something or there's a good chance we're at risk here."

Staring at him, Leah felt herself quiver inwardly. Oh, it wasn't him she was worried about. It was her! Mouth dry, she saw the unhappiness in his eyes. Okay, maybe Kell didn't want to do this, but he was making the best of a bad situation. His logic was sound. "I have no idea if it would stop me from having a nightmare."

"I know," Kell admitted heavily. He had to go with his gut. Every time he'd held her before, she settled down in his arms. Leah relaxed. She trusted him for whatever reason. "I'm open to any other ideas you have. I can see you're uncomfortable about mine. I knew you would be."

Her heart wrenched in her chest. If only Kell knew how much she *did* trust him.

Pushing her hair away from her face with her fingers, a sign of nervousness, she whispered, "I don't have another idea, Kell." She gave him a rueful look. Leah couldn't live with herself if she screamed out in the night. It would put both of them in serious jeopardy.

"I'm sorry," Kell offered quietly, holding her fearful stare. "Can you do it, Leah, or not?"

Could she? "There isn't a choice…"

CHAPTER SIX

LEAH'S PULSE RACED. She was tense as Kell placed his bag next to hers. Frightened in so many ways, Leah tried to hide her reactions. Most of all, she didn't want to put them at risk.

She saw the serious cast to Kell's face, his brows drawn down, his mouth thinned. He probably didn't like this any more than she did. How long had it been since she'd lain with a man? *Three years. Not since Hayden.* Not that she'd lain in bed with him that much. He liked sex, took what he wanted then left her and went into his own bedroom afterward. In college, she'd been stupid enough to have two affairs, neither of them satisfying. Both men had wanted sex, not a meaningful relationship.

But this was new. And different. They both wore T-shirts and trousers, boots off but socks on their feet. She sat there, feeling trapped again. Fiercely reminding herself Kell had held her before and nothing had happened, Leah forced herself to believe nothing would happen this time. It couldn't. Feeling shaky inside, Leah watched him lie down on his back. Kell laid his long arm across her wool blanket pillow and shut off the flashlight.

Darkness enclosed them and Leah breathed a sigh of relief. She was sure she looked scared. Hands damp, she sat there unmoving, trying to control her breathing, as if nothing were going on. The past slammed into the present.

"Come on," Kell coaxed quietly, his fingers curving around her right forearm. "I'm not going to bite you."

His soft Kentucky drawl loosened the fear around her pounding heart. Leah felt a rush of shame. Her inexperience was making her question herself as never before. "Kell?"

"Yes?"

"I'm...uh..." Leah shut her eyes tightly, feeling the dry warmth of his hand on her arm. She absorbed it like a starving thief. "I'm nervous," she admitted, the words coming out with embarrassment. Leah tensed, waiting for him to call her a bitch as her husband had often done when she'd shown hesitation or hadn't wanted to do what he wanted her to do.

Kell released her arm and sat up, hearing anguish in her voice. He couldn't piece everything together yet about her ex-husband, but he went on his intuition that had never led him wrong. He slid his arm around her tense shoulders. "It's all right. We'll make this easy for you. We'll sit up, prop our backs up against the wall and sleep. Come on, I'll just hold you like this. Put your head on my shoulder like you've done before. You trusted me then, didn't you?"

His warm, moist breath fell across her brow and cheek. Feeling his arm move around her, Leah released a ragged sigh. This wasn't Hayden. This was Kell Ballard, her heart whispered to her. He wasn't pulling her toward him to hurt or control her. Her mind was racing back and forth between the past and the present. "You must think I'm crazy," she muttered, forcing herself to relax.

The T-shirt lay between her cheek and his heavily muscled shoulder. Tonight, Leah could smell his male scent strongly, the cleanliness of his flesh. It sent spirals of yearning deep into her body. She'd never felt so sensual, or so hot and bothered, in her entire life. Could just the smell of a man send her into some crazy orbit of aching yearning? Leah didn't have the experience to answer her own question. Plus, when Kell had held her before, she'd been wounded, the concussion lowering her protective walls, and she hadn't had this reaction. Now that she was much improved, her walls were up and she struggled with her past overlaying her present.

"You're not crazy," he reassured her, quietly. *Just scared.* Maybe not of him in particular, but rather men in general? Her ex-husband? Kell leaned his back against the wall, feeling Leah slowly relax against him. He had to make damn sure she never became aware of his erection. There had been veiled anxiety in her voice, and he sensed her trepidation. "That's it," he crooned, "just relax. I'll hold you safe tonight, Leah."

She hesitantly allowed her left arm to move across his slab-hard belly, angling her hips against his to get comfortable. The slow rise and fall of his chest and the lazy thud of his heart against her ear conspired to calm her. With every breath he took, she relaxed a little more. "You can't hold me all night like this, Kell," she protested softly, worried. "You'll get so cramped up from it—"

"You'd be surprised to learn I can stay in one spot for twelve hours straight and never move a muscle."

Because that's what a sniper did when he had to do it. They had infinite persistence and he had that same patience with Leah.

She closed her eyes, feeling his warmth stealing into her. Leah felt him bring up a blanket over her shoulders and tuck it around her. "Thank you…" His scent was perfume to her, lulling her toward sleep.

"Close those beautiful green eyes of yours and let the wings of sleep take you," Kell told her in a gruff tone. Leah's tension dissolved beneath his voice and he was grateful.

Kell's senses honed in on her. The hesitation of even touching him as she laid her left arm across his belly told him a helluva lot. She had a distrust of men. Due to her ex-husband? She'd screamed out Hayden's name the first night.

On the second night, Leah was fighting and struggling, terror in her expression as he'd awakened her. And she nailed him with a right hook to his chest. What had that bastard done to her to make her react like that?

Oh, he could understand some hesitation because of her being a warrant officer and him an enlisted man. But that wasn't what had driven her to be so damned tentative with him just now. Something bad, very bad, had happened between Leah and her ex-husband. That much Kell knew. He just didn't know what. And anger burned in him as he thought of anyone touching this woman in a way that hurt her. She was brave, caring and intelligent.

His fingers moved more firmly against her upper arm and he wanted to pull her deeper into his embrace, to give her protection she hadn't asked for but that he wanted to provide, anyway.

Leah's hair, soft and silky, tickled his jaw and chin. Her breasts were pressed against the left side of his chest and he could feel their fullness. Kell ached to slide his hand beneath that T-shirt and move his fingers up her long rib cage and gently hold one of those breasts in his palm. Frowning, Kell allowed himself to feel her lush, curved body against his.

Very soon, Leah was asleep. He could feel her body sag against his, her breath softening and becoming slow and shallow. Yeah, she trusted him. It sent a giddy joy through Kell but he tried not to celebrate it.

With the Taliban practically next door, Kell set his body cycle up to catnap. It was important Leah got some seriously healing sleep. Judging by her slow breath, her breasts barely rising and falling against his chest, she was doing exactly that. His mind revolved forward to their present danger. This was close-quarters contact with the enemy. He didn't tell Leah, but for all intents and purposes, they were trapped. There wasn't anywhere to go if they were discovered except out that exfil point, then making their way carefully down a two-thousand-foot cliff on the backside of this mountain. And he didn't have rappelling gear with him to do it, either. Worse, he was sure Leah had no climbing experience whatsoever.

THE NEXT TIME Kell awoke was because he felt Leah shift in his arms. She had almost crawled across him, her head near his right shoulder now, her left arm stretched limply across his waist, her breasts fully pressed against his chest. Taking a slow, deep breath,

Kell savored the full contact. She must have shifted but he'd not felt it until now.

What would it be like to feel her naked against him? Just like this. The fullness of her breasts against his chest. Her long, tapered fingers touching him, sensing him, sending hot, scalding signals down into his lower body. He could feel the silk of her hair across his chest. *Breathe*, he ordered himself. *Just breathe.*

Ballard wanted to absorb this moment, understanding it would never happen again. Her cheek was warm against his T-shirt. He could feel the moisture of Leah's breath lightly across it, tightening his skin beneath the fabric. Her left hand had curved over his left shoulder, her fingers wrapped around the nape of his neck. She trusted him. At least, in her sleep she did. She might not in her waking hours, however.

Kell lowered his left hand, smoothing the wrinkled T-shirt gently down along her long spine. Leah moaned. Nothing loud, just a soft moan of pleasure, maybe? Yeah, Kell knew he could give Leah pleasure, make her wild with need. He knew how to please a woman, make her first in his life, make her happy to be with him, sharing the same bed. Becoming one.

He had it bad for her, disgusted where his mind and body were going. Leah didn't deserve this from him. She'd given her trust. And it was sacred to Kell.

His memory turned to the past, looking at his fated marriage to Addy. They'd had a great sex life, but the marriage fell apart because he was gone so often and for so long. She was a high-maintenance woman who wanted to be courted, pleasured and have everything life offered her. She loved his body, told him how beautiful he was, appreciated his strength and power.

But in the end, sex could never hold a marriage, indeed, a relationship, together for the long haul. That was what Kell had learned from the experience.

He and Addy were still friends. She had remarried and was happy. And he was happy for her because she was a bright light in the world, wanting to make a positive difference. It was just that her passionate light required full-time attention. Sadly, Kell couldn't give that to her. He couldn't give that kind of attention to any woman right now.

Sometimes, especially with Leah lying across him, Kell missed the warmth of a good woman in his arms, beside him in his bed. He missed talking with a woman because they saw life so differently than he did. Kell didn't see that as a minus. He'd always found it a plus. He'd always wanted a woman in his life, but somehow, it hadn't happened since his divorce.

Without thinking, Kell moved his hand gently across Leah's shoulders. It wasn't sexual. It was simply an act of care, of happiness on his part, that she was sharing life with him in this crazy place called Afghanistan.

Could he have ever imagined a woman dropping in like Leah? Here? Out in the middle of some of the worst fighting in this country? *No way.* Not in a million years. And yet, here she was, sprawled like a sated cat across his body, fully trusting him, sleeping soundly in his arms. He felt his erection and released a ragged sigh, looking at his watch. It was 0300. In another hour, he'd have to awaken Leah and they'd have to quietly make their way out of this place and go to work.

Leah felt the calloused warmth of roughened fingers against her cheek. Her sleep was so deep that all she did was sigh and absorb the tender touch. It felt so good, so safe. The hand left her cheek and she felt his fingers moving slowly down the strands of her hair, her scalp tingling, the pleasure increasing beneath his strokes.

"Sugar?"

It was Kell's low accent near her ear. Leah felt his hands slide beneath her arms as he lifted her upward. The movement forced her lashes to slowly rise. Moaning, she pressed her face into Kell's strong, thick neck, not wanting to wake up, wanting to continue to enjoy his grazing touches. She felt him laugh. There wasn't a sound, but she could feel the reverberation through his massive chest. Dragging her hand up, she groaned and drowsily rubbed her eyes.

"Time to get up, sleepy head," he told her, amused. Kell had lifted her off his body and eased Leah up beneath his left arm, her face pressed against his neck and shoulder. She was sleeping so damned hard he felt bad about rousing her. But they had to get going.

"Mmph."

His mouth curved as he slid his fingers into her hair. "Come on, darlin', we have to get moving."

Half-awake, all Leah wanted to do was luxuriate in the intimacy strung hotly between them. It felt so natural. So real. So good. Turning she struggled into a sitting position. Her hair was mussed, falling across her face, and she slowly moved the strands aside with her fingers. Kell's arm was loose around her waist. She could feel her body coming alive. Wanting him. Wanting something, but she had no idea what.

"Okay?" Kell asked, turning on the penlight. The blackness fled to grayness and he saw her groggy features as she struggled to wake up.

"Yeah…okay…"

Her voice was thick with sleep, a little husky, and it only made him harder, wanting her even more. Kell forced himself to his feet. If he didn't move away from Leah, he was going to do something really selfish and stupid. He was going to curve her back into his arms and kiss her until she gave him that sweet, husky moan of hers she'd shared with him last night when he'd stroked her back.

Focus, Ballard.

It was the last thing Kell wanted to do. As he grabbed his boots and pulled them on, he saw Leah reach for hers.

"Drink plenty of water before we leave," he warned her. He walked over to the pool, kneeling down and splashing the icy water across his face. That sure as hell woke him up in a heartbeat. But it hadn't eased the pain of his erection in the least. The danger they faced would force his mind onto other, far more important priorities. He just didn't want Leah to realize how much he wanted her. That would throw a hell of an issue into their relationship. She didn't trust men. Okay, he got that. And if she saw him hard, that would destroy the tentative, fragile trust she had given him, probably thinking he was like the rest of the men who lusted after that sweet, curvy body of hers.

Grimacing, Ballard stood up and turned, walking over to her. Leah had her flight boots on, was taming her hair into a ponytail and had the floppy boonie hat nearby. Somehow, Leah didn't look like a SEAL, but she was damned appealing to him, nonetheless.

"Come on," he urged, holding his hand down toward her. Without hesitation, Leah's fingers curved around his and he eased her to her feet. He smiled a little. "I think I'm going to call you a SEAL-ette." He tugged playfully at the brim of the hat she had picked.

He saw her lips draw into a wry smile, her gaze warm and open. That's how he wanted to see Leah every morning, that trust between them, that heat he felt radiating from her toward him. SEALs had intense intuition because their lives relied on it. And there was no mistaking her wanting him sexually. Kell could read it easily in her eyes and in her innocent smile as she gazed up at him.

A zigzag of scalding heat dove from Leah's breasts down into her core as Kell gave her that lazy, heated smile of his. Did the man know that sensuality dripped off him twenty-four hours a day? Was she the only one to sense and see it? Leah drowned in his aura, that protective energy embracing her along with the arousal she saw banked in his dark, narrowed gaze. "I didn't scream, did I?" she asked, remaining where she was. There were mere inches separating them, and it would be so easy to take one step forward and be in Kell's arms...

"Not a peep," he assured her. He reached out, moving some errant strands near her left eye. Tucking them behind her ear, he added, "You slept without waking once."

"And you would know this how?" She frowned, her hands on her hips.

Caught. Kell grinned. "I slept," he assured her.

"SEAL naps." He saw Leah didn't believe one word he'd said, that lower lip of hers going petulant, almost into a pout.

Damn, he'd like to kiss that lower lip of hers, run his tongue across it and feel her respond. And he knew she would. Kell realized Leah had no self-awareness of herself as a woman when in the company of a man. She was completely oblivious to how she affected him, her natural beauty and the way that T-shirt outlined her breasts, those taut, puckered nipples straining against the material.

Leah was no tease. Kell knew a tease when he saw one, and she was simply being open and natural with him. When he'd touched her ear as he slid the strands behind it, he'd seen her eyes widen. It wasn't a reaction to a threat. Instead, his touch had stirred her fire, and he understood how sensitive she really was. And how much she desired contact with him. Leah could have dodged his hand. Could have told him no. But she hadn't. She'd allowed him the gift of touching her, if but for a few seconds.

Taking a deep breath, Leah stepped away. Kell was far too close, too sensual for her. She was way too vulnerable to him. Her lower body constricted and she felt urges she couldn't interpret and had no experience with. When he'd touched her ear, a strange, twisting, hungry sensation enveloped her. It felt good. It made her starving for more intimacy with Kell. Right now? Leah knew it would be a terrible mistake on her part. Rallying, getting her mind off her awakening body, she asked, "A SEAL-ette?"

Kell chuckled and leaned down, handing her the blouse. "You're not a SEAL, but you're working with one, so I'm giving you a new career title. You're now officially a SEAL-ette. It's a compliment," he assured her, helping her with the blouse. He watched her fingers quickly close the buttons on it, thinking of what it would be like if she slowly unbuttoned his blouse.

Damn. He had to use his powerful focus and just stop this hormonal stuff. If he didn't, Kell knew he could put both of them in damn quick jeopardy if he continued to be distracted.

Leah laughed softly, shrugged into her Kevlar vest and then picked up a bottle of water. "At least you're not calling me any names. I can live with that nickname. Makes me sound like a Radio City Rockette from New York City." She chuckled.

Kell gave her his second radio headset. He placed the thick elastic band around her head, moved the mic toward her lips. He clipped the radio to her collar and then tested it. He'd put new batteries in it the night before. He too would wear one and they could speak quietly to one another and never be overheard. He picked up her ruck after she'd finished drinking water.

"The only names I want to call you are very nice ones," he assured her. "Let's get this ruck on you and get the harness system adjusted for your body height and size."

Leah allowed him to tighten the harnesses over her shoulders, his fingers touching her here and there. Every time Kell did, her flesh responded hotly to his brief, grazing fingertips. He leaned over her, his head close to hers as he shortened the belt around the bottom of the ruck to fit her waist.

Closing her eyes for a moment, Leah allowed herself the pleasure of inhaling his male scent that drove her body crazy. She tried to ignore her heart that seemed like flower petals opening to sunlight. Only, Kell was her sunlight.

Ballard straightened. "How's that ruck feel now? Walk around, move a little, see how it sits on you." Leah did as he asked and he enjoyed the sway of her hips. Damn, she had the sweetest butt he'd seen in a long time. He couldn't help imagining his hands on each cheek... He was in such deep trouble here. Kell saw her frown as she turned, her fingers beneath the shoulder straps.

"Awkward," she murmured.

"Too heavy?" That was fifty pounds of weight. A lot for her frame and size.

"It's okay." Leah hoped he couldn't tell she was fibbing. Kell looked like he probably didn't believe her. But he was carrying far more weight than she was, and she wasn't about to have him carry more.

Unsure, Kell dug into her dark green eyes. "Well," he muttered, "if it gets to be too much, speak up." He turned and shrugged into his ruck. The Win-Mag was protected in a nylon sheath and held by Velcro straps on the outside of it, the rifle barrel pointed downward. Turning, Kell saw that same stubborn look on Leah's face as the night before. He was getting the first taste of the warrior in the woman, not the woman with male issues. Two very different people, and he was fascinated with her either way. Kell knew she'd never utter a peep about the load she was carrying in that ruck. He'd have to spot-check her from time to time if they ever had to hoof it over the rocky, demanding mountain in the future.

Leah took her .45 pistol and buckled it around her

waist so it hung a little low on her right hip in case she needed it in a hurry. She saw Kell pick up the M-4 rifle and snap it into a sling across his chest where it hung, but was still handy if he needed it in a hurry.

"Ready?" Kell checked her out one more time. The smallest SEAL he knew was five feet seven inches, her height. The ruck looked like a huge turtle shell on Leah's back, dwarfing her. She was medium-boned and Kell knew she was strong because he'd felt her muscling. *Wimp* was not a word he'd use with this woman, who had her jaw set and her game face on. Still, she was used to sitting in a seat on a helo, not humping the Hindu Kush daily like he was.

"Rock it out," she told him with a grin.

That was a SEAL term, and he appreciated her humor. "Follow me," he urged, turning the penlight so that they could both see where they were walking.

Leah looked up at the stars still hanging in the early-morning sky as they moved outside the cave. The wind was gusting and cold. She was glad for the Kevlar vest now, even though it was very heavy to wear. It kept her entire torso, front and back, warm.

She stopped when Kell stopped. There was a thin quarter moon on the western horizon. She couldn't see any light yet. She watched him pull down his NVG goggles. Having none for herself, she was at a severe disadvantage.

Kell turned, catching her right hand. "Hold on to my web belt and follow me. If I'm going too fast, tug on it. Never say a word, we're close to the Taliban. Okay?"

"Okay." Leah gripped his web belt, standing a little to his left. The ruck he carried was huge and she knew she'd have to be body aware and not run into it and lose her balance. Looking down, Leah saw it was a rocky surface with hardly any soil, composed instead of mostly small stones. She felt Kell move and she did the same. At first, it was tough because she was sometimes stumbling blindly, the toes of her boots hitting rocks she couldn't see.

Kell stopped. He turned, pulling down his goggles, his lips near her ear. "When you walk," he advised, "don't lift your boot, just *slide* it forward about an inch above the ground. That way, the toe of your boot will encounter the rock and it won't make you trip and fall."

Nodding, she got it. Okay, SEAL walk time. Leah often wondered how they were so silent. Kell turned and started to walk forward, a little slower for her so she could try out this new way of moving her feet.

Her breath came in gulps, vapor jetting out of her mouth. It was damn cold! Below freezing. Now Leah wished she'd had a pair of gloves. Her fingers wrapped around Kell's belt went numb. She was able to stick her fingers of her left hand into her cammie pocket.

Concentrating on her feet, Kell suddenly halted. She slammed into him. He didn't move. Scared, Leah knew Kell saw or heard something she hadn't. Desperately, she tried to see into the night, but it was impossible. And then Kell very slowly crouched down. Leah mimicked his unhurried movement. Her pulse quickened. All she could hear was the wind.

She felt Kell's hand bump into her knee. He pushed down on it. Did he want her flat on the ground? He wasn't speaking, so it meant someone was nearby. Her pulse leaped with fear. Leah carefully moved, trying not to make a sound as she got down on her belly, the sharp rocks cutting into her thighs and lower legs. Kell followed suit. She was scrunched up beside his long body, watching him peer intently at something she couldn't see.

He then reached out, his large hand over her boonie cap, gently pushing her head downward, asking her to go to ground. Oh, God, what did he see? What was happening? She pressed her face against the cold rock and soil, barely breathing, heart skittering with fear.

And then, about two minutes later, Leah heard the faint tinkling of bells. Frowning, her face buried in her arms, breathing through her mouth, she thought she was hearing things.

Kell watched the forty goats being herded by a young Afghan kid on a narrow path fifty feet below them. His mind worked swiftly. The kid was about ten years old. He wasn't looking around, he was just following the bleating goats, wrapped in a dark wool cape, shoulders hunched forward, his small rolled cap over his shaggy black hair.

The lead goat, a nanny, had a damn loud bell around her neck. Kell wondered if it was going to roust out the Taliban early or not. Unable to know, he wanted Leah to lie quiet until the herd passed their location. He could feel her tension, but she'd accurately understood what he'd silently asked of her.

It took ten minutes before Kell was ready to ease to his hands and knees. "Come up slowly," he told her quietly into his mic against his lips.

Leah wanted to groan under the weight of the ruck bearing down on her, but bit down on her lip, swallowing the urge. She struggled to her hands and knees. To her relief, Kell offered his hand and pulled her up to her feet once more. Leah could barely see gray, hazy light silhouetting the peaks of the Hindu Kush mountains. Her heart was pounding and she felt fearful.

Kell stood and looked around, as if nothing had happened. As if this was a daily nonevent in his life. It sure as hell was an event in hers. Yet, she trusted Kell with her life. He seemed unconcerned as he casually searched the area with his gaze. Leah waited, rubbing her hands together, trying to warm them.

"Here," he said, taking off his gloves and giving them to her. Why hadn't he thought of that earlier? Kell had a second pair in his ruck and he'd get them out once they were at their recon-op position.

Leah could barely see Kell's face. He pulled the NVGs down, hanging them around his corded neck. When one corner of his mouth pulled up into that slow smile, she felt heat rippling through her from her toes to her head. All he had to do was look at her and her body was coming unhinged.

Later, they lay on their bellies just below a ridge line. Kell had his binos—binoculars—and he was doing a slow sweep of the cave openings down below them. He could sometimes smell the spices of cooking wafting on the chilled morning air. Chances were everyone was up, eating and having their morning tea. All was quiet for now. He turned, placing the binos to one side, and reached into one of his cammie pockets. Drawing out two protein bars, he handed one to Leah.

"Breakfast," Kell told her. "Sorry, no coffee." He saw her smile and nod. It was pure enjoyment watching those tapered fingers of hers gracefully remove the wrapping. He couldn't help but wonder how her hands would feel against his bare skin. Kell had gotten a taste of it last night as Leah had tentatively laid her hand on his hard belly. Only a thin tan T-shirt had been a barrier between her hand and his taut flesh. Teasing heat had shot downward into his groin from just that light touch of hers.

"What now?" Leah asked in a low voice, hungrily biting into the bar.

"Wait. When they start coming out and mounting up, I want you to start looking at what types of weapons they're carrying. Count how many RPGs among them. And if you see a Stinger missile, that's even more important."

"What are you going to do?"

"I'll be looking for Khogani, the leader of this motley crew," he growled. "He's my HVT."

CHAPTER SEVEN

LEAH'S HEAD THROBBED unremittingly as she continued to count the gathering Taliban below. The sun had just risen. She'd heard voices drifting up toward them as all the soldiers turned to the east, laid out their rugs, knelt on them and said their prayers.

Kell had given her his wheel book, something all snipers carried on them, to make notes, drawings and observations. He had a handheld computer between his large hands. She used the spotter scope with a piece of gray cloth across the lens so it wouldn't reflect the sun's rays and give away their position.

More and more men filed out, talking in Pashto, leading their newly saddled horses. The milling around of men and animals caused her a lot of problems with her count, but she kept an accurate tally.

Kell panned his Night Force scope slowly over the crowd looking for Farukh Khogani. He was the older brother to Sangar Khogani, who had personally started a tribal war with the Shinwari, their neighbors for thousands of years. Sangar had been killed by a woman Marine Corps sniper who'd worked with a SEAL friend of his, Lieutenant Jake Ramsey, from another platoon. She'd blown his head off. Kell found it amusing, in a sick way, that he was going after another member of the Khogani clan who ruled over the Hill tribe.

They were a murdering sort, a powerful opium-dealing tribe who partially controlled the Khyber Pass leading from Pakistan into Afghanistan. The Shinwari, who also owned part of the Khyber Pass area, had signed papers with the US, promising cooperation in stopping Al-Qaeda and Taliban from using the pass to run fertilizer, ammunition and men into Afghanistan.

And therein lay the seeds of discontent: The Hill tribe wanted the money that came from keeping the pass open. The Shinwari were stopping their destructive goods from going into Pakistan. Sangar Khogani had thought that murdering a village of one hundred and fifty innocent Shinwari would make them back off and open up the pass to their munitions. But it hadn't. SEAL teams were routinely sent out to hunt the next Khogani leader, thereby slowing the transfer of munitions to the IED bomb makers in Afghanistan.

Kell didn't want to attempt to take the bastard out right now because it was two hundred against the two of them. He refused to put Leah in such a severely compromised situation. He might have if he'd had his teammate, Brad Doran, whom everyone called Clutch, at his side. As a sniper team, they could gun and run with the best of them. With Leah at his side, they'd never be able to keep the pace he'd have to set in order to hightail it out once he took down Khogani. No, he'd wait. He had infinite patience when it came to stalking his quarry.

Sure enough, Kell spotted the leader, a man with red hair and a thick, unkempt beard wearing a black roll cap, a black wool cape and trousers. He watched with curiosity as the soldiers surrounded him, cheering, waving their AK-47s in the air, calling his name like he was a minor rock god. Rocks was right, Kell thought, looking through the crosshairs at Khogani's head.

He rode a white horse, typical of a leader in these parts. White horses were reserved for chieftains only. No one else could afford such an animal in the first place. The horse's bridle was decked out with red-and-black tassels, and so were the leather reins. This guy really knew how to put on a show.

Kell picked up his camera and made sure the material was over the lens so it wouldn't flash and alert anyone below. He had a long-range lens on the Canon camera, and he took a number of shots of not only Khogani, but the officer corps who surrounded him. Every piece of information was important. Every identity and picture, vital. Puzzle pieces that eventually would yield a much larger picture to Intel.

Soon, they all rode off to the south. When they were out of sight, Kell rose up and moved stiffly.

"We're safe," he told Leah. "They're gone."

Leah nodded, folding up his wheel book and handing it over to him. She'd been lying on her belly for three hours. The stiffness from the helicopter crash made her move slowly. She finally sat up, crossing her legs after making sure her head wasn't above the ridge. Otherwise, she'd be a target for a passing Taliban sniper. No place was really safe.

"How are you doing?" Kell asked, noting she looked pale.

"Headache is all."

Nodding, Kell took off his ruck, opened it, found the Motrin and handed her two tablets. "It's going to come and go for a week or so," he warned her.

"Thanks." She took her CamelBak hose and turned it on, sucking water into her mouth. She'd been unable to drink while taking observations of the Taliban below. Popping down the Motrin, she drank even more water.

Kell reached into his ruck and pulled out the sat phone, making a call to Master Chief Axton. Taking the notes that Leah had made in his wheel book, plus what he'd placed on his handheld computer, he called in his report on the weapons—number, type and make—to his boss.

"Good intel," Ax congratulated him. "How's Chief Mackenzie doing?"

"Improving," Kell answered, not willing to tell Ax that she had been on this mission with him. He'd have a bird and a half. Plus, he'd chew his ass out.

"Look, I'm getting hell rained down on me from this asshole, a Major Hayden Grant. Did you know Mackenzie is his ex-wife?"

"Yes, I knew that."

"Well, he's demanding she get picked up like yesterday. I told him no. And now, he's got the commander of the 80th on the horn with our LT Dragon, ripping him a new asshole. Can you tell me if there's any way we can exfil her today? Tomorrow?"

Kell scowled. He felt protective of Leah. She didn't like her ex and even though he didn't know why, it didn't matter. "No way. We just gave you figures on two hundred Taliban right under our noses. You want to send a Shadow helo into this kind of moving mess?" Kell knew Ax wouldn't.

Axton breathed hard and cursed. "You know I don't."

"We've already lost three crewmen and a bird trying to pick up two of our brothers a few days ago," Kell said. "Have you picked them up yet?"

"Hell no. Things are too hot out there and there's just too much activity."

"Then tell that major to shut the fuck up." Kell felt strongly that Leah was getting manipulated. Why, he didn't know, but his thoughts went dark when Ax mentioned Grant's name to him.

Ax laughed. "Yeah, I'll do that. I'll lct LT Dragon know, and the ball's in his court."

"If you want more proof, park a satellite over this area. Head counts don't lie."

"We got drones up and they're showing us what you're telling us. The place is unsafe as hell. Are you all right where you are?"

"We're okay. And until I can get Chief Mackenzie safely exfilled out of here, I'm not going to actively pursue hunting Khogani. Are you okay with that?"

"Fine. Just keep to your little spot in paradise, do your day ops and hide at night. That's as good as it gets for right now."

"Roger. Out." Kell shut off the phone and noticed Leah staring at him. She'd heard the whole conversation. And she looked upset. He wanted to know why. He pulled out a bag of M&M's and offered her some.

"Dessert for a job well-done," he told her.

Leah dug in and got some. "Thanks."

He munched on a few of them, savoring the sugar

shot. He told her about the conversation. He watched her closely as he covered the fact that Major Grant had gotten her father involved in trying to exfil her—she paled. "Care to tell me what's going on here?"

Leah felt her stomach turn. Kell's voice was low with carefully veiled feelings. She sensed his guard-dog-like sense of protectiveness was up and in place for her. And she'd heard his voice grow utterly cold on that call. "My ex-husband thinks he can control me, my life and anything else he damn well wants to," she muttered angrily.

"He's dragged your father into it," Kell said evenly, popping a few more M&M's into his mouth. "Does Grant have him wrapped around his finger, too?"

Snorting, Leah stared down at the ground, getting a grip on her emotions. "Hayden is a sociopath," she whispered, her voice trembling. "A manipulator when it comes to what he wants." *Her.*

Kell looked at Leah sharply. "Are you just throwing that word around?" He saw Leah lift her head, her eyes bleak. What the hell had Grant done to her?

"He's never been seen by a shrink, but he should be." She'd needed two years of psychiatric counseling to get her head out of the hole she'd allowed Hayden to bury it in. "My...counselor. She said he was a borderline-sociopathic personality," she muttered, shame riffling through her. She couldn't stand the sharpened look in Kell's gray eyes. There was rage in them. Not at her, she hoped. Maybe at Hayden?

Leah knew Kell had put some of it together. And just now, he'd argued for her to stay with him. Here, she felt safe. Even out in the middle of the badlands with Taliban surrounding them, Leah felt safer than she would if Hayden flew into Camp Bravo to confront her about the loss of the helicopter. She *never* wanted to see him again. *Not ever.*

Kell saw the way her full lips tucked in at the corners. Yeah, she was hiding a hell of a lot of secrets. Why? He could see disgust in her eyes toward her ex-husband. And banked rage. What did he have on her, if anything? Did she have something on him? Was she hiding a secret? What was it?

"Why does your ex want you back to Bravo so damned bad?"

"He probably wants to pin the crash of the helo on me."

"You were copilot. You said Captain Larsen was at the controls when the RPGs were thrown at you."

Shrugging, Leah said, "He was." She picked up a small rock between her hands and rolled it around for a moment. "Hayden wants to destroy me any way he can. He's afraid I'll talk. And if I do, I could bring down his career and his dreams of being the next commander of the 80th."

Scowling, Kell heard the carefully veiled terror in her voice. "Talk about what?"

Leah dropped the rock near her boots. Emotion welled up through her. Maybe the shock from the crash was still working out of her. Maybe she saw the sincere care and worry burning in Kell's eyes; she didn't know. But it made her speak up. "I've never told anyone this, Kell. Just my psychiatrist, Judy Fontana," she admitted. "Hayden doesn't know about my two years of therapy to get my head screwed on straight after he divorced me, either. I got as far away from him as I could. I had my father transfer me to another battalion. I told him I never wanted to be anywhere near Hayden again."

Kell's mouth quirked. They were out in the open, it was daylight and this wasn't the place to continue such a serious conversation. "Look, let's get back to the cave. We can talk about it there, later."

Leah shrugged. "Yeah, fine." She moved, her knees feeling like they were eighty years old. She'd hit them egressing out of the cockpit window. They were bruised and swollen. Kell picked up her ruck and held it open for her to slide her arms through the straps. He was so damned thoughtful.

"Follow me," Kell said. And then he softened his voice because it was still hard with anger. "You don't need to hold on to my belt this time." He saw Leah rally over his teasing tone. She was still pale, her eyes dark and wounded looking.

"Even out here in the middle of one of the most godforsaken, lonely places on earth, my ex is still after me," she rasped. "He will haunt me until the day I die." Tears burned in her eyes and Leah angrily swallowed them. "Let's just get out of here." Her emotions were getting the best of her; unusual because she could normally control them. Kell would probably tell her it was shock making her more vulnerable than usual, less able to put those walls up. Medically, shock unraveled a person, dismantled them mentally and emotionally. Yeah, she was feeling dismantled, all right. She could mentally feel Hayden begin to tear down her protective walls.

"Wait a minute," Kell growled, gripping her gently by the shoulders, halting her. "Those are pretty strong words, Leah." He searched her moist eyes, saw her lower lip quiver. Ah, hell, he was a goner. Without a word, he swept her into his arms. Not very close with all their gear on, but he could feel her flying apart inwardly. Now, Kell was sorry as hell he'd made that sat phone call in front of her. But how could he have known Leah would have a violent reaction to it? Kell wouldn't do that again.

He pressed a kiss to her hair after he removed her hat, his hand moving across her cheek. "Look, you're safe with me, Leah. You understand that? And whatever the hell is going on with this ex-husband of yours, I'll make damn sure it's handled when we get back to Bravo."

Leah leaned wearily against Kell's chest for just a moment. She was tired to her soul of running from Hayden. She absorbed Kell's low voice, felt his rage toward Grant and his fierce protection enveloping her. The tears wanted to come. They couldn't! She was afraid if she started crying again, she'd never stop.

When he pressed a kiss to her hair, her entire body quivered inwardly. Leah pushed away, looking up at him, taking the hat from his fingers and pulling it on her head.

"This is way beyond you, Kell. You don't want to get involved. Do you hear me?"

He gave her a tender smile, grazing her cheek with his thumb. "I hate to tell you this, but you never tangle with a hill boy."

Blinking, Leah didn't understand what Kell meant, but she could see the deadly look in his eyes and it shook her. She'd been privy to his kind and gentle side. This was a different side to the man. The SEAL sniper side. "We can talk later," she said, and her voice cracked. It rocked her world that she trusted Kell, and Leah suddenly felt torn apart in a different way. One she had absolutely no experience with.

"Okay, Sugar, we'll wait until then," Kell soothed, skimming his thumb down the line of her jaw. He turned around because if he didn't, he was going to kiss the hell out of her. And he wasn't coming up for air when he did it, either. He wanted to pour his soul into that sinner's mouth of hers and take Leah into a paradise they both deserved. He wanted to remove that terror set deep in her flawless green eyes.

By the time they reached the cave complex, Leah's headache had mostly disappeared thanks to the Motrin. They went to work like the team they were, getting out of their gear, setting it aside and removing their heavy Kevlar vests.

Leah's hands shook as she stripped down to the T-shirt and cammies. She could feel bottled-up rage around Kell. She sensed it. But it didn't show on his face, in his voice or how he treated her.

Kell saw how despondent Leah had become. When she sat down on the bag, her back against the wall, he came and sat facing her, their legs against one another. He picked up her hand, which she'd placed over her torso.

"I think I can put some of this together," he began quietly, searching her desolate looking eyes. "The first night you were here, you had a nightmare and you screamed Hayden's name. You were fighting him because your right hand was in a fist, and it looked to me like you were trying to hit someone. Probably him?" Kell swallowed and watched her closely for a reaction. Her lower lip quivered almost imperceptibly. He was on the right track. Kell gently turned her hand over in his. "The second night, same thing. Only this time, you screamed like an animal that had been trapped, Leah. I know the differences in a person's screams. You were terrified. Weren't you?"

She barely nodded her head, caught in a web of so many dark emotions from her past. Kell's slow Southern drawl took the pain out of his words. Oddly comforted, she forced herself to meet his narrowed, intent gaze. She felt him searching, trying to put it all together. It wasn't threatening, but she could feel him putting a lot of her past in perspective. Things she never wanted to give voice to ever again. He was a sniper. He saw patterns. He cobbled pieces together all the time. Kell was observant in a way few people could ever be.

"You've hinted that your marriage to Hayden was a bad one." Kell lowered his voice and he struggled to find the right words, not wanting to harm Leah any more than she was presently hurting. "Correct me on this if I'm wrong, Leah. But my sense, and it's only my sense of things, is that he abused you."

Leah stared at him, the silence thickening between them, weighing down on her shoulders. The gentle look on Kell's face, his care, and his low, vibrating voice, gave her the courage to speak. "Yes." It was all she could choke out. There was no way she could say any more about it. The suffering, the memories—it was simply too much to bear all over again.

Kell scowled and stared down at her long, beautiful hand and lightly stroked her fingers. Rage soared through him. His mind was analyzing all the clues, their conversations about Hayden Grant. He felt Leah become so damned vulnerable, as if she had been skinned alive, with no way to protect herself.

Lifting his chin, Kell assessed her expression. His heart broke. Leah had gone pale. Her eyes were black holes, bottomless pits, the green of the irises a mere crescent around her huge pupils. He wanted to find that bastard ex-husband of hers and take him apart, one limb at a time. Right now, Leah was literally the color of white marble, unmoving, frozen in time, paralyzed by her past. His own selfish need to know had placed her in this position. Kell hadn't expected this kind of reaction from Leah. Now, he was sorrier than hell he'd ever brought it up for discussion.

He couldn't take back the words, so he continued to stroke her hand, knowing it was an anchor point for Leah as she tumbled through whatever horrific past she'd experienced with Grant. Finally, her lashes dropped and Kell felt her retreat deep inside herself, as if it was just all too much for her to bear.

His mind ran through all of his medical training, all his experience, trying to find something that would pull her out of it. Bring her back to him. Back to the present instead of being imprisoned in a past that appeared to still have its hooks buried deep into her soul.

Kell released her hand and whispered, "Come here, Leah. Let me hold you?" *Never make a command to an abuse survivor. Always give them the choice and control.* He remembered that from his classes. He saw Leah open her eyes; the vacant look in them scared the hell out of him. Kell reached toward Leah, offering to hold her. He held his breath, unsure of his tactics, unsure she'd respond. He was following his senses and they'd never led him wrong. No matter how much book learning he had, it always came down to his heart and gut making the final call. He knew she needed to be embraced, to feel protected.

Kell slowly lowered his arms, realizing Leah wasn't going to move. He was staring at a beautiful, vacant doll. Not a human being with passion, with emotions or a personality. The silence lengthened as he held her sightless stare. He'd pushed her too hard, too fast. All it had achieved was probably a horrendous flashback, yanking her back into her painful past. And he'd done it. *Dammit!* In his need to know, Kell had been a bulldozer, shattering her walls, taking advantage of the trust she'd given him.

He'd recalled moving through many Afghan villages, the women who had vacant-eyed stares just like Leah. They'd been raped by Taliban soldiers. They were ashamed, hiding their eyes, turning away, beaten. Broken.

Clutch's sister, Tracy, had been raped, and nearly died from the assault. Brad could always tell which Afghan women in a village had been raped. It was easy for him to spot them because Tracy, who had had her spirit broken by the violent attack, shared the same look. Kell wished Clutch were here right now. He'd know what to do. How to help Leah. Would know the right words to say.

Rubbing his face wearily, Kell slowly unwound and stood up. He took a blanket and settled it over Leah's legs and tucked it around her waist. She had closed her eyes, shutting him out. Shutting the world out, because she could no longer cope. The helo crash had ripped her life apart. She'd lost three men she was close to in that crash. And he'd just ripped her life apart some more because of his selfish need to understand Grant's toxic stain upon her.

Kell cursed himself, striding out of the cave and moving into the other one. He was running through one of many conversations Clutch had had with him about his sister, Tracy. She'd been raped while they were in Coronado, two months before deploying to Afghanistan.

Kell sat down on a box of water bottles, elbows on his knees, hands against his face, trying desperately to remember all the details of that attack upon her. Tracy was twenty-one and a paralegal in San Diego. She was Clutch's baby sister, three years younger than him. Kell had met her many times before for a beer at a local bar where SEALs congregated.

Clutch was tight with Tracy. He was fiercely protective of his blond-haired sister with the baby-blue eyes and innocent face. He never let another SEAL get too close to her, warning her off from his kind. Rightly so.

And then, Tracy had been attacked one night, leaving the law firm on B Street after dark. She'd gone to the parking garage to get her car when a man had jumped her from behind.

He and Clutch had been at Coronado SEAL Team 3 HQ when the police had called, asking for Brad. Kell had watched his best friend fall apart. Tracy had been found by another lawyer from another law firm who had been late getting to his car.

He and his SEAL brother had rushed to the San Diego hospital emergency room. The nurses tried to kick him out of ER but Clutch was half-crazed, looking into every cubicle trying to locate his baby sister.

When he'd found Tracy, Clutch had cried and held

her hand. Kell had persuaded the angry nurses not to bother him. Just to let him be with Tracy while the doctor examined her. When the nurses found out they were SEALs, they instantly backed off. Kell calmed the nurses down, got to his friend's side as a woman doctor examined Tracy.

She was unconscious, her face bloodied, nose broken, her lower lip split wide-open. Her slacks were gone. As the doctor lifted the blanket, even Kell could see the vicious purple bruising inside Tracy's thighs. He'd wanted to throw up. Brad did. The woman doctor had given Kell a pleading look to take his emotional friend out of the cubicle. Kell half carried and half dragged his friend, who was sobbing, out of the room and to the men's head.

Taking a deep, uneven breath, Kell scrubbed his eyes with his palms. Clutch had been a mess after that. Tracy'd had a severe concussion, broken nose, broken cheek and needed vaginal surgery to repair the damage done to her. It took Tracy months to recover physically. But that was just the beginning of her journey, Kell discovered.

When Clutch drove her home from the hospital to her condo apartment on the bay, she'd looked exactly as Leah had looked right now. That vacant, haunting stare. No life in her eyes. No…nothing. As if her spirit had been stolen. *Broken.*

Kell visited Tracy at least once a week because the Team was in town. Clutch was there almost every day to look after his sister. Tracy was never the same. She didn't remember the rape and in some ways, Kell was relieved. She'd suffered enough. He'd seen her sunny,

warm and extroverted personality markedly change
after the attack.

Kell began to piece together Leah's previous actions and reactions to him. Damn, they were identical
to Tracy's! He remembered a time when Tracy would
always throw her arms around him. He'd been like a
brother to her. But she was so hesitant to be touched
by any man after being raped. Even him, which made
Kell confused at first. She would almost shrink inside herself for fear of being touched by *anyone*, even
though she'd known him for years. Rubbing his face,
the picture became more clear for Kell.

Three years later, Tracy met a man, Kevin Johnson,
who was a lawyer at another law firm in downtown
San Diego. At first, Clutch was worried sick about her.
But when Kell met Kevin, he was impressed with him.
He was a very kind, quiet kind of guy. And Kell could
see he worshipped the ground Tracy walked on. More
than anything, Kell remembered how patient Kevin
had been with Tracy. He had, over time, drawn her
out of that shell she'd retreated into. By the time they
got married, Tracy was almost like her old self, out-
going, warm and caring once again.

Lifting his head, Kell pressed his damp palms
against his thighs. Clutch had mentioned Tracy needed
to be held sometimes. Kevin had confided to him one
time that she'd had terrorizing nightmares and the only
thing that brought her out of them was being held by
him. Held and gently rocked. And touched in a non-
sexual way. And it had worked. It had drawn Tracy
out of her shell.

Standing, Kell knew now Leah had been raped.
Spousal rape? He'd bet his soul on it, judging from

Leah's nightmares and her reactions toward him. She'd been so damned afraid to come into his arms to sleep last night. Now, it all made sense. Leah was afraid, maybe dealing with flashbacks.

Rubbing his mouth, Kell began to pace back and forth in the cave, searching for answers. Searching for the right thing to do to help Leah. And just like Tracy, she'd probably compartmentalized her rape. She'd no doubt walled the experience off so she could function. To the outside world, these women looked normal. Leah was one of the best pilots the Army had. She'd compartmentalized her marriage, the spousal rape, the abuse, and continued to be a good pilot. But now... Kell halted. His mind was making huge leaps and connections.

Leah was frightened because her ex-husband was unexpectedly barging back into her life. She was absolutely terrified. He'd seen it in her eyes. She'd managed to avoid Grant until now. Until this helo crash.

Kell didn't know why Hayden wanted back into her life. Obviously Leah didn't want him there. And neither did Kell because he was protective of her. He rubbed his bearded jaw, feeling rage so deeply that it shook him. Where Kell came from, the way he was raised, women were sacred. He'd never seen his father raise his voice or hand toward his mother. They were equals. A good team. And there was respect between them. He'd been raised to treat women as human beings.

Pacing the cave, Kell remembered more of Tracy's journey. Today, she had a little girl, Sonja, and was happy. She'd quit her job to become a full-time mother to her daughter. Kevin made a whopping amount of money, so it worked for them.

Leah could be happy someday, like Tracy, but it hadn't happened yet.

Aggravated, he ran his fingers through his hair. Ballard paced and thought, trying to keep his feelings out of the equation. He couldn't help Leah if he was a ball of unraveling emotional yarn, as his mother would say. Cold logic was going to get him the answers he sought.

He looked at his watch. It was noon. And his stomach was grumbling. Kell halted, a plan gelling in his mind, based upon his knowledge of Tracy's painful journey from the darkness and into the light once again.

To make matters really sticky, Leah was a warrant officer. And he couldn't just waltz up to Grant and tell him to go to hell. Which is exactly what Kell wanted to do. He closed his fist, feeling his rage toward the Army major. Somehow, he was going to have to enlist his officers' help from the Navy side. His LT, Nate Drager, Dragon, a first lieutenant, OIC, was a solid leader. Everyone called him Dragon, and it was a good name for the six-foot-four-inch former football player. Dragon was a real quiet guy until something went wrong, and then he lived up to his fire-breathing namesake.

Above him was Commander Brody Lanoux, the team's CO. He was a Louisiana Cajun boy whom everyone had dubbed Rambo. And even though Lanoux's Southern charm was always in place, Kell had watched this Navy officer tear assholes off assholes. He left no one standing. Lanoux was a snake, a venomous one, and he had garnered the reputation to go with it. No one fucked with him or his team. Period.

When Kell got back to Bravo, he had to seek their help. High-ranking help. And before that, he had to get the rest of the story from Leah. Kell knew he couldn't push her. It would have to come out of her because she wanted to share it with him. Then, and only then, could he circle the wagons within the Navy and SOF-COM, special operation forces command, to help protect her in case her sociopathic ex-husband decided to try to destroy her career. Kell just wasn't going to let it happen. No way. No how. Major Grant was going to find out in a helluva hurry how the SEAL community reacted to an abuser and rapist of any woman. Grant was a dead man walking.

CHAPTER EIGHT

KELL MOVED SILENTLY into the darkened cave. He halted, sensing. Before, Leah would have been awake with the penlight on. Feeling her presence in the cave, he pulled the penlight from one of the pockets of his H-gear. The light slashed through the darkness.

He saw Leah sleeping, her body curled up into a fetal position on her right side. The blanket had slipped off, revealing her legs and hip. Grimacing, he knew he was late. It was almost midnight. Not wanting to disturb her, Kell moved to the other cave and shrugged out of the ruck and his H-gear. His mind was on the Taliban next door. But his heart was squarely on Leah.

How was she? Was she all right now? Throughout the day he'd remained in a new hide he'd created above the two caves where Khogani's men were staying. He'd taken photos, sent them from his laptop via the sat phone back to Bravo. He'd counted twenty more men in the ranks. Khogani was amassing a large group. Why? Something was going down, but Kell hadn't put it together yet.

"Kell?"

Leah's drowsy voice intruded on his thoughts. He turned, seeing her standing at the cave entrance, her expression sleepy, her hair mussed. His heart blew open with happiness. Kell saw a soft smile of welcome on her mouth. When he looked into Leah's eyes, some-one was home. She was home. Relief flooded him.

He dropped his H-gear next to his ruck and smiled in return. What he wanted to do was walk over, drag her into his arms and give her that protection she so badly deserved and needed.

"I'm late," he said quietly in apology, pulling off his Kevlar and laying it across a box.

Rubbing her eyes, Leah saw the sharp shadows across his face, that gray gaze warm upon her. She felt heat tunnel through her. Halting about six feet from him, she said, "Your business isn't nine to five."

He grinned a little more, shucking down to his T-shirt and cammies. "Neither is yours." He became serious as he pulled a couple bottles of water from the box. "How are you feeling?"

"Better," Leah murmured. "I could use some water, though."

He gave her two bottles and they walked back into the other cave with his penlight. They sat down on the two sleeping bags next to one another. Kell made sure he gave her some space. Leah seemed calm. Almost at peace. She looked exhausted; there were shadows beneath her green eyes. He watched her twist the cap off the water bottle, her left hand looking stronger, al-most normal. That was good. Tonight, he was going to have to change the dressing and take a look at how the wound was healing.

"Hard day?" she asked, drinking.

Kell tried to ignore her tipping her head back, ex-posing her slender neck. Groaning inwardly, he felt his erection stir. There wasn't anything that wasn't graceful or beautiful about Leah to him. He was com-

pletely under her spell even though she had no clue
how much he cared for her, wanted her. And maybe,
Kell thought, drinking his own bottle of water, it was
best that way. At least he wasn't seen as a threat to
her like Grant was.

He'd had all day and half the night to think about
Clutch's sister, Tracy, and to realize Leah had the very
same actions and reactions as she'd had after being
raped. Though unable to prove it, but with his gut
screaming at him, Kell now knew that the "abuse"
was most likely spousal rape. Though maybe Grant
had beat the shit out of her, instead. Or worse, both.
His gaze moved to the bump on Leah's nose. It was a
bad break, and it had never been properly fixed. Had
Grant hit her? Rage flared in him every time Kell
thought about it.

And tonight, he'd found Leah sleeping in the fetal
position. It was a position of protection a rape survivor often curled up in when asleep. Tracy had for
years after her rape. Only with Kevin in her life had
she eventually stopped sleeping like that.

Kell ached for Leah. He wanted to help her, but
he'd done a damn bad job of doing it. She'd just about
gone catatonic on him last night. The crash, the shock
of her friends dying in it and now Grant haunting her
from the past, it had just been too much for Leah to
cope with. Hell, it would be for anyone. The fact she
looked normal tonight was a testament to her inner
strength and amazing resilience.

"What do you think Khogani's doing?" Leah asked,
capping the bottle. She rested against the wall, filling
her eyes with his hard, rugged-looking face, knowing
how gentle his hands had been on her. Even now, Leah

yearned for Kell's touch. She had been dreaming of him holding her just before she woke up.

Wiping his mouth, he shrugged. "No clue. Just have to wait and watch. He has twenty more men, so it looks like he's calling in favors or, more than likely, throwing cash around, buying more horse soldiers."

"He's an opium drug lord, he should have plenty of cash on hand."

Snorting softly, Kell nodded. "You up to me changing that dressing of yours? It's time."

Her heart leaped. "Sure. Where do you want me to sit?"

He rose. "Stay where you are. I'll get my ruck."

She watched him walk away; that lithe grace and yet that sense of protection he wrapped around her. Leah knew Kell could be a warrior in a heartbeat. She'd seen it yesterday morning. Why did she want his touch when she'd wanted no man touching her since Hayden?

He returned with the medical items and knelt down next to her. As Kell's fingers grazed her arm, positioning it against his thighs, Leah felt her lower body contract. It was a feeling like a gnawing of an animal deep within her wanting out, wanting freedom. She closed her eyes, relaxing and absorbing his quiet nearness. Sponging in his gentle ministrations.

"I'm sorry I melted down yesterday," Leah said softly, keeping her eyes closed. She didn't want to see Kell judging her, to see what he really thought about her abnormal behavior. His fingers moved against her flesh with knowing ease, removing the dressing.

"It was my fault," Kell muttered, holding her lower arm, looking at it beneath the light. The stitches were holding well and her skin was seamed and a bit red, indicating scar tissue was building around the area.

Leah frowned, moved her head to the left, looking at him. "No, it wasn't." She saw him lift his chin, his gray eyes flat and unreadable. "It was me."

"I triggered it with a really badly timed question," he admitted. Kell struggled. Why the hell was Leah shouldering the blame? He was the one who had initiated the questions about abuse. Had Grant beat her down that far? Made her think the reason he hit or raped her was that it was her fault to begin with? That she deserved any type of punishment he decided to mete out to her?

Kell didn't want to get into that discussion tonight because he was too damned exhausted. He wanted to shove some food into himself and then get some desperately needed sleep.

She watched Kell quickly add antiseptic with his gloved finger across the healing cut. Just his tender care fed her breached soul. Did Kell know how much he was helping her? "I don't remember much from last night. Did you sleep with me? Did I scream out during the night?"

His mouth pulled in at one corner as he finished placing a clean, waterproof dressing on. "I didn't try holding you last night," Kell admitted, finishing taping both ends of the dressing. "I lay close enough so that you'd know I was there, but that was all." He met her calm gaze, excruciatingly aware of her vulnerability. "And no, you didn't have a nightmare last night. Or—" he tossed the gloves into his ruck "—if you did, you didn't scream out."

Relieved, Leah whispered, "Good." She lifted her

hand from his thighs. "Thanks. It's feeling better every day."

"It should." He looked at her head. "How about your head injury? Headaches?"

"Less headache today," Leah said, giving him a half smile, touching the stitched area beneath her hair. "You're a healer, Kell."

He wished. Unhappy with how he'd pushed Leah over the edge last night, he gathered up the medical items and put them in his ruck. Getting up, Kell asked, "Have you eaten yet?"

Nodding, she opened the water bottle. "Yes, earlier."

"I'm going to get something, then," he told her, walking toward the other cave. Kell honestly didn't know how Leah was keeping herself together. He'd always known women were a hell of a lot stronger than men. He saw it in his mother, who was the center and hub of their family. It was in their DNA.

Grabbing an MRE, he moved back to the other cave. Always alert, Kell keyed his hearing. The Taliban could still discover them here. He never took these caves as a completely safe place. Ever.

Sitting down opposite Leah, he crossed his legs and opened the MRE, a foot away from where she sat. "I talked to Master Chief Axton late today," he said.

"Giving him your daily report?"

"Yes." Kell tried to brace himself internally for what he was going to tell her next. He had no idea how Leah would react. Would it be another nail in her mental coffin like Grant was? Hell, he didn't know, but he had to tell her, anyway. Kell held her green, shadowed gaze. "Your father is asking to speak directly

with you," he said. "He wants to make sure you're all
right." He saw her eyes go wide with surprise. And
then, she frowned. The feeling around Leah was like
a small earthquake of surprise followed by happiness.
But he didn't see it in her eyes. Just a blank look. "Are
you all right with that?" Kell demanded, his voice
deepening because he wasn't going to force her into
talking to him if she didn't want to. She'd damn well
been forced into enough things by men in her life.

"Seriously? My father asked to talk to me?" Leah's
world tilted a little. She saw Kell scowling, felt his
fierce protectiveness wrapping around her as never
before.

"Yes. I told my master chief I'd leave it up to you.
I was ordered to tell you, but you weren't ordered to
do it."

Taking a breath, she murmured, "I'll talk to him."

"Do you want to?"

Leah gave him a slight shrug. "I rarely speak to my
father when I'm not in a jam like this, so yes, I guess
if he cares enough to see how I am, I'll talk with him."

Wincing internally, Kell had made several decisions after that sat phone confab with Ax. The master chief warned him that Major Grant was blaming
Leah for the crash. That they needed to retrieve the
black box from the bird to prove or disprove the Army
major's charge.

Kell was angry and upset about the false charge.
He had seen Leah egress out of the copilot's window.
He talked to the master chief about getting the black
box recording from the crash site, via SEAL stealth,
to prove who was on the radio. Because if Leah had
been on the radio just before they landed, it proved

conclusively that she hadn't been flying the helo. If Larsen was at the controls, that would also be on the recording.

Ax gave him permission to try to retrieve the black box. He warned Kell that Major Grant was gunning for Leah, for whatever reason. He wanted to destroy Leah and Kell could feel it. That was why he'd gone back to the crash site under the cover of darkness last night, searched and finally dug into the ruptured soil around where the helo had burned and located the black box.

He'd also found five scattered bone fragments from what he thought might belong to the two crewmen or the pilot's femur, as well as two half-melted dog tags from the hapless crew. He'd had to be very careful, exposed in the valley, no place to hide if Taliban came by.

Kell had relentlessly scoured the wreckage. Only when he was walking around the front of the destroyed helo had he seen the partially visible hole in the ground. Kneeling down, he'd dug into it farther. And there was the badly scratched black box. He had no idea if the information on it was intact or destroyed.

Tomorrow, he'd let Ax know what he'd found. But right now, he wasn't going to tell Leah anything about it, or about Grant's desire to implicate her in the crash.

"What are your dreams, Kell?"

The question completely shook him out of his train of thought. Kell stopped eating and stared over at her. There was no guile in Leah's eyes. Just curiosity, maybe? People didn't ask questions like that out of the blue. There were reasons behind them and he knew it. Leah's expression was pensive.

"Well," he drawled, "when I was a skinny little kid,

I used to lie out in one of the dairy-cow fields and look up at the clouds and imagine shapes in them. I always saw myself as a knight on a white horse, slaying all those dragons in the clouds." He grinned a little.

"So even then, you were a dragon slayer?"

"I guess so. My pa loved the classics, especially about King Arthur and the Knights of the Round Table. He used to come in every night when we were little kids and read us a chapter from a book about knights, dragons and damsels in distress."

Warmth flooded Leah's chest as he gave her a boyish look. Kell stole her heart with his soft Southern accent, the kindness in his eyes when he held her gaze. She wanted to know everything about this man. He was so different from Hayden. Kell invited her trust. When he looked at her with those gray eyes of his, Leah felt herself melting, wanting and becoming sexually awakened. Even needy. As her gaze fell to his well-shaped mouth, that boyish grin spread across it, she felt an ache building in her. A starving, gnawing sensation that always leaped to life whenever she was around him.

"Did your dreams change after you grew up?"

Finishing the MRE, Kell put it aside and wiped his mouth with the napkin. "No. I always saw myself protecting weaker kids. In grade school one of my best friends, Bobby, got picked on by some bullies. I took them on." He gave a dark chuckle. "Came home that afternoon with my best white shirt torn, which upset my ma plenty. And when she saw the blood on the shirt and around my nose, she figured it out. She asked me what happened and I told her. That night, Pa found out about it and he told me I'd done the right thing, that there were people who were weaker in our world, and sometimes, they needed protecting."

"So you didn't get chewed out for the torn shirt?"

"Nah. My pa is a very strong person, believes in right and wrong. Doesn't put up with lies or deceit. We boys learned early on to be truthful even if it killed us." Kell smiled fondly, holding her warm gaze. "The SEALs are the same way. At least in my platoon. No one lies to anyone else. We lay our cards out on the table. It's just a better way to live and survive."

Lies. Yes, Leah knew about lies. Hayden had been the consummate liar and she hadn't even fully realize it until after the divorce. She'd been so young, so gullible. Maybe the word was *ignorant.* "And what are your dreams today?"

Kell fell silent, thinking his way through the softly asked question. "Find the right woman, settle down and have some kids."

"You'd leave your SEAL family?" she asked.

Opening his hands, Kell said, "I've seen a lot, done a lot, Leah. I've seen the belly of the beast since I was eighteen. I'm twenty-nine now. And I'm tired of always seeing the dark side of humanity. Loving a good woman, loving the child she carries in her belly, loving the little tyke when she or he is born. Those are the good things in life."

"That sounds like a wonderful dream," she whispered, touched by his honesty and sincerity. Leah didn't think Kell could ever lie. He had always been open with her. She could feel his vulnerability, and something else, but she couldn't define it.

"What are your dreams?" he asked.

"Mine?" Leah gave a ladylike snort. "I stopped

dreaming when I was eight years old. I really miss dreaming because I used to have beautiful, colorful, happy dreams before that."

Kell remained silent, weighing the emotion in her voice. "Well, maybe things will work out here and you'll start dreaming again," he told her. "We aren't meant to go through life without dreams." Because if a person didn't have dreams, it meant they were technically dead inside, no hope, no vision, no wanting to reach for that brass ring life gave everyone a chance to grab.

Leah studied his shadowed face in the silence. She felt no anxiety, no worry when Kell was here. Why? She always felt safe with him around. The first and only man to make her feel like that. Getting up her courage, she whispered, "Would you sleep by me tonight?" She saw his mouth soften.

"Anything you want," he promised, unwinding and picking up the empty MRE. "I'm going to wash up and then I'll join you."

"Yes," she said, "I'd like that."

BY THE TIME Kell joined Leah, she was asleep. This time, she had turned on her left side, her back to him. Turning off the penlight, he brought the blanket up over them. He didn't make the mistake of holding her. There were six inches separating them. Kell could feel her body heat, the fragrance of her. Inhaling it, he felt his entire body begin to relax. And very quickly, he slid off into an abyss, physically exhausted from the ten-mile run he'd had to undertake to get to that crash site and retrieve that black box.

His last thought was of the sweet fragrance of Leah's

hair; so close to his face. Did she have any idea of the woman she was? He wanted to be the man to show her just how sensual, how beautiful, she really was.

Leah felt darkness eating at the edges of her sleep. She felt it was Hayden, like the predator he was, stalking her, watching her, wanting to kill her. A whimper escaped her as she turned to run away from him. She couldn't see him, but she sensed him. She could feel him wanting sex from her.

Kell felt Leah turn over, seeking shelter. His arms automatically curved around her shoulders as she snuggled closer. Dragging himself out of badly needed sleep, he heard a whimper escape her, her face burrowing into his neck, her left arm moving over his rib cage, drawing herself up against him, as if he were a shield that she could use to protect herself from the nightmare she was captured within.

His whole body flooded with heat as she curved into his long, lanky body. Groaning, Kell knew she wasn't looking for sex even if his body was reading her signals wrong. Silky strands of her hair fell across his jaw and chin. He could feel her breasts against his chest, rising and falling sharply. She was caught in a nightmare.

Forcing himself to full wakefulness, Kell felt her quiver, her breathing going erratic. "Shh, Sugar, it's okay," he rasped, sliding his hand across her hair, stroking her shoulders and back. "Nothing's going to hurt you. It's all right…just hold on to me and you'll be okay…" Leah clung to him, as if he were her last hope on this planet. It tore at Kell. She was breathing irregularly, almost hyperventilating. *Dammit!*

He'd give anything to be inside her head, to find

out what was scaring her out of her mind. Wrapping his arms tightly around Leah, he hauled her against him, tangling his legs among her own, just trying to protect her from whatever was chasing her.

He kept moving his hand slowly up and down her back, feeling how damp the T-shirt she wore had become. It reminded him so much of the flashbacks he'd get from time to time. How real they were. He'd be completely transported to the violent event, the present no longer existing, utterly imprisoned in the past, just as she now was.

Kell whispered her name against her ear, kissing her temple, pressing small kisses across her wrinkled brow. Leah whimpered again. Feeling helpless, he knew he couldn't have her scream. Not now. Not tonight with the Taliban so close. He rolled Leah onto her back, trying to shake her awake. Maybe that would pull her out of it. But she didn't awaken.

She's trapped in the event.

Kell's heart was pounding with urgent concern for Leah, wanting her safe but being unable to give her any safety at all because the monster was in her mind, from her past. And then, Kell followed his heart, which had never led him wrong. He curved his mouth against her lips, inhaling a cry that tore out of her. He felt Leah jerk awake in the middle of the scream, felt her suddenly freeze against him. He moved his mouth gently against hers, feeling the softness of her lips, the cry fading away in her throat. His nostrils flared, dragging in her scent.

As he moved his mouth more deeply, rocking her lips farther open, tasting her, he felt her suddenly relax, felt her arms slowly ease around his shoulders.

She felt so damn good beneath him, her lips responding shyly to his.

Kell felt her heartbeat change, strengthen, and then
she melted into his arms as he moved his mouth teasingly across hers. Now, her breathing became shallow, her fingers digging into his shoulders, telling him
she liked what he was doing. Had she ever really been
kissed? Because Kell could feel the subtle shift of her
entire body beneath his, felt her awakening, wanting,
asking for more without quite knowing how. Somewhere in his deteriorating mind, he knew she was innocent…

There was no going back. Kell cradled Leah in his
arms, molding his mouth to her lips. He heard a little
moan of pleasure vibrate in her slender throat, indicating that she was enjoying their kiss as much as he
was. How far to go? Was he like Grant? Pushing himself on her? Was that what was happening right now?

Yet as Kell sipped her lips lightly, inviting her to
come to him, she did. This wasn't one-way. Leah
wanted what he was sharing with her. She was awake
now. Kell could feel it. He eased from her mouth,
breathing raggedly because his erection was so
damned hard and he was in so much pain, he wanted
to double over.

Leah's lashes barely opened. Kell saw desire burning in the shadowy depths of her eyes, felt her hands
restlessly moving against his shoulders, opening and
closing. Wanting. Not knowing what to ask for, but
wanting it all the same. She didn't give the normal
signals a woman would if she wanted more. As if…
as if she honestly didn't know how to communicate
with a man when it came to her needs.

Staring down at her, lost in the soft curves of her, her body warm and supple, Kell closed his eyes for a moment, exerting control over himself. How far to go? How far did Leah want to go? Where did nightmares end? Dreams begin? Kell wasn't at all sure as he opened his eyes, studying Leah with intensity, trying to read her mind.

He moved his hand, pushing strands away from her face, holding her slumberous gaze. He'd barely kissed her. He was more just stopping her scream from ringing throughout the cave than giving her a real, hot, long, deep kiss.

"Leah…Sugar…you've got to tell me how far to go here…" His voice was thick and ragged.

Her breath was chaotic, her body tense, hungry and restless. Leah had awakened in Kell's arms, his mouth against hers absorbing the scream that had torn out of her. Drowning in his dark, intense gaze, Leah could feel him straining to hold himself in check. Her mind gyrated. The past haunted her. But this was Kell. And this was *now*.

Fragments of the nightmare hung before her. She saw the tightness of his mouth, the desire kindled in his eyes for her. Her lips moved and her throat constricted. It felt so good to be in Kell's arms, to feel his long, hard body solidly against hers. Leah could feel his erection pushing against her belly and the sensation burned into her, making her feel wanted, desired. Not hunted. Not stalked. But desired. She could feel his hand cradling her head and neck. He was holding himself very still, asking her what she wanted. No man had asked her that before.

"Just," she whispered unsteadily, "kiss me?" Because she didn't know what else to ask for. She saw his eyes change, grow warm, the hardness leaving his face. Felt his arms loosen slightly around her, making her more comfortable beside him. He guided her to his side and she missed his warmth and weight pressing against her wildly throbbing body.

"I can do that," Kell rasped, studying her expression, trying to get a read on Leah. There was such innocence in her expression. A kiss? That was all she wanted? Okay, that was fine with Kell. It was something to build upon, a slow, easy way to introduce her to himself in a sensual way. He moved his fingers across her cheek, feeling the softness, the velvet quality of her flesh. "Leah, if something doesn't feel good to you, stop me. You understand?" Kell saw confusion in her eyes. Leaning down, he moved his lips against her cheek, her brow and then barely grazing her lips. "Tell me you'll say something?" he rasped against her wet mouth. "This is about pleasure, not pain, darlin'. I want you to enjoy every second of this with me. Okay?"

"I—will…"

Satisfied, Kell grated, "Just a kiss…" He moved his fingers across her scalp, felt her lips open in response, her lashes sweeping closed. Kell sensed Leah didn't really know the kiss of a man who loved her, who cherished her. She'd known Grant's abusive hands and body, but had never experienced real love. He whispered her name against her mouth, as if it were a prayer shared between them, sliding his fingers in a light massage across her scalp.

Barely touching the corners of her mouth with his tongue, Kell felt her arch and moan, trying to capture his mouth with her own. Smiling, he whispered, "Sugar, we're taking this nice and slow…let me show you just how beautiful you are…" He touched her lower lip with his own. Moving his fingers from her scalp, he trailed them around her slender throat, feeling her pulse fluttering wildly beneath his fingertips. He left her mouth, moving to her ear, tasting the lobe, hearing her take a sharp intake of breath.

She couldn't lie still against him, her hands needy, gripping him, releasing him, as if she didn't understand what her body was asking of her. Kell knew she wasn't a virgin, but dammit, she behaved like one. Untrained. Her own body hidden from her sacred womanhood.

Moving the tip of his tongue around the outer edge of her ear, lightly nipping her lobe, he felt her tense, her hips reactive, pushing hard against his.

Clenching his teeth for a moment, Kell throttled his urge. She was whimpering, her body making ancient, unconscious moves, her hands not knowing, but somehow searching for him, asking for more. Much more.

Kell moved back to her mouth, opening his eyes, looking down into her drowsy green ones. Yeah, Leah was hot. Really hot. Bothered. Needy. He could feel her quivering and tensing, her hips urgent against his. Did she really want just a kiss? Kell didn't know and he wasn't going beyond what she'd asked for. He didn't dare. To take Leah without her express permission was to take control away from her. And dammit, he wasn't going to be that man. Her body was sacred to her. To him. If she wanted more, she'd show him, somehow, someway. Give it voice. And Leah might be a neophyte at making love, but Kell was going to be content to cherish her mouth, kiss her senseless, let her know how a real man should treat her.

He cupped her cheek, angling her mouth so he could take their kiss deeper. She was bold, unafraid, and he smiled to himself. After all, Leah was a warrior woman. Not someone who flew a desk. Her lips were hungry, wanting, strong and demanding against his mouth.

Her hand slid up the column of his neck, fingers curving around to his nape, pulling him against her. Oh, yeah, she liked this. Just as much as he did. Kell slowly slid his tongue inside her mouth. For a moment, she quieted, as if not knowing what to do next. It told Kell plenty.

He started all over again, easing from her mouth, her irregular, moist breath sporadic against his cheek. Moving his tongue to one corner of her mouth, he teased her. She liked it, moaning, pressing her breasts against his chest. Then, the other corner. He kept his hands away from her breasts, though he was burning to touch them, to tease her and pleasure her.

Just a kiss.

As Kell moved his tongue to the other corner of her lips, Leah automatically parted them more, turning her mouth toward his. Yeah, she got it, and she liked it. She was a fast learner. He felt pleasure thrum through him, her enjoyment everything to him as he slid his tongue along her slick lower lip.

A whisper of a cry vibrated through her throat and Kell lavished her lower lip. She trembled against him, her fingers digging into his shoulder. Nothing gave him pleasure like feeling his woman respond naturally, openly to him. There was no guile and no manipulation with Leah. A woman who knew her body could employ artful teasing and knew how to set a man on fire. Leah was completely unaware of her own body's needs and wants. She had no idea of how to pleasure her man.

He could feel her frustration building within her, the mewling cries trapped in her throat. His erection was killing him. He was going to have to do something about it after this was over. He'd never sleep the rest of the night. Hell, he wasn't going to sleep with her in his arms, anyway. It was like holding a wild woman who was artless, hungry, and she had no idea what she was triggering within him, or what he was generating within her.

As Kell left her lower lip, he moved his tongue gently inside her mouth once more, and this time, felt her respond, not stiffen. He groaned as her small pink tongue shyly touched his in return. A deep, ragged tremble rolled through him as her tongue became bolder, more curious, more hungry for the new pleasure she'd just discovered.

He captured her, splaying his fingers against her jaw, deepening their connection, moving his tongue provocatively in an ancient rhythm against hers. All of a sudden, he felt a violent tension release within her and she tore her mouth from his, her back arching, her body pressed hard against him, groaning.

Oh, hell!

Kell held her, realizing Leah had just orgasmed. He could feel the rippling sensation tearing through her, heard it in her panting breath, her palm flat against his chest, keening sobs tearing out of her.

He eased his hand down her back, cradling her

hips, pressing her against his erection. She bucked against him, gasping. He could feel her panic, her confusion coupled with the raw pleasure undulating wildly through her lower body. He felt her surprise over the gift her body had just given her. Yeah, a woman's body was one hot fire to handle. And simply by kissing her, emulating the rhythm of sex against her tongue, she'd orgasmed.

Kell took a deep breath, holding Leah tightly against him, allowing the sensations to roll through her until finally she quieted, her breathing growing raspy. *Just a kiss.*

He released her, moving his hand across her hips, smoothing the rumpled T-shirt against the damp skin of her back. Taking Leah onto her back, his arm beneath her neck, still holding her close, he smiled down at her.

"Helluva orgasm you just had," he growled. Strands of hair clung to her damp brow and cheek. He saw the confusion, undisguised pleasure, in her widening gaze. Her mouth was soft, parted, slightly pouty from the intensity of their shared kiss.

Kell lifted his hand, smoothing the strands behind her ear, grazing her cheek in a soothing motion. It was too dark to see her skin, but Kell would bet the farm she was flushed in every part of her luscious, hot body. He moved his hand across her belly, allowing it to stay there. Claiming her. She was his whether she knew it or not.

"What—what just happened?" Leah managed, her voice sounding light-years away to her. Every single cell in her lower body was tingling, clenching, unclenching, and she felt a golden river of fluid and heat rushing through her channel, dampening her thighs. She stared uncomprehendingly up into Kell's glittering eyes, saw a very pleased male smile on his mouth.

"The most beautiful gift a woman can give her man, darlin'. You had an orgasm from what I could tell."

His large hand splayed out across her belly felt comforting. She placed her hand over his. "I—I've never felt anything like this before, Kell. Not ever…" Leah sighed, sinking into the heat glowing deep within her, feeling satisfied, released and utterly confounded by her body. Oh, she'd heard from women friends in college who would talk about their orgasms, but she was too ashamed to ask them what it really was. Or what it meant. The way her body was now glowing, the pleasure radiating through her, Leah now understood why they were all smiling when they talked about experiencing an orgasm. This was the most wonderful physical feeling in the world!

Her mind canted back to the past, to Hayden. She'd never experienced this with him. Ever. All Kell had done was kiss her and her body had blossomed in response.

"We have a good connection with one another, darlin'," was all he'd say, and Kell shared a tender smile with Leah, holding her exhausted but radiant gaze.

"We must," she whispered in awe, her voice growing weary. "I feel as if someone pulled the plug on my energy, Kell. I'm so tired. Does an orgasm do this to you?"

Kell remained nonreactive to her question. Obviously, Leah hadn't ever had an orgasm until just now. He knew that not all men knew how to coax an orgasm out of a woman. It required physical knowledge on the man's part, an understanding of a woman's body. Plus, many men were in a hurry. And women were slower to come online sexually than men. Grant must have been like that, in a hurry, not caring if he pleasured Leah. Not concerned for her trust in him. And now, he knew Leah trusted him wholly, on every level. If he'd had any question about whether there was something good and powerful between them, it had just been answered in the most intimate of ways.

"Yes, it can make you feel tired, Leah. A good kind of tired, Sugar. Go to sleep. I'll be here. I'll hold you." She gave him a soft, drowsy smile, her eyelids beginning to droop.

"I've never been kissed like that, Kell. Not ever… Thank you… It was wonderful…"

Her voice trailed off and he watched Leah's lashes close. In two heartbeats, she was asleep. And so damned beautiful, her face utterly relaxed, her lips well kissed. By him.

Kell shook his head, never having experienced a woman who orgasmed over a simple kiss. It surprised him. And he'd been right in his initial assessment of her: Leah was one hot, fiery woman, completely natural, trusting him with her body, with her heart and with her soul.

CHAPTER NINE

"WE HAVE TO TALK," Kell murmured, holding Leah's gaze. He'd just come back in as night had fallen and eaten a meal with her.

She'd looked incredibly beautiful this morning as she slept, no tension in her face when he'd left before dawn to head to his hide for the day. The soft, vulnerable beauty of Leah sleeping hovered in his memory all day.

Kell had stood there for a moment, feeling emotions he'd never felt for another woman before. Now, tonight, his emotions were twisted and his mind was filled with hard choices. Did Leah want a relationship with him? It wasn't his call to make. Leah had to be heard and Kell had to know where she stood.

"I know," Leah said, holding his somber gaze. The penlight threw a grayish light around them, enough for her to see him, but not much else. "What happened last night was my fault."

Kell scowled. "There's no fault in this, Leah. At least not from where I stand."

Struggling, she said, "If I wasn't having nightmares, if I wasn't screaming, giving away our position—"

"And you think that's what caused our kiss?" Kell saw the desperation and confusion in her eyes. Over what? Them? Kell didn't know, but he was going to find out.

He watched Leah deflate, all the fight going out of her. She was reacting emotionally, not thinking clearly. Hell, he'd had all day sitting and doing cover surveillance to think through everything from beginning to end a thousand times regarding her and last night. He'd felt gut-wrenching emotions, and had looked at everything with a knowing and realistic eye.

Leah pulled her knees up against her chest, leaning back against the wall. Her voice was strained and soft. "The kiss…I won't ever regret that, Kell."

"There's no fault in me wanting to kiss you."

"You kissed me because I was going to scream. By doing that, you absorbed the sound of it. You could have put a hand over my mouth but I think, unless you tell me differently, that you thought it might upset me even more? So you kissed me instead."

He gave her a patient look, silently applauding her logic. It was faultless. "I was afraid that if I put my hand across your mouth it would have scared you even worse." He held her unsure gaze. Lowering his voice, he said, "I did kiss you to absorb the sound, but it's more than that, Leah, and I have to be honest with you about that. That kiss had been coming from the moment I met you." Kell saw desire in her eyes, knew his touch had gone far deeper, reaching inside her in so many more ways than he'd first realized.

Leah dragged in a deep breath, holding his calm, penetrating gray gaze. Kell was so damned open. Honest to a fault. She had to respond to him on that level and not as she might have in her past, when Hayden had lied to her all the time. She was just too gullible, too stupid, to realize it at the time. "I wanted to kiss you, too, Kell."

There, the truth was out. When she'd tried truth on Hayden, it had gotten her beaten. Kell simply looked at her, and she saw one corner of his mouth hitch upward into that lazy smile of his. It warmed her heart, fed her soul. This was a man who was utterly fearless when it came to emotional high stakes in life.

"Thanks for admitting it, Leah. I expected it of you, and you didn't disappoint me."

"I'll never lie to you, Kell. It's not my nature to lie. But I think you know that already."

"Yes," he said, resting his elbows on his knees. "Now, I'm going to tell you where I stand, Leah. And I need to hear where you're at in all of this with me." He opened his hands. "I wasn't looking for a relationship. When you dropped into my life, it changed me." His drawl became more evident as he went on. "There is something about you that touches my heart. I've been wrestling with it for days now, trying to understand what was going on between us. I wanted to kiss you for some time, but kept telling myself it was wrong to think in that direction. I know you're a warrant officer. I know the UCMJ. I never thought I'd fall for a woman officer." He gave her a wry, amused look. "But I have."

"What does that mean?" Leah asked, her voice barely a whisper. Her pulse was bounding, she felt vulnerable and was unable to shield herself from Kell in any way.

"It means I want to continue what we have. I have no idea where it's going, Leah. I've always followed my heart. I know I want you. I like what we have. I want to build on it, see where it leads us. I'm not the kind of man that does one-night stands. I'm in for the long term with a woman or it's a no-go. And I have to know what you're thinking and feeling. If there is an us or not."

A quiver moved through Leah as she sat there digesting his words, her heart wide-open, wanting him in every possible way. "I'm so screwed up, Kell. I'm just not a good bet for a relationship." Hayden's words came back to her. He'd always said she was damaged goods. That no man would ever look at her if she divorced him. Leah had believed him. Until now.

He frowned. "Who isn't?" And then, more gently, "It doesn't matter to me, Leah. I know we haven't had much time together, and it's been a pretty stressful, intense time for us at that. There's no one in this world who is perfect. We're all wounded, Sugar. It's just a question of where, what kind of wound and how much you let it run your life. I want a relationship with you. What do you want, Leah?"

Compressing her lips, she felt tears stinging the backs of her eyelids. She couldn't cry now. Not now! "I don't want to hurt you, Kell..."

"The only way you could pull that off, is if you tell me you don't want a relationship with me." He smiled a little sadly. "Is that what you're telling me?" Because he had to know.

Rubbing her face, Leah rasped, "I'm...not whole, Kell."

Kell didn't move. But he wanted to. He heard the broken tone in her voice, felt it stab him in his heart. "No one is, Leah. Not even me. But I learned a while back that I make do with what I have. I don't cry over what's gone. I make a point of trying to learn from my mistakes and not repeat them. I'm only concerned with what's left of myself after my marriage. I'm divorced. I learned a lot from Addy, my ex-wife. All I can do is move forward and try to do right by others." The suffering in her eyes tore at him.

"I'm a failure in so many ways," she whispered, voice strained.

"I don't care," he said patiently, holding her moist, confused gaze. "I'll take whatever you want to give me, Leah. It's on your time. Your schedule. I won't push you."

Tears blurred her vision and she made a strangled sound in her throat. The tears fell. "You don't know me!" Leah quavered, afraid to raise her voice.

"That's true, I don't know everything about you. But I'm willing to find out, Leah. I feel I know enough about you to want a closer connection. And I'll always let you define what that connection is between us."

"How can you be so damn sure of us, Kell?"

"I kissed you last night. It told me everything I ever needed to know about you, Leah."

She angrily wiped away the tears, glaring at his passive expression. It was his eyes that held a burning look that seared her body, made her feel weak and sexually needy, wanting to have him kiss her like that once more. "I'm afraid, Kell. All right? I'm really afraid!"

"So am I, but I'm not going to stop listening to my heart where you're concerned." He held her glittering stare, saw the deep anguish in her eyes, the terror of making a mistake in another relationship. "We're in a risk-taking business. If we're so willing to put our physical bodies on the line, knowing we could die, what's so different about us putting our hearts on the line, too?"

Covering her eyes with her hands, Leah tried to stop tears from falling. She hugged her knees to her chest. "I'm not good enough for you, Kell."

"Who the hell ever made you believe you were less than a whole woman?" He couldn't keep the anger out of his voice. She looked as if he'd slapped her, but he hadn't touched her.

"I just know!" Leah pushed to her feet, walking away, unable to stand the care she saw in his eyes. She took three more steps and Kell was beside her, gently capturing her arm and turning her around. The next moment, Leah was staring up into his turbulent gray eyes. His hands settled on her shoulders, holding her, not hurting her.

"Hayden Grant told you that," Kell growled, his voice low with feeling. "It's *not* true, Leah. He hurt you. I know that. I can tell by how you respond to me exactly how he treated you."

Her lower lip trembled. "I told you, I wasn't—"

Kell took her mouth, anchored her against him, tried to kiss away her fear that she was no longer whole and didn't deserve him or a possible relationship. He molded his mouth against hers, felt her start to protest and then, suddenly, she buckled against him. Leah moaned and surrendered. She tasted so damn good, so clean and sweet. Her hand curled against his chest and he softened the kiss, not wanting to bruise her lips.

Holding her, Kell slid his hand against her hips and pulled her against him. There was no denying his erection. She had to feel it and had to know what it meant. Or who the hell knew what she was thinking? He had no idea of how severely Grant had abused her. And he needed to find out.

Releasing her mouth, breathing hard, Kell held her stunned-looking eyes. "I want you in my life, Leah. I don't give a damn how broken you think you are. I see your heart. It's whole. I see a good person in there. A kind person. From where I stand, there's nothing wrong with you at all." His words became guttural. "Grant brainwashed you. He's a sick bastard and you know that now. But you didn't know it then. You were younger and probably pretty naive. Hell, Leah, you didn't have a mother to teach you about sexuality, about your own body or being a woman, what it feels like to be one, or how you should be treated by a man." Kell saw her face crumple and he cursed himself. Diplomacy was not his specialty. Obviously.

Leah closed her eyes, feeling gutted by his truth. Kell was a sniper. He was an alert observer of the human condition. She felt his arms around her, felt his lips resting against the top of her head, letting her silently know he wasn't going to throw her away or abandon her.

As Hayden had told her, she was a cold, screwed-up bitch who couldn't please a man if she tried. He'd beaten her down in every way. And even now, the way Hayden saw her is how she saw herself. It was a frightening realization. Leah thought she had recaptured her self-esteem from the past, her confidence in herself. But that wasn't true because she was fighting Kell's invitation to try a relationship with him. And here she was, trying to make him believe she wasn't worth wanting, desiring or loving. Anger rose in her, pure and hot.

Hayden had stolen pieces of her spirit. And now that she'd met a man, a real man, she felt incapable of being who he saw her as: a woman who was worthy of being loved, being cared for and being protected, if necessary.

"Come on," Kell rasped, turning her around. "Let's sit down. We need to hash this out."

Her knees were mushy. Leah leaned wearily against Kell, needing his strength as he led her over to the sleeping bags. She sat down, wanting to curl up into a fetal position of protection. Her mind was like a wild animal careening into the darkest corners of her wounds. Kell sat opposite of Leah, his leg resting against hers, his arm spanning her lower legs, his gaze tender as he watched her.

"I don't know where to begin," Leah managed.

"Start with me," he said. "Do you want a relationship with me?"

Sniffing, she brushed the tears away. "Y-yes."

"Okay, then there's reason for us to continue our talk, Sugar. I need to know what's got you so spooked about yourself. When you were in my arms last night, I couldn't believe how warm and loving, how hot and hungry you were. I liked every bit of you." Kell reached out, wiping a tear from her cheek with his thumb. "There's *nothing* wrong with your body, Leah." He managed a half smile. "Your body knows exactly what it wants. The only thing in the way is that mind of yours, how you see yourself. Or maybe, how Grant taught you to see yourself."

"I need to start at the beginning," Leah choked. "I thought two years of psychotherapy had helped, but I was wrong."

"We all need some help now and then," Kell said gently. "Where do you want to start?"

Giving a painful shrug, Leah said, "With me. I only had two one-night stands in college. I just hid from boys because they scared the hell out of me. I didn't understand them. I hated that they followed me around. In high school, I was a shadow. When I got to college, it was easier to hide in my dorm room. I got tricked twice by boys. I'm not very proud of it, Kell." Leah waited for his judgment and censure. None was forthcoming.

"In my freshman year, I met this guy. He came on strong and kept telling me how hot I looked. Maybe I was lonely. I don't know, but I went out on a date with him. I didn't know what to do. He kissed me and I didn't know how to—respond. He got angry with me because when he tried to touch my breasts, I pushed him away. I felt so embarrassed and scared. I got out of the car and walked home. It wasn't that far back to the dorm, but I was so shaken up, so scared, that I felt like a loser. Stupid."

"You weren't stupid," Kell said, his hand moving across her shoulder. "You didn't have a mother to teach you a lot of things, Leah. And I'll bet your father never talked about your menstrual cycle with you? Or when you needed to start wearing a bra? All those things moms talk to their daughters about?"

She took a ragged breath. "I was in high school, my freshman year, when a couple of girls took me aside and told me I needed to start wearing a bra. Before that, I was blind, deaf and dumb. I didn't know…"

Kell felt her pain. "But you survived it, and you learned."

"I did," Leah said. "In my sophomore year at college, I met this guy and he kept after me for nearly half a year. I finally gave in and he took me to his dorm room. Tried kissing me, touching me. It was the same horrid situation all over again. I was terrified, pushed him down and ran out of his room."

"Did you ever have any talks with your father about this? About relationships? Boys?"

"No. I was afraid to. He was always so busy and I didn't want to bother him. I learned early on not to take my problems to him. He was so uncomfortable when I'd ask him something."

"What about Grant?"

"I don't know," Leah muttered, shaking her head. "I look back to when I was twenty-three. I was trying to please my father, to get him to be proud of me for joining the Army and graduating from flight school. I was at the top of my class. I wanted him to praise me. Hayden was in his Shadow Squadron. We met at a squadron picnic. I just felt like a fish out of water, Kell. All the wives and girlfriends were there, and I was alone. I guess Hayden saw my discomfort and came over and made friends with me. He was nice... kind, then..." Her voice trailed off.

Kell allowed his hand to travel lightly down her left arm. He took her cool, damp hand into his and said nothing. Leah was struggling and it was tearing him up. Grant was a wolf in sheep's clothing. He'd really wanted Major David Mackenzie's attention. What better way than zeroing in on his shy, innocent daughter? Using her to get what he really wanted, which was more power, a higher rank in the squadron.

"I fell for him. He was so worldly, so polished and

he was paying attention to me. In six months, we were married and my father couldn't have been happier. I found out on our wedding night that whatever I had read about, whatever brides and grooms normally did, wasn't what would happen to me."

Kell tried to steel himself against whatever she might say. His fingers stilled on hers.

"I'm so embarrassed to tell you this…I had a hard time telling my therapist." Rubbing her face, Leah couldn't meet Kell's gaze. "He tied my wrists to the headboard. He told me that's the way he liked his women, helpless. I thought he'd try to kiss me, like those boys had. Or try to touch my breasts. But he didn't. He pushed his fingers up into me and I remember the pain and I screamed, trying to get away from him. He covered my mouth with his hand and all I felt was terror."

Kell felt black rage roll through him. He held her hand a little tighter. He wanted to tear that bastard's heart out of his chest.

"He said I was dry. I didn't know what that meant, what he was talking about. He got angry with me. I didn't know…" Leah forced herself to look at Kell, his eyes flat and hard. "He just entered me. And I remember he nearly suffocated me because his hand was so large and it was across my nose and mouth. I was screaming. I think I lost consciousness…I don't know…maybe fainted." She shook her head. "When I came to, my hands were untied and I was in bed alone. I found him out on the couch, asleep." She looked at him. "I wish I'd had experience. If—if I had some earlier, someone to tell me what 'normal' was, but I didn't know…"

He picked up her hand, kissing the back of it. "He raped you." The words came out low and tight.

Leah's face scrunched up with pain. "Yeah, I finally figured that all out later. I thought that's what husbands did to their wives. What the hell did I know? It felt wrong. It hurt. I was afraid to tell anyone because I was so ashamed. Hayden told me he'd kill me if I told my father or ever spoke to anyone about our sex life. I believed him." She drew in a pained sigh. "About three months after we were married, I tried to fight back. I told him he wasn't going to keep hurting me like that anymore. That's when he hit me in the face."

Kell stilled his rage, his gaze going to her nose. "That's how your nose got broken?"

"Yes, and he fractured my cheekbone, too." She touched it with her fingers, remembering that day. "I thought he was going to kill me right there in the kitchen. He swore if I ever fought back again, I would die. He's a big man, Kell. I believed him."

"Of course you would. Why didn't you go to your father?"

Snorting, Leah whispered, "Hayden had situated himself with my father by marrying me. I finally realized what he was doing. My father, because he always felt guilty about Evan drowning, began to see Hayden as the son he'd lost. Hayden replaced Evan in my father's world." She grimaced, pushing strands of hair away from her face. "He wouldn't have believed me."

"But what about your broken nose and cheekbone?"

"Hayden told me to go to a civilian hospital off base and tell the medical staff that I'd fallen down a flight of stairs. I was too frightened at the hospital to ask for help. He was so violent…"

"So, he hoodwinked your father for three years?"

"Yes. I just partitioned off my personal life from my career. I wanted my father to be proud of me. And Hayden was jealous of me. He'd punish me by raping me. He didn't do it often, just when he felt threatened. And if I didn't go to my father and ask him to put Hayden up for a task that would make him look good in the squadron, he'd rape me that night." She rubbed her cheek dry of tears. "I told you, I'm screwed up. I can look back on those three years and wonder where the hell my head was at."

"He beat you down fast," Kell said, his voice vibrating with rage. "He knew exactly what he was doing, Leah. The guy's a sexual predator. I've seen his type before. They look for someone who's not worldly, someone they can manipulate and scare into submission. They use fear and physical abuse to control you." His voice dropped to a rasp. "You were only twenty-three and what did any of us know at that age?"

"Not much," Leah muttered. "But I knew a lot less than normal. I tried two more times to escape him. The second time, he broke this arm." She held up her right arm. "He did it on purpose, I think, because by then, I had joined the Shadow Squadron and was making really good grades. I was showing him up. I figured that out after the fact. With my arm in a cast for eight weeks, that put me behind in the ratings because I couldn't fly, and it made his scores look good. I was out of the way. Looking back on it with my therapist, I saw I was focused more on pleasing my father than trying to survive Hayden's machinations."

"You said there was a third time?" He saw Leah's face close up, her mouth tighten.

"I don't want to talk about it, Kell. It's just too painful. Maybe someday. But not right now."

"I understand," he said, trying to get a hold on his rage. "And you say Grant is at Bagram right now?"

"Yes, he's the CO of the Shadow Squadron."

"How did you manage to get into his unit?"

"Not by choice, believe me," Leah said, frowning. "I got picked by the general to stand in for a pilot at Bravo who got appendicitis. It's only a temporary slot and assignment. As soon as they can get a permanent replacement, I'm gone. I want nothing to do with that son of a bitch. I don't *ever* want to see him again, Kell. He scares me to this day."

Kell could understand why. His mind turned over the sat phone calls with Axton. "He has jurisdiction over you, though?"

"Right now. Yes."

"And did he see you when you flew into Bagram to take this assignment?"

"No, he was out on a mission. His XO signed me in and gave me my orders for Bravo. I was so damned scared I would have to face him." Leah shivered. "I wish I could get over my fear of him, Kell. I've tried so hard."

Kell knew Hayden was gunning for her right now. He was damned if he was going to bring it up. Leah had enough on her plate. Gently, he said, "I want to hold you."

She held his gaze, a trembling smile on her mouth. "I'd really like that."

Kell stood up and scooted her away from the wall and sat down behind her, easing her back against his chest, her legs inside of his. "Just rest right now," he urged her thickly, bringing his arms across her waist. Leah placed her hands upon his. He was sure his erection was pressing into her lower back. She didn't move, but simply melted against him, their trust in one another in place. He was grateful to Leah for giving him a chance. She could have turned him down for a hundred good reasons.

His gut was tied in painful knots of rage. Grant had gotten away with abuse and spousal rape. He understood Leah being innocent and untrained in the ways of the world. A mother who hadn't even had a chance to teach her daughter anything about her budding body. A father who didn't care for his daughter as much as he had his son. Plus, most fathers would never be able to comfortably teach their daughters things about a woman's body. Grant manipulated her to get what he wanted out of her blind father. Kell wasn't sure who he was more angry with.

And tomorrow, Leah was supposed to talk with her father. He'd like to rip him a new asshole. His arms tightened around her for a moment and he leaned to his left, pressing a kiss to her cheek.

"Better?"

"Much." Leah sighed. "Did you know, Kell, that all my anxiety goes away when you come into the cave? If I'm with you, I feel fine. I feel strong. Confident."

"And if I'm not around?" he asked, nuzzling his face into the soft ginger strands near her temple, inhaling her scent.

"I have too much time on my hands around here." Leah partially laughed, opening her eyes and looking up at his shadowed gaze. "I think too much. About the past. About my many, many mistakes. You take my mind off all of that."

"That's because," Kell rasped, pulling her around so that she could rest in his embrace, kissing her mouth tenderly, "we share something good. Something special."

Her whole body went hot. His kiss enflamed her, tightening her breasts, and she could feel that gnawing sensation between her legs. "It's not going to be easy."

"Nothing worth having ever is, Sugar. We'll figure it out as we go."

"You are always so damned confident."

"I don't like the alternative." He chuckled, feeling her laugh with him.

"I don't know how long I'll be at Bravo. It's a temporary assignment."

"And then where do you go?"

"Back to Hunter, Georgia. I was taking advanced flight training. I'll pick it up where I left off. When do you go home?"

"We return to Coronado in November. Just in time for Thanksgiving."

"Maybe we could spend it together?"

"Even better," Kell said, smiling down at her, "I was planning on going home for turkey day. Why don't we try to plan to get you there with us? I'd like you to meet my family. My two brothers, Ty and Cody, will be home on leave, too, so it's sort of a special holiday this year for all of my family."

"I'd like that. I'm sure I can request leave for a week and be with you."

"Then it's settled," Kell murmured, holding Leah close. But so damn much could happen between June and November. Kell had deployed too many times, knew the drill, knew that life was never even or a constant. Not in their line of work.

He worried about the phone call to her father. Was he going to bring up the fact that Grant was laying blame on Leah for the crash?

THE SUN WAS barely edging the peaks, the wind cold as Leah sat with Kell outside the tunnel. He'd patched David Mackenzie through to her and had handed her the sat phone.

"Leah?"

"Hi, Father." She crouched down, her back to the wall of the cliff outside the tunnel opening. Knowing all sat phone conversations were taped, she wanted to keep this call short.

"Are you all right?"

"Yes, sir, I am. Chief Ballard is a good combat medic. I'm up on my feet and I'm almost a hundred percent." Leah heard real concern in her father's voice. That was a change. Or maybe she wanted to hear care in his voice, like how Kell cared for her.

She looked over to see Kell standing guard, his gloved hands on the M-4 across the front of his body, looking around, remaining alert.

"Can't you get out of there?"

"No, sir. We have two hundred Taliban camping two caves over from where we're at." She heard the frustration in his tone.

"Major Grant needs you back at Camp Bravo."

Her stomach clenched. Her voice went low. "This is a SEAL op. I have no say in when I get picked up, sir."

"All right. I just wanted to make sure you were all right and you are."

"Yes, sir. I'm fine."

"Roger. Out."

Snorting softly, Leah pressed the button to end the call. She felt rather than heard Kell approach. Slowly getting up, Leah handed him the phone. "It's Hayden bugging my father," she growled. And she told him about the short call. Kell's face turned stony. That powerful sensation of protection wrapped around her.

"Don't worry about it" was all he said. "Go back in. I have to call Ax and give him my report."

Nodding, Leah turned and walked into the tunnel.

Kell released an uneven breath, his stomach like a nest of angry, disturbed snakes. He needed to tell Ax he'd found the flight recorder. That valuable piece of evidence would clear Leah's good name and reputation once and for all. He wanted to talk to Clutch, but knew he'd have to wait until he got back to Bravo.

Right now, Kell felt the like the Sword of Damocles was hanging over the two of them. He felt trouble brewing for Leah. Knew Grant was responsible for it. Knew he'd come after her. And then, all hell was going to break loose because Kell wasn't going to let that sick asshole get anywhere near her ever again.

CHAPTER TEN

MAJOR HAYDEN GRANT was pissed as he stalked into his office at Ops at Bagram. His young assistant, an Army private first class, blonde and stupid, had interrupted his meeting with his pilots, saying the call was urgent. The only thing that bitch was good for was sex when he needed it. At least she didn't fight him. Slamming the door to his office, he picked up the sat phone.

"Major Grant here."

"Master Chief Axton, Major. I have some news about your helo crash. Our operator took a grave risk and went back down to the crash site the other night. He's retrieved the following items, the black box, two sets of dog tags and five bone fragments."

Hayden's blue eyes narrowed, his hand tightening around the phone. "He found the flight recorder?" *Shit!*

"Yes, sir, he did. Once our operator returns to Bravo, I'll have it sent directly to your office."

Cursing mentally, Hayden said, "Good work, Master Chief."

"Sir? About the body remains. Aside from those few bones, my operator said nothing was left. He spent hours in the dark searching for the remains of your crewmen. The dog tags are somewhat melted and partially destroyed. Commander Lanoux felt the families of these men would appreciate anything that could bring them some closure."

Shrugging, Grant said, "Yes, of course." He could care less about that end of the crash. Right now, he had Leah in his gunsights, and this was his chance to destroy her career. He'd essentially already made light colonel, so he didn't care what her father said or did. This was payback with that bitch. "When can I get that flight recorder?"

"When my operator can get into a safe enough area to be picked up, Major."

"But, dammit, this is important!"

"So is my man's life, sir. And he's the one that is protecting Chief Mackenzie, so our commander is taking a conservative route, because this is an unusual situation."

He wanted to curse the master chief, who sounded like he was dealing with a petulant child. *The bastard.* "Well, you keep me informed on the progress with this black box."

"I will, sir. Out."

Clicking off the sat phone, Hayden sat down at his desk, thinking. He'd already gotten the evidence on the helicopter communications for that night, and destroyed it. Sweet-talking an Army sergeant, a redhead who had eyes for him and probably thought she was going to marry him, had done the deed.

Rubbing his chin, Hayden smiled a little. Without that tape to prove that Brian Larsen had the controls when they went in to pick up those two SEAL operators, he could then blame Leah for it. If there was no record of the comms, it became a he said, she said. And because he was the head of the squadron, his word carried a helluva lot more weight than Leah's ever would.

Smiling, he moved his hand across the desk, anticipating the coming confrontation with his ex-wife. He'd promised himself over the years that if he ever got a chance to sink her career, he'd do it. Well, it was here, and he sure as hell wasn't going to pass up this golden opportunity.

Standing, Hayden knew he had to get back to the meeting. Once that black box arrived, he'd make sure the evidence in it was destroyed, if it hadn't been destroyed already by the heat of the crash. Hayden wouldn't know until after it arrived, but he'd get his redheaded bitch to find out. And if there was anything in it, she would make sure it wasn't available to anyone. That way, he had Leah where he wanted her.

Moving out of his office, he glared down at the blonde. "No more interruptions," he snarled at her as he passed her desk.

"Yes, sir."

Hayden hadn't counted on the black box being found, much less successfully retrieved. He was already hating the thoroughness of the SEALs. Too bad that operator hadn't been killed, and Leah along with him, during his rescue attempt. That would tidy up everything. With any luck both of them would be killed out in the badlands, and Leah would be off the face of this planet.

Hayden was worried she'd someday turn him in for what he'd done to her. He'd never felt easy about it, and was always looking for an opportunity to take her out of the Army. If she ever testified against him, he'd be court-martialed...or he would have been, if there'd been enough evidence. Smugly, he knew there wasn't, but he didn't want Leah to ever file a report on how many times he'd hit her and broken her bones. That would stop his career in its tracks. He dreamed of becoming a general, and only she stood in the way of it happening.

As he swung down the hall toward a room at the end where his pilots were waiting for him, Hayden thought about his mentor, Leah's father, David Mackenzie. He was getting ready to retire and Hayden had his eye on that prize. Now that he knew he was officially going to become a light colonel next month, at a special ceremony that Mackenzie would be presenting for him here at Bagram, Hayden smiled. He knew his mentor doted on him, had once said he was the son he'd wished he'd had. Well, the son was now going to take the mentor's throne. He was in perfect alignment for the career plum and knew Mackenzie would be suggesting that he become the next commander of the Shadow Squadron.

Rubbing his hands, Hayden put on his game face as he swung into the room. No one would know how damned happy he was. Tonight, he'd take the redhead to his favorite place and screw her royally. She liked rough sex and he liked making it painful for her. He'd celebrate his good fortune.

Tom Axton listened intently on the sat phone to the report by Ballard. Things were heating up near his hide. The Taliban were back in those caves, and more riders were joining Khogani. Writing down the intel, he said, "Let me talk to the LT and the commander. We have Khogani and we want him taken out."

"Roger."

"What are the chances you can move Chief Mackenzie and yourself out of that immediate area?"

"We may be forced to move if Khogani keeps returning to these caves. It appears he's using them as a central meeting place. For what, I don't know."

"Do you have another place in mind?"

"Yes. But it means a five-mile hike down the mountain to reach it."

"Is Chief Mackenzie up to it?"

"I think so. She's no longer dizzy and her headaches are receding."

Ax grimaced. It would be one thing if it was only Ballard. He was a mountain goat and knew the Hindu Kush intimately. Plus, he was in top shape; five miles was no challenge for him at all. But the pilot? It was a prickly situation because she was an Army warrant officer, and the commander had no wish to get entangled in a showdown between Army politics and the Navy SEAL way of doing things. Yet, Ballard was courting real danger, with Khogani seemingly setting up shop right next door to the cave where he was hiding the chief. "Are you sure she's up for this?"

"I think she can handle it."

"Okay, start making plans to move, because if Khogani keeps adding men to his army, they're going to run out of room in those two caves and yours is right next door."

"I'm way ahead of you on that."

"Good. If you have to move, call me immediately. I want your GPS."

"Will do, Master Chief. Out."

Ax scowled. He'd just set the sat phone aside when Commander Lanoux poked his head into his office.

"How's Ballard doing?"

Ax leaned back in his chair. "Sitting on a bad situation." He caught his boss up to speed. Lanoux sat scowling at his desk.

"That woman pilot is our Achilles' heel," Lanoux muttered.

"Ballard thinks she's good to go."

"Yeah? When was the last time she played goat on a mountain in total darkness for five miles?"

Ax picked up his mug of coffee and took a sip. "Ballard's a good judge of character, so I think if they have to move, he'll get it done."

"I just got another call from that asshole, Major Grant," Lanoux griped. "What the hell is *his* problem?"

"He's one of those brownnosers who can't keep his nose out of our shit," Ax growled, unhappy.

"He's the kind I like to put on a hook and troll down a bayou with, dragging along in the water, inviting gators to lunch."

Axton didn't disagree. "Funny thing, maybe odd," he told Lanoux, "but I spoke to Grant earlier. Ballard retrieved the flight recorder for that MH-47, two sets of dog tags and five bone fragments of the crew. You'd think that as a squadron CO, he'd have been a little emotional and a helluva lot grateful that Ballard found dog tags remains of his men. Those things are important to the families of those lost men. DNA will sort out the bones and who they belong to. At least the families can have some sense of closure. But this asshole was far more excited about the black box shit than anything else. Doesn't make sense to me."

"Takes all kinds," Lanoux deadpanned, shaking his head. "Ballard shouldn't have taken the risk. He was out in the open for hours that night. He was a sitting duck if Taliban were around."

"He wanted to do it. He's a SEAL. He understands what it means to give these families closure."

"I know. It was damned risky with all the Taliban crawling around that area right now."

"Ballard understands what it means to have found those remains."

"Yeah, Kell's like that. He's a damned good man." Lanoux stood up. "Any chance of getting them picked up today? Tomorrow?"

"No."

"I want that Army major off my ass," Lanoux growled, leaving the office. "Or I'm gonna drop kick his ass into a Lousiana swamp."

Ax snorted. So did he, but he couldn't push the Taliban out of that area to get a Shadow helo in there to pick them up.

Lieutenant Nate Drager, Dragon, knocked on Ax's door and popped in.

"Hey, Master Chief, what the hell is going on with this Major Grant? I just got a call from a Colonel Mackenzie, head of the Army 80th Shadow Group."

"Sit down," Ax motioned. Draeger was the OIC for Ballard's platoon. He caught him up with the latest intel from Ballard. "That's his daughter out there. That's why you got the call."

Drager rolled his eyes. "Like we don't have enough

to do without babysitting these candy-assed Army types?"

"They don't know how good Kell is. He'll keep Chief Mackenzie safe out there, or die trying." Not that Ax wanted any of his SEALs dead. That wasn't the point. But he saw the first lieutenant become grim.

"I was just on the phone with Bagram SEAL HQ. Their intelligence section has two drones up in that area. If anything, it's a hotbed of Taliban activity right now. There's just no way we can risk a helo and crew to drop in there and try to safely exfil them."

"It's a very dynamic, fluid situation right now," Ax agreed. "And it's gonna stay that way for probably the next week. I was thinking that maybe we could get some Apaches in there to wreak havoc on Khogani's gathering army. It would mean Kell and that woman pilot would have to leave the area because all hell would break loose after that."

"It's a thought," Draeger agreed. "Knowing Kell, he's got Plan B, C and D already lined up, too." He grinned a little. "He's not a sniper for nothing."

"Yeah, I talked to him about that already. He's prepared to move if we tell him to. Or if Khogani's growing army decides to take up immediate residence near his hide area."

"It's too damn close for comfort," Draeger agreed.

"Kell knows those cave systems. If he tells me they're safe, I believe him."

Draeger ran his hand through his long, dark blond hair, not looking like an officer at all. The thick beard covering his face made him look like an operator out in the badlands. "I'll sleep better if I know they're out of that immediate area. It's too damned dicey for all of us."

"Yeah." Ax sighed, leaning back in his protesting chair. "But Kell's a poker player. He knows the odds. He'll move if he thinks it's getting too dangerous. He knows his top priority is to get that warrant officer back to Bravo alive and in one piece. Then, he can go back to hunting our HVT down."

Snorting, Draeger muttered, "Ballard cleaned me out a month ago in that Texas hold 'em game in the big room. I lost forty bucks. That guy has a set of steel balls and a poker face to match it."

Chuckling and watching Draeger rise, Ax said dryly, "That's why I don't play with him. He's got poker luck."

"Yeah, well, he'd better have that luck holding right now," Draeger grumped. "The Intel people at Bagram are worried. There's more enemy flowing across the border. Forty to fifty men per group. That's never a good sign for any of us."

"No," Ax agreed. "But it's the spring offensive. The Taliban does this every year." They had three other SEAL teams out there, placed at important gate points where the inflow tended to go, with eyes and rifles on the situation.

By far, the most important target was Khogani and his growing army. This was a new development and Ax knew every black ops group was watching the Hill chieftain with a wary eye.

"Later," Drager said, leaving the office.

Ax heard a couple of his SEALs out in the big room. Clutch's laugh was deep and booming. The men were out there cleaning their weapons. Another of his

SEALs was working up a DA, direct action, mission for him at the desk in the same room.

The kidding and teasing going on between his men made him smile a little. He had a good platoon of SEALs. They'd been together for three years and were tight as hell. As he rummaged around for some paperwork on his messy desk, his biggest worry was Kell Ballard. He was in a hell of a spot. And with Khogani around, his concern grew. The red-haired Hill leader hated Americans with a passion. He would kill any and all of them. It didn't matter if the American was from an NGO or charity, either. Everyone was fair game to him and a target.

Worse, and Ax tried not to dwell on it, but if Chief Mackenzie was ever caught, all hell would break loose. Yeah, women were in combat, no argument there. What worried him was someone like Khogani, who was wily and very plugged into the internet, knew its use and power, would parade the woman pilot around for the world to see in carefully placed videos. And then Americans would throw their hands up in shock and demand she be rescued.

In the shock-and-awe opening to the American intervention in Iraq years earlier, Jessica Lynch was captured by Iraqis. It had taken a SEAL team to rescue her. In the meantime, Ax remembered the hue and cry from Americans that a woman had become a prisoner of war.

Shaking his head, Ax thought they'd better get used to it. There were women who were equals in combat right alongside the men, but they also shared the same fate if it came to that. And with Major Grant acting like a Harpy eagle, circling their SEAL world because of Chief Mackenzie, Ax wanted nothing more than to get that woman warrant officer picked up and brought the hell out of the badlands.

LEAH WAS NEVER so glad to see Kell as when he silently appeared in their cave long after dark. There were Pashto voices drifting up the long tunnel from below. She saw him turn on the penlight, hiding it with his hand as he approached her.

"How long have they been down there?" he asked her quietly, seeing the concern in her eyes.

"Since midday." Nervously, she said, "I started getting our gear ready." She pointed to his rolled-up sleeping bags.

Nodding, Kell turned and listened to the voices. He knew Pashto well enough. "They're making dinner and tea," he muttered. Turning, he briefly touched her cheek. "You okay?"

"Yes. I was getting ready to bail if the voices started getting any closer."

"Right," he rasped. He looked around, keeping his gear on, the heavy ruck pulling on his back. "Have you eaten yet?"

"Yes." Leah felt wired. She'd put her Kevlar vest on, strapped the .45 in the holster on her hip with a bullet in the chamber, safety off. "I wished I could have gotten ahold of you today."

"I know," he said, apologetic. "Only one sat phone and I've got to have it when I'm out on recon."

"I understand. What do we do now, Kell?"

"Leave as soon as possible." He moved around the cave, checking here and there. Coming back to her, he asked, "Have you packed your ruck? Got plenty of bottles of water? MREs?"

"Yes to all the above."

There was nothing in the other cave except supplies and food. If the Taliban discovered it, they'd be happy about it, but there was no intel for them to find, either. His mind whirled with options. "Okay, get one of my jackets and put it on, and then we'll get you saddled up and ready to leave with me."

Leah nodded and walked to the other cave, where he had extra sets of cammies. Relief that they were leaving drenched her. She shrugged on the huge jacket and rolled up the cuffs so her hands stuck out of the sleeves.

Hurrying back, she tried to quell her fear. Kell was calm. Leah could see the look on his face, that superalertness, his senses online. It made her feel safer in a completely unsafe situation.

Kell lifted her ruck and helped her with it. She put on her boonie hat, her hair already in a ponytail. As he moved his fingers beneath the shoulder straps, standing close, he said, "You're going to have to grab my belt and follow me. We're heading down the mountain, to the west, where there's another set of caves I know about. There's no water in it, and it's five miles from here. I want to put distance between us and them."

Nodding, Leah felt the strength of his fingers as he untwisted one of the straps, smoothing it out against her shoulder. Her skin prickled beneath his touch. "I can do it." She pulled on her set of gloves.

Kell studied her in the gray light. He grinned a little. "You look pretty perky tonight. Good day? No headache?"

Leah responded to his slow, heated smile. Hell, they had the enemy in their backyard and he looked so calm. "I'm okay. Feel almost normal."

He moved his hand across her cheek, leaning down, kissing her quickly. Kell saw the fear recede in her eyes. "Everything will be fine." And he wanted to kiss Leah again. Hell, he wanted to do a lot more than that, but now was not the time.

His drawl was like a blanket of serenity settling around her. Leah's lips tingled with his grazing kiss. She saw care burning deep in Kell's dark eyes as he cupped her cheek. His fingers were calloused, and her flesh reacted wildly to his fleeting touch. "I'm ready," she murmured.

"Okay, let's rock it out…"

Leah knew it was going to be dark outside the exfil tunnel. Kell had his sniper rifle strapped on the back of his ruck, the M-4 in a harness across his chest.

Once outside the cave tunnel, he made a call into Bravo by radio, but his voice was so low, she couldn't catch the conversation. After signing off, he tucked the radio back into his H-gear and they took off.

She tried to remember how to walk, to not make any noise. Below, she could hear laughter and talking floating up through the tunnel system. When he pulled her outside, Leah drew in a deep breath of relief. She'd felt cornered in that cave from noon onward. In some ways, it felt like being trapped by Grant. She hated coming home in the evening, never knowing what kind of mood he would be in. She always felt as though she were walking on eggshells with him, never knowing what he might do with her.

Today, in the cave, the walls had closed in on her

and she'd wanted to run. But there had been no place to go.

Kell caught her right hand and settled it on the left side of his belt above his hip. He patted it, letting her know he was ready to go. The wind was fierce, blowing in gusts. And it was cold. Leah was glad to have the thick warmth of his other jacket. The gloves would keep her hands warm. She adjusted the mic to her lips.

"Test?"

"Roger. Read you loud and clear. Let's hoof it."

Leah couldn't see anything in front of her. But above, the starlight was spectacular, the sky alive with dancing, winking, cold white lights. Shuffling her boots along like Kell had taught her, she was grateful he wasn't hurrying. They were moving slowly downward and she thought it might be a path of some sort because there weren't as many rocks hitting the toes of her boots.

She could feel Kell on guard. Every once in a while, he slowed to a halt and looked around. He had on NVGs and could see into the night. She was absolutely blind. Breathing hard, Leah knew they were at ten thousand feet. Her lungs were burning already and she pressed her hand against her chest, wishing it would stop.

"How you doing?"

"Out of breath."

"To be expected. Want me to slow down?"

"No. I just want to get away from there." She heard Kell laugh lightly and she felt his hand settle on hers where she gripped his web belt.

"You're doing fine, Sugar. We've gone about a mile

and we're heading down to about eight thousand feet. Your breathing should ease a bit."

Grateful for his thoughtfulness, Leah buoyed. "I'd never want to be out here without you."

He chuckled softly. "This is my area. I know it well. Ready to go? Or you want to rest a bit more?"

"No, I'm ready." She felt him move out, probably cutting his stride in half for her. He had such long legs and she was glad he'd slowed down.

Leah knew they were targets out here, although as Kell had said, the Taliban moved at night only when absolutely necessary. They had no NVGs to see through the night and were essentially blind without them, so they made camp instead.

She stumbled and tripped a number of times, always catching herself, sometimes falling into Kell's strong back. And always, he would slow down, put out his arm to steady her. Then, he'd stop, waiting for her to regain her balance once again. Talking wasn't a good thing, either, so she blindly followed him, trying to stay in some kind of rhythm with him. He acted as though he were taking a stroll in the park. It served to help her settle down, to concentrate on where her feet were at instead of worrying about getting jumped by Taliban.

Kell halted and he turned up the trail. "In about two minutes, some Apaches are coming over the mountain. They're going to go after the Taliban in those caves next to where we were hiding."

Leah heard a faint *whump, whump, whump* in the night. "That was the radio call you made back there?"

"Yes." Kell took her gloved hand, easing it out of his belt and into his hand. "Maybe I'll get lucky and they'll take out my HVT, Khogani. Then, I can come back into Bravo and get a hot meal. And see you."

Her heart skittered in response to his low voice, the intimacy, the sensual suggestion in it. Leah squeezed his hand. "I'll see you anytime I can, Kell."

"We'll work it out," he promised her confidently. "Here they come. Look up at about eleven o'clock. That's where they're going to send rockets into those two caves."

The night sky suddenly lit up and Leah watched in awe as the two Apaches began firing systematically into the caves. She shuddered, knowing men and horses would lose their lives beneath the fiery onslaught. But if the Taliban weren't taken out, they would turn around and kill Americans, as well as the peaceful Shinwari villagers who lived in this area.

She felt Kell's hand tighten briefly around hers as the sound of the rockets, and then gatling guns, rippled through the air, tearing through the night.

"Let's go, Sugar. No use watching Sodom and Gomorrah burn…"

CHAPTER ELEVEN

KELL SCREWED THE sound suppressor onto the end of his M-4 barrel. He sat near the entrance of their cave. He'd cleared it earlier. Leah was in a second cave, located via a tunnel, and was already asleep. He had to stand guard, hidden behind a piece of rock that was sticking out. If he had to shoot, the sound would be muffled, likely wouldn't draw attention from any nearby camping Taliban in the immediate area. Through his NVGs he saw the goat path in front of the cave beyond the brush. This was a well-used cave because he'd seen not only goat prints, but horses' and men's tracks, as well. It was not the safest place to be, but it had to do for now.

His mind revolved back to Leah. She had to have been limping along on those cramped leg muscles for at least a mile and she'd said nothing. One corner of his mouth moved slightly upward. She'd make a good SEAL.

He'd broken his ankle during a mission. Once he'd determined he had a closed fracture, he pulled out the dark green duct tape from his ruck and tightly taped it up. And kept on going. Motrin dampened the pain, which sure as hell cleared his head, and the mission was accomplished.

SEALs worked with broken bones, strains, sprains,

YOUR PARTICIPATION IS REQUESTED!

Dear Reader,

Since you are a lover of our books -- we would like to get to know you!

Inside you will find a short Reader's Survey. Sharing your answers with us will help our editorial staff understand who you are and what activities you enjoy.

To thank you for your participation, we would like to send you 2 books and 2 gifts – **ABSOLUTELY FREE!**

Enjoy your gifts with our appreciation,

Pam Powers

SEE INSIDE FOR READER'S SURVEY

For Your Reading Pleasure...

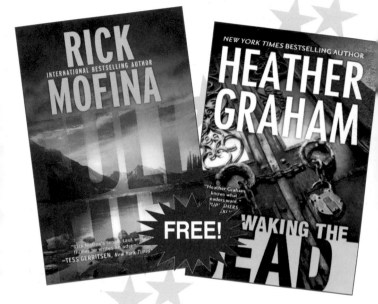

We'll send you 2 books and 2 gifts
ABSOLUTELY FREE
just for completing our Reader's Survey!

YOUR READER'S SURVEY
"THANK YOU" FREE GIFTS INCLUDE:
- ▶ **2 FREE books**
- ▶ **2 lovely surprise gifts**

PLEASE FILL IN THE CIRCLES COMPLETELY TO RESPOND

1) What type of fiction books do you enjoy reading? (Check all that apply)
- ○ Suspense/Thrillers   ○ Action/Adventure   ○ Modern-day Romances
- ○ Historical Romance   ○ Humour   ○ Paranormal Romance

2) What attracted you most to the last fiction book you purchased on impulse?
- ○ The Title   ○ The Cover   ○ The Author   ○ The Story

3) What is usually the greatest influencer when you <u>plan</u> to buy a book?
- ○ Advertising   ○ Referral   ○ Book Review

4) How often do you access the internet?
- ○ Daily ○ Weekly ○ Monthly ○ Rarely or never.

5) How many NEW paperback fiction novels have you purchased in the past 3 months?
- ○ 0 - 2   ○ 3 - 6   ○ 7 or more

YES! I have completed the Reader's Survey. Please send me the 2 FREE books and 2 FREE gifts (gifts are worth about $10) for which I qualify. I understand that I am under no obligation to purchase any books, as explained on the back of this card.

191/391 MDL GH7A

FIRST NAME	LAST NAME

ADDRESS

APT.#	CITY

STATE/PROV.	ZIP/POSTAL CODE

torn ligaments and muscles. Nothing kept the team from their objective. Except death.

He'd brought the sat phone out with him. Kell walked silently to the path out beyond the tall brush hiding the opening. He looked up and down the goat path, seeing nothing.

He called Bravo SEAL HQ and Ax answered. As quietly as possible, Kell gave him an update and their GPS location, plus his next step he planned to take tomorrow. Ax suggested he head toward Bravo, which had been his intention. Kell asked for a drone. Ax said he'd try to get one, no promises.

He switched off the phone, tucking it back into a pocket of his H-gear around his waist. Without the sat phone they'd be in such deep shit, completely blind, no help or support. It wasn't a place he wanted to be. Not with Leah at his side. He could survive without it, but she might not.

Kell sat down, M-4 across his lap. His hearing was keyed, all his senses alert. He prayed that Leah wouldn't wake up screaming. That was the only downside to them remaining hidden from the Taliban in this cave. He wished he could hold her in his arms tonight.

He spent the rest of the night envisioning how he was going to introduce her to how a man loved his woman. She'd never experienced that, and it felt damn good to know he was going to be the one to open those doors of pleasure for her.

LEAH FELT A HAND on her shoulder, slowly squeezing it. Instantly, her eyes flew open. She saw Kell leaning over her. She was groggy and disoriented, and he held her down, shaking his head. Light was coming into the tunnel. Daylight.

Confused, she saw him put his finger to his lips and then point toward the cave beyond the tunnel. Her pulse raced with dread. She saw the cold look in his eyes, his face expressionless, his gaze toward the tunnel where it fed into the first cave. Soundlessly, he rose, the M-4 fitted to his shoulder as he crouched and moved silently down the tunnel toward the cave opening.

Leah didn't move. She could hear men talking in Pashto. God, they were close! Reaching for her .45, she slowly and quietly sat up, getting ready to use it. How many Taliban were out there at the entrance area? Her heart lurched into her throat as she saw Kell suddenly move and disappear around the corner. There were shots fired. Muffled sounds. Fear gripped Leah and she jumped to her feet, pistol held in both hands, aimed at the opening. Was Kell all right?

Her heart was trip-hammering as she cautiously moved down the tunnel.

Just as she got near the opening, Kell reappeared. She saw the gleam of sweat on his icy features. His eyes scared her. They were flat and hard. When he saw her, his expression changed. Softened.

"Come on," Kell urged her quietly, gripping her arm. "We need to get out of here."

As she turned the corner, Leah saw two men lying dead near their horses. Taking it all in, she saw a third animal, a packhorse carrying a load beneath a dark brown tarp. Halting, she saw Kell walk over and start removing the outer clothing the dead men wore. He quickly stripped one and then the other, throwing the clothes into two piles.

"Get dressed in these clothes," he ordered her.

Leah's hands shook as she pulled the voluminous brown trousers over her cammie trousers. Everything hung on her but by the time she was done, she looked Afghan in dress. Looking up, she saw Kell pulling trousers on and slipping a dark blue shirt and a dark brown vest over his shoulders. He took the brown-and-tan *shemagh*, wrapped it around his head, and then pulled more cloth across the lower half of his face so there was only a slit for his eyes visible.

He came over and fashioned her a makeshift headdress with another *shemagh* of the same color, making sure her face was also covered except for her eyes.

"What do you need me to do?" she asked.

"Go back into the tunnel and get our gear. We've got transportation here and we'll hide the rucks and our weapons under that packhorse's tarp. Hurry!"

She ran, fear spiking through her. Had someone head his gunfire? Quickly, Leah gathered up everything, trotting back to the cave entrance. Kell had taken off the tarp. To her amazement, there were two heavy loads of ammunition boxes in the panniers on each side of the horse's back. He quickly tied their rucks in place, got the sniper rifle hidden, as well. He pulled the tarp back into place, making sure it was secure.

"You need to sling this AK-47 on your back," he said, picking it up and handing it to her. "Keep the cloth across your face at all times. Taliban have binos and spotter scopes just like we do. If they see we're

Americans or the fact you're a woman, all bets are off."

Leah nodded and quickly pulled the AK-47 across her back. "Okay. What else?"

He smiled but she couldn't see it; only his dark gray eyes that looked like an eagle staring at her. "I'll take the lead and tie the packhorse rope to the back of my saddle. You ride next to me."

Leah watched as he picked up the reins on a small brown horse and handed them to her.

"How are you at riding?" he asked, pulling over the taller black horse.

"Does riding a Shetland at a carnival when I was seven years old count?"

He laughed softly. "It's got to. Come over here, I'll give you a leg up."

In moments, Leah was in the uncomfortable wooden saddle that had a piece of a small, red-and-yellow Persian rug draped across it. There was another rug of the same colors beneath the saddle, hanging down over the horse's rump. Kell showed her how to make the horse move and how to guide it.

More than anything, Leah didn't want to be a drag or cause Kell disruption. She could see he was fully engaged, knew what he was doing and had a plan, even if she didn't know what it was. She watched him mount the black gelding, all male grace. He'd obviously ridden before.

Kell pulled his horse around so he faced Leah. "Now, we're going to ride like we're Taliban. At a walk. No hurry. If we're caught trotting and galloping then they'll know we're the enemy. These are strong, sturdy Afghan horses and they cover a lot of ground at a walk. I'm going to take us as far as we can get and we'll hope like hell we can carry off this disguise."

"And if we can't?" she asked, fearful.

"We'll make a run for it." Kell patted his H-gear beneath the Afghan clothing. "I'll be on the sat phone with Bravo. They'll know our GPS once we take a rest somewhere that we can't be seen by the tangos. Do you know how to use an AK-47?"

"No."

"At our first rest stop, I'll show you."

Gulping, Leah nodded, a lump of fear in her throat. Flying above the land was a helluva lot safer than having to ride across it. "I'm ready."

He winked at her. "Let's go, Sugar. We're on an adventure."

The sunlight was bright. Kell told her not to use sunglasses because it was a dead giveaway they were American black ops to the Taliban. She squinted, wishing she had a baseball cap, but that, too, would give them away. Her horse was happy to be next to the horse Kell rode. Their feet would occasionally brush against one another as they walked across the desert floor. There were huge boulders to go around, brush and long barren patches of fine dirt the color of ocher.

The sun was cresting the mountains, sending long slats across the valley where they rode. The chill in the air was dissolving quickly.

Kell told her to keep her hand down on the saddle, to ride like a Taliban man would. He corrected small things and she knew it was vital to their welfare that they looked and acted the part.

They had covered the valley and were moving into the hills, following one particular goat path. Over the past three hours, some of Leah's trepidation and fear had dissipated. The heat of the day was building and she was sweating heavily beneath all the clothes she was wearing. Her butt ached, the saddle a true pain in the ass. Her legs were chafing against the rope stirrups and she felt like a complete amateur compared to Kell. He knew how to ride and looked like a man who knew what he was doing.

To her relief he angled them up into a wadi. Once down inside it, hidden by the trees and tall brush, he dismounted. Kell put his finger to his lips, indicating to her to remain silent. He pulled the AK-47 off his back, fitted it into his shoulder and left her alone with the horses, disappearing into the brush higher up in the wadi. Leah sat there, glad to be not moving at all. Her horse was pulling sparse sprigs of grass from the surrounding area.

Kell reappeared ten minutes later. He pulled the cloth off his face, indicating for her to do the same.

"We're clear," he told her, slipping the AK-47 on his back. He walked over to her, holding out his hand. "How are you doing?"

"My ass is so sore," she muttered. Trying to lift her right leg up and over the horse, she lost her balance and grabbed for the horse's mane. Kell held her firmly by the arm and helped her get her leg up and over the rump of the horse. She groaned and he guided her feet to the ground. Leaning over, hands on her knees, she grimaced. "I think I'd rather walk."

Kell chuckled. "In three days, you'll be fine." He went to the packhorse and pulled out bottles of water and some protein bars.

Leah sat on a nearby rock, pushing the cloth away

from her face, dragging in a breath of fresh air. Kell crouched next to her as she drank deeply, surprisingly thirsty. Kell handed her a protein bar. Leah was touched by his thoughtfulness. He wanted her to eat and drink first.

"Thanks," she murmured, opening it and giving him half of it. Grinning, she met his gaze and said, "Like deserves like."

He nodded and gave her a lazy smile. "We're going to rest for about half an hour. I have to check in with Bagram Intel. Find out if they got a drone over us yet."

"A drone?" Hope filled her voice.

"Yes. I requested one via the master chief. If they got a drone available, we'll get it." *We're in so much damn danger every minute because we're out here riding during daylight hours.* But he said nothing more.

FOR THE REST of the day, they dodged groups of Taliban, thanks to the intel officer at Bagram who was working with the pilot of the drone circling high above them. Without that extra set of eyes, Kell knew they'd run into an enemy group sooner or later. And then, it would become a shoot-out and a run for their lives.

The place was crawling with Taliban who were gathering for future assaults against Americans deep into Afghanistan. He knew the area well, knew where to pull up and hide and wait until a group rode by them, completely unaware of their presence.

By the time dusk came, they were climbing the flank of a mountain. At nine thousand feet, Kell found the trail he'd been looking for. Leah had suffered badly beneath the hundred-degree heat on the desert floor.

He'd seen her perk up a bit as they climbed high, into the cooler temperature zones.

Finding a small path, he nudged his horse forward and soon the animal was forcing its way through thick brush. When Kell came out on the other side, he smiled. Dismounting, he got the horses out of the way so Leah could come through the thick, overgrown brush near the entrance.

Tying the animals on some branches, he opened the tarp and pulled out his M-4 rifle, unsafing it.

Leah rode through, looking around. In front of her was the mouth of a cave. She managed to dismount, her legs so bruised and tired that she had to hold on to the saddle to stop from collapsing to the ground. Kell walked over to her.

"Stay here. I'm going to clear this place."

She nodded, holding on to the saddle, getting her legs under her once more. Up above her, she could see clouds turning pink as the sun set. It was beautiful in the Hindu Kush, but so deadly.

Kell came back fifteen minutes later. He gave her a smile and untied the horses.

"Come on, I'm going to give you a five-star cave for tonight."

Leah wondered if Kell ever lost his sense of humor. She tugged at her horse's reins and wearily followed him into tunnels with twists, turns and switchbacks. Leah felt as if they walked at least half a mile up a slight, ascending trail. It was dark after a while and she pulled out her penlight, not wanting to stumble on the rough limestone tunnel floor.

The clip-clop of the horses' hooves echoed and re-echoed up and down the various tunnels as they continued to climb.

Finally, they stopped. Leah couldn't believe her ears. Water? It sounded like a waterfall! Here, in this desert? She waited by the entrance, holding the reins of all three horses as Kell moved deep into the cave and then disappeared. Soon enough, there was bright yellow light emanating from around the corner of it. Surprised, she saw Kell walk toward her with a lantern that threw plenty of light around.

"I'll take the horses," he told her. "Follow me."

Leah was led into yet another chamber. There were two stone walls jutting out in the cave, reminding her of wings of a sort, and they enclosed the area where Kell led her and the horses. The light was bright and welcoming.

She saw a grate and a teakettle. Someone had lived here. Or *was* living here. She started getting out of all the Afghan clothes and then was more than happy to rid herself of the heavy Kevlar vest and her weapon. It was wonderful to strip down to a damp, soaked T-shirt that clung to her skin, and her cammie trousers.

Kell had taken the horses and tied them on metal rings that had been placed into the limestone wall. She saw there was a smaller cave near the horses. Kell went into it and came out carrying flakes of alfalfa hay. What was this place? Curious, Leah walked down the tunnel toward him.

"Does someone live here now?" She watched him take the saddles off the horses and set them on the floor.

"Did. A woman Marine, a black ops sniper by the name of Sergeant Khatera Shinwari lived here for five years. Now, black ops groups traveling through this area use this cave as a sort of safe house." Kell removed the tarp and unpacked the heavy load on the horse, setting all the items in the small hay cave.

"Am I hearing things? Is there water running nearby?"

Kell smiled. "That's the five-star treat. Soon as I get these animals fed and watered, I'll take you over to check it out. Why don't you get us some MREs out of that box?" He pointed to one on the ground near the horse.

Leah chose two. "Have you been here before?"

"A number of times." As Kell gave each of the sweaty animals their hay, he picked up three buckets from the other cave. "Why don't you make yourself at home in her kitchen? There's all kinds of stuff in those cave holes in the tunnel on the other side of where the horses are at. Each black ops group leaves canned food and other items for the next operators who hole up here for a day or two."

She was stunned by the cave. The fact a woman lived here for years made Leah's brows rise with surprise.

She set the MREs down by the metal grate and began to investigate the holes in the cave wall. In some, she found cans of food: vegetables, salmon, sardines and just about everything else. There was a can opener with them, as well.

In another, she found sugar, flour, salt and pepper in aluminum tins. In a smaller one she found bags of candy, chocolate bars and chewing gum. She smiled, thinking about the men and women who had passed through here. She wondered what Kell would leave to restock the place after they left.

Kell hauled three large wooden pails of water, one for each horse. When he was done, he caught her hand, took the lantern and said, "Come on…"

She held his hand, feeling its strength, knowing how gentle he could be. In one way, it felt strange to be with a man. Could it last? Leah wasn't sure. But she wanted a chance to find out.

As Kell rounded the corner, a whole new cave opened up before her. It was twice as large as the other one. Leah gasped, halting, her eyes widening. There in front of her was a waterfall at least ten to fifteen feet high, coming out of the ceiling above and flowing into a huge pool that took up a third of the cave. She saw a wooden bench sitting near it.

"What do you think?" Kell asked, watching her expression.

"Five stars. You were right. I never imagined something like this here in this desert country."

"The mountain surrounding this cave is fourteen thousand feet high. It has year-round snow on its summit and in the summer, some of it melts and this is where it flows."

"This…is so beautiful," Leah whispered. Kell's arm slid around her shoulder, pulling her close. It felt so natural to be with him. Leah wondered how she'd lived all these years without him. But she wasn't sure whether their relationship, which had taken root under the worst of circumstances, would continue to bloom once they arrived at the FOB. She felt tentative, yet hungered for what he effortlessly shared with her.

"Let's go eat and then you can take your shower under that waterfall."

As they ate, Leah asked, "What's the plan for us?"

"We're going to reach Camp Bravo by horseback." Kell didn't want to give her any more information than necessary. Leah was still working out the shock of the crash, and the news that her ex-husband was sticking his nose into her life once again. She was under a lot of ongoing stress. He could see the fragility in Leah's eyes, although she didn't say anything. She was a lot stronger than he'd given her credit for. Mentally, she was tough, and that's where it counted. Anyone who could keep moving with painful leg cramps like she had gained his respect. With most people, it instantly crippled them and they fell to the ground, screaming in pain.

"How far is Bravo from here?" Leah remembered his face, the tight tension, the focus in his expression just before he killed the Taliban who had wandered into their cave. Now, Kell was relaxed, and it touched her deeply. Hayden always wore a game face and never let it down around her. Kell was himself around her. Not the SEAL. Not the military man. Just a Kentucky-bred boy whose natural warmth oozed out of him like warm honey in sunlight.

"Roughly twenty-five miles."

"That's not far."

"No, but it's not a straight shot, either. We're going to be riding and making changes all the time, based upon what the drone sees. We have to avoid Taliban at all costs."

"It's dangerous."

His mouth lifted a little. "Anything we do falls into that category, Sugar."

She sighed and put the MRE aside after finishing it. "I've really been protected by being up in the sky." She held Kell's somber look. "It's very different here on the ground."

"It's always a game of cat and mouse," he agreed. Worse, because of intense Taliban activity, if they got into trouble, they were on their own. Kell was going to have to use his considerable experience over here, his knowledge of the land and mountains, to thread the eye of this particular needle and get them safely back to the forward operating base.

Leah leaned back against the protruding wall, her hands wrapped around her drawn-up knees. "Sometimes," she admitted softly, "I don't want to go back." She saw Kell lift his head and study her. "I know it's immature to say that. Since meeting you, my life has changed so dramatically. When we go back to Bravo, everything will change again. I won't get to see you that often and I know it."

"We'll make it work, Leah. Don't forget, I'm black ops." Kell smiled a little. And then he became serious, placing his empty MRE aside. "You've given a lot of thought to us? About the fact you're a warrant officer? If you ever get outed by someone in your squadron who discovers that you're consorting with an enlisted man, it could hurt your career very badly. You've worked hard for years to get where you are." He saw Leah nod, her expression placid, as if she were at peace with the threat.

"I've thought about it, Kell. I know the danger.

The guys I'm with at Bravo have my back. It's my ex-husband who doesn't, but he's at Bagram, thank God."

"But you're putting your *entire* career on the line." Kell dug into her green eyes. As much as he wanted to continue to explore what they had, the price would be steep.

"Are you trying to get rid of me?" Leah teased, seeing the worry in his eyes, the concern in his voice.

"No. Not even."

"This cuts both ways and you know it. What if your officers find out you're in a relationship with an Army warrant officer?"

Kell shook his head. "SEALs operate differently. I'm not saying they'd like it. But as long as I do my job, I'm accountable to my team, they don't care. If I were to flaunt it under their noses, that would get me in hot water. The team is everything, Leah. But if I do my job, keep us under wraps, they will look the other way."

"Wish the Army had that live-and-let-live attitude, but they don't."

"No, and that's why we really need to be sure of what's going on between us. Because once we make it back to Bravo, you've got a thousand men watching you whether you like it or not. Not many women, especially good-looking women like you, are out here in the badlands. And that means we're going to have to be extra careful, because if there's fallout, it's coming your way, not mine."

She tipped her head back and listened to the music of the waterfall. "I'll roll with it, Kell. Take it a day at a time." She felt the danger of what could happen, how military regulations could tear them apart. Was she being wise? Foolhardy? Leah had taken very few risks in the emotional department with men. The three times she had, they had all ended in disaster.

Was she seeing Kell accurately? Would he change once they were back at Bravo? Hayden had seemed so warm and open to her until they'd gotten married, and then her life became a nightmare. Leah had thrown those experiences around, trying to compare those men to Kell. He was just so different from them that she felt hopeful. Maybe she was idealizing their relationship? Only time would tell.

Leah wasn't going to rush into anything. Hayden had taught her that. They had time at Bravo to slowly move forward and she could, by being more mature, handle this relationship differently. Better.

"Your ex is gunning for you," Kell warned, not wanting to say any more than that. "He could get one of the pilots at Bravo to watch you. Report back to him. If he found out we had a relationship, would he put you up on court-martial charges for it?"

She snorted. "Hayden is vindictive. He's been wanting to trip me up for years, ever since he divorced me. He's filled my father's ears with all the things he can find that I've done wrong, and then he tattles on me." Leah held his dark gaze. "I don't care anymore, Kell. This crash has done something to me." Leah hitched one shoulder upward. "I can't put it into words. Since the crash, I just don't care."

"It's shock," he muttered. "It's going to take you a month or more to shake it off. You almost died." *You should have died. But didn't.* And Kell knew better than anyone, because he'd cheated death too many times himself. It changed a person's outlook forever.

Usually, they realized it months after the event. With Leah, she was already there. "I don't want you making snap decisions right now because of it," he warned her. Kell had seen other team members, once they almost died, walk away. Quit. Others just sucked it up, internalized the experience and kept on moving forward. A person never knew what they'd do until it happened to them. In Leah's case, she was reviewing her life as a pilot. Kell had no idea where it would lead or what Leah would decide because of it.

"I know." She gave him a sad smile. "The past few days have been so different from the life I knew. It's you, Kell. I know that. And I *want* you in my life. I want to explore what we have." She opened her hands and added, "I know we haven't had much time with one another, but I'm serious about you. Maybe I'm crazy. Maybe it's that shock you're talking about. I don't know. What I do know is I want you in my life."

Kell sat very still, listening to her impassioned words, absorbing her expression, the urgency underlying her admission. "I'm serious about you, too, Leah," he said. He'd never expected in a million years that a woman would drop out of the sky, drop into his arms, and he'd fall so damned hard for her, body and soul. "I don't know where we're going, either, Sugar. I want you in my life as much as possible. It's going to be tough to do at Bravo. Most of the time, I'm out on missions for a day, maybe a few days, at a time. Sometimes longer. And you have your flight schedule, too."

"Distance makes the heart grow fonder," Leah said, giving him a tender look. Just the idea that their close intimacy with one another might be coming to an end, that she'd not have this with Kell at Bravo, made her heart ache. Leah had never felt so emotionally connected to a man in her life as she did with Kell. It was inexplicable. It was heady. Scary. And the future wasn't bright. It looked like a minefield to her, and Kell realized the same thing. They were older, mature, and realistic about themselves and the issues confronting them. Leah knew it didn't look good. But something deep was driving her toward him, not away from him.

"I'll find ways for us to be together," Kell assured her, and he saw her perk up and smile a little. He wasn't going to tell Leah that he'd have her six, that he'd either watch out for her himself or one of his team members would. Kell was going to let Clutch and a few of his other SEAL brothers know the truth. If he was off on a mission, he was going to make damn sure Leah wasn't left in the lurch, alone and possibly having to face Major Grant by herself if the bastard suddenly showed his face at Bravo to confront her.

One of his brothers would have her back, would protect her in his absence. That's how SEALs worked; they protected those that they loved. Kell didn't swerve from the word. He knew what love was; had had it once. But through his own mistakes, immaturity and from being gone so much, he'd lost Addy.

What he felt for Leah was even more powerful and life-altering. There hadn't been time for him to absorb it all, or even work through his feelings toward her. One thing he did know, however, was that she was his woman and nothing else mattered. So long as she felt the same way toward him, the path was clear for both of them. But nothing was guaranteed and Kell knew that. Leah was right, they'd take it one day at a time once they got back to Bravo. He was unsure what the outcome would be.

"This crash," Leah began quietly, "has really thrown me."

"In what way?" Kell asked. The expression on her face was one of confusion. Yeah, major shocks sure as hell did that to a person. He'd seen it far too often.

Rubbing her brow, Leah muttered, "It's forced me to start looking at my whole life, Kell. How I've always wanted my father's approval. How he introduced me to his world of flying and I leaped at the chance to join it." She looked at her hands for a moment and said, "I do love to fly. I didn't know it until he took me up that day. I just wonder, Kell, if he hadn't taken me up, how my life would be different." She held his gaze, his expression thoughtful.

"You think that if he hadn't given you that opportunity that your life, your own choices, might have been different?"

Damn, Kell always went straight to the heart of what she was floundering around and trying to discover within herself. Leah guessed it was his sniper mind, recognizing the patterns and seeing the big picture fully. Only, she didn't feel wounded by his question, his summation of her admission.

"Yes," she finally said. "Would I have gone to college for a couple of years? Or just gone out in the world and gotten a job at a hospital? I've always loved medicine. I've always wanted to help people who had less than I did. Help the sick, the injured."

"If you woke up tomorrow morning and someone told you that you could do or be whoever you really wanted to be, what would you tell them?" Kell felt her searching, felt her taking a good, hard look at the patterns in her life, slowly sorting through them, asking questions, comparing them. He understood their coming together unexpectedly like this, on top of the crash, had created a tear in her world. The crash was bad, but he didn't consider their relationship as anything but positive for her. Leah was finding out about her body, herself, without Grant still brainwashing her at such a critical stage of her developing maturity.

Kell held on to the anger that always simmered hotly within him. Leah was sensitive and innocent, and Grant had used her, knew exactly what he was doing. Now, maybe the crash was allowing her to see herself differently.

Leah's mouth twitched. "Honestly? If I could really choose what I wanted to do?"

"Sure," he drawled, giving her a half smile. Kell saw hope suddenly come to her eyes, as if she'd never thought outside that box she called her life before.

"I'd love to go back to college and get a degree to become a registered nurse. I love working with the elderly. I guess I see myself in them. I know I'll be old one day, too. And I know I'll need help."

If he had anything to do with it, she'd grow old with him, but Kell remained silent. It was too soon for that. Too many other obstacles were present in both their lives right now. Too much danger. Too much uncertainty. "Then why not do it?"

"It's not that easy," Leah muttered.

"I've found we make things as hard or as easy on ourselves as we decide to," he told her. "When is your time up in the Army?"

"I've got six months more to go before I re-up."

Shrugging, Kell said, "Maybe you should seriously consider not doing it. Give yourself the freedom to go explore some of what you hold in your heart. I've always believed if you live your passion, it's the right career and job path for a person."

Leah dragged in a deep breath. "I've thought about it," she admitted hesitantly. "What about you, Kell? Are you living your passion? Being a SEAL?"

He nodded. It was his passion…or had been up until very recently, when he met Leah. "I've been doing this since I was eighteen. But I'm twenty-nine now. I've been looking at other options, to tell you the truth. My two younger brothers are in the military, both in black ops. Tyler is a SEAL and Cody is in Army Special Forces. I was planning on talking with them when I got home at Thanksgiving."

"About?"

Kell gave her a gentle look. "I'm just considering some possible alternatives. It hasn't gelled in me yet." He wanted to say that meeting her made a hell of a change in his life; like a lightning bolt striking him. Suddenly he was looking at what he wanted in a completely different way. He loved his SEAL family, but he was also falling for Leah. Kell wasn't sure if it was completely mutual or not. He felt her wanting him. Saw it every time she looked into his eyes. His senses were so finely honed that it almost bordered on mental telepathy between him and those close to him. And Leah was the closest in his heart. "I just need to see where certain things land in the coming months, and then I'll be more clear about my options, what I want to do."

It wasn't a lie, but it hinged on Leah. They were

both in a state of transition. The crash had hit both of them in unexpected ways, whether he'd realized it or not the night he'd picked up her unconscious from that burning crash site.

Leah got to her feet. "I'm going to get cleaned up," she murmured.

"I'll follow after you're done."

Leah felt her body respond to the burning look in his gray eyes. There was this living, vibrating, heated connection between them. It was always palpable; so alive, so incredibly scary for her, but equally attracting.

Leah's gaze settled on Kell's mouth and instantly she felt needy. As she moved down the tunnel, collecting the towels, washcloth and lye soap that Kell had laid out for her earlier, Leah felt shaky with need. For Kell. What would happen tonight? She didn't know, but her body wanted him. So did her heart. But the past stood in front of her like the biggest wall she'd ever come up against.

Did she have the courage to transcend the past? Move into Kell's arms, trusting him with her broken soul? Feeling shaky inside, Leah walked down the tunnel toward the waterfall, unsure.

CHAPTER TWELVE

LEAH WALKED BACK from the waterfall, her hair wet and needing to be dried. She had wrapped the large bath towel around her body. Her pulse was beginning to beat harder. Her gaze lingered on Kell, who had purposely sat down, his back to the waterfall, to give her privacy while she bathed naked beneath the cold streams.

Heat swept through her as she approached him. Kell heard her approach and twisted a look up in her direction. She halted and watched him unwind to his full height.

Kell smiled and touched her wet, sleek hair. "Now you're a mermaid," he teased. She looked so damn hot to him. That white towel hung halfway to her knees. He couldn't help but notice her cheeks flush as his gaze narrowed upon her. Moving his fingers through her hair, Kell wanted her. But the game had changed. Leah had to want him. Had to speak up. It was the only way any intimacy between them would work. Kell unconsciously held his breath for a moment, searching her wide, trusting green eyes.

Leah inhaled deeply, already shaky with need, his fingers creating pleasant, dancing shocks across her scalp. She could feel her breasts tightening. Her nipples pressing insistently against the terrycloth towel.

"I want you, Kell... I want more of what we shared before..." she whispered, holding his gaze. It had taken every scrap of her dissolving courage to ask him. She'd never asked a man something like this in her life. All the tension fled out of her as his mouth curved faintly, his eyes gleaming with pleasure. His fingers caressed her naked, damp shoulder and she quivered, her lashes dropping as she felt heat searing from there directly to her breasts and then downward, stirring up more need below.

"I want you, too, Sugar." Kell dropped a quick kiss on her lips and said, "Let me get cleaned up first?"

Leah stood there, feeling like she would collapse and melt into a puddle. Kell had barely touched her and yet she felt such inner starvation for him that it tore at her mind, leaving her thoughts scattered while her emotions radiated wildly throughout her.

She walked a bit farther and saw that Kell had spread out the two sleeping bags, one against the other. How had he known? She saw two pillows and several thick wool blankets spread neatly across them. The temperature in the cave was probably a constant seventy-five degrees.

Leah knelt and took the smaller towel and dried her hair. She tamed the damp strands into some semblance of order with a comb. Her pulse was going crazy. She stole a look into the other cave. A lantern sat on the wooden bench and clearly showed Kell's powerful male body glinting in the yellow light beneath the falling water.

She felt instant heat burn through her. Kell was incredibly beautiful to her. His shoulders were so broad and heavily muscled, and his chest well-sprung. The dark hair across it narrowed into a line down across his rock-hard abs. She gulped, realizing he had an erection. Unable to stop staring at him, Leah didn't feel fear. Maybe she should have, but she didn't, and for that, she was grateful. Kell was not Hayden. Her mind knew it. Her body sure as hell did, as well, and she felt her heavily guarded heart opening, feelings of anticipation and eagerness flowing strongly through her. Her mind waffled between the past and the present. Was she making the right decision here or not?

Now, she understood how Kell could have carried her the distance he had over some very rocky, challenging conditions. He was tall, well proportioned, his long, curved thighs thick and hard. Fascinated with how his muscles moved and responded, she saw how tanned his face, neck and hands were. The rest of his body was a pale golden color beneath the lamplight.

Leah couldn't help but compare Hayden to Kell. Her ex-husband was powerfully built and muscled and reminded her of a bull's body. Kell was long, lean, his angles sharply defined and with graceful movement. His muscles slid with a smoothness that told her he was in unbelievably good shape, unlike Hayden. Absorbing him as he washed himself, she sensed Kell knew she was watching him. Her thighs tightened.

As Kell stepped out of the pool and walked toward the bench, she turned away. Calling herself a coward, Leah waited. Her body was already attuned to him even though she never heard him approach her. Kell wore a towel tucked around his waist to his knees. He came around and knelt down in front of her.

She saw water dribbling down the sides of his face, the beard making his face more dangerous looking. Without thinking, she gripped the edge of the towel above her covered breasts. Kell was intoxicating, nearly naked before her, his flesh gleaming with water. It was nearly overwhelming to Leah because he allowed her to look at him. Leah felt coiled tension radiating from him even though he appeared relaxed, his hands resting on his thighs, following her gaze as she drank him in.

Her breath was uneven. Kell seemed to enjoy her inspection; a man fully confident in himself. There was no threat between them. He made no move toward her. Leah's mind was torn between the past and the present. One man had terrorized her. This man, Kell, was waiting, not making a move to touch her, to control or entrap her. He was allowing her the time she needed to feel comfortable with him. With herself, in the tense situation.

Her heart was pounding so loudly she swore he had to hear it. Leah hesitantly reached out, her fingers brushing the beads of water away from his right temple. She saw his pupils grow larger. It was the only reaction she saw or felt around Kell. Her fingers, now wet, followed the curve of his corded neck, feeling the muscles leap as she glided her fingertips across his damp, clean flesh.

Moving her hand, spreading her fingers slightly, Leah traced his broad, thickly muscled shoulder. Again, his muscles contracted swiftly beneath his moist flesh. Leah was mesmerized by how his body responded to the lightest of her touches. Hayden had never wanted her to touch him in this manner.

Lifting her lashes, Leah met Kell's burning gaze, her breasts growing taut beneath his hungry look. Her fingers traced his collarbone, felt his chest sharply rise once in response. It gave Leah a sense of power. Her power as a woman to affect the man she desired. She could touch Kell, and he responded, and yet there was no threat present. Just…heat…so much heat gathering and pooling in her lower body that she felt an ache building once more. An ache that she wanted eased.

She remembered that very same sensation from when he'd kissed her before, that pressure that had built into an orgasm, her very first. Leah had nearly fainted from the release, it was so violently pleasurable and long lasting.

It felt so right to lean upward, slide her hands against Kell's hard jawline and tentatively touch his mouth with her lips. Her breath caught as his mouth opened, cajoling her lips to move more surely against him. A soft moan rose in her throat as she trusted herself to languish against his chest, sinking into his welcoming mouth.

His arms lifted, encompassing her. The instant her breasts pressed against his chest, she felt a prickling sensation radiate from them, her nipples so hard that the material rubbing against them caught her off guard. The fire and raw pleasure flowed like a surge of sizzling heat down between her legs, and a whimper caught within her throat. She drowned in Kell's mouth, feeling his hands settle lightly on her naked shoulders, his fingers gliding across their expanse, eliciting more tingles and triggering more intense arousal.

Kell eased from her delicious, hungry mouth. He smiled down at her, thinking how natural, how guileless, Leah was. She was artless, but she was following her own womanly intuition about him. "Before we start," he told her, his voice roughened with lust, "I need to know if you're protected or not."

Blinking, coming out of that cocoon of scalding heat, she managed to whisper, "I'm on the pill. It's okay…"

Nodding, Kell saw the bloom of heat in her cheeks, the way her lower lip drew into a natural, sultry pout. "Tell me what you want, Sugar. Tonight is yours…"

His soft Kentucky drawl was like warm honey flowing across her sensitized nerves. "I want…" Leah tried to think, but couldn't. Out of frustration, she held his dark gaze. She could feel the heat and roughness of his hands upon her skin. "Just…make me feel like you did the other day when you kissed me."

"I can do that," Kell promised her, his voice a low growl.

"I don't know that much," Leah admitted, feeling shame. At twenty-nine she was probably acting like some gawky, idiot teenage girl. She didn't want what Hayden had done to her. That much she did know. But what else was there? She didn't have a clue. Hayden had never kissed her mouth or touched her breasts. Shame plunged through Leah and she struggled to overcome it, to tell herself that Kell was different. Tears streaked down her cheeks, and she sat back on her heels, angrily wiping them away.

"I'm sorry," Leah whispered in a quavering voice. "I feel so stupid here…so ignorant…"

Kell cupped her face between his hands, his thumbs removing her tears. "There's no sin in being innocent, darlin'. Making love is between two people. What's making you cry?"

Sniffing, Leah closed her eyes, unable to stand the

gentleness she saw in his eyes. "I'm stupid. I don't know anything, Kell. I can't even answer your question about what I want." She opened her eyes, his face blurring for a moment. "Do you know how that makes me feel, Kell? I feel like an alien who suddenly got transplanted down here before you, and I don't have a damned clue as to how to—to love you, to touch you... I don't know anything, and it's painful for me to sit here and admit it to you..."

"Then," Kell rasped, taking her and guiding her down on the blankets, "let's just take this time to explore one another. You were touching me earlier. It felt good to me, Leah. I liked your touch. I liked your curiosity because I can see you want to explore my body. I want you to do that all you want."

She lay on her back gazing up at him. He was massive compared to her size, and yet Leah felt nothing but protection and care radiating off Kell, like sunlight, surrounding her, invisibly embracing her. "Okay," she said, her voice hoarse. "I'm just so..."

He smiled a little, kissing the tears from her cheeks. "Darlin', just do what comes naturally, what makes you feel good. And I'll touch you in return." His gaze turned serious as he held her moist gaze. "Remember what I said the other day? If I do something that doesn't make you feel good, or makes you uncomfortable or scared, tell me to stop and I will."

Leah nodded, feeling less tense. "I remember... but you've done nothing but make me feel good before this, Kell." She licked her lower lip, watching the corners of his mouth draw upward. "I want to feel that orgasm again. I loved that feeling. Will it happen again? What do I have to do to make it come back?"

He grinned. "A woman always enjoys that release." He slid his fingers through her drying hair. "And it made me happy you got to discover your own pleasure as a woman. That's what a man's supposed to do, Leah. He's supposed to pleasure his woman first. Not himself. And yes, it's always there, ready to come. Even better? You can have more than one. A man can only come once, but you ladies can have as many as you want."

Her mind wrenched back to Hayden. And then she nodded. "You gave me incredible pleasure."

"Let me give you some more, then," Kell urged huskily, taking her mouth, tasting the sweetness that was only her.

Fire exploded down through Leah's body as Kell moved his tongue slowly, teasingly against hers. She felt his other hand glide from her shoulder, skimming over her back, hip and to her thigh, pulling her slowly against him, giving her time to protest or ask him to stop if the move frightened her. But it didn't. She could feel his erection pressing against her belly, hard and insistent.

His mouth dissolved her fears as she felt his hand move beneath her towel above her knee. Her breath became uneven as his long fingers moved slowly up the outer curve of her thigh, her skin leaping and tightening beneath his slow exploration. Kell moved his hand upward, to her hip, to her butt, and then slowly down her thigh once more. She felt cherished, as if he were memorizing her inch by inch, sponging her in through his exploring hand. It was the most incredible feeling of being claimed and desired. Every graze was slow, giving her time to acclimate, to decide whether

she liked it or not. But there was nothing Kell did that
Leah didn't like.

Mindless, his tongue moving deeper into her
mouth, sliding against hers, cajoling her, Leah arched
upward, wanting, needing closer contact with him.
The moment her nipples brushed against his chest
from beneath the towel, she gasped, a jolt of electric
current radiating down throughout her in wild, grati-
fying shocks.

Kell eased from her mouth, his hand beneath her
neck, exposing her slender throat to his lips. She was
trembling as his warm, moist breath skittered across
her sensitive flesh. Leah felt his small nips making her
skin ripple with deeper pleasure, and then he would
lick the area and finally kiss her in that very same
throbbing spot.

Leah's mind liquified as his mouth trailed a path
of slow, expanding fire from her neck, across her collarbone and then downward. She felt him ease open
the towel across her breasts, felt the nubby fabric removed to bare her sensitive, aching breasts. Her fingers dug into Kell's shoulder, her other hand gripping
his thick, flexing biceps, twisting up against him, not
knowing what she wanted, only that she wanted the
ache growing deep within her to stop. To somehow
be released again.

A soft whimper tore out of Leah as she felt his fingers graze the curve of her breast. The impact of his
calloused fingers stroking her flesh made her gasp.
The moistness of his breath caressed her nipple and
Leah cried out, unable to know what it was she was
wanting. Only that she was needing so badly that frustration was building within her.

The moment Kell's lips settled on her tight nipple, a ragged cry tore out of her and Leah arched her hips against his. The searing jolts shafted down through her body as he teased her nipple. The suckling sensation completely unhinged her in every way. An uncontrollable fire leaped to life within her, an ancient knowing that didn't need any teacher to tell her what to do from now on.

As his teeth tugged gently on the nipple, she writhed in his arms, the feelings so intense that she bucked her hips demandingly against his. All Leah could do was sob as he waged the same sweet assault upon her other nipple. She was barely aware that he had disrobed her completely until she felt his hard erection against her belly as she twisted herself upward against him. It didn't scare her. Her memory had been dissolved by the molten heat that leaped and churned throughout her entire body.

She trusted Kell. And that was all her mind needed to know. It released her from the terror of the past. It allowed her to focus solely on Kell.

Leah made an exasperated moaning sound as his mouth left her breast. She almost cried out louder, wanting him to return to suckle them, the exquisite sensations leaving her trembling in the wake of his skilled mouth. Instead, she felt his hand move beneath her arched back, pulling her upward, his mouth trailing fire down the center of her damp, quivering body. Leah gripped his thickly muscled shoulders, fingers pressed deep into his flesh, opening and closing them as if in spasm as each kiss lavished her torso, her abdomen.

And then her world started flying apart as she felt

his mouth kissing her soft curls, his hands easing her thighs apart. It was such a slow-moving, burning path he created as he followed the crease of her left thigh, then kissed and licked his way down to her aching entrance.

Kell laid her down, moved between her thighs and cupped her hips, lifting her slightly, and as his mouth touched her outer entrance, Leah gasped, a low, tearing moan caught in her throat. Her entire body bowed upward at the scorching pleasure his mouth, his tongue, was giving her.

The impact of his mouth caressing her, giving her such intense, violent pleasure, ripped away her mind and Leah could only respond with her heart as he welcomed her in a way she'd never before experienced.

She began to sob, gripping Kell's shoulders, wanting the pressure, the building ache, to release once more. His tongue moved inside her and she groaned as her entire lower body violently convulsed and contracted. Dazed, she felt a flood of thick, fluid, intense, rippling sensations flowed through her.

She sobbed with relief as the pressure discharged from within her. The trail of singeing blaze moved outward in radiating circles, overwhelming her senses, pleasuring her, rocking her to the edge of some unknown, beautiful, floating universe. And yet, as her body orgasmed, she could feel another building pressure right behind it. But he waited, soothing her with his hands across her belly, her outer thighs, giving her time to absorb all the satiation throbbing through her.

Kell kissed her gently, as if she were sacred to him, and Leah was lost within his arms as he worshipped her. She was coming out of that cloud of intensity when he slid his hands across her hips, kneeling between her thighs, his tongue moving deeply into her once again. The sensation was exquisite and she welcomed his return, hunger coursing through her once more. As he lavished that swelling knot just inside her entrance once again, she gave a hoarse cry. Within moments, her body gifted her once more, sending her into a faraway place of scalding, flames and undulating ecstasy that completely embraced her.

Kell eased away from Leah, filled with her sexual scent and the taste of her. He kissed her curly mound and then he teased one of her nipples, feeling her buck against him, wanting him all over again.

He smiled to himself, luxuriating in her innocent reactions. Once Leah put that troubled mind of hers on the shelf, she became his fierce, passionate woman in his arms. There was no holding back with her, and now Kell wanted to give her what she'd been wanting all along, but hadn't discovered until now.

He placed his knees between her thighs, gently parting her, pressing himself against her wet entrance. She was so ready, her body flooding with nectar, the sweetness flowing out of her. He slid his hand beneath her lower back, her breasts against his chest as he lay against her. She was breathing in sobs, her hands against his hips, pulling him, wanting him inside her. Kell knew what she wanted even if she didn't understand what she was doing. The last thing he wanted was to traumatize her. She was wet, slick and warm, and he pressed just inside of her gate and waited for her reaction.

Leah suddenly froze, and he was glad he'd waited, leaning his damp brow against her brow, feeling her breathing change, feeling her hands suddenly still against his back. He moved just slightly, enough to engage that pearl-like bundle of nerves at her entrance. She suddenly quivered and Kell released a held breath of air. It was all right…all right, and he stroked her slowly, teasing that pearl, feeling her loosen and relax once more in his arms.

Damn, she was so tight. He was afraid to move deeper, feeling her body trying to accommodate him, convulsing, tightening and releasing. And yet, her sweet hips rocked against his, silently asking for more of him to enter her. It was such a risk. Kell felt as though he was going to explode any moment, not used to being gripped like a tight glove. Leah moaned, her head thrashing from side to side, her eyes closed, her mouth open in a silent cry, wanting him.

Kell felt brutalized by the wait. He could feel the tortured ache in his body, the heat and juices of her body flowing in eager welcome around him, relentlessly teasing him. He wanted to surge into her, take her hard, take her fast, but that couldn't be done. *Not tonight.*

Easing farther into Leah, he finally got her body to slowly accommodate and accept all of him. And as he began to thrust into her with a slow rhythm, he felt her hips return that rhythm. As he increased the thrusts, her fingers sank deeply into his back. Yeah, she was going to come again, and he had to control himself for her sake. Her powerful contractions as the orgasm released nearly did Kell in; her hot, scalding flow around him made him lock his teeth, groaning, trying to stop himself from coming.

But it was impossible, and as Leah cried out his

name, he took her with a swift, deep rhythm. In moments, Kell tensed, growled and gripped her against him, burying his face against her neck and shoulder, feeling his release tunnel out of him like a scorching fire. He shook violently, holding her hard to him, feeling her chaotic breath and soft sobs against his ear. She clung to him as if she were going to fly free and disappear. But she wasn't.

Kell held her, eased his grip around her, allowed her to lie down, her dark ginger hair a frame around her deeply flushed face. Her eyes drowsily opened, awe and satisfaction gleaming in their depths. Kell couldn't speak, still caught up in his own release, still inside her, feeling her body massaging him, still keeping him hard despite the release.

He struggled to elevate himself with his elbows on either side of her head, taking most of his weight off her except where they were joined. He could feel the sweat and wetness shared between them. And he couldn't help but thrust his hips slowly forward, twisting and drowning in the welcoming heat of her once again.

Watching Leah's luminous eyes widen, those pupils huge and black, he absorbed the pleasure and satiation shining in them. It made him feel strong and good as a man to be able to give his woman this kind of unadulterated, seamless pleasure. But Leah deserved so much more.

He eased his hand beneath the small of her sweaty back and angled her hips up just enough as he thrust slowly into her once more. Her lips parted, a soft mewl that sounded like music to him escaping her throat as she tipped back her head, her eyes closing as she absorbed each of his slow, measured strokes.

"That's it, Sugar," he crooned, "just enjoy the ride..."

He twisted his hips to tease her inwardly. Her hands wrapped around his biceps, her sweet sounds filling him. More than anything, Kell wanted to show her a man could pleasure her, not hurt her as he filled her.

He continued to move, reaching that other group of nerves high and deep within her, a second trigger point, to coax her to orgasm once more. And as limp as she was, as exhausted as she had been, Kell brought her back, saw that spark of surprise return to her eyes as he continued to stroke deeply and tease her.

"That's it, take what you want," he urged her in a guttural voice.

Her hands slipped around his hips, pulling him hard against her, arching, whimpering.

Kell smiled inwardly, letting Leah get used to controlling her own pleasure with him. And very soon, he felt a swift, tight contraction around him, felt her body convulse and then that boiling release of her fluids swiftly surrounding him. And this time, he knew exactly how to prolong that deeper orgasm for her. He sent her right over the edge of the universe into a hot, floating cloud of burning pleasure. He watched her fly apart beneath him, the powerful arch of her back, the surprised, husky cry tearing out of her slender throat, the pink flush flooding her skin during the prolonged, powerful orgasm.

Leah collapsed against him, spent, breathing raggedly. He eased out of her, knowing for sure she was going to be very achy come tomorrow morning. Kell wasn't exactly small to begin with, and he knew it spelled soreness that Leah would have to endure.

He gathered her up against him, bringing her head to rest against his neck and jaw. Moving his hand down across her hip, he pulled her fully against him, his long leg tangling among hers, holding her close.

Reaching up, Kell snagged a blanket with his fingers, pulling it across them. The cave wasn't cold, but he didn't want her to get chilled. She was warm, damp and pleasantly limp in his arms. Moving his fingers through her hair, he kissed her smooth brow, content.

Leah didn't know when she'd fallen asleep, but as she drowsily awoke, she felt alone. Kell was no longer beside her. Barely turning her head she saw him walking toward her, a towel and washcloth in his hands. Following him with her eyes, he came and knelt at her side. He removed the blanket and gently opened her thighs.

"You're going to be sore tomorrow," he warned her quietly, moving the warm wash cloth and gently wiping the insides of her thighs and her entrance. He then placed the warm, moist towel across her abdomen and between her thighs. "The heat will help, Sugar." He smiled a little and caressed her cheek. "You feeling okay?"

Okay? Just okay?

Leah felt as if she'd splintered into a million throbbing, exploding pieces of intense pleasure that were still surging through her lower body like banked coals on a fire. Her mouth was dry and she was thirsty. Licking her lower lip, Leah rasped, "I feel so good I don't even have words to describe it, Kell." She reached out, catching his hand, bringing it to her lips, kissing the back of it. "Thank you…I just never realized how good this could be…"

Kell felt joy thread through him. "It's the best, darlin'. Nothing else even begins to compare to it."

Throwing her arm across her eyes, Leah groaned, "Tell me about it." She managed a little laugh, never having felt as good as she did right now.

Lifting her arm away, she saw the happiness burning in Kell's dark gray eyes. That male smile was there, too. Pride. Confidence. Love? Was that what she saw in his eyes for her? Leah thought it was too soon to know, but whatever it was, it made her feel cherished. And so well loved.

CHAPTER THIRTEEN

LEAH LINGERED IN a heated world of pleasure even after she woke up much later. She was in Kell's arms, her body fitting against the harder planes of his. Where she was soft and giving, he was angular and unforgiving. In her groggy mind, still captured in the web of pleasurable, ongoing sensations, she luxuriated in his strength and the sense of being cherished. Her arm was curved across his narrow waist, her cheek resting on the soft hair across his chest. Just the slow, deep beat of his heart against her ear lulled her into a delicious space of happiness she'd never realized could exist between a man and a woman.

Leah didn't want to move. She wanted to fiercely remember this night, this moment in Kell's arms. Her life felt altered forever by his loving her. She didn't skirt the word or the sensation opening in her heart, flowing through her, healing the fracture in her soul that Hayden had created.

The more she awakened, the more Leah realized how much she'd allowed herself to be used by her ex-husband. The question of why was glaring. Why had she allowed herself to be manipulated first by her father and later by Hayden? Leah lay with her eyes closed, soaking up Kell's warmth against her flesh, his moist breath slow and shallow against her hair.

In those sweet moments, Leah became aware of the waterfall's music echoing throughout the cave, feeling in another way her life had been rerouted by Kell's entrance into it. She'd only been half-alive, she realized, until he'd opened his arms and asked her to come to him.

Where was all of this going? Leah felt as if she were teetering on the brink of a massive change in her life. There was no way she couldn't draw stark comparisons between Kell and Hayden. New anger toward Hayden began to uncurl from deep within her.

Hayden had taken everything away from her, never sharing, never even thinking of giving back to her in terms of emotional pleasure, intimacy or nurturing. Leah's heart shrank in grief over what she'd allowed him to do to her.

If only she'd had more experience, more worldly awareness of sex, of relationships, she would have known. And by knowing, she would have instantly realized Hayden was sick and abusive. She would have left him as soon as she realized her mistake. He'd initially hidden the ugly, abusive side of himself. She hadn't had the astuteness to realize that he was wearing a disguise. An uneven sigh broke from her lips as Leah felt the anguish and shame of her own ignorance flow through her.

Kell's fingers grazed her cheek, his touch removing her anger and disappointment with herself. Leah stretched languidly against him, leaning up, kissing his bearded jaw. Absorbing his tenderness as he caressed her shoulder and back, her skin tightening wherever his exploring fingers skimmed her skin, Leah didn't want this to ever end.

She moved against his hips, feeling his erection against her, absorbing the moment, his power coupled with his gentleness. Leah felt well loved, cared for and treasured.

"Is this how it is?" she whispered, her voice husky with sleep.

Kell propped himself up on one elbow, easing Leah onto her back so he could study her. "Always," he murmured, removing strands of her hair from her cheek and brow. Her eyes were wide with wonder, a rich green, pupils large and black. His gaze dropped to her mouth, her lips slightly parted. Sliding his hand across her jaw, Kell leaned down, barely grazing them, feeling their softness, feeling her lush response. He wanted to make love to her again, but knew it would have to wait.

Tasting her, placing small, lingering kisses on each corner of her mouth, he eased away to hold her drowsy gaze, his heart lost to her in every possible way.

"I don't want this to end," she admitted softly, reaching up, sliding her hand against his jaw, watching his eyes grow intent, feeling him desiring her once more. It was a delicious, empowering feeling, so new and satisfying to Leah.

Groaning, Kell nodded and said, "Me, either, Sugar." He lifted his hand and looked at his watch. "It's 0400. I'm going to have to get up and get out to the cave opening and call in by sat phone to see what's going on around this area."

Leah grimaced and nodded. "You're right. I was being selfish."

Kell kissed her cheek and then her mouth. "I want you to be selfish about us. It's never going to be easy

with our military demands and responsibilities." He
saw a somber look come to her expression. In some
ways, she was like a young woman who had just awakened to the beauty and amazement of her own body, of
understanding the pleasures to be gained and enjoyed
with the right man at her side. Kell hated to bring it up
because he knew her father had imprisoned her in a
world of responsibility and loyalty only to him, leaving no time for what Leah wanted for herself.

"I wish," Leah whispered, "I could stop time. Just
to stay here for another day… Is that being selfish,
Kell?" To want to be with him? To savor his touch,
his mouth, his body once more? Leah saw his eyes
change and grow softer. A sad smile that came to his
mouth tore at her newly opened heart.

"Someday. But not now, Leah. My only priority is
getting you safely back to Bravo."

She nodded and moved her length against him,
watching his eyes grow narrowed. Feral. The sense
of power she felt she had over him was a new and
wonderful discovery filled with so much possibility.
"Then," Leah whispered, trailing her fingers across
his shoulder, "I'm going to remember Thanksgiving,
being with you, meeting your family."

"That's the plan," Kell agreed, a slow smile coming
to his mouth. "It's something to dream about, Leah.
Something to hold close to your heart when things go
bad, or when we can't see one another as much as we
might want at Bravo." Kell grazed her smooth brow,
her skin soft and velvety beneath his thumb.

He almost said, *I love you.* The words damn near
tore out of his mouth. But it was too soon. So much
had happened in such a short, intense period of time,

and Kell wanted Leah to absorb the important feelings he'd coaxed to life within her. And if he was accurately reading her luminous gaze, Leah was falling in love with him, too. What they shared was serious. His heart soared with giddy hope.

There were many months between now and getting home for Thanksgiving. He worried about Leah. Worried that Major Grant would do something to hurt her. She still didn't know that he was trying to blame her for that helo crash. There were way too many unknowns, and Kell wasn't going to discuss his concerns with Leah.

Right now, all he wanted was that soft, fulfilled look in her eyes, the curve of her luscious mouth softly tipped upward, feeling her fingers trail deliciously across his shoulder, exploring and appreciating him.

Leah sighed and nodded. "We need to get up and get going," she agreed. What she really wanted was more of Kell and to learn how to please him, too. He would have to teach her because she was completely ignorant. Time wasn't on their side.

Kell heard the disappointment and the yearning in her husky tone. He spread his hand across her belly. "How are you feeling?"

"Happy. Satisfied."

He moved his hand across her belly. "Sore?"

"A little. Nothing to worry about."

Nodding, Kell leaned over, placing a slow, wet, lingering kiss over her belly.

Her breath caught, and Leah closed her eyes, feeling the heat build instantly between her thighs, remembering his mouth, his lips and tongue, and how it had sent her into such intense pleasure last night.

As he moved his lips up the center of her body, she gripped his shoulders, needy and wanting him all over again. Her breasts tightened instantly, her nipples hardening in anticipation of his touch, his mouth. A moan slipped from between her lips as his mouth settled over the first peak, suckling her, sending her body into crazed, hungry heat. It was so easy to push her hips against his, feel his hardness, his hunger for her. The dampness collected into warm, thick fluids at her entrance and Leah wanted him so badly, wanted that pressure gnawing at her to be released. And as he suckled her other nipple, she quivered violently, a hunger flowing powerfully through her as she felt his hand drifting across her belly.

She was wet and needy. Leah wanted to cheat the time just once. Kell must have sensed it, must have wanted the same thing for her, because she felt his fingers move down her cleft and skim the slickness near her gateway, and he growled her name, pleased. That rumbling sound moved through her and she sobbed against his mouth as he took her lips. He encircled her rim, opening her thighs, asking her to trust him. And she did. Her heart hammered, her channel achy and in need of relief once more. Kell slowly entered her with his skilled fingers.

Memories of Hayden flashed across her melting mind, and then the pleasure being wreaked from within her erased it. This was not painful. It was hot, desirable and incredibly satisfying instead.

Kell's breath was hot and moist against her cheek as he deepened their kiss, his tongue moving strongly against hers. A shattering explosion occurred deep within her body as she felt him trigger her orgasm, that sweet, hot contraction around his fingers, her juices flooding through her. Leah tore her mouth from his, arching against him, head tipped back, a hoarse cry tearing out of her. Her body shimmered and radiated with the singeing fire engulfing her.

Kell continued to move within her, showing her how a man could pleasure her in another, new way. She felt him suckle her other nipple and then fell into melting pieces within his arms as he pressed her tightly against his body. The earthquake of another orgasm shook her, sent rivulets of burning fire radiating in every direction within her. Leah could only sob, feeling his mouth against her nipple, suckling strongly, milking her body, triggering every intense sensation she had never known existed until this moment.

Kell slowly eased his fingers from within her, watching the flush spread silently across her body, her eyes dazed-looking, her lips wet and pouty from his kiss. He moved his hand across her curved thigh, up her flank, feeling each of her ribs, the dampness of her flesh beneath his fingertips. She was trembling and he smiled, absorbing the ecstasy still moving through her awed expression.

Leaning over Leah as he laid her on the blankets, he rasped, "I've got to get moving and make that sat call. Stay here, just rest. I'll be back soon..."

Leah swore she couldn't move, her body saturated with such potent, swirling sensations. She could only breathe unevenly and continue to be consumed by the heat boiling through her lower body. She closed her eyes after Kell left. Her mind fused with her heart. He'd given her one last gift, showing her that a man's touch didn't have to be hurtful or assaultive. Leah threw her arm across her eyes, absorbing it all, feeling intense love for Kell. But did she know what love really was? No. She had no guidepost to tell her so she allowed the bright, sparkling feelings to swell in her heart and called it nothing right now except happiness.

Leah lay there remembering what she'd thought was love for Hayden. Oh, he'd romanced her, brought her gifts, made her feel good about herself because he always complimented her beauty, the color of her hair, and said how much he was looking forward to loving her once they were married. He'd kissed her often before marriage. And he'd respected her chastity.

Yeah, she'd fallen for his lies. How stupid, how young and innocent she'd been. Hayden, she realized now, had stalked and manipulated her. In the end, Leah realized he'd done it to get close to her father, not to her. She was a means to an end.

Dragging her arm off her eyes, Leah slowly sat up, alone in the cave. The waterfall beckoned her. The water would be freezing cold because it was snow melt, but right now, it was an opportunity to get clean before they rode out into the harsh environment of the mountains. She could smell Kell's scent on her, not wanting to wash it away. It was a perfume to her, making her lower body glow in a new and wonderful way. It made Leah acutely aware of him. And she wanted him all over again. Was it possible to store up years of orgasms? Leah shook her head and smiled a little. She didn't know. *Again.* She could fly a helicopter, meet bullets being hurled at her bird and crew, head-on, and not flinch, but she didn't even know her own body. Or a man's body.

"ARE YOU READY?" Kell asked Leah. There was the gray light of dawn, enough to see by while riding down the trail toward their next destination.

She made final arrangements to her hajji costume. "Yes."

Kell walked over and cupped his hands so she could put her boot into the stirrups. "Up you go," he said, lifting her so she could throw her leg over the horse. He saw she was focused. That was a good thing. Wishing they weren't on the run, that they could spend quality time with one another, Kell knew it wasn't going to happen. He patted her lower leg. "Just follow me."

He didn't like Leah bringing up the rear for fear of Taliban riding up behind them on these narrow goat trails. He had a map left by Sergeant Khat Shinwari. She'd made detailed drawings of all the paths in this area of the Hindu Kush. With the drone overhead, Kell felt somewhat better about their situation, but not much.

Mounting his horse, the packhorse rope tied to the back of his saddle, he pulled the mic close to his mouth. "How do you read?"

"Loud and clear," Leah said, gathering up the reins on her horse's neck.

"Let's mosey on down this mountain, then."

She smiled a little, absorbing his soft Kentucky drawl. He sat straight and confident on his horse, moving the animal out at a fast walk. After they rode through the brush opening that hid the cave, they were once more out on a narrow goat trail.

Leah looked up at the scree slope rising sharply above them. She saw snow at the top of the mountain.

Down below them, a five-hundred-foot drop-off into a rock-strewn wadi. It wasn't pleasant to think about her horse stumbling or falling into it. They'd be killed on impact. There was nothing forgiving about these mighty mountains. How many times had she flown in and around them, never fully realizing their stark beauty or the danger on the ground?

By the time the sun rose over the peaks, Kell had followed another wider, more traveled goat path that would take them into the valley far below. He would look back from time to time, to make sure Leah was doing all right. His body tightened as he thought about loving her. The time spent in that cave was a gift to both of them.

He turned around, always moving his gaze over the slopes, never totally trusting the intel of the drone or the operator flying it. Even they would sometimes miss the Taliban. While drones were useful, they weren't perfect, nor were the pilots. Kell didn't allow himself to think about Leah. About their blossoming relationship or the rage he now held toward Major Grant. All of those thoughts were distractions he couldn't afford to indulge in right now.

Leah continued to look behind her every ten minutes or so, making sure she saw no riders or goats or goat herders on the trail coming up behind them. The horses were fresh and well rested, moving out at a steady, fast walk. Kell had told her that there were Taliban crawling everywhere in these mountains. He'd talked with the master chief at Bravo, planning a route that would hopefully help them avoid meeting any of the enemy. But nothing was guaranteed.

Near noontime, Kell took another, less used goat

path that was steep and narrow. The heat of the day flowed through the Hindu Kush and they were now at seven thousand feet, heading down to a cave marked on the map. He knew that without Sergeant Shinwari's careful mapping of the area, he wouldn't have a clue as to which path to take. Finally, the path opened up a bit and Kell stood in the stirrups, looking to the right. There was a wadi gouged out of the mountain from above, slicing to the right of them, the trail becoming rocky and uneven as it flowed downward past the path they were on, for another thousand feet below them. Eyes narrowing, Kell spotted what he thought was the cave, hidden next to the wadi with a cover of brush and trees. Pulling up, he dismounted.

"I'm going to check this cave and clear it," he told Leah, tying the horse's reins to a sturdy bush.

"Roger."

Removing his AK-47 off his back, he turned the selector to single-shot and went quickly into the brush, making little noise. Kell moved and crouched by the opening. The cave had a five-foot entrance, narrowing upward. The light was good and he looked around before entering. As he cleared the oval maw, stepping to the rear, Kell spotted another tunnel leading off to the left. In this cave, according to the map, there was water. He heard nothing, moving down the smooth, white tunnel. Finally, around a curve, he heard the water dripping and saw a small pool. No tangos in the cave. They were safe.

Leah saw Kell emerge ten minutes later.

"It's clear. Let's go on in," he told her, leading his weary horse through the brush.

Leah followed. She was glad to get out of the daylight and hide. Once inside, she dismounted and followed Kell down a large tunnel, the horse's hooves making clip-clopping sounds that echoed and re-echoed around them.

She smiled as she spotted the pool of water. The horses eagerly surged forward, desperate for a drink from their half day of working. Leah stood next to Kell as they allowed the horses to drink their fill. He gazed down at her.

"Holding up?"

"I am."

"Butt sore?"

She grinned. "That's a given." Leah opened her hand, touching his. She felt his fingers draw around hers, gently squeezing them. Her heart did flip-flops beneath his dark gray eyes. She was turned on just being near Kell.

"Hungry?"

She laughed a little, feeling heat rush into her face. "Yes."

Kell gave her a wicked grin. "Maybe not for food but for something else?"

"Stop reading my mind." She laughed, embarrassed. "I think you've created a monster."

He slid his arm around her shoulders, drawing Leah against him. "Never a monster," he admonished, leaning down and giving her a kiss. "You're like a flower, Sugar. You're finding out what it's really like to be a woman. And to enjoy being one. Opening one petal at a time in my arms."

Her body was already hotly responding to his mouth, the way his lips engaged hers, coaxed her mouth open and enjoyed her response. "Okay, not a monster. Maybe a horny woman who wants to explore?"

Chuckling, Kell said, "Yeah, that sounds about right."

"All I want to think about now is sex. And you." Leah eased from beneath his arm as her horse finished drinking. Off to the left was an alcove where they could tie up the horses and get something to eat.

Kell gave her a good-natured smile. "Both compliments. I'm going to get us some MREs and we'll sit down and take a breather. The horses can use a time-out, too."

As they sat near the pool and ate, Leah asked, "What's our destination today?"

"I'm hoping we can get down to about six thousand feet," he said. "There's another cave, no water, but we'll stay there the night. After that, we can make a run for Bravo. We'll be within fifteen miles of it, a good day's ride, but doable." Providing they didn't run into groups of Taliban. Providing the drone was still available and working. Nothing could be relied upon a hundred percent and Kell knew it. He kept all of it to himself, not wanting Leah to be stressed out.

"Do you have to check in with the master chief?"

"Soon as I'm done chowing down, I'll raise him on the sat phone. Gotta see if that drone's still active around this area, and find out where the Taliban have moved and if we've got a clear shot at that cave or not."

Leah grimaced. "I'm so afraid of running into a group. There's no place to turn around on these paths. No place to hide or protect ourselves."

"I know. It's a dicey way to travel." But they didn't have any options. Kell saw the anxiety in her eyes even though Leah didn't say anything. A little fear was a good thing because it kept them sharp. "How's your head injury? I forgot to ask this morning."

She touched her hair. "Fine. No headache." Leah lifted her arm, the dressing still on it. "No problem here, either."

"What will happen with your flying status once we get back to Bravo?"

Shrugging, she said, "I'm sure a flight surgeon will check me out, make sure I'm ready to fly again."

"Does that mean you have to go to Bagram?"

"God, I hope not," Leah muttered, finishing off her MRE. She set it aside. "I'm hoping one will come to Bravo to check me out. I don't want to go to Bagram. I don't want to have to interface with Hayden." She felt an ugly chill down her spine, trying to ignore it.

Kell saw her eyes became dark. "Be proactive and when we get back to Bravo, make a call and request the flight surgeon come to you."

Snorting, Leah said, "You're right. I'll do that." She grimaced. "Kell, I'm feeling a lot of anger toward Hayden. It's never happened before."

"That's not a bad thing, Leah. You have a lot of banked rage over what he did to you. Maybe long overdue? Anger isn't a bad thing, you know. It's how we handle it that counts."

Leah looked around and then her gaze settled back on Kell's thoughtful expression. "My marriage, if you can call it that, was a total sham. I see that now more than ever. Hayden used me. And—" she rubbed her hands down her pants "—I don't know what to do with my rage. I'm afraid if I see him, I'll hit the son of a bitch."

Kell said nothing. If he ever saw Major Grant, he'd be hard-pressed to do nothing, either. Leah was struggling. He could see it in her eyes and hear it in her tightened voice. "Maybe part of healing is working through this anger, Leah. Talkin' about it is good."

"Maybe," she muttered. "Right now, all morning, I've been thinking about him, Kell. What he did to me. How I stupidly allowed him to maneuver me to get to my father." She gave him a frustrated look. "Why didn't I see it coming?"

"I don't know, Sugar. It's more important you learn from it, remember the signs, the way he manipulated you, so that you never let it happen again."

Rubbing her face, she rattled, "I swear, I want to put my fist right through his mouth."

"Glad you're angry at him and not me," Kell drawled, teasing her a little.

Leah stood up and started to pace. "I've never hit anyone, Kell. But the feelings coming up in me are full of unadulterated rage."

"It's okay to feel that way." Because he wanted to kill Grant, pure and simple. Kell wouldn't act on it, but damn, he wanted to deck the bastard for all he'd done to Leah. As a SEAL, his hands were considered lethal weapons. He knew many ways to kill. And all SEALs were under orders to never allow their training, even in a bar fight, to escalate. They had to stand down. Stand back. Hopefully de-escalate the conflict.

He'd been in bars before when the local guys found out he and his team were SEALs. They never started fights, but they sure as hell finished them. And of course, when it happened, the master chief had to get involved, convince the local police not to press as-

sault charges against them. It always worked, but Kell
was more than aware of his lethal capabilities. Still, it
would feel good to take Grant down. The bastard was
a sexual predator and an abuser. And he was still on
the loose, still able to do it again. That's what really
bothered Kell. He got away with it once, with Leah.
How many other women since her had suffered a similar fate?

Leah continued to pace. It actually felt good to
move and get rid of the pain of riding in that awful
wooden saddle. Finally, she came and sat down next
to Kell.

"Tell me something about your growing-up years
that I don't know already."

He held her curious look. "So you can compare?"
Or maybe just to talk about something more positive,
to get her mind off the anger rolling through her?

"Yes."

"That's tough to do, Leah. Your life took different
twists and turns than mine did." He touched her cheek
and felt her pain. She was wrestling with not only her
marriage, but how she saw herself in relation to her
family. He'd told her most things a few days ago, but
added in a conspiratorial tone, "We grew up in rural
Kentucky. I went barefoot until my ma told me I had
to have shoes in order to go to school."

Leah smiled, lulled beneath his accent, the warmth
in his gray eyes. "Really?"

He leaned against the wall and put his MRE aside.
"Yeah, we three boys were wild hellions when we
were young. We tracked, we hunted and we got into
all kinds of adventures."

"Maybe that's why you're in black ops now."

Shrugging, Kell said, "It didn't hurt that we already knew how to recon an area, live off the land, track and shoot like snipers," he agreed, smiling a little.

"Where are Cody and Tyler now?"

"Ty is with Seal Team Eight and Cody is with his A team in southern Afghanistan, near Kandahar."

"And are they married?"

"Them?" He chuckled. "No, not by a long shot. Cody is a partier by nature. He likes women and they like him, but no moss is growing under his feet."

"And Tyler?"

"He's the youngest among us," Kell said. "He's introverted, but sees the positives in life. Loves adventure. And he dearly loves blowing things up. My youngest brother wants to live life to its fullest and have no regrets."

"And you?" Leah asked, holding his gray gaze. "How would your brothers describe you?"

"The quiet one," Kell admitted. "I'm the introvert. The loner. The one who gets touched by the beauty of the earth, the kid who lay on his back and watched clouds form and shape and drift by for hours at a time." He smiled a little, tipping his head back on the wall. "You'll hear a lot of other things—" and he gave her a wicked look "—when you come home with me for Thanksgiving. They'll fill your ears with tales about me."

"True stuff?" Leah asked, smiling, feeling warmth open her heart, because the look he gave her was intimate. She felt as if she were his woman. She *wanted* to be his woman. But was it really possible? Leah didn't have an answer.

"Oh," he murmured, chuckling, "part truth, part a big windy."

"Big windy?"

"Lies," he said. "Hill-speak for not telling the truth."

"You're the oldest?"

"Yes, I am. When we were little, they hated that I was older than them. Cody and Ty were always trying to make me look bad in front of my parents. I was responsible for them, and if I couldn't keep them on the straight and narrow, my folks would land on me with both feet."

"You've always been the responsible one." *Like me.*

"Someone's gotta do the duty," Kell drawled, meeting and holding her stare. "You'll find out plenty about my two brothers when we're at home. They play hard and they work hard. They're good men. They have integrity and their word is their bond."

"Your mother and father are like that, right?"

Nodding, Kell said, "Yes. Even though we were like little wild animals growing up, we were taught right from wrong. To tell the truth and not lie."

"Does your Mom ever want you boys to get married and settle down?"

Kell grinned. "All the time. She comes from a big family of ten. She was used to having a mob of aunts, uncles and two sets of grandparents around her growing up. We keep trying to tell her that being in the SEALs or in the Special Forces isn't good on a marriage. Too many of my SEAL friends who have married, have broken up, like we did. It's a hard life on a woman or a woman with children. The man just isn't around that much, and it all falls on her shoulders."

Leah absorbed his words. "Worse," she added, "because you're black ops, you can't tell your wife anything. Not where you are. Or what you're doing." How would it feel to live with a man when he could never share half of his life with her? Leah didn't find that very positive. Why get married if the two were never together? Or rarely?

"Right. My ma thinks we're telling her a big windy about it, but we're not. She saw my marriage self-destruct. There's a ninety-percent divorce rate among my kind, so that sort of says it all."

Leah roused herself. "Are your brothers as good-looking as you are?" She saw his cheeks turn a ruddy color. Kell was blushing! And her heart opened fiercely to him. He didn't see himself in that way.

"Actually, to hear my brothers talk, you'd think I was the underside of a lily pad." He laughed.

"And that's Kentucky-ese for what?"

"They consider me plain looking in comparison to them," he said, his smile broadening. "When you meet my brothers, you can make up your own mind. My ma always said Cody and Ty are heartbreakers. And they are. Women flock to them like bees to the flowers."

"Well," Leah said, turning and kissing him lightly, "you are eye candy in my book."

He held her close, took her mouth more surely against his, kissing her deeply. As he eased away, Kell rasped, "Your opinion is the only one that counts with me, Leah."

CHAPTER FOURTEEN

KELL SCOWLED AND punched his sat phone off. He stood near the entrance to the cave, the noontime sun overhead. Things were going to hell in a handbasket according to Ax.

Pushing his fingers through his hair, he leaned against the opening, thinking about strategies and alternatives. *Damn.* His heart was in the mix even though it shouldn't be there. He worried for Leah and didn't want her in jeopardy—again. What the hell was he going to do? This wasn't a situation where he could call in his team and they'd be there for them. Camp Bravo was between fifteen to twenty-five miles away, depending upon avoiding Taliban riders. Taking a deep breath, he pushed off from the wall and walked silently back to where Leah and the horses were resting.

Leah looked up, sensing Kell's presence before she saw him. They had an invisible connection to one another. She felt it in her heart. His face was set and his gray eyes dark. Something was wrong. She watched as he came and crouched opposite her, the sat phone dangled between his long, spare fingers.

"What's wrong?"

Kell saw the sudden wariness come to her eyes. Leah could read him like a book, but he wasn't surprised. Their time with one another had been short, but intense and concentrated. And he'd allowed himself to become vulnerable with her, something he'd never done with another woman this soon after knowing her. "We got some strategy to figure out," he said, keeping his voice calm and unemotional. "We've lost the drone overhead due to a higher-priority order. It got called to a firefight north of here. And we won't be getting it back soon enough to help us. The last streaming video from the drone showed there's three major groups of Taliban on horseback between us and Bravo."

"Can we stay here and wait until we get the drone back?" Leah saw him frown. He sat down, crossed his legs after pulling out the map he'd taken from Sergeant Khat Shinwari's cave, studying it.

"No. We have a group of Taliban on the path I was going to take to get down to that other cave," he murmured, having committed part of the map to memory. "They're on their way right now, and we're going to have to get out of here in the next thirty minutes. I'm trying to figure out where best to go now in order to avoid them."

"How many?"

"Forty men."

She swallowed against a dry throat, her pulse beating a little harder. "Can't we get help from Bravo?"

"No," Kell said quietly, intently studying the map. "All the Apaches are out on other missions. It's the spring assault and every piece of equipment that will fly is assigned elsewhere to firefight missions. The Taliban, according to Ax, is ramping up, and they've got three major assaults underway within thirty miles of the border. We're right in the middle of that area."

He didn't want to upset Leah, but he wasn't going to lie to her, either. Just not tell her the whole truth. Being a pilot, she never had to concern herself with ground combat. Kell glanced up. Her eyes were filled with concern, her mouth set. She was a warrior and he saw her moving that side of her to the forefront.

"Then we're on our own."

"Yes."

Leah felt her stomach clench. She lamented that their intimacy, their time with one another, was gone. It would be a race to get to Bravo without getting killed or captured. And without air assets available, no drone eyes in the sky, everything was landing on Kell's broad shoulders and years of experience as an operator to get them home. She said nothing, watching him stare at the map in his hands. If anyone could get them out of this situation, he could.

"How can I help?"

Lifting his chin, Kell stared at her serious demeanor. Gone was the soft, vulnerable woman he'd made love to and had cared for. He got up, moved to her side and spread the map out before her. "This small path is a very steep descent, but it can get us down to a lower elevation and we can avoid this Taliban party coming our way by taking it."

"The lower we go, the more trees and brush are around," Leah said. "It could provide us cover."

He gave her a proud look. "Now you're thinking like us ground pounders."

She smiled a little, inwardly anxious and not wanting to let Kell know about it. He had enough on his shoulders to contend with right now. "I'm trying.

Tough for a pilot who is used to flying in the sky, not surviving combat on the ground, believe me."

He moved his arm about her shoulders, pulling her close for just a moment. It was a selfish act. Kell knew things were going to get tense very soon. And when, not if, they made it to Bravo, their time together there was going to be severely limited. He also worried about Major Grant flying into Bravo to meet Leah. "We need to stay in our hajji gear for now. I don't like riding in broad daylight. SEALs operate better at night, but we don't have a choice right now."

"When Ax gave you the positions of those three Taliban groups...?"

"Yes?"

"That doesn't mean he knows where they're heading, right? That they can change course? We could possibly intercept them by accident?"

He moved his fingers across her nape, feeling the tension in it. Massaging the area, he said, "All that is possible."

Leah wanted to melt beneath his hand, groaning as he loosened those tightly corded muscles. All she wanted was to fall into his arms and forget everything else. A purely selfish and dangerous wish. "Okay, let's mount up."

He gave her a nod and stood up. Holding out his hand to her, Leah took it and he pulled her to her feet. She stood inches away from him. Kell was in complete SEAL mode right now. His game face was in place and she could feel him thinking, strategizing and preparing for all kinds of what-ifs they might be challenged with during their journey.

She moved over to her horse, tightened the loose cinch and saw him do the same with his bay gelding.

They gave their mounts water and then led their animals out beyond the cave, the sunlight hot and bearing down on them. Kell helped Leah mount up and then he threw a leg over his larger, taller horse. He turned, checking the packhorse rope, making sure it was tied. Their rucks and their weapons were on that horse and he wanted to make sure it couldn't get loose and run away. That would be a disaster for them.

Kell squinted and found that smaller, less used goat path. It led almost to a 7 percent grade down through brush. The trail had a lot of loose rocks on it, telling him it was rarely used but making it impossible to move quickly. He pushed his horse forward and then began the very steep descent.

Leah felt the sweat running down between her breasts and her shoulder blades. Kell kept up a fast walk, pushing the horses on the narrow, slippery path. The rocks were a pain in the ass and Leah kept looking back up the long sloping hill. The air was hot, the wind sporadic. It would climb to over a hundred degrees down on the valley floor far below them.

Off in the distance, she saw a Shinwari village. She wondered if they could reach it, because that tribe had a peace pact with the States. Was Kell planning on going there? The village was barely visible through the rippling heat waves dancing like floating, transparent horizontal ribbons across the desert landscape. She adjusted her mic near her mouth.

"Are we going to that Shinwari village in the valley?"

"No. The area is crawling with Taliban. If they

see us and suspect we're military and not one of their kind, it would be dragging the war to their doorstep. Those people are farmers. They have a few antique firearms, but if we led the Taliban into their village, a lot of innocent people would die. We're going to avoid going anywhere near it."

Made sense to her. As they moved down, the path became less steep, the brush now growing six to ten feet tall around them. Leah felt a little safer simply because it gave them some cover from prying, alert Taliban eyes. They'd been moving for three hours on switchbacks, the horses stumbling sometimes due to the rocks. This land, Leah thought, was incredibly barren and lifeless. She didn't know how the people managed to survive in this harsh climate.

She saw Kell hold up his right hand into a fist, which meant "stop." She pulled her horse to a halt, its nose almost resting on the packhorse's rump. They were hidden by tall brush on one side. Her pulse leaped as she saw Kell stand up in the stirrups, looking intently at something up to their left. Up where they'd been hours ago. Leah turned, looking, trying to see what he saw. And then, she froze. A large group of Taliban was riding on the trail. Feeling adrenaline beginning to pump into her bloodstream, Leah automatically pulled the robe she wore aside, unstrapping the .45 in case she needed to grab it in a hurry.

"We'll just stay quiet here," Kell told her in a low tone. "If we don't move, they won't see us."

"Roger." Her voice sound tense. Hoarse. It would take them hours to reach them but that wasn't the point. Leah knew these different Taliban groups could be in radio contact with one another. They might spot them from above and radio another group somewhere else, unseen, and they could swoop down upon them instead. She leaned down, rubbing her horse's sweaty neck.

Kell dismounted and moved to the packhorse, opening up one side of the tarp. Her heart raced as he pulled out his M-4 with a grenade launcher attached to it beneath the barrel. Was he expecting trouble? She watched as he took off the AK-47 and replaced it with the M-4 rifle. The look on his face was intense. It scared her. It was one thing to be in an MH-47 helicopter with all kinds of capability, with the ability to defend herself and shoot back. Here, on a horse, not so much.

She glanced up, watching the forty men walking their horses along the path. It was a large group.

Kell looked up to see Leah's glistening face, her eyes watching the Taliban group. He tied down the tarp, gave the horse a pat on the rump and walked over to her. She came close so they could talk in low voices.

"I just spotted a second Taliban group down there." He pointed below them. "Maybe fifteen riders. We're staying put for right now because we've got good cover."

"Are they on the same path we are?"

Shaking his head, Kell said, "I don't think so. They're coming up out of the valley where we want to go." He put the rifle on his back, barrel down, and opened his cammie pocket to pull out the map to study it. He felt the tension in Leah and knew she was worried. Looking up, Kell pulled a compass out of his H-gear, opened it and studied their position. And then he studied the map some more, not liking what he'd realized. He pulled the sat phone out of his gear and made a call to Ax at Bravo.

Leah listened to the quiet conversation. Kell set the map on the ground, kneeling over it, speaking to Ax about alternative routes. She had a terrible feeling the Taliban coming up from the valley were utilizing the same path they were on. Leah held the leather reins a little tighter. They were trapped.

Finally, Kell finished the call and tucked the sat phone away in his waist gear. He turned to Leah, who was frowning and looking worried. Placing his hand on her thigh he said, "As soon as that group above us disappears, we're going to turn around and go back about five hundred feet. There's a smaller path we'll take." He pointed across her saddle toward the northwest. "It goes off in a direction that will avoid this group coming up from the valley."

She wiped the sweat off her brow, hating the wool clothes she had to wear. "Will it take us down to the valley?"

Kell nodded, his eyes narrowing. "Yes."

"Couldn't we get a Night Stalker in here?"

"No. Way too active. I asked and Ax said it's a no-go."

"At least you asked." Leah managed a tight smile, placing her hand over his.

"Never hurts," Kell said. And then he grinned slightly. "All they can do is say no." He patted her thigh and said, "I'm going to turn the horses around. I don't see the Taliban up on that upper path. Time for us to make our move."

They found the barely used path. Leah wondered how Kell could even follow it through the scrub and rocks—it was almost invisible to her eyes. She reminded herself he knew how to track, how to see things most people wouldn't. Right now, she was blessing his Kentucky background, the fact he'd been an untamed little boy hunting and growing up in the wild mountains near his home.

By the time they reached the valley floor, the sun had shifted near the western horizon. Kell found them a small cave and Leah breathed a sigh of relief. They never ran into the other group of Taliban and little by little, relief replaced her tension. The cave was hidden, like so many were, by tall, thick vegetation in front of it. Kell dismounted and handed her the reins to his horse as he went to clear the cave with his M-4.

Leah felt more relief as he came back, took the reins of his horse and led her through the brush and into the opening. Every cave was different. This one was barely eight feet high and she had to dismount to lead her horse into it. Once inside, Kell joined her.

"We got lucky. There's water down off to that tunnel on the right. Follow me."

Water. Leah's spirits rose swiftly. She could tell the horses could smell it because they started walking faster down the tunnel, wanting to reach it. Kell turned on his penlight as the darkness grew. Always worried about the horses and the inability to find them water often enough, Leah stepped aside as the tunnel opened up into a much larger cavern. She saw the water dripping off the walls, a trough of liquid below it. The horses swiftly covered the distance, thrusting their muzzles deep beneath the water's surface, gulping in great draughts.

Kell kept the penlight on. He saw Leah looking

tired. The heat of the day bled everyone of their energy. The horses sucked noisily, their muzzles dripping with water as they finally raised their heads, sated for now.

"Let's go back where there's some light," he told Leah, pulling on the reins and leading his horse out toward the tunnel.

Leah followed. The gray light got brighter as they approached the cave.

Suddenly, she saw Kell crouch at the entrance, swiftly bring up his M-4 and begin firing.

The tunnel shattered with the roaring sounds of bullets. The horses reared, panicked. The reins were ripped out of Leah's hands. Kell started firing again. Screams drifted down the tunnel. She jerked the .45 out of its holster, running toward him as the horses ran back into the other cave. Bullets were ricocheting off the walls. Leah threw herself down on the floor, next to Kell. Her eyes widened. Six Taliban had just come into the cave!

She didn't think, just aimed and fired. The soldiers were just as surprised as they were. Kell fired, taking down all of them with head shots or body mass shots. Leah gasped as he moved like a shadow toward the bodies. He passed by them, moving to the cave opening and then disappeared outside of it. Scrambling to her feet, Leah followed, her .45 held high, ready to fire.

Just as she ran by the last Taliban soldier, his hand shot out, grabbing her by the pant leg. With a grunt, Leah fell, the .45 bouncing out of her hand. She fought, kicking with her other boot at the man's strong, sundarkened hand. He lifted his head, blood running

down his temple, his eyes filled with rage and hatred. Adrenaline surged through Leah. She was being
dragged closer! With a cry, she slammed her boot into
the man's head. He snarled, trying to get up on his
knees. Twisting, Leah jerked hard, trying to get free.
Panic struck her and she saw him get to his knees,
jerking her closer to him.

Leah suddenly saw a flash; so fast that at first she
thought she was imagining it. Kell moved like a striking snake, the heel of his palm smashing upward into
the Taliban soldier's face. She heard the sickening
crunch of bones snapping and breaking. The soldier
screamed and collapsed, falling backward, unmoving.

Kell turned, his eyes on hers. She was sobbing for
breath, frightened and trying to get up. He grabbed
her beneath the arm, hoisting her to her feet.

"Oh, God," she rasped, quickly moving to her pistol and picking it up.

"You all right?" Kell asked as he surveyed the unmoving group.

"Y-yes. I've never been so glad to see you," she
choked, breathing hard, her hand against her chest.
"I—I thought they were all dead."

Grimly, Kell shouldered the M-4 and turned, moving through the bodies, searching for anything of
value. "They are now," he growled. "Their horses are
all tied outside," he told her, leaning down, pulling
cloaks and vests aside, searching in all their pockets.
"Stand watch. I'll be done in a minute."

Kell was so calm. Heart hammering, Leah did as
he ordered. She picked up her pistol. There were six
horses tied to brush nearby. Who had heard the shots
fired? In a cave, the sounds had been amplified many

times over. Gaze darting around, Leah felt suddenly shaky, her knees feeling weak. She'd almost died— again. Unable to shake the image of the soldier's rage and hatred of her, she wiped the sweat off her temple, her .45 in her hand ready to fire. She had no idea if she'd killed any of them or not.

Kell joined her. He was stuffing items down into the lower pockets of his trousers.

"Anything?"

"Yeah, some good maps," he muttered, frowning. He looked over at her. Leah was pale, her eyes dark with fear. Reaching out, he touched her cheek. "It's over. You did fine."

Just his grazing touch, that soothing drawl of his, smothered her fear, slowed her heart rate down. "That scared the shit out of me," she managed.

Grimly, Kell nodded. "They got the drop on us. We were in the other cave, and we didn't hear them come in. They didn't know we were here, either. I heard a noise out in this cave and knew we'd been compromised."

"Really glad you're a good shot," she whispered.

"You were, too. You took one of them down."

"At least I'm able to help."

Kell nodded. "You did what you were trained to do, Leah. I'm glad you're with me. Come on, let's get our horses and get the hell out of here. Those shots are going to alert every Taliban within a two-mile radius that a firefight just went down here."

Leah had never been so glad to leave a cave as right then. By the time they were riding away, following that same nearly invisible goat path, the sun had set. There were some long clouds hanging around the peaks to the west, and shortly they turned from orange to pink. She was too worried about their situation to appreciate their color and beauty. Kell moved his horse at a trot now and she bumped along on the saddle, always off balance, having to grip the horse's mane to stay upright and not fall off.

She saw Kell talking on the sat phone as they trotted down the switchbacks. Leah was scared and kept looking around. The dusk was deep, the shadows dark, and she tried to watch for Taliban. Her heart wouldn't settle down and her pulse bounded erratically. The bliss of a few days of safety in Kell's arms, learning about a whole new world that had made her vulnerable and happy, came to a slamming, abrupt halt.

Kell seemed to be able to move between those worlds with ease. At no time did he look scared or worried. He'd been confident, a silent ghost, lethal and deadly accurate with his rifle. If there was any chance of getting out of this alive, Leah knew Kell could do it.

Night fell. Kell had his NVGs on and Leah was content to let her horse's nose follow the rump of the packhorse. She allowed the reins to relax in her hands, feeling safer because of the pitch blackness that had hidden them from the eyes of their enemies. She heard the wind blowing off the mountains, and was now glad for the thick wool cloak over her cammies.

Kell kept up the brutal pace. Her butt was so sore it never stopped aching now. Not really knowing how to ride, Leah just kept bouncing around. She didn't complain. Kell had a plan even though he'd given her strict orders not to talk on the mic. Voices carried. Whispers were even easier to pick up on with sharp-eared tangos nearby.

Kell finally halted somewhere near midnight. Leah was so grateful the horses had finally stopped. Her horse's flanks heaved with exertion. She lifted her butt out of the saddle, rubbing it and wanting to groan. Hearing Kell approach, she could see nothing. When his leg touched hers, he halted his horse.

"How are you doing?"

"Okay," she lied.

"Butt sore?"

"That's a major understatement. Where are we?"

"In the valley. Have you been drinking water? Staying hydrated?"

"Yes." She heard an edge in his low voice. "What's going on?"

"We're going to keep moving," he told her. "I've been on the sat phone with Ax. An Apache coming back for fuel had its thermal imaging on over this area. They spotted four Taliban groups settled down for the night. I've got their GPS positions and we're going to thread through all of them. You up for this?"

Leah grimaced, thinking of her butt. "Yes. Are we trotting?"

"No, too risky. We'll walk. Whatever you do, don't sneeze, don't cough, and breathe through your mouth. Our biggest worry is if one of our horses decides to whinny because there are other horses nearby. If that happens, we're in deep shit because the Taliban will know someone is moving nearby. And when they set up for the night, they don't travel. Only black ops do, and they'll know we're the enemy."

"What will they do?"

"They could fire indiscriminately in our direction, hoping to hit us, because they don't have night-vision goggles. Or they could mount up and try to find us, but again, they can't see in the dark. Probably just throw a lead curtain our way."

"Great," Leah grunted.

"We're fifteen miles from Bravo. This valley is pretty flat, but still has some ups and downs, some draws and deep washes."

"Fifteen?"

He heard hope in her husky voice. "Yeah. Providing we can get through these small camps in the area, we should reach Bravo by dawn." Kell reached out, sliding his hand over her jaw. He could see her face, her wide eyes. "Hang in there, okay, Sugar? We're almost home."

Did that ever sound good to Leah. She reached out, sliding her hand against his. Kell was so strong and self-assured. Right now, she was terrified but didn't want him to know it. "Home sounds good," she choked, sudden emotions rising in her.

"I'll get you there," Kell promised, wrapping her hand in his, kissing the back of it and then releasing it. "Let's go…"

LEAH FELT AS though her body were going to break from riding so long. Her butt had gone numb. The insides of her knees were raw and bleeding. Dawn was edging on the peaks of the Hindu Kush. She could barely see the land around her, glad to have the coming light. Her horse stumbled every once in a while, weary. She could see Kell in front of her. He guided them into a huge wash, tall enough to hide them, and he dismounted.

Leah wasn't sure she could get off the horse and

was grateful when Kell walked back to get her. He placed his hands around her waist and lifted her out of the saddle. She bit her lip, trying not to groan as he placed her feet on the ground. Wobbling, she reached out, gripping his arms.

"Damn," she muttered, "I feel like I'm going to fall apart."

Kell laughed softly and began removing her hajji gear. "Just think of a hot shower back at Bravo. That will ease our aches and numbness."

"What are you doing?"

"We're getting out of this stuff. I'm going to get our rucks and weapons off the packhorse. We're going to ride in cammies with our gear. I'll take the harness off the packhorse and let it go. It will survive out here on its own just fine. When we make a run for Bravo, I don't want to be slowed down by it."

Nodding, she quickly divested herself of the Afghan garb. "Sounds good."

"Come on," Kell urged, his hand around her upper arm. Leah walked bowlegged and he smiled a little. He knew she'd never ridden a horse before, and she'd been a trooper, never complaining.

Opening the tarp, he helped Leah into her ruck and quickly got it situated across her shoulders. He took his ruck, laid it on the ground and then pulled the Win-Mag sheath off the packhorse and strapped it barrel down on his ruck. Standing, he hauled the gear over his shoulders and strapped up.

Leah stood back as he got rid of the harness and removed the halter from the wet, weary animal. He slapped it on the rump and the horse moved away, but remained with the others because he was a herd animal.

Kell looked over at Leah. He put his M-4 in a harness over his left shoulder and approached her. She glanced up and smiled at him. Groaning inwardly, he slid his hands around her face, leaning down, kissing her, feeling her return it, her hands against his chest. Her lips were soft, giving, taking, and he felt himself missing her so damn much already. Easing from her mouth, Kell smiled into her glistening eyes. "I'm going to miss what we had back in those caves," he told her.

Her legs felt shaky and it wasn't because she'd been riding. "I'm afraid, Kell. I'm afraid when we get back to Bravo we'll never see one another again."

He gave her a very confident smile. "That's not going to happen." He grazed her cheek with his thumb. "The first couple of days after getting back are going to be hectic. I'm going to have to devote a lot of time to sit reps, writing up a report on this whole journey of ours. But I'll be around. And I'm going to hunt you down, so don't worry."

She frowned, feeling uneasy. "You can't come over to the squadron office, Kell. They'll suspect something between us…"

He chuckled and dropped a kiss on her lips. "I'm black ops. Remember? I'll find you before you even know I'm there."

She felt her heart expand with love for him. Leah almost spoke the word, but was afraid. Their lives were huge holes of unknown everything. Combat guaranteed nothing but chaos, no normality, nothing either of them could count on. "Okay," she whispered, her voice unsteady. Digging into his amused gaze, she said, "Kell, I *like* you. I don't care if I'm an officer and you're not."

"Shh," he said, placing his finger against her lips. "You're a part of my life, Leah. That's not going to change unless you say differently." Kell lost his smile and wanted to reassure her because he saw her concern. "When we ride into Bravo, you stick with me, all right? We've got a small barn and corral on the other side of the SEAL HQ and we'll take the animals over there. And once that's done, I want to introduce you to my master chief and the men in my team."

"Because?"

"Because you're my woman and I want my team to know you on sight. We take care of our own, Leah. You can ask any SEAL at Bravo for help, and he'll give it to you without question because you're mine."

All her worries dissolved. His voice was deep with hidden emotion but she saw it in the hard glitter of his eyes. "I want to meet them," she told him.

"Good," Kell murmured. "Come on, I'll help you back into that torture rig we call a saddle."

Just as Leah turned, she gasped. Kell whirled around, going for his M-4.

"Hey, Ballard, we've come out here to rescue your sorry ass."

CHAPTER FIFTEEN

"It's all right," Kell reassured Leah, turning and placing his hand on hers, which was going for her pistol. "It's my team. Stand down."

Leah felt her heart galloping in her chest as four SEALs appeared silently out of the surrounding brush. She pressed her hand to her chest, feeling her fear dissolve. The men were all grinning at Kell. They were dressed in cammies and boonie hats, and carried M-4s. They all wore camouflage face paint to blend into the surrounding environment. The man who had spoken was smiling widely and walking toward Kell. He had an oval face, was at least six feet tall with long-ish blond hair and a beard. His eyes were hazel. He walked with purpose, his face hard and those eyes of his glinting fiercely. Leah decided this SEAL wouldn't be someone to mess with. He gave new meaning to the word *intensity*.

"We're giving you a Protective Service Detail, Ballard." He moved his rifle aside and slapped him heartily on the back.

Kell snorted and muttered, "Bullshit, Clutch." He slapped him on the back good-naturedly and then released his best friend. "Did Ax send you out here?"

"Yeah, you know how he is, a mother hen." Clutch's

eyes lit up and he stared over at Leah. "Is this our pilot? Chief Mackenzie?"

Kell gripped his friend by his thick shoulder. "Stand down, she's taken."

Clutch's blond brows rose and he stared up at him. "No shit?"

"No shit." Kell gestured for the rest of his men to come over. He pulled Leah to his side.

"Leah, you need to meet my notorious team." He pointed to the tallest, "This is Brad Doran, but we call him Clutch because he's someone you can rely on in a hot firefight. You can call him Brad if he's being nice to you, if you want."

Snickers abounded, Leah noticed. She felt the camaraderie between all of them, as if they were, indeed, a group of brothers.

"And this is Grayson McCoy, who we call Trace," Kell said, pointing to the SEAL with brown hair and hazel eyes. "He can disappear, literally, without a trace, which is how he got his name."

McCoy smiled and lifted his hand in hello to Leah. She liked the bearded SEAL, his eyes warm with welcome.

"This is Jerry Stadler, who we sweetly refer to as Breach."

Breach snarled, "Jesus, Kell, curse me out, but don't call me sweet."

The team snickered again, enjoying getting under Breach's thin skin. Leah didn't know what to think, never having been around SEALs before like this. Yes, she ferried them to and from ops, but never engaged with them personally. They looked like a group of hormone-ridden teenage boys out on a risky lark, more than ready for a little adventure and wanting to leave some mayhem in their wake.

Kell ignored Breach's bad mood and said, "This last dude is Andy Domanico. We call him Dom."

Leah lifted her hand. "Nice to meet all of you." She saw they simply stared at her, nodded, but that was it. These were toughened, uncompromising men. Good thing they were on her side. Kell, in comparison, was easy to read, but she figured these four men had their game faces on. Plus, they were in enemy territory.

Clutch said, "Ax wanted us to escort you in. I'm going to put us out in a diamond pattern around the likes of you and your ponies. We'll be making sure the area's clear so you two can ride into Bravo safe and sound."

Kell nodded. "Sounds good. Go for it."

Clutch tapped the mic near his lips. "We're all on the same channel just in case something happens. There's been a ten-man Taliban mortar team harassing the camp nightly, and we know they hide somewhere out here. We didn't want you running into them and raising hell." He gave Kell a wicked grin.

Kell sent them on their way and turned to Leah. "They're nice guys but right now we've got Taliban hiding out here," he told her. Cupping his hands, he helped her up on the horse. He saw her grimace as she carefully sat down on the saddle. Patting her thigh, he said, "Remember that hot shower? It's not too far away, Sugar."

Leah groaned and nodded, picking up the reins. It felt freeing to know they were surrounded by four other SEALs. Leah tried to see them, but never succeeded. They blended into the landscape and disappeared. The dawn was getting brighter. Some of her tension melted just knowing they were close to the forward operating base. It represented security to her.

KELL SAW THE SECURITY gate open as he rode with Leah at his side up the slight incline toward Bravo. His team had remained behind, continuing to search for that Taliban mortar team. He lifted his hand to the two Marines who guarded the gate. Leah rode at his side and he guided her off to the right toward the low, concrete one-story building that housed the SEAL contingent.

As they drew close, Leah saw at least ten SEALs waiting outside to meet them. She smiled to herself, understanding that Kell was one of their own and they were glad to have him back inside the wire, safe. Her heart felt heavy because her time with Kell was over.

The SEALs were all dressed in desert cammies. When Kell dismounted, he was instantly surrounded, his brothers clapping him heartily on the back, shaking his hand, welcoming him back among them.

She sat in the saddle, smiling, seeing the relieved and happy expressions on the men's faces. She wished her squadron had that kind of tight-knit, positive feeling, but it didn't.

Kell turned and made his way between his friends to where Leah sat on the horse. "Ready to get out of that torture trap?" he teased, grinning and holding up his hands to her.

Leah saw a number of the SEALs hanging around, curious and listening. A few of them gave her looks that made her blush. She felt as though she were among a pack of male alpha wolves. "Yes." She didn't want to embarrass herself in front of them and dismounted under her own steam. She felt Kell's hand settle on her upper arm, steadying her as she pulled her boot out of the stirrup. And then she looked up to see all of them watching her. It was disturbing because when they looked at her, she felt as if they had X-ray vision, looking straight through her. As if they knew everything about her lurid past.

"Why are they staring at me like that?" she asked in a whisper, turning away from them.

Kell smiled. "I told them you're my woman. They're checking you out. They asked me if I dirt dived you yet and I told them I had."

Heat crawled up into Leah's face and she rolled her eyes. "What does dirt dive mean? It sounds…rude…"

He laughed heartily. "No, it means to know someone really well, that it's not a one-night-stand kind of thing. It means I'm serious about you, that this isn't a passing fancy." He squeezed her arm and said, "It's a compliment, not meant to embarrass you, Leah. Don't worry about it." Kell lifted his head and walked at her side. "My brothers will take care of the horses for us. Let's go inside. I need you to meet Ax and to introduce you to everyone else."

Leah wasn't so sure about being surrounded by all this high-octane male testosterone. She could feel the stares in her back as the group followed them into the building. The first place Kell took her was to the master chief's small, cramped office.

Ax looked up as they came in. He stood and offered his hand to Leah. "Welcome back, Chief Mackenzie."

His hand was huge! Scarred with lots of calluses, but when Leah took it his grip was gentle, even though he must have stood a couple inches taller than Kell.

"Thank you, Master Chief. It's good to be back." She released his hand. "If it wasn't for Kell, I would be dead." Choking up a little as the master chief stood there watching her, she explained, "I never knew what SEALs did, really. But I do now. Kell is a hero. You need to know that. He deserves to be written up for a medal." She saw Ax give her a slight smile, his gaze pinned on Kell.

"He was just doing his job, ma'am."

Just doing his job? Leah stared at him and sputtered, "But he saved my life."

"Yes, ma'am," Ax rumbled. "That's the nature of what we're trained to do." He tried to sound less abrasive. "Can we get you a cup of good coffee? Can I make a call over to your squadron commander and let him know you're safe here, inside the wire?"

"That would be very nice, Master Chief. Thank you."

"Ballard, why don't you get the chief some coffee while I make that call?"

"I'll be right back."

"Sit down," Ax invited her. He picked up the phone and made a short, terse call to the CO.

Unsure, Leah warily sat. This man had real power. His office was a mess, with three sat phones and a number of different types of radios near his right hand. There were reports in leaning stacks that looked like piled-up pancakes all across his desk. Ax was a huge man, the chair creaking loudly in protest when he sat down.

Kell returned and Leah gave him a grateful look as he handed her the cup of coffee. She thanked him.

"Close the door," Ax ordered Kell.

Kell did so and sat down with his own cup of coffee in the other chair.

"Ma'am, if it's not too much trouble, would you humor me by filling out a sit rep on your experience with us?"

Leah shrugged. "No problem, Master Chief. First, I need to talk with Captain Markley, my CO. I could get to it after that. Is that all right?"

"Yes, ma'am, that's fine. Whenever one of our men performs a rescue, planned or not, if the survivor is willing, we like to have him or her fill out a sit rep for our files. It's routine SOP."

Kell grinned and sipped his coffee. He gave Leah a sideward glance. "Ax likes making paperwork for everyone." He made a flourish toward the desk. "You can tell."

Leah grinned.

Ax scowled. His mouth tightened. "Ma'am, there's a special reason I'm asking for this, and you need to know, we've got your six on this. Major Hayden Grant, the battalion commander, has accused you of being at the controls when that bird went down. Now—" Ax looked over at Kell "—Chief Ballard already told me his side of what he saw. But I need your sit rep because your CO is pissed up to the gum stumps, and he's gunning for you."

"I didn't have the controls," Leah stated coldly, defensively, stunned by the information. Damn Hayden!

Kell watched as color drained from Leah's face. She sat up, her mouth hardening. He wanted to touch her, reassure her, but he couldn't. "I was informed by Ax that Major Grant had made the accusation against you," he quietly told Leah.

"You didn't say anything about it to me," she said, her voice strained as she stared over at him.

"You had enough on your plate out there. You were dealing with shock from the crash. I made the decision to wait and let Ax tell you after we got you back to Bravo." Kell gave her a look he hoped she realized was caring. He saw the sharpness in her gaze disappear, her mouth soften as she nodded.

"I understand," she choked.

Ax sighed heavily and looked at both of them. "Ma'am, I don't know what's going on here. It's none of my business unless one of my men gets sucked into it, and then it does become my business. I asked Chief Ballard to go back to that crash site and retrieve anything and everything he could. All that evidence is going to be turned over to Major Grant. Kell found the flight recorder. I'm going to send Clutch to Bagram with it tomorrow morning and have it delivered to him in person. That should clear up this little tempest in a teapot and I can get back to running the platoon instead of dealing with a pissant major who likes to stir up shit just for the pure joy of doing it. That twerp wouldn't last two seconds in my platoon with that kind of game playing. We have far better things to do with our time than play grab-ass politics with a sister service."

"That tape will clear me," Leah said strongly. She tried to keep the anger out of her tone.

"Well," Ax grumbled, "that Army officer is on a mission."

"He's my ex-husband."

Ax's brows shot up and then he made a grumpy sound and sat back in his chair. "It's personal, then?"

"Very," she breathed. Leah saw the master chief's beefy face grow less hostile and irritated.

"Sorry to hear that, Chief."

"I'm sorry this happened, Master Chief. I wouldn't be sitting here if it weren't for Kell."

"I need to get Chief Mackenzie over to her squadron," Kell said.

"Do it."

Leah felt tired and deflated as she walked across Bravo with Kell at her side. "Why didn't you tell me Hayden said that?" she demanded.

"You didn't need any more stress on you than you already had, Leah." He dug into her worried gaze. "I figured Grant was blowing hot air. He wasn't at that crash site. I was. And so were you. It's our two eyewitness accounts against his hot air."

"He's just trying to cause me trouble," she muttered irritably.

"Why now?"

"He's going up for early colonel recommendation. I'm sure he wants me to put in some kind words to my father for him." Her mouth flattened. "Like hell I will."

"So he's trying to blackmail you?"

"Exactly."

"Look, why don't you check in with your CO and we'll meet for lunch over at the chow hall? Maybe he'll have more intel on this accusation."

She tiredly rubbed her brow. Right now, all Leah wanted was to crawl into Kell's arms and hide. She could feel that powerful sense of protection washing over her. It was in his eyes, in the set of his mouth. "That's a great idea." She looked at her watch. "Two hours. That will give me time to check in, grab a shower, a clean flight suit, and I'll probably feel halfway human."

He smiled down at her, wanting to touch her, graze her mussed hair in a ponytail. "You look beautiful right now." Hell, she looked beautiful with or without clothes on.

Wanting to reach out, but stopping herself, Leah had to get used to the fact they were now in civilization. "I wish," she said softly, holding his warm gaze, "we were back in that first cave where you rescued me."

"But we aren't," he said gently. "There will be other times and places, Leah. Right now, I want to get you cleaned up, and I want some food in that belly of yours. We've been on the run for days and we've both lost weight we can't afford to lose."

"You're such a big, bad guard dog, Ballard."

"Better believe it, Sugar." He winked at her. "See you over at the chow hall in two hours."

Leah watched Kell turn around and leave. He wore a black baseball cap and his M-4 was in a sling across his chest. She looked at other men, comparing them to him. The way he walked, the boneless animal grace, stole her heart. He had confidence she'd never seen anywhere else, other than in the men at the SEAL HQ just now.

KELL WAITED OUTSIDE the chow hall. His heart hammered briefly as he saw Leah walking confidently down the avenue. She looked good in her desert-colored flight suit, although it didn't show off her curves, which he knew so well. Her hair was loose and he could tell it was damp, barely touching her shoulders. When he met her eyes, he smiled a silent welcome to her. There were a lot of people milling around the entrance to the chow hall and he stepped out of the way of the traffic.

Leah smiled up at him. "I'm starving. How about you?" She him gave him a wicked look.

Kell's smile widened. "Oh, I'm starving all right."

"Poorly phrased," she admitted, feeling heat sweep up her neck and into her face. "Hungry for *food*," she admitted with a soft laugh.

Leah turned away because of the intense, burning look in Kell's eyes after her remark, remembering their intimacy with one another. Around him, her shields dissolved and she was fully vulnerable to him in every way. Swallowing hard, she walked with him into the busy facility. Just being with Kell made her needy for him again.

"It's okay," he soothed, giving her a teasing glance. Kell held the door open for Leah and followed her in. The place was packed with the noontime crowd, mostly men in uniform, although there were civilians among them.

As they stood in the chow line, Kell saw her remove her baseball cap and stick it into the thigh pocket of her uniform. He inhaled Leah's scent along with the fragrance of the soap she'd recently used. "What? You traded in my lye soap for almond-scented shower gel instead?" he teased.

Turning, Leah nodded. "You bet I did," she said. Pushing her fingers through her damp hair she added, "It feels so good to be clean." And her body was responding to his quiet, powerful presence whether she wanted it to or not. She knew Kell well enough to see that gleam in his eyes that was meant solely for her. It wasn't obvious, but she felt heat course through her in response to that look. The man could turn a rock on. Hell, he'd turned her on, a major miracle in and of itself.

"How are things in your neck of the woods?" Kell picked up two trays, handing one to her. He didn't really care if the men, who always watched the few women that came to the chow hall, knew he was with her or not. But maybe it'd go a long way to make a subtle statement to other males that Leah was taken. She was his. And there would be no hiding the fact that if they met here every once in a while to eat together gossip would start. Forward operating bases were magnified fishbowls of the human condition. One of the worst kinds. There were a thousand personnel here at Bravo and 95 percent of them were men.

Leah spotted a hamburger and added it to her tray. Her stomach was growling. She ignored the looks she always got from the men. With Kell behind her, maybe she wouldn't get hit on, which usually always happened.

Once they were through the line, Kell said, "Over here." There were two empty seats at the rear of the chow hall. They could sit together and he would have his back to the wall so he could see everything out in front of them. SEALs never sat with their backs to an entrance or exit, or near windows.

Leah took the end seat at the long table filled with the Marine security force that kept Bravo safe. She recognized the two sentries who had let them in earlier in the morning and nodded a hello in their direction. Kell sat between her and a Marine Corps sergeant.

Settling in, Leah put a lot of ketchup on her fries. "Our first real meal together," she teased, grinning. She liked the way his mouth curved at the corners. On Kell's tray were four hamburgers and twice the amount of French fries she had on her tray. She had one hamburger. He was a helluva lot taller and weighed much more than she did.

"One of many to come," he promised her, picking up a hamburger. Kell noticed the men at the table looking longingly at Leah. He wondered how women in general handled this kind of alpha-male, testosterone-laden environment. Leah completely shut it out, busy eating. He could feel she'd put up her shields, so maybe that was her way of dealing with it. Women out here on the frontier were few and far between.

Leah had waited until the men across from her had eaten and left. She didn't want to have a private conversation with Kell that could be overheard by others. Finally, the table cleared as she ate a huge piece of cherry pie for dessert. Sometimes, her elbow would accidentally graze Kell's elbow. Every touch felt good to Leah. She yearned to be in his arms, to kiss that wonderfully male mouth of his, to sink against him as the world melted away.

"How's it going over at the squadron?" Kell asked her, pushing his tray to the other side of the table.

"My CO, Captain Markley, told me Hayden is gunning for me."

"Is this the first time?"

"No." Leah finished her cherry pie and put the tray to the opposite side of the table. Picking up her mug of coffee, she said, "Hayden gets this way when he wants me to put in a good word with my father to have him considered for the next early rank selection. He's up for light colonel, so he thinks I'm going to aid and abet him." Her voice turned to a growl. "Not this time."

Kell nodded and picked up his coffee, sipping it. "That flight recorder leaves tomorrow morning. Clutch's been assigned to hop a flight into Bagram and personally hand deliver it to Grant. I'll be interested in what Clutch sees in him." In more ways than one. Kell wished it had been him that Ax had assigned to take the recorder to the bastard. He wanted eyes on Grant to ferret out his weaknesses and strengths.

Leah smiled a little. "You guys go by such funny names."

"The master chief gives everyone a nickname when we first enter our platoon," Kell told her. "Clutch got his name because he's good in the clutch. He's solid, steady and reliable." He chuckled. "And if you knew Clutch, he gives the name new meaning."

"How so?" Leah asked, enjoying his closeness, his Southern drawl.

"Clutch and I went through the same class at BUD/S to become SEALs. He came out of a very rich family. And he has a mind like a razor. He's a good man, Leah, someone you want on your mission. Clutch trusts no one, sees their weaknesses and can exploit the hell out of them. He always goes for the jugular when it comes to a tango."

"When I saw him appear out of those bushes, he scared the hell out of me," she admitted.

"Yeah, he's pretty intimidating when he wants to be." Kell agreed. "But no one will have your back like he will, either. Clutch's loyalty is to his SEAL brothers. Everyone else comes second." And then Kell smiled a little. "Except for you, of course."

She felt heat rising into her cheeks. "Why did you have to tell everyone we're a couple?"

"Because it's how SEALs work. No one will hit on you. If one of the team guys is around and they see you, they'll keep an eye out for you. And if you have a problem or a question, you can go over to our HQ and ask Ax. He's our manager, so to speak, and he's the go-to guy if you need anything. He'll make it happen."

"But does Ax know about us?"

"No. But he will shortly. When I get back to the HQ after lunch, I intend to tell him."

"I don't think he'll take it well."

"Probably not, but he'll get over it," Kell murmured. He held her worried-looking green gaze. "And he won't throw you to the dogs, Leah. He'll protect you. Even though he's going to raise hell with me and give me this parent-child talk about officers not consorting with enlisted men, he'll do right by me and you. He'll have our six."

Leah wasn't so sure. "Are you sure you won't get in trouble, Kell?" She knew of other mismatched relationships in the military, had seen an officer lose rank and an enlisted woman court-martialed and kicked out of the Army.

"Nah, don't worry about it, Sugar. You just keep getting well." He looked at her arm. The bandage was off and he could see the red line indicating where the original gash had occurred. "You getting a flight surgeon to check you out?"

"Markley's calling Hayden to see if he'll cut loose a flight surgeon to fly out here to examine me."

"Think it will happen?"

Leah frowned. "I don't know." She moved the cup slowly around in her hands, studying it. "I just don't want to get cornered by him again, Kell."

He heard real concern in her voice, saw it in her face. "Keep me posted on that, okay?"

"Why?"

He straightened and rolled his shoulders. "Because, if you are forced to fly into Bagram, I'll make sure I'm going with you."

Relief plunged through her. "Really?" She saw Kell's eyes narrow and felt the energy shift around him. That protective embrace was once more in place around her.

"I'm not leaving you alone with that bastard." *Never again. Not ever.*

"I could use the moral support." Leah knew she'd get called into his office behind closed doors. Just knowing that Kell was nearby was good enough for her.

"You'll always have my support." Kell cut her a serious look. "I have your back, Leah."

"Well," she muttered, "let's just cross our fingers Hayden approves the flight surgeon coming here."

KELL KNOCKED ON the master chief's door and stuck his head in. Ax looked up and gestured for him to enter.

"What's up?"

Kell closed the door. "I need a few minutes of your time."

"Sit down."

Kell sat and said, "A lot of shit went down with that crash."

"I'm waiting for your report on it."

"These are things that aren't going into my report," Kell warned him. And as quickly as he could, he filled in his master chief on Major Grant Hayden.

"So, where's all this leading?" Ax demanded, scowling.

"First," Kell said, his voice flat and hard, "Grant is not only a sexual predator, but he was also abusive toward Leah, as well."

Ax stared at him for a moment of stunned silence. "Dammit, Kell, what the hell have you gotten your-self into?"

He had anticipated this reaction. Kell knew Ax's hot buttons and he'd just pressed one of them. "I haven't gotten myself into anything I didn't want to get myself into," he told him calmly, holding the master chief's frustrated stare.

"She's an *officer*, dammit!"

Kell took his growl in stride. "I knew that from the beginning."

"Shit!" Ax got up, running his thick fingers through his hair, glaring down at him. "This isn't good and you know it."

"I'll be careful, Ax."

He shook his head, muttered some more curses and sat down. "Her ex-husband is Major Grant."

"Yes. That's the point in all of this. Grant's ac-cused her of being at the controls of that bird when it crashed."

"We're sending that flight recorder to him. That should clear her."

"I don't trust him, Ax." He told the master chief how Hayden manipulated Leah to get to her father.

When he was done painting the ugly picture he added, "Now, Grant wants early colonel's leaves and he's trying to pressure her into saying something positive about him to her father."

Rubbing his jaw, Ax studied him darkly in the growing silence. "That's why Grant came here, planting seeds."

"Yes."

"Asshole."

Kell knew Ax, as master chief, didn't like anyone screwing with his kingdom as the head of the platoon. Especially someone from another military branch trying to maneuver him for their own political purposes. He sat without saying anything. Ax was a strategist and he knew how military politics worked inside and out.

"You know," Ax growled, "that if Grant even *suspects* something between you and her, all bets are off. He'll use it to put the screws to her, big-time. Maybe even get her court-martialed and you along with her. Dammit all, Kell."

"I'm aware," he told Ax.

"Then," Ax muttered more to himself than to Kell, "I need to pull in a favor from that woman Intel officer, Lieutenant Sinclaire, down at Bagram SEAL HQ. I'll have her check out the flight recorder first. I'll send Clutch over there with it. Then—" and Ax looked across his desk at Kell "—she'll make a copy of it, and only after that is done will I have him take the original to Grant."

"Do you think Grant would try to deep-six that flight recorder?"

Snorting, Ax gave him a deadly look. "I met the

bastard once. He's a snake oil salesman. Didn't like him on sight and was really pissed off with him after our little conversation. He's *not* to be trusted."

"Why can't I deliver that flight recorder to him instead of Clutch?" Kell wanted a bead on Grant.

"Are you nuts?"

"He won't know I'm connected with Leah."

Ax cursed softly. "Your ass is staying right here. I'll send Clutch down. He's good at this sort of intrigue."

"Light fingers," Kell agreed.

"I'll clue Clutch in on a need-to-know basis."

Nodding, Kell said, "It sounds like a good plan."

"I'll get Clutch to find out if the radio calls that are always recorded at TOC in Bagram are available. That's another way to avoid a crisis here for Chief Mackenzie. Even if Grant thinks he can wipe that recorder clean, we'll still have the original radio calls on TOC record. That can clear her, as well."

Kell felt some relief. "Good, because she needs to be protected."

Ax shook his head. "So do you."

Kell grinned a little and stood up. "I'm still alive and breathing pretty well, Ax." Master chiefs took care of their men. They were like old broody, protective hens about their platoon charges and would rearrange the world to get their SEALs out of harm's way. Master chiefs knew the military universe better than anyone. "Thanks, Ax."

Ax glowered at him. "This is really serious between you and her?"

"Very."

"Jesus, Kell, you're killing me. You've got to be damned careful and so does she. This is a small base!

We have maybe eighty women at the most around here. They're easy to spot and they're constantly watched by nearly a thousand horny males."

"I won't bring any problems to your doorstep," Kell promised him somberly.

"You'd better not. If Commander Lanoux hears about this, he's going to go ballistic."

Kell reached for the doorknob. "Black ops, Ax. Black ops."

Snorting, he said, "Is there anything else you're not telling me that isn't going to be in your report?"

"No, that's it."

"Thank God, that's enough. Dismissed."

CHAPTER SIXTEEN

KELL TOOK LEAH out back, to the barn and corral at the rear of the SEAL HQ. The barn and paddock area looked out across the flattened hilltop.

It was Kell's first chance to be alone with her, removed from prying eyes. They sat on a bale of hay in the barn, the door open to allow a breeze. There were the three horses, the same ones they'd rode in on plus the packhorse, contentedly munching hay in a small nearby paddock.

Leah sat next to him, no doubt feeling raw. Kell put his arm around her, and she sighed, resting her brow against the column of his neck.

"How are you feeling?" he asked her. It felt good to have Leah in his arms once again—and in private. The only way anyone could see them was if they made the effort to walk around the end of the SEAL building. And that wasn't going to happen unless it was another SEAL wandering out this way. He'd asked Clutch to stand guard near the end of the building so they would not be interrupted.

"Like hell," Leah murmured, inhaling Kell's scent, lifting her hand and sliding it across his chest. "Scared to death." She cast him a look. "There's a new female pilot that I just met earlier today at the squadron office. Her name is Lieutenant Harper Corliss. She's very pretty, very nice, but something awful happened to her."

She rubbed her brow, the words rushing out of her. "I met Harper, gave her some papers to fill out and then took off for a briefing meeting. Later that day, Clutch brought Harper back to my office. He'd found her crying. Clutch became concerned, stayed and asked her what happened." She closed her eyes, dragged in a deep breath and whispered, "Hayden lured Harper into his back room right after she'd checked into the squadron at Bagram. He had a bed in there, Kell. He threw Harper onto it and tried to rape her."

Instantly, Kell straightened, staring at her.

Holding up her hand, Leah rushed on, "Harper fought back and got away. The next day, she found herself ordered to Bravo. Hayden got rid of her. But, God, she's got bruise marks all over her shoulders and neck, Kell. I immediately took her over to the dispensary. I had them take photos of her injuries, and had the physician on duty fill out a report." Grimly, she said, "And Harper wants to press charges against Hayden."

Stunned, Kell sat there, seeing the ravages of anger and fear in Leah's eyes as she nervously moved her hands up and down her thighs. "What are you going to do about this?"

"I'm not only backing Harper on her charges, but I'm going to ask the JAG assigned to this case to talk to me, also." She stared up into Kell's shadowy face. "I'm coming clean, Kell. I'm throwing my weight into this ring and I'm going after Hayden. I didn't do it before because I was so young, scared and beaten down by him, but I'm doing it now. Because of me not going to the police when I was younger, he's continued to be a predator."

Kell nodded and pressed a kiss to her hair. "You're doing a brave thing, Leah." He sighed. "Your whole career is on the line now."

"Tell me about it." Leah sat up and faced him. "But if Harper has the titanium ovaries to move forward with this, I need to do it, too, Kell."

He moved his fingers through her loose hair, wanting to touch her, knowing his contact was calming to her. Leah's green eyes were fraught with fear and anger. "Sometimes, we're called on to stand up and be counted, Sugar. This may be your time."

"I didn't realize Hayden was doing it to other women, Kell." Her voice broke. "That son of a bitch! If—if I'd just told the hospital doctor, the police, what he was doing to me when I was married to him, maybe it would have stopped him right then." She hid her face in her hands and mumbled, "I've screwed up so damned badly, Kell. Because I was scared of losing my rank, getting kicked out of the Army if I testified against Hayden, I allowed him to turn around and do the same thing to God knows how many other women." Tears streaked down her face as Leah pulled her hands away and gave him a miserable glance. "I've failed myself. I've failed these other women."

"Hey," he cajoled her, kissing her temple, enfolding her into his arms, "don't go there." He felt Leah sob once, struggling to hold it together. She buried her face against his shoulder. Moving his hand across her hair, Kell felt her anguish. And he wanted so damned badly to personally take on Hayden Grant.

Leah finally pulled away. "I'm not going to do anyone any good if I sit around crying," she muttered fiercely, wiping her cheeks dry. She absorbed his quiet strength, his arm around her waist.

"Tears are always a good thing," Kell drawled, giving her a tender look. "Never bad. Gets the poison out of a person's system."

"Tomorrow is going to be a bitch of a day," Leah whispered. "The JAG will take everyone's statements."

"Will Grant know he's being implicated?"

"No, not yet. The JAG has to decide first if there's a case against him, which I know there is."

"What part are you going to play in this?" Kell asked.

"I'm going to come clean with the JAG and tell her everything. It will show her a pattern of abuse that Hayden kept up for years with me when we were married, which he's now carried forward. He *has* to be stopped and held accountable once and for all. And it's up to me, for the most part, to stop him, because my testimony will be the most damaging to him. I also had rape kits and photos taken of my injuries Hayden gave me. I never went to the police with them, but I kept them as proof. All of that information is going to the JAG. It's proof that Hayden has a pattern of abuse."

"You are two very brave women," he murmured, kissing her wrinkled brow. "And you have us standing with you. You know that?"

Leah nodded, twisting her fingers together. "Yes, and I'm forever grateful. I don't know if Harper is, but I am." She looked up into his hard, weather-beaten face. His gray eyes were so clear looking and she felt the serenity he afforded her. "Will this hurt your career? Clutch's career?"

"Doesn't matter, Sugar. There are times in everyone's life when they have to stand up and be counted."

"C-could you be disciplined?"

"Doubtful," he said. "Ax is pissed off to the hilt. And I'm sure he's going to the CO of our Seal Team Three with this, Captain Johnson. He knows how to circle the wagons. And SEALs are probably the most protective group in the black ops community when it comes to one of our women being threatened." He squeezed Leah a little, to reinforce her and give her support. "Any father who's a SEAL, who has a daughter, is going to react to this situation just like Ax has."

"That's good to know." Leah gave him a sad look. "I miss you so much, Kell. We get back here, and my whole world blows up in my face. I had that time with you and you helped me…and now, it's come full circle. I never had the strength to stand up to Hayden before. And I thought I'd just keep it all buried, all the abuse, the anger, the pain…"

"We'll get through this together, Leah."

His words were a balm over the guilt and anger eating away at her. "Why didn't I have the strength then, Kell? Why?" Her voice broke as she searched his eyes.

He held her tightly. "Listen, you came out of a twisted family situation to begin with. You had no mother to guide or support you. You had a ghost of a father in your life who never really cared for you. He never took the time to teach you things you needed to know about life, about men and about relationships. There's no going back to change any of that, Leah. What you have to know is that you're older now, you've matured, and you didn't try to deep-six Harper's assault. Instead, you stepped up to the plate and you're doing the right thing for the right reasons, even if it means hurting or ending your career."

Kell eased her away and gazed into her teary eyes that held so much anguish in their green depths. "You've been given a second chance to get that son of a bitch removed from the Army, get his ass thrown into prison, and it makes the world a safer place for all women. You have to know in your heart that you're making a better choice this time around, Leah. Don't you?"

She nodded. "Yes, I see how this is playing out now. And you're right, I've grown and matured." Nuzzling against his neck, Leah whispered, "Thank you for saying what I was thinking. And thank you for being here for me, for believing in and supporting me…"

Kell wanted to tell her he loved her. But it was far too soon. He placed his finger beneath her chin. "I care very much for you, Leah. And that's what is going to get us through this."

He leaned down, taking her lips gently, tasting the salt of spent tears, feeling her warmth and response. She turned fully toward him, sliding her arms across his shoulders, her warmth sending sheets of heat down through his body. Her breath was moist against his cheek and she strained against him, as if to melt into his body, heart and soul. Kell would continue to dream of Leah becoming a part of his life and, someday, telling her that he had fallen in love with her.

Easing from her wet lips, wanting to do so much more but knowing it was the wrong place and time, Kell emphasized his support. "I have your six, Sugar.

You just need to do what's right for yourself and everyone else who is involved." He kissed her brow, her temple, then skimmed his mouth against hers. "And it's okay to be scared as hell. You just don't let the fear stop you from doing the right thing."

Leah closed her eyes, needing Kell's strong mouth upon hers. She slid her hand across his bearded cheek and held him tightly against her. "Yes," she whispered against his mouth. "It's past time to stop Hayden. I've been given a second chance. The first time, I was too scared to turn him in. This time, I'm still just as scared, but I know it's the right thing to do, no matter what he might do to my career."

Kell held her painful gaze and caressed her cheek. "Life always gives us second chances like this one. It's going to be tough, but you've got a backbone of steel and you'll gut through it. And I'll be standing right beside you all the way."

"Just having you makes all the difference," Leah admitted.

"No one gets through life alone. No one," he said.

"I wish...I wish we were back in that cave." Leah studied him, thinking how handsome he was, how courageous and how much she loved him. She'd not spoken those words to Kell because they needed more time together. Looking into his stormy gray eyes, Leah knew he would be there for her. But this was her fight, not his. She was willing to fight this time, and it wasn't just because of Kell's support. It was because she'd seen the damage done to Harper. Hayden had done that and more to her. Leah would be haunted by Hayden's attack upon the young lieutenant for years to come if she didn't stop him right now.

"Have chow with me tonight. How about 1800?" Kell asked, enjoying touching her velvet skin, watching her eyes grow drowsy with desire.

"I'd like that. Don't you think gossip will start, though, Kell? The *last* thing I want to happen here is for Hayden to realize we have a relationship."

"Don't worry. Everyone on this small base knows I rescued you. They would expect us to have a friendship of some sort. I don't think there's anything to worry about."

Leah roused herself, not wanting to leave the circle of his arms and knowing she had to. "Okay, I'll see you at 1800."

He gently tousled her hair. "With bells on, Sugar."

"It's done," Leah told Kell, weariness in her tone, the next evening. She sat with him on the hay bale in the barn, darkness surrounding them. Her head ached and she rubbed her brow, wanting to will away the pain. "How did the JAG session go for you and Clutch?"

Kell slid his arm around her shoulder. "Probably a lot less stressful than when you and Harper were grilled by her." He heard the exhaustion in her voice, wanted to hold her.

"Major Reid is like a laser-guided rocket," Leah told him, allowing her hands to drop into her lap. "She questioned Harper first, then me and then Markley."

"And then she came over here and talked to Clutch and me. She asked Ax questions, too."

"Do you like her?"

"Yeah, she's fierce. Seemed really focused. But she's a woman and she's been harassed and knows the drill. I think you're lucky she was assigned to Harper's case and not some male JAG."

Leah could barely see Kell's darkly shadowed face except for the glitter of his alert, intelligent eyes. "Did she ask about us?"

"No, only in terms of the rescue. Nothing else. She was more interested in me going back to get that flight recorder. I'm sure she knows about Grant wanting to hang you for that crash. Ax knew about it, had talked to Grant directly, and he said he told Major Reid about his allegations that you were at the controls when the helo crashed."

Rubbing her arms, she was cold. At night, at an elevation of eight thousand feet, the forward operating base could dip to freezing.

"Relax," Kell whispered against her hair. "Everything's going to work out in the end." He maneuvered her across his lap and guided Leah's head to his left shoulder.

She sighed, closing her eyes. "It feels so good being this close to you, being held by you..."

Hell, he thought the same thing. She had to feel his arousal, but this wasn't the time for what he really wanted to do. Leah kissed his neck and nuzzled against him, her hand sliding slowly up across his chest. Though he'd like nothing more than to strip off their clothing, lay her down and take her in the barn, Kell knew he couldn't. Not here. Clutch was already in place, guarding their six from around the corner of the building. Still, Kell would never open Leah up to the possibility of being embarrassed if they were caught.

Kell eased her away just enough to drown in her wide, sultry-looking eyes. Leaning down, he took Leah's mouth gently, knowing that was what she needed on such a hard-edged day, the events of which were probably going to spin out of control sooner or later.

Grant wouldn't take the charges lying down if the JAG decided there was a case. He'd come after Leah. And that was when Kell would start standing between her and that sick, perverted bastard.

He cupped her jaw, angling her slightly, taking his kiss deeper, making her forget today and the tomorrows to come. Her mouth tasted of chocolate and he smiled to himself, coaxing her lips open even more. His mother had sent him a package of her homemade fudge this morning. Kell had kept some for Leah, who had been delighted with the gift. Women seemed to love chocolate, no question.

"Mmm," Leah said as he broke their kiss. Her whole body was on hot alert. The man was such a good kisser. Her breasts were tight, nipples achy from wanting Kell's touch, his mouth upon them. She felt his large hand reverently gliding down her back, coming to rest on her hip, pulling her tightly against him. Opening her eyes, Leah drowned in Kell's glittering, narrowed gaze. Her body vibrated with desire and she felt so damn tense, so ready to experience another climax. "I wish this were a cave…"

Kell smiled faintly, bringing her against him, burying his face into her loose hair that smelled of almond shampoo. "You know we're desperate when a cave sounds good."

Leah shook with laughter and lifted her head, smiling up at him. "You're good for my soul. Do you know that?" She leaned up and kissed his jaw, the beard beneath her lips.

"You're good for my heart."

Leah became serious. "I never told you, Kell," she began, her throat tightening, "but I want to continue to build on what we have with one another. I don't know where it's going…what will happen. But I want to find out what we have, even though I've stepped into a hornet's nest just now." She saw his eyes change, tenderness burning in them.

"I knew that from the first night I got you into that cave. When you opened your eyes, darlin', you stole my heart."

She was touched by the sincerity in his voice. "But—how?"

Shrugging, Kell made her comfortable in his arms and said, "I just knew. My ma always said to us boys that one day, we'd meet the right woman and we'd know in our heart she was the one." He caressed her lips and whispered, "You're the one."

Her whole world fell away as she languished in his strong embrace. "It isn't that easy for me," she admitted. "I was drawn to you, Kell, but I was so damned afraid. I was still running from my shadow."

Leah opened the first button on his cammies, moving her fingers below the material and across the soft hair of his chest, beneath the strong column of his neck. "But you—" she shook her head, feeling his flesh tense, the muscles leap beneath her fingertips "—you make me want to live again…to hope…"

"Kentucky boys are a pretty persuasive lot when we want to be," Kell drawled, holding her radiant eyes. He groaned as her hand moved lightly across his upper chest. Leah's fingertips felt so damn good across his skin. He wanted her to explore every inch of his body. And he wanted the time, the space, to love her properly. Not in a cave. Not in a barn. But at his condo, in his bed, back in Coronado.

"I'm torturing you," Leah apologized, sadness in her tone as she pulled her hand from beneath his cammie shirt. She felt him laugh, heard the rumble in his chest, saw the gleam in his eyes, wanting her. Now.

"It's the sweetest torture I can think of," Kell admitted, kissing her brow as she rebuttoned his blouse with trembling fingers.

Leah rested her head on his shoulder, her arm curving across his torso. "I worry what will happen when Major Reid decides to move forward with Harper's case."

"You're here at Bravo. Grant is at Bagram," Kell reminded her. Leah was tensing up, as if trying to protect herself from her ex-husband. "You've got forty badass SEALs who would do anything necessary to protect you and Harper. Okay? You two are not alone, Leah. Not ever."

Closing her eyes, Leah clung to Kell, the beat of his heart so strong and solid beneath her ear. She nodded, but she knew how much of a monster Hayden really was. He was going to strike out at her and Harper— but mostly at her. Hayden would blame her for all of this. He was more than capable of killing her. He'd put her in the hospital too many times already. One day, he wouldn't pull his punch. One day…

LEAH WAS IN the squadron office near noon, taking over for Markley while he went to the chow hall. Where had three weeks gone? She had passed her physical and been approved to go back on flight duty by the flight surgeon two weeks ago. Major Reid was instrumental in the request for the surgeon, Major Armstrong, and he'd agreed to fly in to Camp Bravo to see Leah. After the hours of examination, she'd been cleared to fly once more, to her utter delight and relief.

Leah had taken Harper under her wing, and she became her copilot trainee. Together, they'd been flying nearly every day or night, working with black ops groups in the area. She was putting the finishing touches on her night-mission report on her laptop when the door opened. She looked up. Her heart banged into her throat. It was her father!

"Leah?" David Mackenzie snapped tightly, shutting the door. "We need to talk."

She stared, stunned for a moment. Her father was in his Army BDUs, a cap in his left hand, his face hard and unreadable. *As always.* At forty-nine years old, he looked every inch the soldier he'd always been. His black hair was short, his dark brown eyes narrowed upon her. He was five feet nine inches tall, standing only two inches taller than her. In her opinion, Colonel David Mackenzie was the perfect soldier for recruiting drives. His thin mouth was a hard line and she could see anger in his eyes.

She stood. "Why didn't you let me know you were coming here?"

"You're part of my command," he said. "I can drop in without any announcement."

The door opened.

Leah's eyes widened. Kell. Why was *he* here?

Kell closed the door and noticed the confusion on

Leah's face. He turned to see the man, "Mackenzie, D., Colonel, US Army," above his pocket.

"Sir," he said, coming to attention.

So, this was Leah's father. Kell wondered if he'd dropped in on her without notice. Judging from the look on Leah's face, he had. And he knew the connection between him and Grant. What was he snooping around for? The protector in him was on alert.

Mackenzie glared at him. "You have official business here?" In the awkward silence, the man looked back at his daughter, making the connection. And then he stared at the SEAL again. "You're Ballard. You're the one who rescued my daughter?"

"Yes, sir, I did." Kell stood a lot taller than the colonel and he was glad to be putting eyes on Leah's father. He didn't like the man's authoritarian attitude.

Mackenzie offered him his hand. "I'm in your debt, Chief Ballard. Thank you for saving her life."

Kell gripped the man's hand and found it strong. "She was worth saving, sir." He released the colonel's hand and gazed over at Leah. She appeared to be in mild shock.

"Chief? If you don't mind? I need some privacy to speak to my daughter."

Kell glanced over at Leah. "You know where to reach me if you need anything." He wanted to stay, but knowing he couldn't he respected Leah's nod, excusing himself.

Out in Ops, Kell moved to the opposite side of a large area where the Shadow Squadron office was located and sat down in one of the many rows of chairs. He had a perfect line of sight on Leah and her father. A bad feeling moved through him. Kell picked up his radio and called Ax, alerting him. Ax told him to stay where he was, play sniper and observe. That, he could do.

"SIT DOWN, LEAH," Mackenzie said, gesturing to the chair behind her.

She sat down and watched her father set his black leather briefcase on the desk in front of her. He remained standing. Adrenaline was coursing through her.

"This is about Hayden, isn't it?" she demanded grimly. Her father's thin black brows drew down in reaction to the question.

"Here," he said tightly, pulling a manual out of his briefcase, "just tell me what the hell this is all about." He threw the JAG indictment of Hayden Grant down on her desk between them.

Containing her shock over her father's closeted anger, Leah turned it around and studied it. The indictment listed all the names involved in Hayden's assaults. "Where did you get this?"

"I'm the battalion commander. Major Reid *had* to send me a copy of the indictment."

"I haven't seen this yet," Leah muttered, riffling through the pages. Hayden was indicted not only for the assault of Harper, but rape of one of the other Army women who were named on the document. Her heart started to pound. Twisting her head, she stared up at her father, who was so damn tense she thought he might snap and shatter at any moment.

"Everyone will get their copy tomorrow," he grated. Jabbing a finger down at her, he said, "What in the hell is going on? Hayden's a good man! He's a damn fine officer!" He sat down opposite her.

"Why the hell didn't you ask me that years ago, Father?" Leah stood up, hands rigid at her sides, breathing unevenly. He was blaming her for this?

"What do you have against Hayden?"

Her nostrils quivered. "Stop yelling at me. If you can't talk civilly to me, I want you the hell out of here." Leah watched him react, as if she'd slapped him.

For a moment, her father looked contrite. And then he snapped the briefcase shut and said, "I apologize."

Her heart wrenched with pain. "I know I've been a pain in the ass to you since I was born," Leah told him in a growling tone. "And I know when I married Hayden, he took the place of Evan in your life."

"That's not fair, Leah."

"Yes, sir, it is," she ground out, her hands clasped tightly in front of her. She held her father's narrowing gaze. "You have no idea what Hayden is like. I spent all those years getting abused, getting raped by that sick bastard. I was too afraid to come to you and tell you about it because you made it very clear Hayden was first in your life. I was not." Leah's voice quivered. "If I'd had the guts to turn him in after I was married to him, Father, he wouldn't be out there prowling around like the sexual predator he is, raping other women. But I was too damned beat down. I worried you'd believe him, and not me." Her voice broke, and she fought back the tears. "I was afraid you'd side with him. Do you know what that did to me? It made me feel alone. Like I had no one who would believe me, who would believe what Hayden was doing to me on a weekly basis."

Leah pulled out a file from a drawer, opened it and spread out the color pictures of Harper's bruises that Hayden had inflicted upon her. "Did you see these, Father?"

He scowled. "Yes."

"This is what Hayden was doing to me every month! You didn't see any of my bruises. Hayden was always smart and gripped me where it couldn't be seen by anyone. I wouldn't show them to you, anyway. I knew Hayden had your trust and that he'd tell you that, hey, it was a little rough sex between the two of us was all. You'd believe *him*, not me."

David Mackenzie sat there watching her. His hands moved over the briefcase in his lap. He opened his mouth to speak, but then shut it.

Leah stood stiffly, her fingers curling into fists at her side. "You *still* believe him, don't you?" Hurt rifled through her, tore at her heart as she saw her father's gaze and read it accurately. "That's fine. You believe the sick bastard and not me. I know you'll be there for the trial. You're going to hear four women, including me, giving evidence that your golden-haired boy, the one you consider your replacement son, is not innocent."

"Now, look here—"

"No," Leah snarled, leaning forward, her palms flat on the desk, "I get it, Father. I really do. Your whole life was wrapped around Evan. You had so many big dreams for him. You never once saw me, much less had a dream for me. You never held me, or kissed me. You paid attention to your son, not to your daughter. Well, I'm done with you, but the sad truth is, you were done with me from the minute I was born. Go defend

Hayden and see just how far it gets you. I hope this not only brings him down, but you, too. You're alike in some ways, do you know that? Always chasing the brass ring, the next rank. It was always more important to you than your own family."

Leah eased out of her hunched position and stood, struggling to remain strong. Collecting the pictures and sliding them into the file, she said, "We have *nothing* more to talk about. But then, we never did."

The colonel stood, his face pale, his eyes intense with anger. "You can't speak to me like that."

Leah put her hands on her hips, giving him a challenging look. "What are you going to do, court-martial me? Well, you do whatever it is you think you have to do. I can be kicked out of the Army and still fly a helicopter in civilian life and I won't have to answer to you or the Army anymore."

Colonel David Mackenzie said nothing, turned on his heel and strode out of the office.

Leah sat down after he left, tears burning in her eyes. She heard the door open. Thinking it was her father again, she jerked a look toward it.

"Rough?" Kell asked quietly, walking over to her. He placed his hand beneath her elbow and helped her stand up. "Let's go back to the ready room. We can be alone and talk there."

His drawl tamped down her anger and heartache. Leah nodded and Kell followed her down the hall toward the rear of the building. She pushed the ready room door open. Her heart was broken regarding her father. As she shut the door, Leah turned and Kell opened his arms to her. Her heart swelled fiercely with love for this man. He offered her sanctuary. He believed in her, believed what had happened to her at Hayden's hands. Without a word, she made the step forward, wrapping her arms around his waist and pressing her face against his chest, her eyes closing.

CHAPTER SEVENTEEN

HAYDEN PLACED A bullet into the chamber of his .45.

It was time.

At dusk, he'd hopped a ride from Bagram to Bravo on board a medevac helo returning from delivering a gunshot-wounded Delta Force operator to the hospital. No one thought anything of him asking for a hop. People did it all the time. After he showed his fake identification, he was happy to sit in the rear jump seat of the Black Hawk. He'd brought a duffel bag with food, water and enough ammo to fulfill his plan. His emotions seethed with a mix of hatred and rage.

As the helo neared Bravo, he smiled. Very shortly, Leah and that bitch, Harper Corliss, would be dead. With them out of the picture the other two women would not testify. With the two officers dead, they'd read the handwriting on the wall. Enlisted testimony didn't rate like an officer testifying against another officer. He knew how scared those two enlisted Army bitches would become. And they would fear being shot, too. The two worst accusers would be dead. Already, Hayden had his lawyer digging up plenty of dirt on the other two enlisted women to bury them. No jury would convict him on their flimsy testimony. There were no rape kits, no DNA evidence. It became a he said, she said. Leah's rape kits and photos were damning but if she were dead, Hayden would paint an ugly picture of her. He would explain she was into kinky sex and that she liked pain and being hurt. And the broken bones? She fell. Without her alive to testify, he knew he could put enough doubt into the proceedings to protect his rank and position. By that time, he would have found and dispensed with them. He'd already arranged a return ride to Bravo, departing near 2300.

Hayden had memorized the tent layout for the Shadow Squadron at Bravo. The last two tents in the row housed Corliss and Leah's billets. He rubbed his hands, smiling in the darkness, feeling the shaking and shuddering around him. The sensations of a helo in the air were always calming to him. His mind leaped forward, to the plan to get on that return flight without being caught after he killed the two women.

He'd arrive on an already scheduled Medevac flight from Bravo back at Bagram after killing them. This was a night flight that would be dropping off surgical and medical items to the Dispensary. He'd have plenty of time to sneak into his quarters, get to his room and bed down. He smiled a little, thinking about what Major Reid would do when she found out her two main witnesses were dead. Of course, he'd be suspected, but the .45 he was using was owned by another pilot in his squadron. Hayden would make sure it was back in his locker, fingerprints wiped off it. He'd purchased a Ti-RANT pistol suppressor for it. A .45 had a damned loud report and Hayden didn't want the sound to draw the whole damned camp to where he was after he shot the two women. That way, after he arrived at Bagram and the MPs checked his personal .45 he wore for flights, there would be no

gunpowder residue on it. And he'd make damn sure
to take a shower and wash away any evidence on his
flesh or his flight suit. And he'd hide the suppressor
so no one would ever find it.

The Black Hawk landed and Hayden headed for
Operations at Bravo. The stars were bright and looked
close. The wind was cold, and made Hayden wish he'd
brought a jacket, forgetting the forward operating base
sat at eight thousand feet in the Hindu Kush. No one
would think anything of him moving through Ops. He
was in his flight suit with the fake name velcroed over
his real name, and he carried his duffel bag in his left
hand. It was 2100, and Ops was pretty much deserted.

It was the perfect time to find them, Hayden
thought, swinging out the doors. He pulled on his
NVGs because there was no light whatsoever at the
FOB. Roving Taliban always wanted to send mortar or
RPGs into the base. Any type of light within the camp
was like an open invitation because they targeted it.
He settled the goggles over his eyes, flicked them on
and got his bearings. Unfamiliar with Bravo, he wandered around for about thirty minutes before he found
the dirt street where the Shadow pilots were billeted.

Voices! He quickly leaped between two tents and
crouched down in the darkness. His heart was thud-
ding in his chest, his hand on the .45. Hayden heard
two men talking and laughing. The men's voices subsided and he slowly rose to his feet, waiting and listening.

"DAMN," LEAH MUTTERED, flipping through the files
spread out across her bed in Sarah's room.

Ax had practically ordered her and Harper to stay

at night at the SEAL HQ in Sarah's room. Leah loved that it had been painted and fixed up for a woman medevac pilot who had fallen in love with a SEAL from the last deployment.

Ax didn't trust Hayden, so Kell and Clutch had asked the women to stay from dusk till dawn with them. At night, they would make Sarah's room their sleeping and working quarters, which was wonderful because the large chamber had an air conditioner.

"What?" Harper asked, sitting on her cot in the corner of the room.

"Oh, hell, I left one of my files I need and it's back at my tent." Leah looked at the watch on her wrist. It was nearly 2130. "I've got to get next week's roster of flights and pilot assignments done by tomorrow morning." She'd promised Markley they would be ready to be put up on the big corkboard in their ready room.

"Come on, I'll walk over with you," Harper urged. She unwound from the cot, still in her flight suit. Leaning down, she dug into her helmet bag and pulled out her NVGs.

Leah hesitated. Outside the door, she could hear many of the SEALs in the big room down the hall. This was their poker game night, and judging from all the yells, curses and laughter, some were winning and others were losing very badly. Kell was a part of the winning group—he'd told her that he never lost at Texas hold 'em. She smiled faintly as she climbed off the bed and picked up her helmet bag. Kell didn't want her going anywhere alone after dark. Not without him. But she didn't want to go out there and ask him to quit the weekly poker game just to walk about four hundred feet over to her tent to grab a single file.

"Yeah," Leah said, throwing her helmet bag upon the bed and opening it, "let's do it."

"Won't take long," Harper murmured. She pulled the NVGs over her head and they rested against her neck. They didn't go anywhere on base without a pistol, either. She stuck her .45 in the flight-suit pocket at her lower thigh with the safety on.

Leah pulled her flight suit on, strapped the .45 around her waist, put a bullet into the chamber and left the safety off. They were ready to go. Technically, they weren't supposed to go anywhere without their Kevlar vests, but it was such a short trip. It would only take ten minutes, total. And, aside from the poker game, the base had been quiet.

"I hate that vest," Leah muttered, giving it a distasteful look as it hung over a chair. "I'm leaving it here because it's so heavy to wear."

"Makes two of us," Harper enthusiastically agreed, opening the door.

They stepped out into the hall, the noise from the big room raucous, curses drifting down along with laughs and jibes. Leah smiled a little. It was good to hear the men having a little fun, blowing off some steam. Harper led, and just as she got to the back door, Clutch entered.

"Hey, where you two going?" he demanded, standing in the doorway.

Leah wrinkled her nose. "I need a file from my tent, Clutch. It's only going to take a few minutes."

"I'll go along," he said.

"Don't bother," Harper said, frowning. "We've got pistols. We know how to shoot if we have to."

"I didn't want to bother Kell," Leah admitted, giving him a pleading look. "He's having a lot of fun with the other guys. It's only ten minutes. The base is quiet. Really, Clutch, we'll be fine."

At that moment, Ax, who was in his office, called to Clutch.

"Be right there," he called to the master chief. Hesitantly, Clutch looked and saw her pistol on her waist. "Okay, but stay alert. I'll go see what Ax wants and then catch up with you. This will only take a second…"

"That's fine," Leah agreed. The two women left the building, walking quickly and taking short cuts over to their street.

"I swear," Harper muttered, "Clutch thinks he has to be our shadow."

"I know." Leah agreed. "Sometimes I think those guys see ghosts where there aren't any."

Harper nodded as they made the turn down their street. "It gets kind of claustrophobic to me. I'm not used to having a guard dog on my heels all the time."

Leah agreed. Either Kell or Clutch always escorted them after dark without missing a beat. This one time, they'd just chance it without them.

Leah slowed and pulled open the flaps on her tent. "Come on in, I'll need my flashlight to find that file in the drawer. I'm sure Clutch will be dropping by shortly."

Harper pulled her penlight from her pocket. "Lead on," she said, climbing up on the plyboard platform and moving into the tent with her.

Switching on the penlight, Leah took off her goggles, letting them hang around her neck. Harper did the same, looking over her shoulder as Leah walked over to a four-drawer file cabinet in the corner where she kept squadron paperwork. The lieutenant held her penlight high, the entire tent filling with a grayish cast.

Opening the top drawer, Leah said, "Could you hold your light on the files, please?"

Harper lowered the beam, illuminating the many files, watching as Leah quickly thumbed through them, head bent, absorbed in her task.

Leah suddenly felt the hair on her neck rise. She warily lifted her head, glancing toward the opened flaps. A gasp lodged in her throat as she saw a man with NVGs move inside, a .45 with a suppressor on it pointed at them. It wasn't Clutch!

Harper jerked a look toward him, confused.

Hayden smiled and pulled off his goggles. "Well, well," he snarled in a low voice filled with pleasure, "two for one. What luck."

Leah slowly dropped her arms to her sides. Her pulse skyrocketed. In the light, she could see Hayden's hatred-filled face, his colorless eyes with huge black pupils.

"What are you doing here?" she rasped, her voice unsteady. Her mind whirled with options. Hayden had the pistol pointed at them. Where was Clutch?

"Dropping in to see you two bitches."

Leah broke out into a cold sweat. How well she knew that tone, that hatred. And she saw it in his face. Her mouth compressed as he swung the pistol from her to Harper and then back to her. "Hayden, this isn't any way to—"

"Shut up!" he rasped, glaring at her. "You're both

going to pay for ruining my career. You two thought you'd be alive to testify, didn't you?"

Harper gasped.

The only thing Leah could do was remain frozen, staring at this vicious bastard. But then the anger started to burn through her. She began to think. She knew enough not to goad Hayden. Maybe, if they didn't show up at SEAL HQ shortly, Clutch would come looking for them. She had to keep him talking.

"This isn't the way to end it, Hayden. You know that. They'll find out who killed us." A bolt of anxiety shot through her. If only Clutch would get here! She lamented that they hadn't waited for him.

He smiled a little. "Do you think I'm that stupid, Leah?"

"No, you're not stupid, Hayden." Her voice sounded hoarse. Leah's heart was galloping, adrenaline plunging through her bloodstream. "Why don't you let Lieutenant Corliss go? I'm the one you really want."

Hayden grinned, his lips pulling away from his teeth. He snorted. "She's the one who got the ball rolling! No, you're both going down."

He fired the pistol, the bark harsh.

As Leah went for her .45, she heard Harper scream and then collapse at her feet. But Leah wasn't going down without a fight. She lifted her .45 in both hands and fired at the same time Hayden fired at her.

Leah felt herself being knocked backward as something hit her upper left arm. Hayden screamed out and she watched him fly out between the flaps of the tent. Oh, shit! She was hit! Slamming into the rear of the tent, her legs buckled beneath her.

The penlight Harper had dropped to the floor,

rolled crazily across it, light arcing and wobbling up through the tent as it moved. Leah felt her entire left arm go numb. She tried to get up, to reach the lieutenant, who was moaning on her back and weakly trying to lift her hand. Where was Clutch?

Hot blood was running down Leah's arm as she staggered to her knees, trying to get to the badly wounded woman pilot. Dark red blood was spreading swiftly across the center of Harper's uniform.

Oh, God...

Outside, Leah heard sudden commotion. Men's voices. Shouting. She knew the gunfire, even suppressed, would wake up those closest to their tent area. Someone ripped open the flaps. Leah nearly sobbed.

"Kell!" she cried out. "Harper's wounded! We need help!" Clutch came barreling into the tent behind him, his SIG raised.

The world started to spin and Leah stopped herself from falling forward, throwing out her right hand against the plyboard floor. Her vision grayed. She watched as Kell kneeled over Harper, his face tight with worry. There was a huge red patch eating rapidly across her entire stomach region.

No! Oh, God, no!

Leah sobbed for breath, fighting off unconsciousness. Clutch roared for help outside the tent flaps as men swiftly gathered around him. There was a lot of noise surrounding her right now. Her hearing was going. The blood was running down her left arm, dripping off her fingers as she tried to remain upright. The tension on Kell's face indicated to her that the lieutenant had been critically wounded. And that was the last thing Leah remembered.

CLUTCH LEAPED OVER CORLISS, kneeling at her side.
"How bad?" he gasped.

"Critical, gut wound," Kell growled before glancing over at Leah. "We've got to get them to the dispensary. Now!"

"I'll take the lieutenant," Clutch gasped, already
scooping her up into his arms. "You get Leah."

Kell gently turned Leah onto her back. His gaze immediately went to her left arm. Blood had soaked her
entire sleeve and left shoulder. She was bleeding out,
an artery hit. Another SEAL, Breach, entered the tent.

"What can I do?" he demanded.

"She's blown an artery here," Kell rasped. "Put
your hand over it, squeeze the hell out of it and stop
the bleeding while I carry her."

"You got it." Breach wrapped his lean hand around
Leah's upper arm. "Kell, her arm is broken, too."

"Do it, anyway," Kell ordered roughly, lifting Leah
into his arms. "Let's go!"

Clutch was the first one to reach the dispensary. He
kicked open the doors bellowing, "Gunshot wounds.
Two coming in!"

Instantly, the quiet dispensary of one doctor and
two nurses leaped to their feet from behind their large,
U-shaped desk.

Two cubicles opened. Clutch hurried to the nearest,
placing the female pilot gently on the gurney. "Over
here!" he yelled to the approaching doctor. "She's critical!" He kept his hand on her shoulder. Harper's eyes
were wide, shocky, and she was dazed. He watched
the blood eating up the tan of her flight suit, spreading quickly across her torso.

"It's going to be all right," he rasped to Harper,

leaning down, his lips near her ear. "You're going to be okay. Just stay with me, Harper. Stay with me…"

Kell arrived a minute later with Breach holding Leah's arm. Everything was in a state of barely controlled chaos. He knew there was no surgical unit here, and that both women needed to get to Bagram.

As soon as he placed Leah on the other gurney, Kell shouted, "Call a medevac! Stat!"

One of the nurses ran to make the radio request to get a bird out of the hangar and ready for flight.

Another nurse rushed over to him.

"She's taken a GSW to the left upper arm," Kell rasped. "The artery is severed and her arm has a fracture." Kell threw on a pair of gloves and took a pair of scissors from a nearby metal tray, using them to begin to open up Leah's blood-soaked sleeve. Glancing down at her, he saw her becoming conscious.

"Leah? Stay with me. It's Kell. Can you hear me?"

Leah's mind was rolling like a loose ball around in her head. She heard shouts, yells and snarls. Someone clamped an oxygen mask over her nose and mouth. The white of the ceiling blurred, and she closed her eyes, trying to hang on to Kell's strained voice. Pain began to drift up her arm and into her shoulder, sharp and hot.

"Get an IV into her," Kell ordered the nurse.

Breach held her arm until Kell needed to fully open up the sleeve, then he let go. "What do you want me to do now?" he asked.

"Get over to the lieutenant. She's got a GSW to the gut. Get an IV line into her." All SEALs knew how to push an IV, thank God. Tonight, it would really count. Breach could possibly help Harper survive.

Kell grimaced. The bullet had struck Leah's bone
and there were pieces of it poking up through her
flesh. The blood was pumping out of the openings.
Cursing softly, he grabbed his blowout kit tourniquet
he kept on his upper left shoulder, bound in velcro
to keep it in place. His hands shook but he grabbed
the tourniquet, swiftly wrapping it in place above her
wound. He tightened it down. Leah groaned. His gaze
was on the wound. Blood was still pumping out too
quickly. He tightened it down even more.

Leah cried out. The blood slowed to a trickle.
He looked over at the nurse, who had put a line into
Leah's right arm.

"You got any O type blood around here?" Kell demanded.

The nurse nodded. "Yes, but the woman next door
needs it worse. She's lost at least two pints. We only
have so much here to use, Kell. Only two pints on hand
and they need to go to the other patient."

"You got Celox on hand?" It was a blood coagulant
that all SEALs carried in their medical gear.

"None. It's on order. Sorry."

Kell nodded and moved his hand across Leah's
ashen face. She'd passed out again, either from the
pain of the tourniquet or from the blood loss. He
wasn't sure which. His mind raced through options
and priorities. "No surgeons here?" Sometimes, one
flew in from Bagram to perform minor surgeries that
didn't require someone to be put under.

"No, I'm afraid not," the nurse said apologetically,
holding her stethoscope to Leah's chest.

"What are her numbers?" he demanded.

"Not good. 70 over 50. She's lost a lot of blood. Her

pulse is sixty and steady. And her heart sounds good so far." She raced out of the cubicle and to the desk, making a radio call.

Kell cursed. Both his medical kits were in his ruck back at HQ. There was Celox, a blood coagulant, in the larger kit. If he had it, he could sprinkle it into the wound area and help stop the bleeding. Kell covered Leah with a blanket, immobilizing her left arm with a pair of splints and some gauze that he tied off around her neck to stabilize her entire arm.

Rage boiled in him. Hayden Grant had lain dead outside the tent when they ran up to it. He looked down to see that Leah's holster was empty. She must have shot him. Corliss wore no weapon that he could see.

The nurse ran back over. "The medevac is ready!"

"I'll carry Leah," Kell said. He hooked the IV bag to his shoulder so it would be high enough to continue to feed Leah the fluids she desperately needed.

The nurse ran next door.

Kell saw Clutch carrying the unconscious pilot in his arms, a nurse running at his side, holding up her IV bag. He turned and walked swiftly, not wanting to jostle or possibly aggravate Leah's broken arm. Breach continued to stabilize Leah's arm with his hands.

The man on watch at Ops opened both doors leading out to the tarmac. The Black Hawk was ready, the blades beginning to turn, the pilots up front and a medic and an air crew chief waiting for them. Kell stood aside, allowing Clutch to hand Harper off to the two men on board. They strapped her into a litter attached to the inner fuselage wall and instantly went to work on her.

Clutch climbed in, moving toward the other litter

above Harper's. Kell pushed into the medevac with
Breach, the place tight, not much room to maneuver.
They put Leah up on the litter above Corliss. Breach
wished them luck and hopped out of the Black Hawk.
The air crew chief slid the door closed and tapped the
pilot on the shoulder, a signal to let him know it was
all right to take off.

Turning, Kell worked to strap Leah in. She was
still unconscious. As he pulled down his NVGs, the
cabin went dark. There were never lights on in the
cabin at night. The medevac would become a target
for the enemy.

Once Leah was strapped in, he turned and searched
around for helmets. Finding a couple in the rear, Kell
handed one to Clutch and then pulled one on himself.
They plugged their connections into the ICS system
so they could hear all the radio talk between the pilots, the medics and themselves.

Kell hung the IV on a hook above Leah's litter.
He leaned over and borrowed a stethoscope from one
of the medics. As he listened to her heart, his alarm
grew. Her pulse was growing weaker. Son of a bitch!

"Hey," Kell called out, "I need an IV! Get me one?"
Leah had already gone through the first IV bag and
needed a replacement. It was vital to get fluids into
her body, even if it wasn't blood, but saline instead.

One of the medics reached into his canvas bag and
tossed it up to him.

"How bad is Lieutenant Corliss?" Clutch demanded, watching the the medic work on her as he
stood aside.

"She's critical," he muttered.

Kell got another line into Leah's lower left arm.

She'd lost too much blood and if she didn't get enough fluids back into her quickly, she could go into cardiac arrest. Kell turned, looking down at the medic.

"Is there anything I can do to help you?" he asked. "I've got this patient stabilized."

"Yeah," he muttered, "pray."

Kell lifted his head, looking into the helo's darkened rear. Clutch got out of the way of the working medic by sitting down in one of the two jump seats bolted to the deck in the rear of the cabin. His face was set and grim.

The Black Hawk was at top speed, the bird shaking and shuddering as it thunked through the night air, heading as swiftly as possible for Bagram.

Kell asked, "Are you 18 Delta?"

"Yeah," the medic said, "I am."

Kell felt some of his fear dissolve. He looked deep into the dark cabin and told Clutch, "Then the lieutenant has got a chance."

CHAPTER EIGHTEEN

KELL WIPED HIS smarting eyes as he stood near Leah's bed. He watched the monitors on the other side of where she lay unconscious. They'd just brought her out of surgery an hour ago. Looking at his watch, he saw that it was 0300. Exhaustion pulled at him. They'd given her a private room after she briefly became conscious in Recovery. Her face was serene, her lips parted. Kell gently pushed some strands of her ginger hair away from her smooth brow. Her left arm had been repaired and was now in a sling across her body.

Worried about Lieutenant Corliss, he took a risk that it would be a while before Leah would awaken again, and left the room. He took the elevator down to the surgery floor where Clutch was still waiting to hear anything about the pilot's surgery.

He walked into the lounge and saw his SEAL brother sitting, staring into nothingness, his face tense.

"Anything?" Kell asked, going over and sitting down opposite him.

"No," he growled. And then he looked up. "How's Leah doing?"

"Sleeping. It will probably take another hour before she's awake again." Kell saw the worry in his friend's eyes. "You did tell the charge nurse that you're Harper's fiancé, right?"

He nodded. "Yeah." It was an old black ops trick. If someone was wounded and in ICU, the other operators always told the nurse on the ICU floor they were a brother or cousin of the wounded man. That way, they could get in to see their teammate, stand vigil and be there for them when they became conscious.

"Why do you think it's taking so damned long?" Clutch demanded.

Kell shrugged. "She got hit in the stomach. Could be other organs involved." He didn't want to go on, seeing the bleak look in Clutch's eyes. "It's all fixable," he reassured him quickly. Kell didn't even want to think about her chances of ever flying again if she survived. He felt rage bubbling up within him toward Hayden Grant.

"I'm staying here. No one should be left alone at a time like this," Clutch told him quietly, clasping his hands between his thighs, staring down at the waxed green tile floor.

"I understand," Kell said. It was a SEAL thing, never leaving a man abandoned by his team. In this case, because Leah was his woman, Lieutenant Corliss, her copilot, she would automatically fall under that protective umbrella SEALs accorded to women and children.

Running his fingers through his hair, Clutch muttered, "I asked the nurse if they'd been able to contact her family."

Kell snorted softly. "They'll probably wait to see if she makes it through surgery first."

Clutch gave a bare nod. "I know."

Kell watched his friend prowl the lounge, walk out into the hall, stare at the operating doors, as if to mentally force them to open. The SEAL turned on his boot heel and stalked back into the lounge. "It's a good sign she's still in there."

"How so?"

"If she'd coded or died, someone would have been out here a lot sooner, so this isn't a bad sign, Clutch."

Clutch's lips pulled away from his teeth. "She's not going to die. She's got a steel spine. She's a fighter." He continued to pace and look at his watch. "Corliss is engaged. Did you know that?"

"No. Leah mentioned she had a guy, but nothing beyond that."

"He's an Apache pilot stationed stateside, an instructor."

Kell looked at his own watch. "Bad luck," he muttered. "I need to get back up there to Leah," he told Clutch. "I'll check back here in an hour with you."

Clutch nodded and halted. "Thanks, Kell. It means a lot. Go take care of your woman. She needs you."

Kell slapped him on the back. "Harper's going to make it. I have a good feeling about it."

Leah was conscious when Kell moved quietly into her room. He walked over and saw her eyes were barely open.

"Welcome back to the land of the living," he told her, leaning over, skimming her mouth with a hello kiss. He ached to tell her that he loved her, that he wanted forever with her. "How are you doing, Sugar?"

Leah raised her right hand and it weakly dropped back to the bed. Her voice was raspy. "Harper?"

Kell picked up her hand. Her fingers were cool and damp. "Still in surgery. Critically wounded in the stomach but I think she's going to make it." Leah's expression changed, relaxed a little. Squeezing her fingers gently, he asked, "Are you in pain?"

Barely conscious, Leah licked her lower lip. "No… just…exhausted…" She blinked and tried to become more alert. "What happened to my arm?"

"Hayden shot you in the left arm," Kell told her.

Leah frowned, as if digesting the information. And then she pulled her hand from his. Her fingers moved to explore the sling her left arm was in.

"Oh… I remember now…" she whispered, closing her eyes. "H-he must have been waiting for us." Her brow wrinkled and she placed her hand against her eyes, her lower lip trembling.

"Hey," Kell soothed, picking up Leah's coolish hand, holding her tear-filled gaze, "it's all right." He wanted to hold her, crush her against him and make things all right, but he knew he couldn't. Leah was emotional right now and anesthesia made a person horribly vulnerable, their feelings like raw, exposed nerves.

"Harper can't die," Leah whispered, tears trailing down her cheeks. "Sh-she didn't deserve this…"

"I know," Kell whispered, his voice unsteady. He released her hand and framed her face, removing her warm tears with his thumbs. "You didn't deserve it, either."

"I—I feel terrible, Kell. She is young, engaged to be married. She had her career, her whole life in front of her—"

"Shh," he whispered thickly, holding her dark, grief-stricken gaze. "Corliss is strong. Clutch is holding a vigil for her down on the surgery floor. She's not alone. What I want you to do is focus on you. Okay?"

Kell's roughened hands framed her face. Leah felt like a top spinning out of emotional control. Every time she closed her eyes, she could see Hayden silently sneaking into her tent, that .45 aimed at them.

Hot tears ran down her face and she couldn't stop them. She was alive when she thought she'd die.

"Hayden?"

"You killed him," Kell told her, seeing her eyes flare with surprise.

"H-he shot at Harper first," Leah whispered, missing his touch as he removed his hands. "It gave me a chance to jerk my .45 out of the holster. Thank God I had a round chambered in it and left the safety off." She swallowed hard, closed her eyes and whispered, "We both shot at the same time at one another."

Kell smoothed her hair, the strands strong and shining beneath the low light. "You took him out," he said, trying to keep the anger out of his tone.

Leah opened her eyes and choked out, "I was so afraid I'd never see you again, Kell." Her heart expanded and she felt a rush of love for him as he gave her a tender look. Leah no longer cared if they'd had the proper amount of time with one another. Love was love. And she knew now, with a clarity that overwhelmed her, she wanted this man in her life forever— if he would have her.

"I thought that when we ran over to your tent area. Clutch came and got me out of the poker game. Said something didn't feel right and told me you and Harper were walking over to your tent a few minutes earlier. We took off from HQ at a dead run, heard the first shot. We'd just turned down your street, our pistols drawn, when you fired the shot that killed him. We saw Grant fly out of the tent and land out in front of it." Kell took a deep breath and held her hand. "Neither of us knew if you two were dead or alive."

"I wanted you to take care of Harper. I knew she'd been badly hit."

"We had enough help, Leah. She had an 18 Delta medic on the flight here to Bagram. That's as good as it gets."

"I remember passing out. That's all. Until now."

He saw the grief in Leah's eyes, the worry for the other female pilot, not for herself. "It's over," he told her. "Grant is dead."

So many emotions collided within her, relief being the most powerful. "Thank you for being here," she managed brokenly. She saw the terror banked in Kell's gray eyes, the realization he had almost lost her.

"I didn't want to be anywhere else, Sugar." Kell grazed her cheek with his finger, her skin firm and warming beneath it. "Are you thirsty?"

She nodded. "My mouth is so dry, Kell…"

He released her hand. "I'll get you some water. Feel like sitting up a bit more in that bed?"

"Yes."

He raised the bed so that she was in more of a comfortable sitting position. He poured her some water from a nearby tray and brought the glass over with a straw in it. Kell held it for her as she sipped from it. The water tasted heavenly. Leah drank all of it and then lay back, feeling more clarity and less wooziness.

"What about my arm?" she asked, touching it lightly with her right hand. Her upper arm was in a removable but waterproof cast.

Kell brought the chair over but didn't sit down. "It was an open fracture," he told her. "The surgeons fixed it and you've got some screws and a plate in the bones to hold them together while they mend back together again."

Leah slowly moved her fingers. They all worked, thank God. "My whole arm went numb when he shot me," she murmured, moving her hand lightly across her bandaged upper arm.

Kell saw how tired she looked. "It would." He squeezed her other hand gently. "I've been putting off something I've wanted to tell you for some time now, Leah." He held her gaze. "Ever since I picked you up at that crash site, I've been falling in love with you." Kell's voice grew thick. "Now this. Leah, I'm not holding off any longer telling you that I love you. Looking back on it, I think I started to love you from the moment I saw you in that cave after I got you to safety." Swallowing hard, Kell rasped, "And I know this might be too soon for you. You're reeling from this latest trauma. I just want you to know I'm here for you, that I hope you love me."

Tears came to her eyes and it tore at him. Kell sat down on her bed, his hip against hers, and framed her face with his hands. "Leah, I dream of a lifetime with you." He leaned forward, his mouth softly brushing her parting lips. Her breath caught and he felt the warm return of her mouth weakly against his, a silent celebration of life over death. Never had Kell wanted Leah more, as a permanent part of his life.

They'd both danced around the issue and he knew it. He'd respected it up until now. Kell had nearly lost her a second time, and he was no longer willing to remain silent.

As he drew away from her wet lips, drowning in the gold and green of her eyes, she gave him a trembling smile. His heart opened wide and intense love for her burst through his chest. "What do you say? Are we a team?"

Taking a serrated breath, Leah felt his hard, calloused hands gently framing her face, his gray eyes stormy with longing for her. "We've always been a team, Kell. Always." She lifted her hand, skimming his bearded jaw. "I love you, Kell. And like you, I was afraid to say it. Afraid it was too soon." She gave him a tender look, watching his face relax, his anxiety dissolving beneath her whispered words. "We've always been a good team. I just had to get over Hayden…the past. I wanted to see *you*, not him."

Kell released her and tucked her hand into his. "I knew that. I was battling a ghost. I could see you struggling to get beyond Grant. But Leah, you always saw me. I don't believe you ever overlaid Grant on me at any time."

She barely squeezed his hand, her heart pounding with joy. "You're right. You're so psychic it's scary sometimes, Kell."

His mouth moved into a faint smile. "It's the part that kept me knowing that you were worth any kind of wait, Leah. I was trying to time my admission to you, but damn, life kept throwing RPGs at us faster than we could duck 'em."

Leah loved his simple, honest Kentucky way of

looking at life. "Yeah, RPGs for sure. This last one was the size of a Hellfire missile," she added grimly. Looking up, her voice dropped with emotion. "But you were always there. You always supported me, Kell."

He scowled. "I'm just sorry I couldn't stop Grant from shooting you and the lieutenant…"

"That was my fault," Leah admitted sadly. "I should have told you, but you guys were having so much fun, laughing so much during that poker game, I just couldn't do it." She shook her head. "How many times do we really get to laugh in a combat zone? Not many."

"Listen," he rasped, touching her cheek, "you saw Clutch. The only reason Clutch didn't walk over with you is that Ax called him into his office for just a moment. You didn't do anything wrong here, Leah. You did everything right. Clutch was going to hurry and catch up with you. He just didn't know it was going to take that long to get back with you gals. This is no one's fault, so don't go there."

Shrugging, she whispered, "Everyone had good intentions, Kell. I'm not blaming anyone for what happened. God knows, we're human…"

"So?" he said, searching her sad gaze. "I want to make this official, Leah. Will you marry me? Be my wife?"

Leah squeezed his hand, feeling his warm fingers surround hers, drowning in the burning love that she saw in his eyes as he stood there, waiting for her answer. "Yes," she whispered unsteadily. "Yes, I'll marry you, Kell."

Such staggering relief came to his face that it made more tears flow from her eyes. Her heart ached with such love for this man. Kell had shown her what real love was, that he cherished his woman, supported her through the good and bad. And always, Kell had been at her side, never abandoning her. Always doing his best to aid her with her tortured past and helping her to finally leave it behind.

"Wise decision," he managed, leaning over, pressing a kiss to her lips. "We'll talk more about this later, when you feel up to it. Why don't you just close your eyes and rest? I'm going back down to the surgery floor and see if we can get a status report on Lieutenant Corliss. Then, I'll come back up here."

Leah nodded.

Kell leaned down and kissed her brow. "Rest. I'll be back in a little bit. I love you…"

KELL SHOWED UP midafternoon at Leah's private room. She had just awakened, her eyes half-open, drowsy looking. And beautiful to him. He closed the door and walked over to her. "Have a good nap?"

"Mmm," Leah muttered, rubbing her eyes. "I feel drugged."

"You're still working out of the anesthesia," Kell murmured, leaning over, kissing her cheek. "Good news. Harper is conscious and the surgeon said she was in fair condition. They're moving her right next door to you as we speak." Originally, right after surgery, she had been taken to ICU, in critical condition. Clutch had remained with her until she improved. Now he sat at her bedside as she slept, continuing to keep watch over her like the good SEAL guard dog he was.

"Really?" Leah's heart thumped with joy. "Harper's going to be okay?"

"She's got a long road to recovery," Kell cautioned.

"They had to remove her spleen and resection her stomach. I just talked to Dr. Pastore, her surgeon. Her fiancée, Lieutenant Carter Boyer, is flying in and will meet her at Landstuhl Medical Center in Germany tomorrow. That will help her a lot."

"That's such good news," Leah whispered. "I wonder when my surgeon will come in."

"Shortly," Kell said. "I saw him down the passageway working his way in your direction." He studied her sleepy features. Leah had more color in her cheeks. Hair mussed, he threaded his fingers through it, taming it here and there.

"I want to get out of this bed, Kell. I need to go to the bathroom and I refuse to use a bedpan." Leah gave him a pleading look. "Can you help me get up?"

"Anything the lady wants," he murmured, taking her hand. There was a wheelchair nearby and he hooked it with his boot and brought it over to the side of the bed. "I'll get you standing, but I want you to sit in the wheelchair. Then, I'll take you over to the bathroom."

Nodding, Leah wasn't going to argue. Kell pulled the covers off and pulled down her wrinkled blue gown that had hitched up midthigh. She had beautiful, long, curved thighs. He went hot remembering skimming his hand over her warm, velvet skin.

"You know," he said with a drawl, "you have a great set of legs…"

Leah laughed a little, and it hurt her arm. "Do you guys ever *not* think of sex, Ballard?" He helped her off the bed, placing his arm around her waist until she felt steady.

"Guilty," he admitted, chuckling. Easing her into

the wheelchair, he guided her feet onto the paddles. "But I'm not that way with every woman," he whispered, kissing her cheek. "Just you."

CHAPTER NINETEEN

"THIS SUCKS," LEAH GRUMBLED. She stood watching Kell pack a rucksack that had all the important belongings she'd need when she left.

"It does," he agreed. Kell closed the ruck and turned around. Tomorrow morning, he and Clutch were heading back to Camp Bravo. Leah and Harper would be on a C-5 flight that would take them to Landstuhl Medical Center in Germany. From there, they would both take another long flight to the USA. The good news was Leah would be receiving therapy and treatment at the Naval Medical Center in San Diego because she was now engaged to him.

Harper would be flown to the East Coast to the Walter Reed National Military Medical Center near Washington, DC. She was Army, and the Army and Navy had combined military hospitals there. When the authorities found out that Harper was not engaged to Clutch, her orders were redirected. The good news was that Carter Boyer was stationed in nearby Georgia and he could fly up to be with her nearly every week. It was a happy ending for them, or as good as it was going to get under the circumstances.

Still, Harper thanked him for being nearby while she was in surgery, calling him a hero. Clutch had blushed, mumbling that SEALs took care of their own.

Leah was in her desert-tan flight suit. Her left arm remained in a sling. She sat in a chair, pouting. Kell came over and knelt down, his hands curving across her long thighs. "In two months, the platoon will be back at Coronado," he told her. She gave him a nod. "And the best news of all is you'll be able to stay at my condo on the island. The senior chief will meet you when you get off the flight, Leah. He's arranging everything for you. I've given you the keys to my SUV, and he'll make sure you get to my home."

"I shouldn't be sulking about this," Leah admitted quietly, reaching out, touching his longish hair at his temple. "We've been lucky."

"We are lucky," Kell agreed. He squeezed her thighs, remembering how they felt naked against his hands, but he couldn't go there. There was no way to make love to Leah right now. She was still in shock and grieving over killing Hayden. It weighed her down, and they hadn't been able to discuss too much during the three days they'd had together at the hospital.

"Come on," he urged, standing and holding out his hand toward her. "I want to buy my favorite girl an ice cream." Leah loved ice cream, he'd discovered. Especially pistachio.

Leah gave him a grateful look and slowly stood up, her fingers curving into his. Out in the hall, they couldn't hold hands or show any kind of affection toward one another. As Kell pulled her up from the chair, he enfolded her into his arms, careful so as not to jolt her wounded left arm. She closed her eyes, leaning her head against his chest, her right arm going around his waist. "This sucks, too, Ballard. I love you so much. I can't even hug you properly anymore."

He laughed and kissed her hair. "I love you, too, Sugar. You're such a mama bear today." He opened the door for her. Kell knew why she was cranky, and he wanted to try to cheer her up. Leah's father had visited her on the second day and that meeting hadn't gone well at all. Kell had reluctantly left the room, but hadn't wanted to, knowing Leah was going to have to face him alone. But she had insisted that this was between her and her father.

When he returned after the colonel had left, he found Leah crying. He hoped that over time some of the bridges between her father and her could be salvaged, but it wasn't going to happen right now. Kell was sure David Mackenzie was feeling a whole lot of guilt right now after realizing his choice of a faux son over his daughter had been dead wrong. Leah had almost died showing him the bitter truth of the situation. The man should be begging for Leah's forgiveness as far as Kell was concerned. That was going to take some time.

In the cafeteria, Kell found a place for Leah to sit. Midafternoon the place wasn't that busy. He bought her a bowl with two scoops of pistachio and two scoops of chocolate for himself, along with two mugs of coffee. He sat down opposite her, handing her a spoon. Leah brightened and dug into the ice cream, her appetite beginning to slowly return.

"Your doctor said that within the next eight weeks you should be almost back to normal," he said. Silently he added, *But you won't be healed from it emotionally.* That too would take time. At least in two months he'd be home to help Leah travel that excruciatingly painful path of healing from shooting Grant.

"Just in time to jump you at the airport," Leah said with a grin. Her heart widened as Kell flashed her that lazy, sensual smile, his eyes burning with desire for her and her alone. She was still coming out of trauma, her emotions skewing within her in so many twisted and unexpected ways. Kell had remained her cornerstone. Her anchor. "Well, maybe I'll wait until we get into your SUV." She grinned wickedly.

"We'll both be counting the days, Sugar. We have email and Skype. The senior chief at Coronado will make sure you can talk to me at least once a week, provided I'm not out on a mission."

Her blood chilled. Leah knew more than most what SEALs did because he'd rescued her from sure death. Kell had risked his life in order to save hers. She'd lived nearly a week on the run with him and he'd kept her safe. "I'm going to look forward to going home to meet your parents and your brothers at Thanksgiving." His eyes lit up with humor, his smile devastating to her wide-open heart. When the man smiled, she felt drenched with his love.

"My brother Cody will be coming through San Diego before I rotate home. He'll be returning from a Special Forces mission. He'll probably drop over to say hello to you when he arrives at Coronado."

"What? And dirt dive me? Make sure I'm worthy of you?"

Kell chuckled. "Oh, more than likely." He pulled out some photos from his pocket and slid them over to her. "I had these made over at SEAL HQ yesterday. Here's a picture of Cody. He's pretty hard to miss,"

Kell said wryly, his eyes crinkling at the corners. "You can see how good-looking he is. Got women hanging off him like ripe fruit 24/7/365."

Leah picked up the photo. Cody was handsome, there was no doubt about it. "I see a little of you in his face."

"Oh, he'd say the reverse. He's pretty full of himself. But he'll do right by you, Leah. Anything you need, just ask and he'll help you. He'll probably want to stay at least a night. Give him the guest bedroom. You sleep in my bed."

A frisson of desire burned through her. *Kell's bed.* Where he slept. "Yes, I'd like that," she whispered, suddenly choking up. Leah set the picture aside and wanted to reach out and touch his hand. "I love you, Kell." She couldn't say it enough now that she knew what real love was.

Hearing the emotion in her voice, Kell sobered and drew in a deep breath. "Nothing worth having is ever easy," he told her quietly. "And I love you so damn much I can't even give it words, Sugar."

What Leah needed was him right now. Not to be sent home. Not to be left alone. But that was the military. It took no prisoners and Kell knew it. Leah was made of strong stuff and he knew she'd gut through it. Not that things were ideal under the circumstances, but there was nothing he could do. He watched Leah self-consciously wipe the tears from her eyes, understanding how emotionally strung out she really was. "We can talk on Skype. I want you to call me, tell me what's bothering you, Leah. You need someone who cares to listen to what's on your plate."

"My father sure as hell doesn't care."

"He's in shock of another kind right now. I'm not trying to defend him, Leah. But that JAG lawyer gave him *all* the evidence. He knows the truth now about Grant and how he abused you in that sham marriage. I'm sure that's hitting him hard. And I'll bet he's feeling a lot of guilt about not being there for you when you really needed him." The pain in her eyes increased and she pursed her mouth, as if to hold back emotions. "Listen, we'll get through this together. I think the physical therapy is going to keep you busy on a daily basis. They'll rebuild your muscles, your strength in that left arm."

Leah shrugged. "Right now, Kell, I just feel like a tumbleweed with no roots, no direction in my career."

"It's part of the trauma. In time, it will ease."

Leah didn't want their last day together to be a complete downer. She rallied and pointed to the other photos beneath his hand. "Is that one of Tyler?"

Kell slid it over to her. "Tyler's a lot like you, sort of an introvert. He says little but sees a lot."

Leah picked up the photo. Tyler was not smiling. He had an intense expression in his hazel eyes, his black hair cut short, his jaw lean and stubborn looking. "He doesn't look like you at all."

"No, he takes after Ma. He's a SEAL like me." Kell gave her the last photo. "This is my ma and pa, Orin and Mary Ballard."

She took the photo, absorbing their brief touch. The photo showed his parents sitting on a red porch swing, smiling. Orin had his arm around his wife. The porch was enclosed with a screen that she imagined would keep the mosquitos at bay during the summer. "They look happy."

"They are. They married young, when they were eighteen. They'd gone through high school together, and fell in love. When they graduated, they married. My pa took over his father's dairy farm because he'd died the year he graduated."

"And when did you come along?" Leah loved hearing happy family stories. There weren't many in the world, but Kell had gotten lucky.

"She had me at twenty-four. Cody came two years later. And Tyler, the baby, two years after that. Ma said three times was enough."

Leah grinned a little. "No kidding."

"Keep the photos."

"I don't have any of you."

Kell grimaced. "I don't like to have my photo taken. It's a black ops kind of knee-jerk reaction."

"Mmm," Leah said, gathering up the photos and tucking them into her pocket.

"Well," Kell relented, "my ma will send you a packet of photos of me when I was younger. She said she would because I told her you'd be staying at my condo. The packet will arrive there and you can see all kinds of photos of me."

"That's something nice to look forward to," Leah whispered, touched by his thoughtfulness.

"I'm sure that when I take you home for Thanksgiving, my two younger brothers are going to give you an earful about me since I'm the oldest," Kell lamented. "You're going to hear so many stories about me. Most of them are big windy, half-truths or embellishments. You'll have to pick and sort your way through my little brothers' bad memories about me."

Leah laughed softly, sponging in the light dancing in his eyes. "I think you'll help me sort out truth from fiction."

"In a heartbeat," he promised wryly. "When the three of us get together, there's no mercy or quarter given between us."

There was hope in her eyes, which made him feel relief. Kell knew Leah really didn't have much family unity, and he hoped that by sharing the photos and the stories, he would let her know she would be embraced by all of them. A new family who honestly loved her. He saw Leah suddenly become pensive.

Reaching out, he grazed her cheek, holding her gaze. "In two months, Sugar, I'll be home and I'll be able to hold you in my arms…"

LEAH ALMOST DROPPED the head of lettuce into the kitchen sink when Kell walked unexpectedly through the door of his condo in early August. Two months had gone by and she was expecting him home a day from now. He was early! Her lips parted as she stood at the granite island. He entered with a huge duffel bag over his left shoulder.

"Kell!"

He grinned and tiredly dropped his duffel on the bamboo floor and shut the door. "Hey, I'm a day early. You okay with that?"

Hungrily, Kell watched Leah move toward him in white shorts and a pink tank top, barefoot, her ginger hair longer. She looked healthy, suntanned, and the smile in her eyes made him go hot with longing for her. He opened his arms as he strode across the living room to meet her halfway.

"Oh, I'm so fine with that!" she whispered, throwing her arms around his neck, pressing herself against him. Leah kissed him blindly, finding his mouth, feeling it curve like liquid fire across her lips. She soaked up his male scent, the perspiration, the dust of Afghanistan, still on his uniform and flesh. Leah didn't care, feeling his arms wrap around her, lift her off her feet, hold her tightly against him until she felt like she was melting into him.

"Look at you," he rasped, touching her hair, feeling the silky strands flow through his fingers. Gently, Kell allowed Leah's feet to touch the floor once more, eased back, staring into her joyful green eyes that had gold flecks dancing in their depths. "A tan California girl, wearing her shorts, showing off her beautiful legs… San Diego has been good for you, Sugar."

Leah wiped her eyes, unable to stop from touching him, his jaw, his shoulder, his chest, as if to convince herself that Kell was really here. Really home. His shoulders were so broad, so capable. Murmuring his name, Leah leaned upward on her toes, kissing him passionately on the mouth, unable to get enough of him. She framed his bearded face, wanting to taste him deeply, feel his strength, his tenderness, all wrapped up within him, feeding her.

"I stink," Kell muttered in warning as he left her lips. "No shower for three days."

"I don't care. You smell wonderful to me." Leah skimmed her fingers across his chest, more than a little aware of his erection pressing insistently into her belly, sparks of heat clenching within her. As his hands ranged down from her shoulders, cupping her breasts beneath the pale pink cotton tank top, she moaned and strained against him, wanting so much more.

"I have to get a shower," Kell rasped unsteadily, "and shave off this beard." Reluctantly, he released Leah, wanting to go straight to the bedroom instead. He saw her pout and he gave her a swift, hard kiss. "You're a wicked woman, you know that, Sugar?" He smiled against her soft, hungry lips.

"I've had two months of dreaming of you in that bed." She pointed down the hall. Leah stepped back, feeling giddy, excited and so very, very ravenous for Kell. "I'd already put extra towels and soap in the bathroom thinking you'd be here tomorrow evening."

He placed his arm around her shoulder and walked with her down the hall toward the bathroom. "When I last called you on the sat phone, we didn't have a flight out of Bagram. But another C-5 came in, unexpectedly, and we got lucky. There was no time to call you." Kell gave her a look of apology.

"That's okay, it's one more day you're home with me." Leah halted at the bathroom and felt her heart expand powerfully with love for him. The look Kell gave her was pure male with so much promise.

"Hold that thought I see in your beautiful green eyes. I'm going to get cleaned up. Could you grab me a pair of jeans, a T-shirt and my Nikes out of my duffel?"

"Are you hungry?"

"Starving," Kell admitted. "For you and food."

"Not necessarily in that order, though. I was just fixing lunch. I was going to have a salad and a grilled cheese sandwich."

"That sounds good," Kell murmured. "If I get clean and get some food in me, I'll feel halfway human." He leaned down and gave her a quick kiss. "And you're dessert," he growled.

KELL SAT ON the stool next to Leah as he ate three grilled cheese sandwiches in a row and finished off three-quarters of the salad she'd made. He'd drank a quart of milk straight out of the refrigerator and she shook her head, thinking of the grocery bill he was going to create by being home. The man did live on his stomach, no question. And yet he was a lean wolf, not an ounce of fat on his hard body.

Leah couldn't get over how handsome Kell was without his beard. It was the first time she'd seen him without one. If he thought his brother Cody was the drop-dead gorgeous one, he was completely wrong. Kell belonged on the cover of *GQ* with his rugged good looks. She could see the dimples now when he smiled, which had been hidden before by the beard. It gave him a decidedly boyish look, someone carefree and fully comfortable with himself.

"Where's Clutch?" she asked, sliding off the stool and taking the empty plates to the sink to rinse them off.

"He's got a condo on the other side of the island. His car was parked at North Island Naval Air Station, where we flew into. Clutch drove me over here after we landed. He's home with his girlfriend, Stacy, who has lived with him off and on for six years."

"That was awfully nice of him," Leah said, bringing over some fresh-baked cookies she'd made for him for tomorrow. His mother, Mary, had sent Kell's favorite cookie recipe to her, told her all his favorite foods, and she was prepared to give him meals that he'd appreciate.

Kell smiled as Leah presented him with a plate of two dozen cookies. "Are these all mine?" He pulled it over in front of him.

"I know you're a growing boy, Ballard, but I'd like a few left for me if you don't mind." Leah laughed.

Kell gave her a teasing look and said, "Okay, here's two. Will that do?"

She threw her arms around his shoulder as he turned around on the stool to face her. "Your ma's recipe," she said against his smiling mouth. Kissing him, feeling his hands slide from her shoulders down to her hips, a purring sound caught in her throat. And when he cupped her hips and pulled her hard against him, she felt heat tunnel through her. It had been so long…so long…and she suddenly found herself picked up and Kell was carrying her down the hall.

"I told you," Kell whispered gruffly against her hair, "you're my dessert…"

Kell's bedroom was spare, just like him. Leah had added a beautiful floor-to-ceiling corn plant near the heavy gold brocade drapes. It brought life to the very masculine dark-brown-and-gold room.

He placed her on the bed and then shoved off his Nikes, pulled off his green T-shirt and began to unzip his jeans. His narrowed gaze never left her face and Leah felt a quiver of anticipation race through her, fire about to erupt within her lower body. She appreciated his well-sprung, dark-haired chest, those incredibly strong, powerful shoulders of his, the muscles in his arms, lean and taut.

As he stepped out of his boxer shorts, her gaze

drifted lower. Leah felt her channel tighten almost painfully with need of Kell. His erection left her mouth dry and her pulse leaping with expectancy. She stood and shimmied out of her shorts and pulled off her tank top, letting them drop to the floor beside his clothes. She wore no bra, saw Kell's face go feral as his gaze locked onto her breasts. Heat flared through them, her nipples instantly puckering. He hadn't even touched her and she was responding.

"You," he growled, "are incredibly beautiful. I like you not wearing a bra." He halted in front of her, his fingers skimming her shoulders, watching her breasts tighten, those nipples begging to be touched, suckled.

"I hate bras. Only wear them if I have to," Leah admitted, her voice a little off-key and breathless. His fingers made her flesh melt as they skimmed her shoulders lightly and devoured her with his eyes.

"And your left arm?" Kell asked, gently cupping her wounded upper arm. He could see the puncture marks where the four screws had been placed into her flesh in order for the bones to knit. There was a long three-inch scar, a line of puckered red scar tissue where the surgeon had operated. He leaned over, lightly kissing the wound. Leah's breath hitched, and she closed her eyes, leaning forward to make contact with him.

"My arm's okay," she managed, her voice wispy. "I've been cleared for flight duty a week from now. The flight surgeon feels I'm ready to go back to work."

"Hmm," Kell growled, lifting his lips away from her arm. "I only have you for a week?" He moved his hands down to her pink silk panties, sliding his fingers beneath the elastic, easing them down her long, slender legs and letting them drop around her feet. Rising, he said, "I'm not letting you out of here all week, then. That's not enough time for what I had in mind for you." Kell lifted her and placed her onto the center of the bed. He pulled some condoms from the pocket of his trousers and placed them on the bed stand.

Leah lay on her back, watching his animal grace, that bonelessness that belied the dominance he had strength-wise. Kell lay down beside Leah, propped up on one elbow, reaching out and grazing her cheek. "You aren't going to get any disagreement out of me," Leah said breathlessly as his fingers trailed down the line of her neck and he cupped her breast with his large palm. Her mind simply went blank as she closed her eyes, felt Kell memorizing her breast, his thumb lazily stroking the peak, making her gasp and then whimper with need.

His lips settled over the first peak and she pressed against his long, hard body, her hips nestling against his, telling him what else she wanted. Kell tensed, his entire body stilling for a moment, savoring her moving sensuously against him. Leah dug her nails into his thickly bunched shoulders as his teeth settled teasingly upon her nipple. Her entire world came apart.

Kell devoted equal attention to the other breast, suckling her until she pressed wildly against his hips. His mouth plundered her lips, curving powerfully against hers, opening her, his tongue taking hers quick and hard. Her breath changed, and she strained, wanting Kell within her, to become one with him.

The tempo shifted like quicksilver and Kell felt the driving ache, felt the sleekness of her flesh beneath his exploring fingers. There was nothing gentle or tender between them right now. It was raw appetite, starvation of a kind that drove him to almost lose his control as her breasts moved teasingly against his chest, those hardened nipples tangling in his soft, curled hair. She bucked against him, demanding. Wanting. He was starving for her, wanting to feel her around him, gripping him, lavishing him with her sweet, hot fluids.

He slid his hand down across her hip, opening her thighs, and her breath hitched for a moment. Kell touched her, felt her wetness, felt her explosive release of breath, her whimpering cry as she buried her face against his neck.

He'd dreamed of a hundred ways he was going to make love to Leah when he returned home. But her wildness, her naturalness, just tore apart any erotic plans he'd planned previously. Leah wasn't lying quietly beneath him, either. Her assertiveness as a lover was a powerful turn-on for him.

She wrapped her fingers around his erection, and a guttural growl rolled through his chest, his entire body stiffening, the exquisite heat and softness of her fingers moving around him damn near making him release way too soon.

Kell appreciated and understood her hunger because he was equally starved for her. Their mouths clashed together, their breaths heavy and ragged, his finger slipping into her wetness, her body contracting powerfully around him. She tore her mouth from his, arching, crying out. Her body clenched, and he felt her heat, knew how close she was. Easing from her, he pushed his knees between her thighs, opening her to him.

Leah's eyes were drowsy with lust, her lips swollen from his bruising kisses. She slid her hands along his flanks, pulling him forward, pulling him into her. His world collided with hers and she quivered violently as he sheathed into her. She enclosed him, so tight, so damn tight, that air hissed between his clenched teeth. His fists knotted into the bedding on either side of her head as she drew him deeply into herself, just wanting what she knew he could give her.

He met her mouth, her tongue tangling with his. His entire body had reached a point of no return. He slid his hand beneath her hips, angling her, her cry drowning in his mouth as he surged repeatedly into her, taking her, establishing a wild, chaotic rhythm between them.

Leah suddenly froze, her body contracting violently in release. Kell groaned, burying his head against her neck and shoulder. The hot fluids spilled like a riptide around him and he could not stop the explosion from being drawn out of his body, hammering him with pleasure. He grated her name against her temple and ear, arching deep into her, the pleasure so intense, his entire body shuddering.

Leah's sweet moan caught in her throat as she curved powerfully beneath him, their hips fused as another orgasm shook her. Kell held her, sliding his arms beneath her shoulders, grasping her tightly, feeling the sweat of her body mingle with his, their chests rising and falling in sync with one another, their hearts thundering as one.

Leah felt the rippling release surge outward, spreading out across her entire belly. Then came the euphoric aftereffects as it continued to flow in relentless, fiery waves. She absorbed Kell's weight, like a warm, living blanket across her. Leah had never felt as loved or

as protected as she did right now. His breathing was
harsh against her ear, his head pressed against hers, his
arms holding her against his taut, trembling body. And
slowly, so deliciously slowly, their breathing began
to ease and become more shallow, less chaotic. Leah
made a happy sound in her throat, sliding her hands
across Kell's narrow hips, lifting hers just enough to
feel him so potent within her even now.

She opened her eyes, feeling floaty and utterly
satisfied, turning her head toward his. Sweat beaded
Kell's brow, his gray eyes burning with desire even
now. She leaned over, sipping from his lips, feeling
his return pressure, feeling him grow inside of her
once more as she languidly kissed him more deeply.
He quivered as she thrust her hips seductively against
his. She placed her hands on his damp chest, asking
Kell to roll over and onto his back. He did and he slid
his hands around her waist, lifting and bringing her
on top of him.

Kell looked lazily up into Leah's sated green eyes,
that ginger-colored hair of hers a beautiful frame
around her flushed face. It was the bloom of orgasm,
of good sex with one you loved, and he luxuriated in
how beautiful she looked. "That was one helluva dessert, darlin'." He grinned as he slid his fingers across
her cheek, watching her lashes drop, her well-kissed
lips part in a faint smile of agreement.

Leah laid her head on his chest, her fingers moving through his damp hair, feeling the pounding beat
of his heart beneath her own. "I love you. I love what
we have. We're so good together, Kell…"

Sliding his large hand down across her damp back,
he whispered, "Better than any dreams I've ever had."

He gave her a feral smile. Her eyes were barely open, yet the heat still lingered. "I think you're an incredibly natural woman. I like you being the warrior you are with me."

She laughed and kissed his jaw. "I never knew I was so assertive." She sighed. "All I knew was I wanted you, Kell. All of you. Every second was wonderful..."

"I liked every second of it, too, Sugar. Don't ever stop being yourself. You're perfect for me, and we're a good match for one another. That's all that counts."

"Just remember that," Leah said playfully, smoothing her hand over his shoulder, feeling the muscles leap wherever she grazed his tight skin.

LEAH SAVORED HER cold white wine later on the back porch of Kell's condo. They'd gone to sleep in each other's arms and slept until an hour before dinnertime. Her body still glowed from their recent lovemaking in the shower. And judging from the relaxed look on Kell's normally tense, hard face, he felt as mellow as she did right now.

He had a beer in his hand and was watching the hamburgers on the grill. There were seven in all, and six of them were for Kell. She'd already brought out the plates, napkins and all the condiments. The evening was balmy, the bay a smooth reflection. She watched white seagulls with black wing tips sail silently over the three-story structure where Kell had his condo.

"This is so peaceful," Leah murmured. She watched Kell handily flip the burgers.

"Something we don't get much of," he agreed, sitting down opposite her at the picnic table.

"I've been doing a lot of thinking, Kell."

He held her serious gaze. "Things we couldn't talk about when I was overseas?" Even though they could talk via Skype, personal things were off-limits.

Leah smiled a little and sipped the white wine. "Yes. It took me about a month to shake off the initial shock from what happened to me and Harper. I had nightmares for a while, too, but they're going away over time." She twisted the slender stem of the wineglass between her fingers, staring down at it. "I'm going to resign my commission to the Army, Kell. Are you all right with that?" Lifting her chin, Leah needed to see his reaction.

"I figured that was coming," he said quietly. "And I couldn't be happier about your decision, Leah." Because he'd have worried himself sick when she was deployed back into a combat theater.

"How did you know?"

Kell shrugged, tipped the beer up and took a drink, then set the empty bottle aside. "I think it goes back to your childhood, Leah. To your father." He held out his hand and captured hers. "I think you joined the Army to try to get him to love you, or at least pay some attention to you."

Hurt drifted through Leah, his strong fingers holding hers so gently. Nodding, she whispered, "You're right." And then she stared into Kell's somber face, searching those gray eyes of his. She saw sadness in them—for her. "You saw it all along?"

"It's easy to see things when you're not swimming in the fishbowl." Kell shared a warm look with her. "I think it's time you decided what's best for you, instead of trying to be something for someone else so they will pay attention to you. You were trapped and you couldn't have realized what you were doing or why you were doing it, Leah."

"I realize now that everything I did was to please my father. To get him to love me…"

"He must have seen you had a lot on the ball to invite you into the Shadow Squadron. Only the finest aviators get asked. So he saw you, Leah, in his own way. Maybe not as his child or his daughter, but he did acknowledge your flight skills."

Leah felt a soul-deep sadness, the abandonment scoring her heart. "I feel like I've lived my entire life for him, not for myself, Kell."

"Sugar, you saved a lot of men's lives by making the choices you did. You braved danger and you were indispensable in the role you played in those operators' lives. You got something of worth out of it."

"You're right," Leah admitted. "I love flying. What I don't like is the violence, Kell. And with Hayden nearly killing me and Harper, it's just pushed me over the edge. I don't want to go back and be in my father's squadron. I don't want to be in violent places or situations anymore. I've had it."

"Then don't. I'll support whatever you want to do, Leah. And frankly, I'm happy because it means you're not going back into harm's way."

Relief flooded her. Kell released her hand and walked to the grill. He took the huge platter and scooped up all the burgers and set them on the table. He picked up the bottle of wine and refilled her glass, and then ambled into the kitchen, to the refrigerator, to fetch himself another cold beer.

When he returned, he sat down, holding her gaze.

"I'm glad you're going home with me to meet my family. There's time for you to sort out what you really want to do with your life." And then he gave Leah a crooked, little-boy smile. "So long as you marry me, of course."

CHAPTER TWENTY

LEAH'S HANDS GREW damp as Kell pulled the SUV rental into the dairy farm run by his parents. The late-November sky was a bright blue and the surrounding hills had mostly naked gray and brown trees. It had snowed the night before and patches of white were still here and there. She saw the huge red barn and two tall red silos next to it. There were miles of pristine white fence, thirty black-and-white Holstein dairy cows in two different pastures. The grass was yellowed and the cows stood out against the color. The family home was a large, three-story, rectangular redbrick structure, probably five thousand square feet in total.

The white picket fence around the huge yard warmed Leah's heart. It represented home. How she wished she'd had a stable one. Kell drew to a crawl as he guided the vehicle through an outer gate and down a muddy road that led to home.

"You grew up in one place," she said to Kell. "You never had to move around." Leah wondered what that kind of stability would have been like. Her father moved every two years. Kell was the epitome of stability and now Leah understood where it had come from.

"No place like home," Kell murmured, reaching over and gripping her hand in her lap. "Doing okay?"

He knew Leah was worried about meeting his family, afraid she would somehow not measure up or fit in. She was anxious, afraid of being judged by all of them.

Kell had tried to tell her that her family would welcome her with open arms, love her and would never judge her. It wasn't in the family genes. Her fingers were clammy. "They won't bite you, Sugar," he teased, meeting her anxious-looking eyes for a moment.

Her mouth pulled in. "I want to believe you," she muttered. "I—I just worry is all, Kell."

He nodded and squeezed her fingers gently, trying to give her silent support. "They're excited to meet you."

Suddenly, two people emerged from the house. Leah's pulse took off in leaps and bounds. It had to be Kell's parents. They opened the screened-in porch door and walked down the steps, coming to meet them. The noon sunlight was bright and it was a coolish forty-five degrees. As they drew closer, she could see Orin Ballard was very tall. Kell had said he was six feet five inches tall. His mother, Mary, was closer to her height.

"See?" Kell murmured teasingly, "they're smiling."

Leah gulped and nodded. Orin was in a denim set of coveralls and wore a red flannel shirt beneath his brown barn coat. His arm was around his wife, Mary, who wore a set of black wool slacks, a white blouse with a red knit cape thrown around her shoulders.

It had been nearly a year since Kell had last visited his parents. Leah wondered how the rural couple coped with three sons in the the black ops community, always in harm's way. Yet, Orin's oval face, although weathered, didn't look worried or anxious. His parents were in their midfifties, but she couldn't believe it; they both exuded youth and vitality. Maybe being out in the country did it?

Leah felt a surge of relief as her gaze rested on Mary's square face. She had her dark brown hair pulled back in a ponytail. Her blue eyes were large and warm with joy. Kell braked to a stop outside the picket fence gate.

"Come on, let's meet my parents. They're going to love you, Leah," he reassured her.

Leah rubbed her hands down the sides of her jeans and Kell walked around and opened the door for her. She gripped his hand, maneuvering out of the huge SUV. The sweet odor of decaying leaves on the ground and the clean, cool air mixed and made her breathe deeply. Kell opened the gate and urged Leah through it to the wet, gleaming concrete sidewalk. She was glad he placed his arm around her waist, drawing her next to him, as if sensing her trepidation.

Leah saw the delight on Mary's face. She walked forward and, instead of hugging her son, she threw her arms around Leah first.

"Welcome home, Leah. I'm Mary." She released her, smiling and bringing her husband forward. "And this is Orin, my husband."

Orin smiled and thrust out his huge, work-worn hand to Leah. "Welcome home, Leah. We're glad to see you and Kell."

His hand was calloused, strong, but he monitored the strength of his grip as he gently enfolded Leah's proffered hand.

"Hi, thanks," she murmured, feeling suddenly foolish for ever thinking Kell's parents would be anything else but kind, like he was.

Mary moved over to Kell. "Son, good to have you home!" She leaned upward and threw her arms around his massive shoulders.

Leah stepped aside so Kell could fully embrace his mother. Hot tears leaked into her eyes and she looked down at her feet, trying not to let them fall. She felt a hand settle on her shoulder, patting her gently.

"Been a long road home for you, hasn't it, Leah?" Orin asked quietly.

Sniffing, Leah glanced up into the man's kind gray eyes. Kell's eyes. She was amazed at the wisdom and understanding Orin had. "Y-yes, you're right." She self-consciously wiped at her cheeks. Orin patted her shoulder, as if understanding. Leah didn't know if Kell had told his parents about her background or not. She assumed he had. After all, he was going to marry her.

Once Mary released Kell, Orin went over and gave his son a huge, long bear hug. Leah felt more tears falling. The love between father and son struck her deeply. She looked back on her own life, her father missing from it, realizing that these two parents had invested their lives, hearts and souls into Kell and his brothers. It showed in so many large and small ways.

Mary came over. "I can see why Kell fell in love with you," she said, smiling into her eyes. "You're so beautiful!"

Heat flood Leah's face. She had never considered herself beautiful. "Thanks, Mary."

"I heard that," Kell murmured, claiming Leah, his arm curving around her shoulders.

Orin smiled and looked over at his wife. "They make a nice couple, don't they, Pet?"

"Surely, they do," Mary said, tears springing to her eyes as she gave them a wobbly smile. "Come in. I have coffee, tea and Kell's favorite cookies waiting for us!"

Kell urged Leah up the wooden stairs and opened the screen door for her and his parents.

There was a big red porch swing at one end. Everything seemed so personal, so family-like. Kell opened the door leading into the house and ushered her inside to a large foyer. There were several rugs for people to wipe off their boots. Kell called it a mud room. And a bench to take them off, as well, if they were caked with dirt or snow. Kell removed her jacket and hung it up on a thick wooden peg next to his. Leah smelled bread baking and she internally shook herself. She felt as though she'd walked back into that old television series she loved to watch reruns of. *The Waltons*. This place reminded her sharply of that famous TV family who had a farm during the Depression.

In the huge, sunny kitchen that faced west, Leah saw a long, rectangular trestle table at one end, with six wooden chairs surrounding it. The pale yellow walls made the place bright and cheery. Kell led her to the table and pulled out a chair for her. Mary came in and brought a big platter of chocolate chip cookies and set them in front of her. Kell walked to the counter and poured them both coffee and brought the mugs over.

"Can I help you at all, Mary?" Leah asked.

"Mercy, no," Mary said. "My sons were taught to take care of themselves around here. I wasn't going to be a kitchen slave to them." She grinned.

Orin made himself and his wife some tea and ambled over, sitting down opposite Leah. He placed a mug of tea opposite him where his wife would sit. "Mary's an RN," he explained. "We have a local hospital nearby and she's the head of obstetrics. Gets to welcome the little ones into the world." He reached for a jar of honey in the center of the table and poured some into the tea. Then he gently nudged it toward Mary's awaiting hand.

"And you take care of the dairy farm?" Leah asked. Orin was a huge man. If she thought Kell's shoulders were broad, they weren't compared to his father's set. Orin was darkly tanned, deep lines in his face from being out in the sunlight, fresh air and inclement weather. She liked his warm gray eyes, that humor lurking in their depths. How much Kell was like his father in that way!

"I do. We have a herd of sixty milk cows," he said. "I've got hired help, but it's still a full-time job."

Mary sat opposite her husband. She pushed the plate of cookies toward Leah. "I just baked these. You'd best hurry and grab some. Cody and Tyler are out in the woods hunting for a couple of wild turkeys for our Thanksgiving meal. I can promise you, they'll smell these cookies on the wind a mile away. And as soon as they do, they'll hightail it back here." She chuckled. "Then, there's going to be a fight to see who gets the most first."

Orin laughed indulgently and took two of her freshly baked cookies. "Now, Pet, if you weren't such a good cook, we men wouldn't be fighting over the leftover crumbs all the time."

Leah watched Kell stack six cookies by his cup, no

fool. There was such warmth in this kitchen, and it wasn't because of the woodstove in the corner, either. "They're out hunting a turkey?"

"Yep," Orin said, savoring his cookie. "One of my sons, at least, tries to make it home for Thanksgiving. I usually go out with him and we find a wild turkey that wants to volunteer to give up its life to us and be eaten."

"Only this time," Mary sighed happily, "all three boys are home at the same time. That's a miracle in itself."

"And Kell's brought his fiancée," Orin pointed out proudly, beaming. "That's a first among our sons."

Kell grinned and looked over at Leah. "All three of us swore on our graves we'd never settle down." He hadn't brought Addison home to meet his family before marrying her. Kell had been young, immature and had promised to rectify the mistake he'd made if he ever got the chance. The joy in his parents' faces told him everything.

"Oh." Leah chortled, giving Mary a look. "Guess that didn't work out, did it?"

Mary patted her hand. "You have *no* idea how long I've waited for one of my sons to get hitched, Leah. Kell's first marriage didn't work out, unfortunately. After the divorce, he said he'd never get married again. I was chewing his ear off a year ago that he was going to end up a lonely, crotchety old bachelor. I'm glad he changed his mind and fell in love with you."

"Now, Pet," Orin soothed, "the boys all have good hearts. I told you, when the right women sashayed into their lives, they'd fall like a ton of bricks, marry them and settle down for good."

"And have some grandchildren," Mary added enthusiastically. "Soon."

Leah smiled softly and felt so much a part of Kell's family. They treated her as a much-cherished daughter-in-law.

Kell held up his hand. "Now, Ma, don't go there. I've barely gotten her to agree to marry me. Leah's a career woman. Family will come, but in time. So give her some breathing space. Okay?"

Mary rolled her eyes. "I can wish, can't I?"

Everyone nodded and smiled.

"Hey, Kell!"

Leah jerked her head up at the booming male voice carrying through the kitchen. She turned, seeing two men, both over six feet tall, entering the kitchen, grinning like fools.

Kell snorted and got up, giving Leah's shoulder a squeeze. "My brothers are loud and noisy, as you can tell," he murmured, smiling into her eyes. "I'm going to say hello to them."

"Noisy?" Cody crowed, placing one of the turkeys they'd shot into the sink. He waved hello to Leah, whom he'd met months earlier. "Hey, Leah, how are you?"

"I'm fine, Cody, thank you."

"Welcome to our noisy brood," he called, giving his older brother a devilish look of welcome. Cody placed the rifle in the corner, turned and took Kell into his embrace, slapping him heartily on the back.

Leah watched Tyler, who was the quiet SEAL, set a second wild turkey into the sink. He glanced in her direction, his gaze inquisitive. Leah smiled a little, feeling the intensity of Tyler's hazel-eyed stare. He had that SEAL look. That instant focus, like a laser.

"I thought you and Leah were coming later this afternoon," Cody said, releasing Kell. He pushed his green Army baseball cap up off his broad brow, grabbing a mug and pouring himself some coffee.

Kell went over and hugged Tyler, who grinned and slapped him on the back. He released him and stepped aside. "We got a flight in a little earlier than expected," he said.

Tyler set his rifle in the corner and then took off his black baseball cap, tucking it in his back pocket. "Introduce me to your lady," he said to Kell, motioning toward Leah.

"Sure," Kell said, walking over to the table.

Leah stood and felt nervous beneath Tyler's focused observation. She'd been around enough SEALs to know he was missing nothing about her. She held out her hand toward him. "Hi, Tyler. I'm Leah. Nice to meet you."

Tyler looked at her hand and then gave her a sudden, pained look. "What is this I hear?" he teased. "You're marrying this troublemaker of a brother of mine? I think this needs more than a handshake, don't you?"

Leah was caught off guard when Tyler stepped forward and wrapped his arms around her and gave her a quick, warm, welcoming hug. She felt his controlled strength, smelled the cold, fresh air on his dark blue T-shirt he wore. And when he pulled away, his hazel eyes were dancing with welcome. His sudden warmth surprised her, but he made her feel sincerely welcomed. That was a relief for her.

"Welcome to our family," Tyler said, releasing her. He turned his attention to his brother and playfully punched Kell in his upper arm. "How'd you get so damned lucky? Usually you're stepping in cow pies, bro. She's hot."

Leah blushed. She watched the brothers tussle with one another and it developed into playful wrestling. Kell stood about two inches taller than Tyler, and he had a wicked grin on his face. There was a lot of love between these brothers, she realized. They were tight with one another. She remembered how attached she'd been to Evan. When he died, a huge piece of her died with him because they had gotten along like these three brothers did with one another. Bittersweetness flowed through her heart for her Evan. She missed him to this day.

"Oh, quit, you two," Cody growled. He stepped around them, threw his arms open to Leah and said, "I get a hug, too."

Leah knew Cody well. He was a brazen, in-your-face Special Forces weapons sergeant, and so confident in himself. Leah eagerly stepped forward and he leaned down and chastely kissed her cheek.

"See? I warned you, didn't I?" Cody whispered loudly so everyone could hear him, releasing Leah. "That it's crazy when all three of us get together?"

"You warned me," Leah agreed, laughing. Cody hung his arm around Leah's shoulders watching Tyler trying to out-wrestle Kell. The two brothers were playing, but they were highly competitive.

"Boys." Mary's lilting voice rang out in warning. "Not here! You want to go roughhouse? You go outside. I'm not having you break any of my furniture with your antics."

Kell laughed and released his little brother. "Okay, Ma, we'll be good." He slapped Tyler on the back, giving his younger brother a friendly look.

Tyler grinned and said, "Ma, we haven't seen each other in a long time. This is how we show our love for one another."

"I don't care. You can show one another in a lot of different ways. If you insist upon wrestling, then take it outside."

Moving his hand through his mussed-up, longish hair that fell almost to his shoulders, Tyler turned to Kell and said, "Later. We're just getting started."

Leah saw the spirited competitiveness among the three brothers. She was glad to have hung out with Cody earlier in the year. He had warmed to her like a long-lost sister the first time he met her at Kell's condo.

"See, Ma?" Cody said smugly, coaxing Leah over to her chair to sit down. "Didn't I tell you how beautiful Leah was? I didn't exaggerate one bit, did I?"

Mary nodded, watching her two sons, who were still eyeing one another as if they wanted to tussle some more. "Yes, you did. And you were absolutely right."

Cody took his coffee and sat down at the end of the table facing all of them. "Leah, Ma was saying that she was happy to have another woman around here. More estrogen to offset all this testosterone she's had to put up with all these years."

Leah laughed and felt Kell's hand on her arm as he sat down next to her.

"Can you blame your poor mother who has had to live in a house full of males for so long?" Mary shot back, tittering.

Tyler eased into a chair next to Cody's elbow. "Tell me something, Kell. Did Leah know what she was getting into when she said yes to you?"

"I warned her," Kell said, giving Tyler a grin. "I spared nothing about you two birds to her."

"Leah, you're a strong woman to take on this guy," Cody said, gesturing toward Kell.

"Wonder Woman," Tyler added, drinking his coffee, a sly grin pulling at the corners of his mouth

"He's a very sweet man," Leah murmured.

Cody and Tyler groaned and rolled their eyes.

"Sweet?" Cody cried out, appearing completely wounded and taken aback by the word. He dramatically slapped his chest. "My God, she's calling a SEAL sweet?"

Tyler shook his head and laughed. "Don't *ever* use that word to describe Kell. Okay?" His smile widened.

Kell shrugged. "Sweet is better than vinegar," he told his two brothers.

"Yeah," Cody grumbled. "But sweet?" He cut Leah a glance. "I can think of many, many words to describe this guy of yours, but *sweet* ain't one of 'em."

"That's because you're not a woman, Cody," Leah shot back, smiling. That brought more roars of laughter and teasing. She saw Mary get up.

"Can I help you, Mary?" she asked.

"No, not unless you want to help me get these birds gutted and then thrown into a hot kettle of water in order to pull their feathers."

"You stay sitting," Kell told her, rising. "I'll go help Ma clean the birds."

"Yeah," Cody jeered. "We killed 'em, and now you guys have to clean 'em."

Leah glanced over at Orin. "Is it like this all the time?"

His mouth pulled into a faint smile as he finished off his mug of tea. "Actually, this is mild in comparison. I think they're all being sweet because you're here."

That brought collective groans, laughter and more raucous teasing between the three brothers. Leah found herself happier than she could ever recall being. Her own family was a cold, lifeless shadow compared to this one. She watched as Kell did all the work while his mother poured water in a large steel pot. There was love in this house.

KELL TOOK LEAH for a walk near dusk down a wooded trail. The temperature was in the high thirties and Leah had bundled up. Kell walked with her on the flat, muddy trail, arm across her shoulders, holding her close. The limestone hills above were clothed with hundreds of naked trees devoid of leaves. Many of them had caves beneath them. The trail was covered with a thick layer of brown leaves. It was a bit slippery and Leah was glad to have her arm around his waist. He seemed impervious to the weather, wearing a denim jacket and no gloves, hat or muffler, unlike her.

"What do you think of my family?" Kell asked as he led her down a slight curve.

"I love them." And then Leah added more softly,

"Right or wrong, I was comparing your family to mine."

Kell nodded. "Two very different worlds, Leah."

Her throat tightened. "Your parents' kitchen felt so warm and inviting. I loved looking at your father because he just watched you three and you could see the love shining in his eyes for all of you. He was present. He cared. And—" Leah shrugged "—I found myself wishing my father had looked like that at me. But he never did. He looked at Evan and then Hayden like that."

His heart contracted with her pain and Kell leaned over and pressed a kiss to her cheek. "My family loves you. You know that? They will all look at you with that same warmth and love in their eyes. You're one of us now. You have a new family, Leah."

She rallied and smiled up at him, her eyes moist. "Yes. I knew when Cody came for a visit, after getting off that op in Afghanistan, that he was so much like you."

He laughed. "Cody is the extrovert. Tyler and I are the introverts."

"He was kind and thoughtful toward me, Kell. It's the way your parents raised you. Even though Cody is full of himself, and he teased me horrendously about falling in love with you, he was never mean to me. He even brought me flowers and a box of chocolates as a gift and told me that if you'd been home, you'd have done the same for me. That told me so much about him, about how your parents raised all of you. He's a decent guy."

Kell grew quiet. "We were raised a certain way. My

ma drilled it into us boys to treat women right. Respect them. That they were our equals, never beneath us."

"Your mother is terrific. And Cody is so sweet. He insisted on cleaning up the kitchen after I made him a meal. Told me to go sit down and get my beauty sleep." She smiled fondly.

"We had my pa as our role model," Kell told her, leading her down another trail that sloped out into a meadow combed with yellowed grass. There was a spring-fed pond about an acre in size and a couple of red wooden benches sitting near the bank. "Pa and Ma adore each other. We grew up watching him love her in so many small but important ways. He works hard as a dairy farmer, but when she'd come home some nights after a long day at the hospital, he'd cook everyone dinner and let her get a bit of rest. He was always bringing her flowers. Sometimes he'd pull them from the pasture, or from along the roadside, for her. And when they had a little money left over, which wasn't often, he'd buy her some flowers from the florist in town."

"You brought me flowers," she reminded him, gazing up in his face, the shadows emphasizing his large, warm gray eyes. "The second day you were home, you brought me flowers and chocolates."

"I couldn't let Cody outdo me," Kell provided, grinning.

Lean smiled and shook her head. "You guys are so competitive with one another. It's got to be your black ops background?"

Kell chuckled. "No, we were born that way. Probably why we went into black ops."

Laugher bubbled up through her throat and she

nodded. "You three must have been a handful growing up."

"Ma says we gave her all the gray hair she's sporting now," Kell said, a smile lurking across his mouth. He eased his arm off her shoulders and picked up Leah's mittened hand. The sun had set in the west and there was a dark blue sky above and a gold strip along the horizon as he guided her to one of the wooden benches. He sat down with her. "The three of us boys always came here to fish. Pa didn't make a lot of money, so we grew up living off the land. The three of us learned to shoot and bring down game from the time we were twelve years old. And if we weren't eating venison, we were eating duck or the fish we caught out of here." He gestured toward the pond.

"You were poor but happy."

"We never knew we were poor," Kell murmured, pulling out a small box from his pocket. "Raising three boys, providing them with the things they needed, left our parents with no savings. That's why now the three of us send them money for their retirement years savings account."

"That's so wonderful of you," Leah said, looking at the small dark blue box he had in his hand.

Kell turned to her and pulled her mitten off and laid it across his thigh. "I wanted to come here, Leah, because this has always been a favorite place of mine." He lifted his chin, holding her gaze. "I want to marry you. I want to see you laugh again, know love, and watch you blossom." He placed the small box in her palm. "Open it," he rasped, his large hand cupping hers.

Shaken, Leah pulled off her other mitten. Prying the box open, she whispered, "Oh, Kell…" There in white satin was a green diamond engagement ring set in gold. Next to it was a simple gold wedding band.

Kell gently pulled the engagement ring free and set the box aside. He held her left hand out and said, "Now, let's see if I guessed the size right." He grinned sheepishly and eased the ring onto Leah's finger. It fit perfectly.

"It's so beautiful," Leah breathed, holding it up to the fading light.

"Like you, Sugar. It's a green diamond," Kell told her. "I wanted something to remind me of your beautiful eyes." He slid his hand along her jaw, drawing her forward, their mouths meeting and melting against one another. She was warm, tasted of chocolate chip cookies and coffee, plus her own sweetness. Warm tears met and flowed between their lips. Kell realized these were tears of happiness, not of pain.

Sliding his fingers through her hair, he held her glistening gaze. "Marry me, Leah?"

Never in his life had Kell wanted anything more than her. Her lower lip trembled, those soft corners of her wide mouth drew upward, and he saw the gold flecks dancing deep in her green eyes.

"You know I will…" Leah slid her arms around his shoulders and felt him drag her as close as he could to himself. Closing her eyes, she nestled her face against his jaw and neck, her pulse pounding in joy, a flood of happiness moving through her. Kell held her tight. Held her safe. Held her with a promise of a rich, happy life with him.

KELL LAY QUIETLY with Leah in his arms. Her breath was moist against his naked shoulder, her fingers languidly skimming his chest in the aftermath of their loving one another. They were in his old room on the third floor. He'd claimed the attic as his bedroom as soon as Cody was born and his parents had turned it into a haven for him. The house was quiet, and it was nearly 1:00 a.m. in the morning. His bed faced the only window, and outside he could see the stars glimmering in the black ink of the sky.

"Happy?" he asked, turning and kissing her lips. Inhaling her scent was like inhaling life. Kell felt Leah stir against him, a satisfied sound vibrating in her slender throat. He smiled and gazed into her drowsy eyes. "I love you," he whispered, lifting strands away from her brow.

Leah nuzzled against Kell's hard jawline, closing her eyes, her body satiated, her heart light with joy. "I never thought I'd ever fall in love," she admitted huskily, her fingers curving around his shoulder.

"Makes two of us." Kell laughed quietly. He got serious and lifted her chin, holding her gaze. "I know you're going to resign your commission when we get back to Coronado. I wanted to talk to you about my new career."

His grave manner made Leah more alert. His eyes glinted in the darkness, like warm, black coals of smoldering heat and desire for her. When her gaze dropped to his mouth, she realized this was a serious discussion.

"A new career, Kell?" There were a lot of feelings in his eyes and Leah sensed his concern over a decision he had made, but hadn't shared with her yet.

Trailing his finger along the slope of her cheek, Kell murmured, "I've been in the SEALs since I was eighteen. I'm thirty now and considered an old man in the ranks." One corner of his mouth lifted over that admission. "Until you dropped into my life, I was going to re-up, but things have changed. I have you." He looked deeply into her eyes. "I don't want to be away for weeks or months at a time from you, Leah. When you see the life my parents have, I want one similar to theirs. And I know from seeing your face, watching you with my family, that you want the same thing. Am I wrong?"

Leah swallowed hard and shook her head. "I wish I could clone what's here, Kell. I know I can't, but I crave this…this sense of family, of belonging…being loved and caring for one another."

Kell understood because Leah had never had it in her family. "There's a lot I haven't told you yet, mainly because time wasn't on our side in Afghanistan. I started back to college when I was twenty. An old senior chief told me to get a degree. Even if I didn't use it to go on and become a Navy officer, I would have a skill when I left the SEALs. And he was right. He was my sea daddy, the man who molded me into becoming a damn good operator. And he pushed me into going to college. It was a patchwork affair, Leah. I didn't graduate with a degree until I was twenty-five because of the rotation and deployment cycles."

"You have a degree?" Leah blinked. Why wouldn't he? Kell was intelligent.

He gave her a half smile. "I'm a physician's assistant. That's one rung below being an MD. I'm a combat corpsman and I've always liked helping people who were sick or wounded. I talked to my counselor at the university in San Diego and she said that with my background, I could get hired anywhere in the US."

He frowned. "There's a shortage of doctors here in our area. As a PA, I can work under a doctor, but be free to diagnose, treat and write prescriptions for my patients. It's something I want to do, Leah. I like helping people, and maybe Ma being a registered nurse was a defining influence on me. I was talking to her before dinner tonight and she was telling me our local hospital is desperate to hire a PA. And," Kell added, hope in his voice, "she said they're expanding their services to add a medical helicopter. They're looking to hire two pilots. Maybe you might consider applying for it?"

A good kind of shock rolled through Leah. She eased out of his arms and turned around, their hips meeting as she looked down at his peaceful features. "Move back here?"

He shrugged. "Would it bother you to do that?"

Her mind whirled with so many questions, so many emotions. Leah knew how important family was to Kell. And how important it was to her. "When is your enlistment up?"

"A month from now."

Leah wrapped her arms around her legs, drawing them up against her chest as she considered his ideas. "Would the hospital wait a month until you got out?"

"Ma told me to call the administrator on Monday morning and go in and meet with her. She feels they would hold the position open for me if they knew I'd accepted their job offer."

"Wow," Leah murmured, shaking her head, drowning in his dark, thoughtful expression.

"Do you want to fly when you get out?"

"I'd wanted to, yes, but hadn't given it much thought." Until now. "I have to earn money. I can't sit at home and expect you to carry the load, Kell."

He reached out, trailing his fingers down across her back. "If you want to stay at home, Sugar, you can. I'll be making very good money. Enough to support the two of us very easily. We aren't going to be in financial stress at all."

Leah bit her lower lip. "What if…what if I told you I wanted a baby, Kell? I'm twenty-nine years old and I'm not getting younger. I sat in your parents' kitchen today thinking how wonderful it would be to have a baby. That baby would get so much love and attention from your parents, from you and me…"

Kell sat up, leaning against the headboard, drawing Leah into his arms. When her head came to rest on his shoulder, he whispered, "You will make an incredible mother," and he kissed her lips tenderly, with all the love he had in his heart for her. Leah might have been cheated of love growing up, but Kell knew in his soul she'd shower any children they had with all that love she held in her huge, giving heart. "I'm very open to making a baby with you," he whispered against her lips.

"Really?" Leah stared into his eyes, her heart bounding with hope.

"Really."

Leah drew in a serrated breath and kissed Kell with everything she held in her heart for this man. She could feel him smiling, felt the tender way he grazed her temple and cheek with his fingers. Kell would make a wonderful healer. Who knew that better than her? He'd helped her heal from festering wounds she'd carried around all her life. His love had opened them up, allowed them to drain and then sutured them closed, making her realize she was worthy. Drawing away from his strong mouth, she whispered, "Let's do it. I want to stay home, Kell. I want to make us a home. I love to cook, and Mary can teach me what I don't know."

"Then you're ready to hang up your wings, Sugar?"

Leah slid her hand across his sandpapery cheek. "I'm ready to fly in another way, Kell. Only this time around, you'll be my wingman."

"That sounds like a doable plan," Kell murmured, easing her down on the bed, sliding against her warm, soft body. There was such peace in Leah's shadowed eyes now. Kell saw joy in them, the way the corners of her mouth drew upward, the hope burning in them. Never had he wanted to give her anything more than what he saw reflected in her wide, lustrous eyes. Leah was so brave and yet didn't see it, but he did. "Then," he murmured, placing small kisses along her hairline, "we should use the time we have here to start looking for a house to buy."

"I like that. A big house, Kell. With a huge kitchen like Mary's."

"You can have anything your want, darlin'. I want you happy."

She moved her hand up his hard, muscled arm. "Will you miss the SEALs?"

"I'll miss my friends. I've given my service to my country. Now, I want to give it to you. To our growing family." Kell splayed his large hand out across her belly. "And I want to be there for any children we have, not gone most of the time."

His hand was warm, strong, and Leah could feel Kell's support in his eyes, his voice and his touch. "I want you near. I want you home every night."

"I'll be there," Kell promised, sliding his arms around her, holding her close. Holding her forever.

* * * * *

Don't miss Lindsay McKenna's next HQN, NIGHTHAWK, available September 2015!

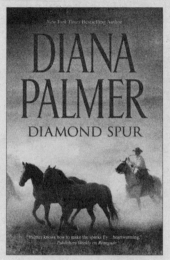

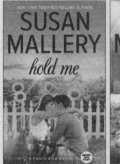

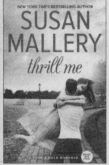

REQUEST YOUR FREE BOOKS!

2 FREE NOVELS
FROM THE SUSPENSE COLLECTION
PLUS 2 FREE GIFTS!